ALL THE KING'S MEN

BLACK

BLACK©
All the King's Men, book eight
Published by Phoenix Press
Copyright 2017 Donya Lynne
Cover by Reese Dante – www.reesedante.com
ISBN: 978-1-938991-19-6

ACKNOWLEDGEMENTS

They say it takes a village to raise a child. I think the same can be said about writing a book. From my beta readers, to my editor, to my cover artist, to my formatter, and, ultimately, to my faithful readers who devour my books with robust enthusiasm, I can honestly say this is the village that helps me raise a book from a nugget of an idea to a full-fledged novel.

Special thanks to Liz, Leann, and Amanda. Your input helped me uncover so many wonderful angles to BLACK that I didn't see on my own. I have the best beta readers ever!

To everyone who had a hand (or both hands) in this book: Thank you so much! I couldn't do it without you.

BOOKS BY DONYA LYNNE

All the King's Men Series

Rise of the Fallen
Heart of the Warrior
Micah's Calling
Rebel Obsession
Return of the Assassin
All the King's Men - The Beginning
Bound Guardian Angel
BLACK
Micah's Bride – An AKM Novelette (Dec. 2017)

Strong Karma Trilogy

Good Karma
Coming Back to You
Full Circle
Good Things Come (2018)

Savage Storm Trilogy

Savage Storm (2018)
Savage Surrender (2018)
Storm Damage (2018)

Standalones

Finding Lacey Moon
Little Things
Suspicion

Stand-Alone M/M Titles

Winter's Fire

Collections and Anthologies

All the King's Men Vol. 1 (books 1-3)
All the King's Men Vol. 2 (books 4-6)
Strong Karma Trilogy Boxed Set
Banger Complete Set

ALL THE KING'S MEN

BLACK

DONYA LYNNE

CHAPTER 1

Approximately 950 years ago

A STEEL-TIPPED ARROW WHIZZED PAST MICAH'S HEAD as he and Malek battled their way through the rush of drecks pouring through the village from all directions. Metal on metal rang out as the village's males took up their swords and engaged the enemy. It was their duty to defend the females and humans against this unprovoked, peacetime raid.

Who was Micah kidding? They weren't in peacetime, anymore. This attack was enough proof that the drecks had risen up against them once more like some kind of fungus rot on their cultivated fields. No matter how many diseased plants you pulled, the shit just kept coming back.

Would the godforsaken war ever end? It had raged off and on for centuries before Micah's birth, and, at this rate, would continue for centuries to come, even under the guise of peace.

Micah whistled to get Malek's attention. When his friend and fellow warrior turned, Micah pointed to the top of a nearby ridge.

"High ground!" He had to shout over the roar of infernos consuming nearly half the cottages in the village, casting blazing heat that scorched his skin and singed his long, braided hair, coating him with soot and ash.

Malek nodded, pulled the strength from only God knew where, and hoofed it up the steep incline behind Micah.

Micah's lungs pumped hard as his legs churned, propelling him higher as the burn and fatigue in his muscles grew so great that his thighs almost locked up in protest. But somehow, he pushed through the pain. The safety of his family depended on him. Katarina had fled to the forest at the first sign of attack, and thank God for that, but he refused to leave even one dreck standing who could pursue her and the other vampires and humans who had escaped.

But he didn't know where his parents were. Surely, his father was engaged with the enemy, but he had yet to sense that his mother had found safety. On the contrary, what he felt vibrating in his soul was impending doom.

Another arrow flew past him, this one close enough to catch the side of his arm, nicking his flesh. Blood already spilled from multiple wounds all over his body, so this one merely added to the collection. None of his injuries were life threatening, but eventually, the loss of blood would weaken him. There was no time to spare.

He and Malek reached the top of the ridge and Micah turned, pulling an arrow from his fully stocked quiver as he brought his bow up in front of him. Malek did the same.

From here, the damage to their village robbed him of breath. It was a total loss. More than half the structures were consumed by flames or already falling into piles of smoldering rubble.

Beyond the steel tip of his arrow, Micah saw a dreck toss a torch on one of the remaining cottages. Calming his breath, he lined up the blue-tinted creature in his sights, held for a moment, and then released the arrow.

It impaled the dreck square between the eyes.

Malek took out another.

One by one, he and Malek sniped the enemy from their advantageous location, killing the drecks gradually but steadily as they worked their way along the ridge that surrounded the village, moving toward his parents' cottage on the far end.

Behind him, he could feel the first sign of sunrise spreading light across the horizon. They needed to hurry so the vampires had enough time to seek shelter in the forest beyond the fields or in any of the remaining dwellings not taken by fire.

As Micah's quiver neared empty, he caught sight of his uncle Rory, engaged with three drecks. Rory was a deadly male, fighting like a banshee unleashed by the devil himself. His skin and clothing were red with spilled blood, streaked with fresh, blue blood of the drecks, which quickly faded to red. No doubt Rory had killed half the invaders himself.

"I'm empty," Malek said beside him.

Micah handed him one of his last two arrows. "Me, too."

The good news was that the number of the fallen enemy was greater than that of the villagers. Drecks were no match for vampires, and their dead and dying bodies littered the cobbled paths and open spaces of their village, their blue blood running in rivers into the grass, where it pooled and gradually turned from blue to purple to red.

Just as he nocked his last arrow, Micah turned in the direction of his parents' cottage. With the faint light of the pending sunrise granting him greater breadth of vision, he found his childhood home. His father was nowhere to be seen, but his mother stood in front of the open door, a sword in her hand, facing off against a pair of drecks.

Micah's heart raced as a premonition of dread shocked his mind's eye.

His mother was not a fighter. Not at the level needed for this kind of combat. Not against a trained enemy, and especially not against two of them.

As one attacked, she lifted the sword, blocking the dreck's blade. But she wasn't fast enough to counter the second dreck as he lunged forward, holding a pair of short swords, and sliced into her abdomen.

"NOOOOOO!" Ignoring the fatigue in his muscles, Micah took off at a sprint, traveling along the top of the ridge like a streak of lightning.

"Micah!" Malek called as he gave chase.

His mother staggered backward, toward the open doorway as if she were trying to block the way inside, blindly swinging the sword at her attackers, unwilling to surrender even as her knees wobbled.

"No! Mother!"

Like a true warrior, she refused to give an inch, despite her rapidly weakening state. Mustering what must have been the last of her strength, she surged with determination, parrying her foe and driving her sword into his belly.

The next seconds flashed by in an instant, even though Micah saw the events unfold as if through a thick, slow-moving fog. The dreck she impaled fell, his body spasming in the throes of death. The second dreck moved in, blades flashing. His mother was left unprotected, alone, and without a weapon. Micah stopped and raised his bow, determined to save her.

Just as he released his arrow, the glint of cold steel dripping with vampire blood rose over her. Would the arrow find home before the dreck's blade did? The firelight reflected off the sword's edge as it fell in a swift descent.

Micah held his breath, his heart and soul flying alongside the arrow blazing a trail in the distance between them.

The sword sliced into his mother a split second sooner than his arrow lodged into the center of the dreck's back.

"NO!" Micah burst into a run, barreling down the steep decline of the ridge, falling, tumbling, then regaining his footing as he reached the base.

With Malek hot on his heels, he vaulted the simple wooden fence and charged into the small square of land surrounding his parents' cottage, leaped onto the dreck, who was still alive, and drove his dagger into the beast's heart, releasing a savage war cry.

And he kept stabbing, long after the dreck was dead, turning the foul creature into nothing but tenderized meat.

"Micah, stop!" Malek remained a safe distance from his swinging dagger, but Micah could feel his desperation.

He couldn't stop. He had to keep stabbing. Had to keep destroying that which had taken what he loved. His anger—*his fury*—required vengeance.

Malek pushed dangerously close, dodging Micah's dagger as it plunged through the air and into the dreck's chest, and grabbed him by the collar as he raised the blade again. "Micah! Your mother! She needs you!"

They were the only words that could have gotten through to him.

The bloody dagger in his hand halted in midair then dropped to his side as he swung his rage-hazed gaze around to where his mother lay in the flattened grass.

"Is she alive?" He abandoned the gore he'd created and lurched toward her.

"Barely." Malek's dismal tone said all Micah needed to know about his mother's fate, and he froze, meeting his best friend's eyes with a sense of foreboding. "She doesn't have much longer, Micah." Malek bobbed his head in her direction. "She asked for you."

The breath caught in Micah's raw throat, scorched by hot smoke and strained from shouting. Then he sprung to life and scurried to his mother's side, falling to his knees. He took her hand. It already felt too cold. Too small. Too . . . lifeless.

"Mother . . .?"

Her eyes blinked open as if just that simple act took too much effort. "Mi . . . cah."

Tears blurred his vision, but he forced down the sob that threatened to break through his throat. "I'm here. You're going to be okay." He squeezed her hand and brushed the bloody hair off her face.

She weakly shook her head as the corners of her lips turned up knowingly. She knew she was dying. This was her end, and nothing could stop it. Then she shifted her gaze to the open door of the cottage. "Your father . . . needs you . . ." Her breath rattled in her lungs like shackles being tugged by the Grim Reaper. "In . . . side." She tried to lift her arm but couldn't, instead pointing in the general direction of the doorway.

Micah glanced toward the cottage.

And that's when he saw it.

His father's booted foot lay on the floor, in the shadows, unmoving, just beyond the door.

"Go . . . to . . . him . . ." His mother's voice was quickly fading, no louder than a whisper now. "Needs to . . . give . . . you . . ." Her hold on his hand weakened. Her body relaxed. Everything in her went slack.

"Mother . . .?" Micah turned back toward her, only to find the light that had been in her eyes moments ago was now gone. *She was gone.* Her soul claimed and taken to the other side. "Mom?" He shook her. But it was useless. She was dead.

Tears trailed down his cheeks as he bowed his head. "I will kill every last one of them, Mother," he vowed on a whisper. "I promise not a single dreck will remain when I am finished avenging you." He bent forward, placed his palm over her silent, unbeating heart, and kissed her dirty, abraded forehead. "I promise."

There was no time for more. The remaining drecks were quickly closing in, and he had to save his father.

Pulling the strength from deep within, he leaped to his feet and rushed into the cottage. His father lay on his stomach in a pool of blood, his hand outstretched toward the large wooden chest against the wall. Its lid was open, the contents scattered as if his father had been searching through them before he fell.

There was so much blood. *Too* much.

"Father?" Micah crouched and rolled the heroic male he had always admired and looked up to over. No less than a dozen wounds seeped his life-giving blood.

"Son . . ." His father's voice rasped from him as if from a ghost.

"Father . . . I'm getting you out of here." He began to lift him, but his father protested.

"No . . . no time . . . I'm not . . . going to make it." His skin was already so pale it was a wonder he had any blood left to sustain him. "Save yourself. Save your mother."

Micah didn't have the heart to tell him she was already gone. Hot tears stung his eyes once more. "I will."

"Take . . . the chest"—his father let out an ugly cough that speckled his lips with blood—"with you." He turned his head toward the large wooden structure only a few feet away.

There was no way he could take that with him.

"It's too heavy."

His father shook his head. "No. Inside. The chest . . . smaller one. The box . . ." He coughed again, and it sounded like his lungs were filling with what little blood he had left. "Take it. Protect it. The ankh . . . inside . . . keep it safe."

Micah looked inside the large chest, and, there, to the side, was a smaller one. No wider than the length of his hand and as deep as three of the leather-bound books Kat enjoyed reading. It was ornately carved and secured by a disproportionately heavy lock. He lifted the chest and secured it under his arm as he returned to his father.

"I have it."

"Take it . . . go . . ." His father held out a key fastened to a knotted length of leather. "Hurry . . ." His father's midnight blue eyes glanced through the open door toward the east. "The sun . . . almost . . . here . . ." He winced and groaned then fell silent as his body went lax.

"Father?" Micah knelt closer. "*Father?*"

"Micah!" Malek's frantic voice shot through the doorway. "Hurry!"

There was no time. The drecks were coming, and the sun was close behind. He had to leave.

He plucked the key from his father's loose grip and tucked it into the pocket of his cloak, stashed the small chest in his father's pack, which he slung over his shoulder, and then crossed his forearm over his chest as he faced his father's lifeless form. "I will avenge you, Father." He glanced out the door at his mother. "I will avenge you both."

With one last sorrowful glance toward his father, he breathed in the last inhale of air he would ever take inside the home he grew up in. Never again would he set eyes on the male who had taught him how to hunt, how to track prey, how to kill, how to be a good mate, and how to lead an army. A male more powerful than a tidal wave, stronger than a gale-force wind, and more respected than even the king. A male who had been, was, and would always be his hero.

His father was dead.

Or so he thought.

CHAPTER 2

WITH BARELY A CURSORY GLANCE AT THE GUARD in the lobby, Micah flew past the security desk of The Sentinel in downtown Chicago. His insides were as raw as if they'd been scrubbed by steel wool, but what was going on between his ears was even worse. It was like a million nano-wasps had been released into his grey matter, and those that weren't stinging his brain were crawling through the grooves and folds like melting shards of ice.

What the fuck had happened tonight?

His father was alive.

Alive!

And Ronan was his brother. The thief who'd broken into his apartment — the very apartment he was fleeing to now — and led him and his team on a wild-goose chase all over Chicago was his goddamn brother!

Micah had almost killed him tonight. He'd put a bullet into Ronan's shoulder and had almost planted one inside his brain before he learned the truth.

He hadn't believed it at first, because for Ronan to be his brother meant either his father or his mother hadn't died, and since he'd been there the day of the raid that killed them both, he knew that wasn't possible. But then doubt had crept in. The family resemblance had been too striking. And then his father had shown up, and that was when everything blinked out inside Micah's head.

Without slowing his long strides as he reached the elevator bay, he smacked the up arrow and continued to pace.

Alive, alive, alive . . .

How was his father alive?

Why hadn't he reached out to let Micah know?

Where had he been all this time?

Who the hell was Ronan's mother?

So many questions blurred through Micah's thoughts he couldn't think straight.

A ding rang out in the elevator bay, and Micah practically leaped through the doors that slid open, immediately slapping the button to close them again.

He couldn't risk anyone else riding up with him. He was too torqued. Too strung. Too holy-fucking-hell-this-has-got-to-be-a-nightmare. If anyone else got closed inside this tiny space with him, they'd be in danger, because he was ready to let loose on something, like right fucking now.

How had his father gone from lying in a lifeless heap on the floor inside the family cottage nearly a thousand years ago to being a walking, talking, breathing, heart-beating SOB inside Ronan's home tonight? Shit like that wasn't supposed to be possible.

And how about Ronan? That little fucker had skills.

Before he could tamp it down, brotherly pride welled up inside him as Micah breezed through his half brother's accomplishments in the past couple of weeks. Ronan had broken into his apartment, stolen the small chest his father had given him, evaded them at every turn, hacked into a system that should have been unhackable, and had even bested Cordray in a hand-to-hand confrontation and tied her up in her own home. That alone deserved brownie points for a good deed done.

But the fragment of respect for his brother was short-lived as his mind refocused on the very large elephant in the room.

Micah scrubbed his hands up and down his face as he paced in the elevator's minimal square footage. "How the fuck is he alive?"

The memories of that night, as well as from the years before and after, continued to flood his thoughts. He could still see the streams of red, blue, and purple blood gushing along both sides of the stone path as he and Malek battled their way toward freedom, cutting down anything shaded dreck blue. He could still smell the acrid stench of burning wood and thatch. Still see the death and loss and destruction all around him. Still feel the rush of adrenaline as he and Malek fled to the forest, racing the dawn with the remaining survivors after killing the last of the raiders.

They had barely reached the safety of the thick, leafy canopy as the sun broke the eastern horizon. He could still hear the moans of those who suffered. Still smell the metallic twang of blood in the air. No detail escaped his recollection.

He had found Katarina, grateful she was alive, and they and the others had watched from their shadowy hiding place as great plumes of smoke rose from their burning homes, as well as from the bodies of the vampires who'd been left to die and be claimed by the sun.

He had spent the decades since mourning his parents' deaths, as well as Katarina's when she was taken from him a few years later in another raid he managed to survive, while more of those he loved perished.

So much loss. So much death. Knowing his father had been alive all along would have gone a long way toward easing his pain, but his father hadn't thought enough of him to let him know, and now it felt like he was losing him all over again as he relived the past inside his mind.

The elevator doors opened on the eighteenth floor, and he gusted out like a hurricane.

As he barreled through the wide hallway toward his apartment, he freed his phone from his pocket and hit Sam's speed dial. He needed his mate, and he needed her now.

THE HOUSE WAS QUIET. It often was when Micah was at work. Not that Sam minded Micah's special brand of noise. His presence alone was loud enough to drown out a symphony. But that's what Sam loved about him.

The phrase, *never a dull moment,* was written with him in mind.

But tonight's quiet had nothing to do with Micah's absence. The kids from Cordray's shelter were finally asleep. They'd been staying with her and Micah after the fire destroyed their dorm at Asylum, the orphanage Cordray ran in the country, miles away from the city proper.

Sam wasn't sure she liked the silence better than the lively cacophony they created while awake. With so many kids from toddler to teenager staying with them, there was always something happening. Cartoons, video games, arguments . . . laughter. The laughter was what Sam liked best. Nothing beat the laughter of a child, especially a toddler.

She would miss the constant activity once their new dorm was finished and the kids returned home.

Having kids in the house and seeing their Crayola-colored artwork stuck to her refrigerator awakened Sam's maternal instincts, making her want children of her own more than ever.

Which wasn't something she could simply talk to Micah about and expect to happen anytime soon. She couldn't just go to him and say she wanted a baby and expect that having a lot of sex would make her dreams come true. That's not how things worked in this still-new-to-her world she'd entered not even five months ago.

Now that she was mated to a vampire, conception wasn't that simple. Fertility didn't rely on her ovulation cycle. It relied on Micah's calling, a phenomenon Micah had told her only occurred once every ten years or so. And since he'd had his first calling with her back in January, and she hadn't gotten pregnant, it would be another decade before they got another shot at becoming parents. Seems that being bitten by a dreck then bitten by Micah to save her life had made her too fragile to conceive during his calling the first time around.

Ten more years. How was she going to make it that long, especially craving a child as deeply as she craved food and oxygen? This was the definition of suffering.

Maybe—*hopefully*—Micah's next calling would bring success. For now, she would have to get her motherly fix from Cordray's orphans.

She made herself a cup of chamomile tea, went to the living room, and was about to kick up her feet with a late movie when her phone vibrated on the end table beside her.

She set down her mug and checked the caller ID.

Micah.

She answered and brought the phone to her ear. "Hey, baby, what's up?"

"I need you." The thick tension in Micah's voice made the hairs on the back of her neck stand on end.

She was on her feet in an instant.

"Where are you? Are you okay?" She was already hurrying toward the mudroom for her purse and keys.

It didn't matter if he was at their penthouse, at AKM, or burrowed inside a rat-infested crawl space in the worst part of town. If he needed her, she was there.

"I'm at the apartment. When can you be here?" He sounded more strung out than a crack whore.

She also didn't miss the fact that he hadn't answered her second question. The one inquiring whether he was okay. Whatever had happened to upset him, he didn't sound like he was in the mood to discuss it.

"I'm on my way. Less than thirty minutes." She snatched her jacket and purse off the hook by the door then darted into the garage. "Are you okay?" she asked again, hopping behind the wheel of her Camaro, which had been Micah's gift to her after they mated.

"Just hurry."

That was twice he'd avoided the question. She wasn't going to risk a third time. With Micah, she'd learned it was better to let him get there on his own. He'd tell her what had happened when he was ready.

The Camaro's engine fired, and she hit the accelerator, backing out of the garage like she was launching into space.

"I'll be there as soon as I can."

She was about to disconnect when Micah called her name. She lifted the phone back to her ear.

"Sam?" he said again. The strain in his voice gave her the impression he was on the edge of losing control.

"I'm here."

Silence drew out over the line.

"Micah?"

He exhaled heavily, remained silent for another moment, and then said darkly, "I won't be gentle."

His voice held no malice or danger, but it most definitely held a warning. One meant to prepare her for what he planned to do to her once she arrived.

Her breath hitched as she braked at the stop sign at the end of the street, and her body warmed in all the right places. She loved this side of him, but she hadn't seen it in a while. They had sex, yes. They had a lot of sex. Hot, torrid, body-melting sex. But there was something about having sex with him when he needed to blow off steam that made her extra weak in the knees.

And it sounded like he had major steam to blow off tonight.

"I don't need gentle," she said.

"Yeah well, I'm not sure you're ready for *this* kind of rough." She hit the gas, pulling into traffic. "I'll be there soon. Just hang tight, baby."

"Sam?"

"Yeah?"

"I love you."

"I love you, too." She disconnected, quickly dictated a text to Brenna and Mya, the two females who worked for Cordray at Asylum, to let them know they were in charge of the house since she had split too fast to find them and tell them where she was going. Then she dictated another text to Trace and Cordray so they knew what was up.

Those two had cordoned themselves off somewhere private in anticipation of Trace's calling. Apparently, Trace hadn't learned how to control his mixed-blood power during sex, and had made quite the destruction zone of Cordray's bedroom and the upstairs hallway at the Asylum house the first time they'd done the deed.

So, yeah, no one wanted them around the kids when his calling hit. There was no telling what might get broken or how dangerous shit could get with the kind of sex forged by a calling, which was a hundred times more powerful than regular sex.

Cordrace, as everyone had begun to call the newly mated pair, should probably hole up in a bomb shelter for the duration. They might be safer that way. So would everyone else.

Once the texts were sent, Sam got down to business using the Camaro in the way intended. For speed.

She didn't know what was wrong, but Micah needed her, and that was all that mattered. Because as much as Micah needed her, she needed him more.

That was what the mating bond was all about. Undeniable, unquestionable devotion to the one who owned your heart.

I won't be gentle.

That's what he had said, and she knew exactly what that meant.

But she didn't want gentle. She wanted whatever it took to make Micah whole. If that meant her body would be covered in bruises after he was finished finding solace inside her, so be it. Because rough with Micah was more glorious and moving to her soul than any of the gentle she'd ever received from her previous lovers, including her ex-husband, the bastard that he was. Except he was never gentle. A man who hits women could never be called gentle.

Micah had saved her from Steve. Now she would save him from whatever haunted his thoughts. And she would continue saving him for the rest of their lives.

"I'm coming, baby," she muttered to herself as she sped toward downtown.

CHAPTER 3

Ronan pulled the Jeep to the curb in front of Alexis's house and shut off the engine.

After dematerializing away from his townhome to put five miles of much-needed distance between him and Micah — and his prick of a father — Ronan stopped by his dad's crib, swiped the spare keys, then took off in the Jeep. He hadn't known where he was going at the time, just that anyplace was better than being near his fucked-up family.

He used the term *family* loosely, because he didn't think of either his dad or Micah as family. They shared genes, but that was about it. And genes alone did not a family make. At least not by Ronan's definition. He thought of Alexis more as family than his own father.

Once he'd climbed behind the wheel of the Jeep, it hadn't taken him long to figure out where he was going. He hadn't seen Alexis in a while, but she was just what he needed. She was his partner in crime, his nurse when he needed mending, the feminine body he wanted when his appetites turned more hedonistic, and the ear he needed to vent to when he'd had enough of his father's shit.

In some ways, she was his mentor. In others, he was hers. But they were equals where it counted.

The one thing she wasn't was his mate. Hell, she wasn't even what he would consider a lover. Best friend, confidante, and fuck buddy? Yeah, that pretty much described their relationship. When he needed sex, he went to her. When she needed it, she came to him. No strings attached. Nobody got hurt that way. After all, you couldn't miss what was never yours, and they'd both already been hurt enough. They didn't need to try to be more to each other than they were.

Alexis was as damaged as he was, and, as the saying goes, it takes one to know one. He got her, she got him, and that was all that mattered. Trust naturally followed suit.

But casual and uncomplicated didn't mean boring or ordinary when it came to the time they spent in the bedroom. After all, she was the one who had taught him rope bondage, an art he'd taken naturally to when she started letting him tie her up.

But bondage was as far as she wanted the kink to go. And spanking. She did enjoy a good spanking. But no flogging. No hitting of any kind beyond a firm hand on her ass. No ball gags. No blindfolds.

Although . . .

Ronan liked the idea of blindfolds. A deep, dark corner of his personality adored the thought of rendering a female helpless and taking care of her. Call it a hero complex, but the fantasy of earning a woman's trust and keeping her safe always got him hard. Alas, that was one sexual fantasy that would never play out with Alexis, because while she liked being tied up, she detested be treated like she couldn't take care of herself.

He hopped out of the Jeep and winced. His arm throbbed as his feet hit the pavement a little harder than he'd intended. He cursed under his breath. Damn shoulder ached like a motherfucker. The bullet was still lodged in the flesh.

Alexis opened the door and leaned against the jamb, her arms crossed. She was barefoot, wearing loose jeans that were torn at the knees and a draping, off-the-shoulder top that fell to midthigh. "What happened to you?" Her straight black hair hung over her shoulders to her waist.

"Bullet." Holding his injured arm against his body, he marched up the steps and pushed past her, into the entryway.

She closed the door and locked the half dozen deadbolts that had probably taken her an inning's worth of baseball to unlock. "Let me see."

He peeled out of his bloodstained shirt, cringing as he lifted his injured arm, and tossed it over the back of the settee a few feet away.

Alexis inspected the wound. "Let me guess. This has something to do with your brother."

She knew all about Micah. She was the only person he'd told about his family problems and his plans to steal the ankh from

Micah's ridiculous penthouse apartment. Then again, she'd been the one to put the final pieces of the ankh's power together for him and show him the map she had created of the portals she'd identified in the Chicago area. At least the ones she was able to locate. Pretty much any structure that looked like a pyramid or obelisk served as a gateway.

Being that she had done most of the legwork and research for the ankh's purpose, she could be considered a co-conspirator in the ankh's theft, whether she saw it that way or not.

When he didn't answer, she peered up at him. "Ro, please tell me you didn't actually go through with it."

"Damn right I did. Fuck him."

She sighed and pushed him toward the back of the house. "Come on, let's get this thing out of you." They entered the kitchen, where she pointed toward the table. "Sit."

He did as he was told while she disappeared in the back hallway, where he heard her rummage through the bathroom cabinets. A moment later she returned with her first aid kit.

Hers wasn't a standard kit. For starters, it wasn't a tiny white and red box. It was a large metallic-grey, multilayered fishing tackle box she'd customized to hold all her medical supplies. You didn't survive off the grid this long without having your own miniature surgical unit in your home, as well as basic medical knowledge. And given Alexis's line of work and who she was hiding from, she was a master at independence and self-preservation.

She plunked the tackle box on the table beside him then retrieved a bowl and several small, stained towels from the linen closet. The towels were clean, but she'd removed a lot of bullets and sewn up a lot of wounds over the years, and Tide could only get out so many bloodstains before it said "Fuck it," and gave up.

"You wanna talk about it?" She pulled another chair in front of him and sat down, studying the bullet hole under the brighter lights of the kitchen.

"Not really." He wasn't in the mood for being Dr. Phil'd, and he already knew what she would say.

She stood and flicked the latches on her medical kit, popping the lid. "I told you going after Micah was a bad idea." She dug out a small bottle of local anesthesia then grabbed a syringe.

"Well, I did it anyway. He deserved it."

"Is he the one who gave you this?" She nodded toward his wound.

He glanced down at the hole in his arm that was still leaking blood. "He surprised me at my house. Popped me before I could pop him."

"Did *you* deserve it?"

He frowned. He knew what she was getting at. She thought he should have left Micah alone, but that wasn't Ronan's style. Micah had been a black mass of oppression in his life since birth, and he was sick and goddamn tired of living under that shroud. The best way to break free was to cut his way out. If that meant literally running the blade through Micah to get out from under his shadow, so be it.

Alexis shook her head and set down the syringe. "Of all the people to rob, you picked him. Have I taught you nothing?" She grabbed an alcohol wipe and tore open the packet. "Never steal from someone in your own family, Ronan, no matter how much you hate him, and especially when he's AKM's fiercest enforcer. He could have killed you. I'm surprised he didn't."

"Must have been my charm."

"It *must* have been *dumb luck*."

"What's done is done—AH!" He flinched and pulled back as she swabbed the bullet hole with alcohol.

She gave him a tart smile. "Serves you right."

He grinned back. "Sadist."

"Only when you're bad."

"Is that how it works?"

She let out a breathy laugh. "Look who's talking." She picked up the syringe.

"I'm not a sadist."

This time she laughed outright. "Are you kidding? My ass is still burning from the spanking you gave me the last time I saw you."

That had been a good night. He'd been especially torqued, having just had another argument with his father.

"That wasn't sadism. That was affection." He hissed as she pierced his skin with the needle and injected the local. It burned at first, but within seconds, he felt nothing.

She capped the syringe and set it back on the table. "Affection?"

"You know how much I care about you." He did care about her, but they preferred to joke about their feelings rather than take them seriously.

"Uh-huh. My ass you do."

"It *was* your ass."

She picked up a scalpel. "Hush. Let me concentrate."

He laid his head back and stared up at the ceiling as she sliced into his flesh then used a pair of forceps to dig out the slug. Despite the local, he could still feel her mangling his muscle tissue. That shit was going to hurt like a bitch come morning . . . or whenever the local wore off. Then he heard the bullet drop into the ceramic bowl beside him and glanced down at it. It always amazed him that such a small object could cause so much damage.

Alexis pressed a towel against his shoulder. "Hold this."

He placed his hand over the towel while she grabbed a small squeeze bottle of saline solution from her kit.

Pulling the towel away, she cleansed the bloody wound, catching the runoff with the towel, then placed a second towel over the injury. He held it in place while she threaded a surgical needle with suture thread.

Several stitches and one large, thick bandage later, she was finished.

"You'll need to change that bandage in a few hours." She stood and began tidying up her kit. "When was the last time you fed, anyway?"

"Are you offering?" They often fed from each other. Like everything else about their relationship, it was simpler that way.

She glanced at him over her shoulder, tucking her hair behind her ear. "You're bleeding too much. That wound should have healed more than it had before you got here. You need to be feeding more, Ro."

"Like I said, are you offering?" He slid his good arm around her hip and pulled her toward him.

Her hands landed on his bare chest as her legs straddled his thighs. "If you need to feed, my vein is yours, but you shouldn't wait until you're with me. You can feed from others."

"I feed from others." He sounded defensive, even though he wasn't. "You're just my favorite flavor."

The corner of her mouth turned up. "I like feeding from you, too, but you need to hit up other sources more often, especially if I'm not available."

"You're available now." He pushed his hand up her shirt.

She wasn't wearing a bra, and her nipple puckered instantly as his fingers brushed over it. She moaned and sank onto his lap, closing her eyes.

She enjoyed the sex as much as he did. Neither was getting it elsewhere, and they were sexually compatible enough to know what the other wanted without having to ask, so it was the perfect arrangement.

Like now, for instance. He knew Alexis loved her breasts played with. It was the surest way to turn her on other than tying her up. If she seemed to be on the fence, all he had to do was fondle her breasts or caress her nipples, and she was putty in his hand.

He pinched both nipples between his thumbs and forefingers, and she rocked her hips against him.

And there she was. The wanton female he had hoped would come out to play the moment she mentioned feeding.

"Come here." He pushed her shirt up and off then pulled her forward, sucking one nipple into his mouth.

She wrapped her arm all the way around his head, holding him in place as he tongued the tight peak of her breast. She groaned and rocked more forcefully against him.

He could make her come this way. He had before. But that's not what he wanted or needed tonight. When he made her come, he wanted to be inside her. He had as much frustration to expend as she did.

With her nipple still in his mouth, he found the fastenings of her jeans and quickly released them while she did the same to his. Within seconds, her jeans lay in a heap on the kitchen floor and his were around his ankles.

She straddled him, guided his cock inside her, then gripped the back of the chair as she rode him, pressing her other breast against his mouth.

Taking the hint, he drew her neglected nipple between his lips, sucking hard then soft, nipping it with his teeth, and swirling his tongue around it.

She whimpered then shuddered, and a moment later, she cried out as she came, shivering violently.

When she was finished, he picked her up, still inside her, stepped out of his jeans, and turned her toward the table.

He laid her on the polished wooden surface, grabbed her

ankles, and levered her legs open, outstretched to the sides.

He had to bend his knees to take her in this position, but it didn't matter. When he came, it still felt just as good when he collapsed over her and sank his fangs into her neck.

Simple.

Casual.

And safe.

CHAPTER 4

MICAH PACED LIKE A CAGED TIGER in front of the windows overlooking the city. Good thing building maintenance had fixed the pane Ronan broke last week, or he might have walked right through the gaping hole and fallen eighteen stories to the sidewalk before he could dematerialize himself out of danger. Then again, maybe the fall and ensuing splat would have awakened him from the nightmare that continued to haunt him on a repeating loop.

My father is alive? I have a brother?

He wasn't sure whether he should curse Ronan or thank him. On one hand, if Ronan had never broken into his apartment and set off the chain reaction that had culminated in tonight's shocking revelations about his family, Micah might never have learned his father was still alive. On the other hand, ignorance is bliss.

Knowing his father was alive opened a huge can of worms. Hell, it opened a baker's dozen of them. In hindsight, he might have been better off not knowing the truth.

He didn't need a half brother who created problems like the ones Ronan had puked all over him since revealing himself a week ago. The guy was already a one-male wrecking ball with a side of natural disaster. Who the hell knew what else Ronan was capable of if he could alter the course of reality in only one week?

Then there was his dad. Drake Black. The male Micah had looked up to as a child like he'd been a god. When he'd been but a boy, Micah wanted nothing but to grow up to be like his father. Strong and powerful, respected by all and feared by the enemy.

Drake and his brother Rory had been vampires no one wanted to cross. Not because they were violent or cruel, but because they were the epitome of what a leader should be. Compassionate and kind to those they were responsible for and ruthless to anyone who tried to harm them.

Micah's father was older than Uncle Rory, and, as such, acted as a sort of governor of their village. He made decisions that affected them all. He oversaw the planting, the harvesting, and the law of the land, as it were. If there was a dispute, Drake Black resolved it. If punishment needed to be meted out, Drake Black served it. If a mating occurred in their small village, Drake Black blessed it.

But if anyone came to the village with the intent to harm, Drake Black destroyed them so thoroughly, nothing remained but the dust of their bones.

Ruthless, dominant, and authoritative. That was his father.

At least, it used to be. Now . . .? Micah didn't know what to think of him.

For the first time since blasting out of Ronan's home like he was launching from Cape Canaveral, Micah recalled how his father looked when he revealed himself in Ronan's home less than an hour ago.

There had been no hint of ruthless abandon. No sign of the ferocious warrior his father had once been, nor of the pragmatic dignitary. Not one glimpse of authority.

No power.

The male who showed up tonight had looked like his father, but the essence of his father hadn't been present. At least, not of the father Micah had known.

Drake Black 2.0 was but a shadow of the male Micah remembered. His body seemed smaller, even though his height was unchanged. But he had *appeared* thinner, shorter, diminutive in stature. Was that because his shoulders had been drooping, his head hanging like a heavy sack of rocks from his neck? Was it because something devastatingly traumatic had occurred? Or was it because his father had simply lost weight?

All of the above?

At his core, Micah was ecstatic to learn his father was still alive, but on the surface, he was furious. All this time, his dad had been out in the world, living and breathing, but he hadn't thought to get in touch to say, "Hey, son, guess what? I didn't die, after all." What the hell kind of sick fuck did something like that to his own son?

A voice inside his head tried to pipe up with a reply that made sense, but Micah stomped it down. Right now, he would much rather be angry at his father than entertain logical answers for why he hadn't revealed himself. Once he spent his initial internal uproar and made room for common sense, he would let the voices of reason give their two cents, but right now he was too fucked in the head to think rationally.

Ronan was his half brother. His father was alive. That was the extent of his ability to comprehend. The details were overflow that got washed away in the slushy current flash flooding his rationale.

He rubbed his palms together as he checked the time. Sam should be there any minute. She might already be inside the building, but he was too torqued to reach out his senses to find her.

He needed her to help him forget. To help him shut off his mind to everything but the most basic of needs. And what could be more basic than lust? Than primal desire? Than the need to feel his mate under him as he claimed her?

Sometimes a male simply needed to fuck, and fuck hard. Because fucking consumed everything else. It brought out the feral animal in every male, shutting down all the peripheral bullshit until the animal was satisfied. The harder the fucking, the greater the escape from reality. And right now, Micah needed to escape. He needed to feel Sam's softness yield to his hardness in every way, inside and out. He needed to expend the pent-up energy twisting his insides into painful knots.

His breath came in tight bursts, his cock already hard at the thought of sinking inside her. His fists clenched and released as he marched back and forth in the darkness, shirtless, barefoot, the fly on his cargo pants undone so it didn't crowd his erection.

He was ravenous with need, panting, overwhelmed with all he'd learned tonight and restrained only by his solitude.

He knew there was more to his father's sudden emergence — as well as his brother's — than he'd been told. A *lot* more. But he'd shot out of Ronan's home before his father could explain. There's only so much space inside a person's head to deal with the kind of personal shock and mental baggage his father had dumped on him, and Micah had tapped out before his dad got to the good part. All he wanted right now was for someone to toss him a tender T-bone and leave him be while he gnawed the damn thing down to the bone marrow.

His head jerked toward the door, his awareness lighting up

with Sam's presence like a flame catching on dry kindling. She was there. Just outside, in the hall.

He started for the foyer as the door slowly opened. She stepped inside, squinting into the dark apartment.

"Micah?"

In a flash, he was on her, slamming the door with the palm of one hand as he spun her and shoved her against the wall with the other.

She gasped, but the scent of her arousal spiked, letting him know she was more than ready for what he required.

He gripped handfuls of fabric on either side of her scoop-neck collar and yanked in opposite directions. Her T-shirt tore down the middle with the satisfying growl of ripping fabric.

He pushed the tattered shirt off her, along with her jacket. Leather and ruined polycotton blend puddled at her feet.

"I'm sorry," he said, growling the words as he tugged harshly at her jeans. The metal button at her waist shot across the room and thumped softly on the carpet.

She kicked off her sneakers. "For what?"

"For not being gentle." He clutched her bra between her breasts and tore it off her as if it were made of nothing more than tissue paper.

"I don't care. Whatever you need." She pushed the waist of her jeans past her hips and wiggled her legs so that the denim fell to her ankles as she pulled him closer. "I can buy new clothes, but you can't be replaced."

"I don't want to hurt you." He hoisted her off the floor.

Her legs locked around his waist as her palm wrapped around the back of his neck. "With you, pain is pleasure."

He thrust his hand between them and released his cock. "Then get ready for a lot of pleasure, baby."

SAM'S BACK SLAMMED AGAINST THE WALL as he plunged into her, making her cry out as her eyes flew open wide. She dug her fingers into his shoulders, hanging on as best as she could as he fucked her like his very existence depended on taking her as hard and fast as possible.

Their flesh slapped together. He grunted like a desperate wild animal with every urgent thrust, releasing a stream of what she imagined were obscenities in a language she couldn't understand. He wrapped one arm around her back and pressed his other hand against the wall beside her head, at once holding her against him while giving his body leverage to take her even harder.

She struggled to hold on, to keep her legs wrapped around his hammering hips. Somehow she stayed with him. A moment later, he let out a vicious growl that made her think of a lion attacking its prey. He pulled her from the wall and threw her face-first over the back of the couch. Without missing a beat, he was back inside her, shoving her face into the seat cushion with one hand as he clutched her hip with the other.

She latched onto the micro suede and pushed upward even as he wrestled to hold her down, pressing his hand between her shoulder blades, gripping the back of her neck like he was a police officer and she was the perp he'd chased down, tackled, and was now frisking on the ground.

But this was no normal frisking. No, sirree! And thank God for that!

The new position caused Micah's cock to hit her at just the right angle as he thrust into her, and with the physical onslaught that was Micah Black, her G-spot didn't stand a chance. Within seconds, a powerful orgasm clenched her muscles, and she fell into violent spasms, crying out as wave after wave of pleasure ripped through her.

"Fuck!" Micah's grip on her strengthened as his thrusts stuttered then renewed with a surge of urgency.

His pace quickened as he drove more deeply into her, and a few seconds later, he slammed forward and shuddered, coming hard, his cock kicking inside her as he shouted his release in one long, primal growl.

Before he finished coming, he yanked her off the couch by the hair, driving himself into her one final, gruff time as he sank his fangs into her shoulder with unceremonious abandon. Micah was never so violent when it came to feeding from her, so whatever had happened tonight was bad. Bad enough to push him to his absolute limit.

She let the venom euphoria take her as his cock continued to empty inside her, and then she became vaguely aware that she was being carried down the hall. As the euphoria began to wear off, she realized she was on their bed, and he was tying her wrists to the headboard's corner posts.

"What are you doing?" she watched bleary-eyed as he adeptly secured her wrists then moved to the foot of the bed and began tying a pair of ropes around her ankles. Then he stood on the bed, his feet on either side of her torso, removed the light shade from the overhead lamp to reveal a hook in the ceiling, and threaded the ropes through the hook.

"Micah?"

He pulled on the ropes, and her legs lifted as if controlled by a puppet master. He pulled again, and her legs opened wide as she forced her body to stay grounded on the mattress. It was either that, or her whole body would lift off the bed, so at least she had that much control. That's when she realized he was still hard. As in raging hard. And his eyes were black as midnight.

"Micah?" She shivered at his heady, lust-filled gaze as it swept over her body the way a serial killer might eye his next victim.

"I'm sorry, baby." The apology didn't reach his gaze as he knelt between her legs, but she heard the sincerity in his tone.

She was so excited, she was panting. "Sorry for what?"

He licked his lips, and his gaze practically swallowed her whole as he looked her up and down, admiring his work. Then he stared between her legs as he pushed his hips forward and breeched her with the head of his cock. "I won't be finished with you for a while."

"Oh." She sucked in her breath as he plunged all the way inside her, and the ride started all over again.

CHAPTER 5

With his shoulder on the mend, his carnal needs momentarily sated, and Alexis's blood recharging him as only a good meal can, Ronan geared up. He still had a lot of aggression to work out, and while sex had taken the edge off, it wasn't what he needed to finish the job.

Which meant he was heading to the South Side.

And what better place to work out what ailed him than Chicago's South Side? Haven of drug lords, turf wars, and enough gang violence to make a vigilante thief like him cop one hell of an adrenaline rush. If you wanted to hurt someone, the South Side was the place to do it without worrying about the local authorities. Hell, the CPD would probably thank him if they knew he was responsible for taking down some of Chicago's worst habitual offenders, even if all his kills were destined for the cold case files.

AKM, on the other hand, wouldn't be as eager to write him a happy little thank-you card. The pansy-assed enforcement agency Micah worked for had to follow certain rules. Rules that bound their hands, preventing them from taking down law-defiling humans, or from shutting down a dreck's cobalt-dealing enterprise permanently . . . due to the untimely death of the its blue-blooded proprietor, for example. As a free agent vigilante, Ronan could issue such life-ending cease and desist notices.

For every vampire who got hooked on the blue shit, the vampire race became that much easier to defeat. If nothing was done, it was only a matter of time before the power balance shifted and drecks claimed the upper hand.

And if that happened, God help the human race.

Not all drecks were bad, but the leadership was, and the dreck race would do what the leader wanted. And if Premier Royce wanted to exterminate humans or turn them into slaves, the rest of his race would have no choice but to comply.

That's where Ronan's special, self-appointed vigilante status came in. Micah had to follow protocol, Ronan didn't. He was Robin Hood. Green Arrow. Batman *and* Robin. He put on his mask, hit the streets, and took out the trash. If said trash ended up dead along the way, so much the better. He was making the world a better place, not playing footsies with political correctness.

Ronan exited the closet, cinching a leather belt around his waist. He was dressed all in black and had one of his skull masks tucked under his good arm. He kept a few changes of clothes at Alexis's place. Like everything else about them, it was just simpler that way, especially when they worked — and played — together as often as they did.

Alexis sat in the center of the bed, the sheet draped over her lap, her breasts shamelessly exposed. "You coming back here when you're done?"

"I can if you want me to?" He wouldn't mind spending the day with her. Nobody knew about their relationship, not even his father, so he didn't have to worry about anyone tracking him down here. He could hide out at her place for a day or two and have a little fun, all while ensuring his loathsome family left him alone.

Alexis looked him up and down then shrugged one shoulder. "Sure, why not? It's been a while since you tied me up." Her mouth curled into a sexy smirk.

He grinned. "Then I'll be back before dawn." He took his mask out from under his arm. "Hey, do you have any more of that tincture? The one that hides my scent?"

She sighed, her eyes rolling as her head tilted to one side. "Are you out again?"

"Not yet, but I'm getting low."

Making a tsking noise, she threw back the sheet, exposing her gloriously naked body as she swung her legs around and got to her feet. He stared at her slight but supple curves then followed her as she passed him and strolled back to her first aid kit, where she fished through the contents on the bottom.

Turning, she held out a small vial. "This is my last bottle until I can make more, so try to make it last."

He plucked the tiny bottle from her hand and stashed it in his pocket. "Yes, Mom."

"Ugh, I am *not* your mom."

Cozying up to her, he set his mask on the table and slid his hand over her hip and around to her bare ass, where he gave her cheek a squeeze. "And thank God for that." He pulled her hips forward as he pinched her nipple with his free hand, relishing the way it made her gasp sharply, and then released her. "Can I take your bike?" She had a kick-ass Kawasaki built for speed and agility. It would be a lot better for hunting targets than his Jeep.

With a lick of her lips and flushed cheeks—because, yeah, nipple play really did work that fast at turning her on—she took a step back and chucked her chin to where her spare keys hung on a rack on the wall. "Just don't wreck it."

He retrieved his mask, snatched the keys from the hook, and twirled the ring around his index finger, catching the keys with a jingle of metal on metal in his palm. "Where I'm going, I'd be more worried about it getting stolen."

"Ro . . ."

He cradled her cheek in his palm, tucking his fingers into her hair. "I'm only kidding." He pecked her on the lips. "I'll keep it safe."

"You'd better."

Seconds later, he was out the garage door and slinging his leg over the saddle of one of the finest pieces of machinery he'd ever ridden as the bay door slowly crawled upward.

A turn of the key, the hungry whine of the engine . . .

Let the hunt begin.

CHAPTER 6

MICAH LAY ON HIS SIDE, watching Sam sleep. Bruises shackled her wrists, and her neck and breasts were covered with bite marks, but she wore a delicate smile, as if, even in sleep, she was content and right where she wanted to be.

He'd used her body within an inch of sanity for over an hour, but with every release, he'd exorcised a few more of the demons that had been awakened by all that had transpired tonight. Learning your pops was still alive and that you had a little bro made for a serious mindfuck, and didn't Micah know it.

But now he was better. More focused. More like his old self again.

His head wasn't exactly a calm sea of ambience, but at least his thoughts were less scattered, and fragmented questions no longer strangled his brain. It was like he'd been a clogged drain that had been Roto-Rootered, Liquid Plumbered, and snaked all at once, letting the water flow freely again. So, yeah, the rough fucking had done its job. All that haunted him now were a few straggling, ghostlike memories.

Rolling to his back, he rubbed his palms up and down his face and stared up at the ceiling as his thoughts returned to his childhood. To the first time his father took him hunting.

He'd been twelve years old.

Oh sure, Micah had gone on hunts before, but only as an observer. Only as a student to learn how to track and corral the quarry for the kill. This had been the first time he'd been armed with his bow and arrow . . . an active participant rather than a bystander.

He closed his eyes, and once more, he was racing through the trees on his skinny, twelve-year-old legs, tracking the wild boar they would roast later for the celebration of the newly mated couple in their village. It was midday, but the thick forest canopy blocked out the sun, keeping his father and the other vampires safe from sunlight. The heavy, hooded cloaks they wore were an added protection.

Darting around the trees, Micah made hardly a noise as his long black hair whipped behind him. Most of the males in the village wore their hair short, but not he and his father. They left their hair long as a sign of status.

Coming to an abrupt stop, he lifted his bow and nocked an arrow with expert quickness, then drew the string back by his ear and held his breath. His young vampire hearing, which was only just beginning to develop, picked up the approach of both the boar and the other hunters driving it toward him.

It was a high honor that they had chosen him to send the fatal arrow into their quarry, and he refused to let them down. To let his *father* down. Because if he failed, it would reflect badly on not just him, but his father, too.

Closing his left eye, he tracked with his right as he stared down the length of the arrow to the deadly tip, following the crashing noises of the boar as it barreled through the forest toward him.

The moment the boar burst through the undergrowth, Micah took a moment to steady himself, girding his courage against the raging, snarling beast, and then released the bow.

The arrow zipped through the air and penetrated the boar straight between the eyes.

A desperate squeal peeled from the animal's throat as it lurched and fell forward. A moment later, his father rushed into the clearing, the others behind him, and drove his knife into the boar's neck, ensuring the beast didn't suffer needlessly. They didn't hunt for sport. They hunted out of necessity, for food and pelts, which they used for a variety of items around the village, from clothes to waterskins to floor coverings. No part of the boar would go unused. Not even its blood, which a member of their hunting party rushed forward to collect in a satchel made of animal skin as it poured from the wound in the beast's neck. The females would use it to make blood sausage for tonight's feast.

"Clean kill, Micah." His father rose and stood tall, his shoulders straight and chest lifted. "I'm proud of you."

Micah lifted his shoulders and chest, too, mimicking his father as pride coursed through him. Pleasing his father was the greatest reward he could hope for. Nothing was better than receiving a pat on the shoulder or a smile of approval from his father.

"Those are some superb skills you have there, boy," his uncle Rory added, joining his father as he wiped the sweat off his brow. Rory turned toward his father. "You've done a good job with this one, Drake. A damn fine job."

His father beamed as he approached then knelt in front of Micah. "You'll make a powerful warrior someday, Micah."

"Just like you?" He would be honored to be only half the warrior his father was.

His father had fought with the king during the war, and from the way the others in the village revered him, Micah knew his father's reputation was legendary.

The elder male placed his large palm on Micah's small shoulder. Its heaviness threatened to tip Micah over, but he forced himself to stand tall. "Micah, I daresay you're destined to become the greatest warrior our race has ever seen."

The greatest? How could that be? No one could ever be greater than Drake Black.

Micah smiled and nodded, accepting the compliment even as he doubted his own abilities to overtake his father's lofty example. "I won't let you down, Father."

His father rose to his full height and shook his head. "My son, you could never let me down."

As his father's words echoed in his memory, a wave of energy jarred Micah from his thoughts. He opened his eyes and frowned up at the ceiling. Sam still slept beside him. But what was that weird humming? Like white noise fuzzing his thoughts.

He lifted his head and scanned the room.

Then the static-like noise was gone.

His frown deepened, his senses sharpening as he glanced around the dark, silent room. The only sound was that of Sam's gentle breathing.

But something had stirred him from the reliving of his past.

And there it was again.

A soft surge of energy touched his mind in a way that reminded him of how it felt when he heard other people's thoughts. Only, no words echoed inside his head, just a subtle vibration and static. Well, it was more like a soft popping or crackling.

And then the sensation was gone again.

With his mind freed from whatever had just reached out to him, he sat up and glanced at Sam. She remained undisturbed, in deep slumber, her eyes moving behind her eyelids as she dreamed.

Maybe that's what he'd felt. He occasionally picked up on her dreams, and doing so did feel similar to hearing people's thoughts. But he'd always caught snapshots of images and words from her dreams, not the Rice Krispies elves doing the Snap! Crack! Pop! thing inside his head.

Shaking it off, he dismissed it as nothing. Just Sam's dreams reaching out to him, only in a new way.

His sweet Sam. His mate. His life. He would be lost without her.

Careful not to wake her, he eased out of bed. After slipping on a pair of sweats, he quietly retreated to the living room, where he stood in front of the wall of windows and stared out over downtown Chicago, his thoughts returning to how it had felt to earn his father's approval when he was still but a little boy.

He had looked up to his father once. Drake Black had been his entire world. His hero. His idol. His mentor. Now Micah didn't know how to feel about him.

How do you see someone as a hero when they've let you believe a lie for nearly a thousand years?

CHAPTER 7

PERSEPHONE PACED AT THE HEAD OF AN ALLEY behind an abandoned building in the heart of Chicago's notorious, gang-riddled South Side. A shot rang out from a few blocks to the west, followed by more gunshots, distant screams, and then sirens.

Toto, we're not in Kansas, anymore. The South Side was as different from the North Shore as a Timex was from a Rolex. Hey, but at least a Timex couldn't kill you. Death was a real possibility on the South Side.

Speaking of timepieces . . .

Stepping farther into the shadows, she checked the platinum Cartier watch on her trembling wrist. She was shaking so badly it took her a few seconds to confirm the time.

The people she was there to meet were late. Then again, they usually were, but only by a few minutes.

She lowered her arms, gripping her left wrist tightly with her right hand, trying to make the shivering stop. No such luck. All she managed to do was transfer the violent tremors from her arms to her teeth, which chattered as she slinked a few steps farther into the alley as a pair of drecks appeared on the street corner, spotted her, and headed her way.

Just the sight of them with their small duffel of yes-please-I-need-some was enough to calm the shakes and bring a sigh of relief.

She'd tried to get off the blue powder, which had become blue rock, and then injectable blue serum. A month ago now, wasn't it? Or was it two? She couldn't think straight enough to put a timeline on when she and Miriam, her best friend and the king's daughter, had decided to enter AKM's cobalt addiction rehabilitation program and get off the crap.

Miriam had succeeded and remained sober.

Persephone hadn't and was back on the blue death.

Then again, Miriam had her new mate and her new and improved father to thank for her clean status. Persephone didn't have that kind of support at home. Lucky her.

Everything was different now that Miriam had Io in her life. She was a recovering addict, in love, and expecting her first young. All because her father had realized the error of his ways.

Almost losing his daughter had made the king reevaluate how strict he'd been with Miriam, which had led him to understand he was to blame for pushing her to use cobalt as a coping mechanism. Once he realized he was contributing to his daughter's near-death overdoses, he quickly modified his behavior, and now he and Miriam were closer than ever, and she was getting the support she needed to stay sober.

Too bad Persephone's own father couldn't drink King Bain's brand of Kool-Aid and give her some slack, too. But, noooo, her father was even worse than Miriam's father had been before he pulled his head out of his ass. At least the king had always desired a *true* mate for Miriam. One who had bonded to her, soul to soul, tied one to the other through biology. It had been his *methods* of finding said biological mate for Miriam that had been the problem, even though his heart had always been in the right place.

But Persephone's father's heart was all wrong. In every way.

He followed the old traditions. Or, as Persephone called them, the *archaic* traditions. Traditions that had fallen out of favor with the king eons ago because of their preference for arranged matings instead of natural ones. Traditions that dismissed the natural order of things and sought to do better what Mother Nature would always do best.

Caring more about social standing and money, her father insisted on choosing a mate for her that met *his* standards, whether she liked the guy or not.

Only a male of proper breeding could bed his daughter, even if said bedding would never result in offspring, because it was well known among the vampire race that unless a biological mating occurred, a male couldn't have a calling, and if he couldn't go into a calling phase, he was practically infertile.

But to people like her father, who still engaged in the practice of arranging unions for their children, pedigree was more valuable than a male's ability to sire a young. All they cared about was that if an arranged couple was blessed with a young, at least the bloodlines remained pure.

At least half of the vampire couples of the upper class who had been together longer than five hundred years still had no children, which was why so many bloodlines had gone extinct. No callings meant no children to pass on the family genes.

That was a fate Persephone couldn't envision for herself. She wanted young. She wanted a *lot* of young. The more the merrier. But with a mate who had been chosen for her rather than one who had bonded to her naturally, a large family was out of the question.

Her father had already tried to pair her with Arion Savakis, the pure-blooded son of Gregos Savakis, another of the king's liaisons.

She had liked Arion. He was handsome, virile, and a member of the king's warrior class. Every female she knew wanted Arion for a mate, and she had been prepared to sacrifice her dream of a large family simply at the thought of feeling his strong, able hands on her body, her breasts, her sex. After all, if she couldn't hope for children, she could at least hope for pleasure.

But Arion had already mated another—the male Severin—and King Bain had upheld the pairing, leaving her like a jilted human at the altar, no groom, no wedding, no honeymoon.

Still a virgin.

But her father—while livid at being robbed of something he felt was his right—simply moved on, scouting the pool of unmated upper-class sons like he was tossing a fishing line into a lake without caring what he reeled in. All that mattered was how wealthy the fish was. The quality of the meat wasn't as important as the size of the fish's bank account, even if what he landed was a slippery eel instead of a red snapper.

She would be mated by summer's end. That much she was sure of. And since it appeared he'd made his selection, because she knew of only one male he was still interviewing, the mating was likely to happen sooner rather than later.

Persephone's gag reflex nearly engaged, helped along by her cobalt withdrawal. She held no desire or fondness for the male in question. He had clammy skin, oily hair, and needed to put on at least a hundred pounds and grow six inches to be of ample size to even *begin* appealing to her sense of physical attraction. Not only was he shorter than she was, his eyes were too close together, his lips as thin as a thread, and his nose small and pointed.

He reminded her of Professor Snape from the Harry Potter movies, but even Snape was better looking than this male.

How would she ever withstand his cold, snakelike touch? The thought of kissing him was enough to nauseate her. Sex would surely make her retch.

But her father cared not for her feelings on the matter. She was but a puppet, a pawn, a token piece on the board game of life, controlled by another, never in the driver's seat. Never allowed to make her own decisions.

Which was why she was in this alley, pulling out a small bundle of cash and handing it to the first dreck who reached her.

If she couldn't make decisions that impacted her life, she would make decisions that could effect her death.

"You want the usual?" the dreck asked, taking her money without counting it.

They'd gone through this drill enough times for him to know she never shorted him.

She nodded, nibbling her bottom lip as she eyed the duffel and began rolling up her sleeve.

The usual was an injection of serum now and a small cellophane bag of rocks she could smoke later. But they had to inject her. She couldn't stomach needles.

The second dreck pulled out a syringe filled with bright-blue fluid and directed her to sit down. You didn't want to be standing when the drug entered your bloodstream. The convulsions and instant euphoria were so strong, your legs went out from under you.

She didn't care that the ground was damp and dirty, or that the alley smelled strongly of urine and something else resembling feces. As she dropped her butt onto the pavement and leaned against the cool brick wall behind her, all she cared about was getting the blue death inside her.

If she was lucky, tonight would be the night. Her last fix. She had gradually increased the amount of serum she purchased, hoping for the overdose that would end her life so she could finally be released from servitude to her father's agenda. But her heart was still beating, her lungs still pumping air, her blood still warm.

She just couldn't catch a break and die.

As the first dreck stood guard, the second knelt beside her, tied rubber tubing around her biceps, tapped the inside of her elbow looking for her well-used vein, and then slid the needle home.

The rush hit her the moment he began plunging the serum into her.

Yeeesssss . . .

Colored lights danced like tiny fairies in her vision. Euphoria not unlike that of venom euphoria — only darker and more robust — hit her. Then the convulsions started. Small at first then with greater intensity. She was flying . . . flying high above the earth . . . free with great white wings instead of arms. Wind blew her hair back from her face, and she smiled up at the heavens, spiraling higher, higher.

She glanced to the side and saw the skull face of Death. He was coming for her, dressed all in black, moving with the stealth of a thief.

Tears blossomed in her eyes. Death. Sweet, beautiful Death had finally come for her. And he *was* beautiful. Glorious even. So much so that her tears of joy flowed freely down her cheeks and dripped off her chin.

Then she began to fade, her vision dimming, her heart growing sluggish, every muscle falling limp like dying weeds pulled from a garden.

This was it. Freedom was finally hers. At last.

RONAN DROPPED TWO DEAD BODIES IN THE CORNER of a dark, empty warehouse and dusted off his gloved hands.

Whoever the hell had made oversized pants that hung halfway — or even all the way — off a dude's ass a fashion craze deserved a round of applause. Not that Ronan liked the look. He hated it, but it made his job easier. If these two vagrants hadn't been fashionistas of the off-the-ass trend, at least one of them might have gotten away. But no, they had tried to run in their silly attire and tripped over their own low-slung, wide-leg jeans, the cuffs of which had bunched up over their feet like coiled rope.

Thank you, thug life.

Chicago was a fractionally safer place now that these two were off the streets. What he'd seen in their minds about what they'd done and what they'd been about to do had made exterminating them an easy call. The little girl—the cousin of one of the boys, if you can believe that shit—in that house they were trying to break into would be okay now. She wouldn't be raped, beaten, and killed. She would sleep through the night, wake up in the morning, put on her school uniform, and head off to class, none the wiser to how close she'd come to being just another statistic.

What kind of human did something like that to another human? A relative, no less?

Even the vampire race had bad eggs, but Ronan had never understood how someone could do something so heinous against another.

Unfortunately, this was par for the course on the South Side. This area was a hive of crime where drecks and humans alike did tragically bad shit to anyone and everyone. Human females were trafficked and pimped out by the quarter hour. Little kids were murdered execution style in alleys as retaliation for a member of one gang offending a rival gang member's mother. Money changed hands for both drugs and weapons hundreds of times a night. And drecks dealt the lion's share of their cobalt here.

In other words, there was no shortage of criminals on the South Side who needed a brand of justice the police couldn't serve, what with all their rules, due process, and the need for tangible proof.

Ronan needed no such proof. He witnessed the crime, he executed the grime, and then he took it out like the garbage it was.

He eyed the two lifeless gangbangers slumped on the grungy floor. It would be days, if not weeks, before the bodies were found, but the most important takeaway from their deaths was that they were two less weapons made of flesh and blood that could be used against the innocent.

Which left only a few thousand still in need of termination.

No sweat. All in a night's work.

Making mental tick marks reminiscent of the way fighter pilots marked their planes with kills or successful missions, Ronan turned to go, his skull mask still shielding his face, ready to dematerialize back to Alexis's Kawasaki.

That's when he smelled them. Drecks. And cobalt. And a vampire. A female who was this very second drowning her blood in blue death.

How was that for lucky? He'd poofed right into a deal going down. He was going to get two kills tonight for the price of one and maybe even save a life.

Whisking silently to the roof, he darted around the perimeter of the warehouse, zeroing in on the activity.

Male voices drifted up from the alley that ran behind the building.

"What's wrong with her?" one voice said.

"Do I care?" said another. "She wanted a little extra, she got a little extra. What do I care if she dies? Bitch had a death wish, anyway, and we got our money, right?"

Ronan vapored to the foot of the alley and slinked toward the sound of rustling, as if the two males were rapidly gathering their shit for a fast exit.

"Yeah, paid in full," the first voice said. There was a pause before he spoke again. "I don't think she's breathing."

"Good. That's one less vampire we have to worry about. Grab the rocks. We can resell them to someone else and pocket the extra cash."

Ronan peered around a dumpster to find two drecks gathering paraphernalia and stuffing it in a small black duffel. He couldn't see the vampire they'd apparently just doped, probably because she was on the ground. Cobalt took the legs out from under a person. That's why you drugged up on your ass, so you didn't crack your skull when you convulsed and toppled over like a crumbling silo.

"Shit, we've got to go before someone catches us," the first dreck said.

"Jesus, relax. No one's going to catch us here. This location is as far off the radar as you can get."

"Not for those AKM fucks. This is just the kind of place they like to patrol."

"Fuck them. We were just filling a junkie's need. We've done nothing wrong."

"Like they'd believe that load of shit."

Ronan pressed closer, still staying in the shadows but flirting with the light. There. He could finally see the victim. Long blond hair. Her head was slumped forward like she was unconscious. She was seated on the filthy concrete, her back resting against the brick wall of the warehouse. The acrid scent of cobalt laced the air.

Nothing wrong? This asshole thought they'd done nothing wrong? Think again.

Ronan knew the score with cobalt. He knew the damage it did and why the drecks were using it against vampires. Maybe he and his dad didn't get along on their good days, but ol' Dad knew things no other vampire did, and he shared his knowledge with Ronan, which was just about the only reason Ronan stuck around. He didn't know where his dad got his intel, but possessing it gave Ronan a leg up in the information war that seemed to plague King Bain.

Stepping into the light, he blasted the first dreck with a pulse of energy from the oscillator strapped to his palm. The same oscillator he'd used to break the window at Micah's apartment over a week ago and the same oscillator that had destroyed the internal organs of the gangbangers discarded inside the warehouse.

The dreck flew backward like tossed meat, slamming into the wall, knocked out cold as he fell to the dirty, decrepit pavement.

"What the—?" The second dreck spun around and went for his gun.

Ronan leaped forward and kicked the gun from his hand then fisted the dreck's jacket and swung him around, slamming him into the wall so hard he heard the asshole's teeth rattle.

"You think you've done nothing wrong here?" Ronan hissed. His modulated voice came through vicious and hushed. He sounded like Satan's henchman.

The dreck scowled at his mask. "What the fuck are you? A video game character?"

Cute. Very cute. If only he knew. "I'm your worst fucking nightmare. And you're about to get Mario Brothered."

The dreck sneered. "Even if you are AKM, you have no jurisdiction over me."

"You just became my jurisdiction, asshole." Behind the mask, Ronan grinned. "And you'd be better off if I *were* AKM." This fucker was in for a surprise. A nasty, demented, torturous surprise.

Worming his way into the dreck's mind, he began stretching his thoughts, turning them, distorting them, twisting them into nightmarish insanity that felt more real than the world around him. He was delivering a fate worse than death. He was gifting the dreck with madness.

The dreck's eyes widened. His body tensed and shuddered, and his breathing intensified, growing ragged and haphazard. Within seconds, abject terror lined his face, filling his eyes with horror.

Ronan had no idea where his gift had come from, being that both his parents were full-bloods. Typically, only mixed-bloods were born with such supernatural gifts. But he'd learned almost twenty years ago, right after his transition, that he could distort someone's reality so drastically that they could no longer decipher truth from fiction unless he allowed them to.

Only one person knew of his gift. Alexis. She'd seen him use it. But he didn't abuse it. Maybe he scoffed in the face of danger. Maybe he laughed at fear and let reckless abandon dominate in ways it shouldn't. But he would never take his gift for granted. Only those he deemed most worthy of a trip through hell suffered its wrath.

Ronan yanked the dreck away from the wall and tossed him aside like a rotten fish carcass. The dreck landed haphazardly and staggered, blabbering unintelligibly, cackling like a crazy person strung out on gasoline-laced PCP as he turned and lurched for the alley's exit. If he didn't get himself killed by stepping in front of a moving car, he might make it to morning before taking his own life.

The first dreck groaned and pushed off the ground, shaking his head, dispelling the brain fog that resulted from being tossed against brick and mortar.

Ronan was on him in a heartbeat, lifting him off the filthy pavement. "Looks like you picked the wrong night to be out dealing cobalt."

He pressed the oscillator directly over the dreck's heart. A split second later, a pulse ripped through the dreck's chest. His arms and legs jerked, and he convulsed as if he'd been struck by lightning. Then he went limp, blood trickling from the corner of his mouth, his eyes lifeless orbs.

Ronan discarded him as carelessly as he'd done with the first dreck then turned toward the female.

Crouching beside her, he gently lifted her head and bushed back her hair, listening for any sign of a beating heart.

As he revealed her face, he caught his breath, his whole body growing lighter, as if he'd been lifted by an angel and his feet no longer touched the ground.

He'd never seen a more beautiful female, nor one so pure. One full inhale was enough for him to know she'd never been touched. Never been violated in the most intimate way.

A virgin? On the South Side? Trying to reconcile the two was like trying to read a book upside down.

So what in the hell was she doing here?

Enchanted to the point of bewilderment, he took in her full pink lips, her rounded cheeks, the way her dainty eyebrows arched over her closed eyes.

He'd do anything for her to open those eyes and look at him, just so he could see what color they were.

Her labored breathing was what finally jolted his wits back into him. Her pulse was sluggish. He could hear her heart thumping hard but slow — too slow — to keep her alive for long. If he didn't do something to save this fair creature, she would die.

Vampires might have been immortal, but cobalt was their Achilles heel. Overdosing led to death, and it was obvious she had way more than OD'd.

Ronan couldn't let her die. He didn't have to see into her eyes or hear her voice to know the world would be a far worse place without her in it.

Casting aside his fascination, he scooped her into his arms. "What the hell are you doing using this shit?" he murmured.

She obviously came from money. No one wore couture to buy drugs unless that was all they had in their wardrobe, and the Hermès scarf and Chanel handbag lying beside her bespoke of wealth.

What could drive such a fine female to shoot up? What was she trying to escape that was so awful? If he could stomach his own abhorrent life without requiring drugs to do so, she could certainly accept hers.

Snatching her handbag and cradling her against him as he connected with her near-lifeless form, he dematerialized and reappeared outside AKM.

If only there were somewhere else he could take her, because AKM was the last place he wanted to be, but this was the best place — the *only* place — capable of treating a vampire overdose.

Rushing through the front door, he shot toward the reception desk. "Cobalt overdose!"

The female behind the desk jumped to attention, her expression contorting into one of terror as she stared at Ronan. Oh, yeah, he was still wearing the mask and using his voice modulator.

"HELP! She's dying!"

She jumped to attention then quickly punched in a series of numbers on her phone.

He probably looked like the Grim Reaper, but instead of taking away the dead, he was trying to keep the mysterious, beautiful female alive.

"We have an overdose in the lobby!" the receptionist barked to someone. "Alert medical and get someone up here *now!*" She disconnected and stared fearfully at him but said nothing further.

He rocked the precious female in his arms and felt for her pulse again. Shit! Where was her pulse? He shifted his fingers on her neck. He couldn't find a pulse! Couldn't hear one, either.

"Help me!" he shouted at the receptionist as he fell to his knees and laid the blonde on the floor.

The receptionist hesitated.

"HELP ME NOW! She doesn't have a pulse, goddamn it!"

The other female rushed around the counter and landed on her knees beside him. "What do I need to do?"

Ronan pushed up his mask and tilted the blonde's head back. "Start chest compressions."

The female clamped her hands together and began pumping on the blonde's chest as he guided her to press down forcefully to the beat of the Bee Gees' "Staying Alive." After twenty compressions, Ronan told her to stop, bent down, pressed his lips against the blonde's—they were so soft—and breathed for her.

"Again," he commanded as he sat back up. "Twenty more compressions."

Back and forth, he and the receptionist performed two more sets. On the third, the blonde sputtered and coughed, blinking frantically as she tried to get her bearings. As she opened her eyes for good, Ronan dropped his mask back over his face and lifted her upper body off the floor.

"You're okay." He brushed back her soft, silky hair. "You're going to make it." He glanced behind him as the double doors leading into the belly of the building burst open and a team of doctors and nurses poured through, pushing a gurney. "See, they're here to help you. You're going to be okay."

Her eyes were the bluest he had ever seen. Light blue. Jamaican-water blue. Clear-sky-after-a-summer-storm blue. Her perfect brows scrunched as her gaze focused on him. Then a faint smile touched her pale lips as her expression softened, and she reached for his face. For his mask. "Death . . . my hero," she whispered weakly.

My hero.

Those two simple words echoed inside his head as if she'd shouted them inside a canyon.

My hero. My hero . . . my hero . . .

He'd never been anyone's hero, and hearing the words lift from her mouth caused his heart to skip a beat. Someone like her, who had everything, who should have wanted for nothing, thought of him as a hero. *Her* hero.

If only she knew. He was no one's hero. If anything, he was a curse. Nothing but trouble and bad fortune had followed him all his life. He'd fought relentlessly just to have anything that resembled a normal childhood.

He stared at her, mesmerized by her eyes. "I'm no hero," he said quietly, trailing his fingers down the alabaster skin of her cheek. "Just someone in the right place at the right time to save the most beautiful female in the world."

Her smile widened in that drunken way a drug addict grins when she's seeing purple elephants dancing in tutus. Then she let out a breathy giggle that quickly turned into sobs as she clutched the front of his hoodie and tried to pull herself up from the floor. "Please help me. Don't let him do this to me. Don't let him take me back. Please."

What was she talking about? Who was *him*? Where was *back*? Why didn't she want *him* to send her back there? And where could he find *him* and rip his heart out for making her so afraid?

He took her hand and pushed her toward the doctors as they reached for her.

"You're okay. They'll take care of you here." He didn't want to let her go.

"Pleeeaaassse . . ." She sobbed and continued reaching for him even as the doctors lifted her from his arms, stripping him of her touch, and placed her on the gurney. As they hurried her away, her eyes locked onto his and screamed silent pleas for him not to leave her.

He watched them whisk her away, feeling an unfamiliar ache stir inside his chest, along with a peculiar sense of loss. It felt like he'd just missed something vital. Something that meant life or death. Letting them take her didn't feel right.

"What the fuck?"

Ronan glanced up as two enforcers joined the receptionist, who had retreated from him and now stood several feet away. One of the enforcers had long blond hair and shoulders as wide as a tractor trailer. The other had high and tight dark hair and a wicked tattoo sleeve down one arm.

Severin and Io. He knew the players inside AKM well enough to identify these two.

"Skeletor! Get him!" Io shot toward him with Sev hot on his heels.

In a blink, Ronan darted out the door and dematerialized, engaging the refilled vapor pod attached to his belt to erase his trail as he flew away from AKM.

Away from *her*.

The female who'd stolen his heart with just one look.

The female who had awakened something inside him he'd never felt before.

My hero . . .

This wasn't going to end well.

For her.

For him.

For everybody.

Weeks from now, he would look back on this night and wish he'd done about a million things differently.

CHAPTER 8

SAM STILL SLEPT, but Micah was a stew of emotions. Some happy, some sad, some downright pissed off.

As he paced in his living room and stared blindly out the wall of windows overlooking Chicago, his thoughts returned to that night from his childhood. To the celebration in the village. He chuckled softly as he remembered his mother chiding him for his dirty feet.

"How do you expect to catch Katarina's eye with dirty feet?" she had said when he entered their small thatch-and-stone cottage, where she and his father remained during daylight hours, except Father had stayed in the forest after the hunt and would return home after sunset, when it was safe.

At the mention of Katarina's name, Micah had scrubbed himself raw in the wooden tub, ensuring not a speck of uncleanliness remained.

Katarina's family had moved to the village the year before, and he had developed an instant crush on her the moment he saw her. If there was even a chance she would look unfavorably on his dirty feet, he would make sure he never walked barefoot again.

At nightfall, after his father returned, he and his parents dressed in their finest clothes and made their way along the torch-lit path toward the courtyard in the center of their village.

Micah trailed behind his parents, looking down at his trousers, embarrassed at how short they were. When had he grown so much?

His mother glanced back at him. "Stop moping."

"My pants are too short. I look stupid." He scowled and hid his face.

His dad stopped and turned around. "I'll have none of that,

Micah." He crouched in front of him. "You are my son, and my son does not look stupid. Never will. Do you understand?"

Micah had been on the verge of tears, but as he looked into his father's ice-sharp navy blue eyes, he immediately swallowed them. "Yes, sir." More than anything else, Micah wanted to be like his father. Brave, powerful, respected. Admired and revered by all who met him.

His father took Micah's shoulders and held him firmly. "If you walk into that courtyard with your head high and your shoulders squared, all anyone will notice is your confidence. They won't even notice the way your trousers hit above your ankles. But if you walk in slouched and defeated, the other children will see your weakness and exploit it." He stood and chucked the underside of Micah's chin. "Stand tall, son. Be proud. You're a Black. Own your family name. Own who you are."

Micah nodded, straightening and jutting out his chin as he smoothed his palms over the front of his dingy, faded shirt.

"That's my boy. Always remember where you come from, Micah. Always carry the Black name with honor." He brushed his long fingers over Micah's cheek. "Appearance is everything. Act like that which you wish to become, and not only will you become it, but everyone around you will believe that is who you are." His father chucked his chin again. "Now, keep your head high."

"Yes, Father."

His mom motioned to take Micah's hand, but his father stopped her. "No. Let him walk on his own, Isabel."

"But, Drake—"

"Let him be strong in his own right." He wrapped his hand around hers and started down the path again. "He is of age to walk on his own now."

They continued in silence, his father the picture of patriarchal pride, as if he owned not only his own skin, but that of Micah's mother, Micah's, and the entire town.

It was then that Micah realized that his father took responsibility for the village. Not because he'd been appointed — his father held no royal or political positions—but because he cared. He felt responsible for the people who lived in the village. He was a figurehead for the community. A pinnacle of strength and justice.

Once they reached the courtyard, Micah slipped away from his parents. A giant bonfire burned in the center of the square, lighting the surrounding stands of food. Musicians played on a makeshift platform. Some of the villagers were already dancing, but many were still busy setting up, milling about in greeting, congratulating the newly mated couple, and setting out heavy platters of food.

Micah wandered from fire pit to fire pit, inspecting the smorgasbord. Grains, meats, breads, wild vegetables, roasted corn and potatoes from the gardens, and, of course, the wild boar dripping fat into the flames beneath it, sizzling and sending up light-grey plumes of smoke.

And then there were the desserts. An entire table made of long planks was set with sweet biscuits, tarts, cakes, and pies, which beckoned every child's eye in the courtyard. Making a quick glance behind him to ensure no one was watching, Micah snatched one of the tarts and darted into the shadows of the trees to eat it.

As he took his first bite, he watched from his hiding place as his father twirled his mother then pulled her against him as they danced in time with the music. His parents were happy. They never fought. They disagreed sometimes, but they always managed to come to an accord without arguing. When he had questioned how they managed to get along despite their differences, his father had told him that it was because his mother was his heart, and how can you argue with your own heart?

At the time, Micah hadn't understood what he meant, but now that he'd become infatuated with Katarina, his father's words were beginning to make sense.

A flash of red hair caught his eye. He turned and drew in his breath. There she was.

His Katarina.

She looked glorious in a simple, pale-blue dress, with her auburn hair hanging in loose curls over her shoulders and down her back. She nodded in greeting at his mother as she passed. His mother smiled and waved back before his father spun her again, making both females laugh.

Katarina would be his someday. Micah felt the truth of it deep inside his heart, which skipped a beat as she glanced in his direction. He quickly ducked behind a tree so she didn't see him, the tart all but forgotten in his hand as he peered back out. She crossed the courtyard then paused to smell a bouquet of flowers on one of the decorated tables only a short distance away.

She looked heavenly, her eyes closing, her nose dipping into the buds as her delicate hand lifted and pulled back her hair.

So perfect and beautiful. Micah swore she had to be an angel.

Then, as if she could feel his gaze on her, she opened her eyes and turned toward him. A humored smile spread over her face as their eyes met.

"Little Micah? Is that you? What are you doing back there?" She straightened and fluffed her skirt as she walked toward him.

Feeling the blood rush into his face, Micah quickly stepped away from the tree, trying to pretend he hadn't been hiding.

"I didn't want my parents to see me." He lowered his gaze to the tart, feeling his cheeks heat even more.

Katarina knelt in front of him. "I see." She giggled. "You snuck back here so no one would know you stole a treat, didn't you?"

With a sheepish grin, Micah nodded, totally transfixed by her luminous green eyes and plump lips.

Demurely glancing to the ground, she looked back up through her lashes. "Can I have a bite? I promise I won't tell."

Nodding eagerly, Micah held the tart out to her, speechless. The female of his dreams was right in front of him, asking him for a bite of the treat he had stolen, making flirty eyes at him even though she was more than twice his age and well into her transition.

No doubt she knew of his crush on her, and like his mother, Katarina sought only to indulge him. But that made no difference to Micah. All that mattered was that her long, elegant fingers wrapped around his skinny wrist as she leaned forward and took a bite of the fruit-filled tart.

Micah could barely breathe. He knew it was an honor to feed a female from his own hand, and here he was, feeding the most beautiful female in the village.

Katarina's pink lips parted, and her perfect, straight teeth sank into the morsel he held for her. As she drew away, sugar crystals clung to her lips, and she quickly licked them off.

"That's delicious." She released his wrist. "I can see why you couldn't wait to eat it." She grinned as she chewed with delicate propriety.

He could only stare, hypnotized by her green eyes and pink cheeks.

"I heard you were the one who caught our dinner tonight," she said, sinking to the ground and sitting back on her heels, facing him. She placed her palms on her lap.

Micah nodded and finally found his voice. "Yes. I'm going to be a warrior someday."

Katarina's eyebrows shot up as her expression brightened. "Really now? A warrior? That's very noble, yes?"

He didn't care if it was noble or not. He just wanted to impress her. "My father says I'm going to be the greatest warrior our race has ever seen." He took a bite of the tart, carefully avoiding the part she had eaten from.

"Well, your father would know." Katarina brushed her palms over her skirt. "He's quite skilled with a sword. I've seen him training you."

"You have?" Knowing Katarina had watched him train filled him with perverse joy. Even at such a young age, he liked knowing she'd been watching him.

"Oh yes. You're quite talented. I'm impressed how well you keep up with your father."

"I'm better with a bow and arrow."

Micah grew more excited. Katarina was talking to him. She was here, alone with him, in the shadows, eating from his hand, and they were talking. His little heart practically beat out of his chest.

"The bow and arrow it is for you, then. Maybe you'll teach me how to use it someday."

Nodding again, he imagined what it would be like to teach her how to shoot with his bow. To be close to her, maybe even touching her. "Absolutely." He quickly blushed, realizing he sounded too eager. "I mean, if you really want to learn."

She shifted on the ground and giggled. "Of course I do, or I wouldn't have mentioned it. Rumor has it you're the best archer in the village, and I want to learn from the best." She leaned forward and tucked his long hair behind his ear and lightly pinched his nose. "Silly you."

Butterflies lit inside his stomach as her fingers touched his face.

She sat back once more. "Can you show me how you killed the boar today?"

He nodded then held the remainder of the tart out to her. "Hold this."

She took it from him, her eyes twinkling from the firelight of the bonfire in the center of the courtyard. She looked like she was fighting a smile.

Micah stepped back proudly and stood tall, just as his father had taught him. It felt odd without his bow, but he pretended he was holding it, nocking an arrow.

"The others ran the boar to me, corralling him." Micah glanced over as he dramatically relayed the story to her. "I heard the beast tearing through the trees and lifted my bow." He lifted his arms in grand fashion, as if he held his bow and arrow at the ready. "As soon as the boar burst from the undergrowth, I took a deep breath" — Micah paused briefly — "and then I let go." He opened his hand by his ear as if releasing an arrow. "Right between the eyes!"

Micah spun back, reveling under her admiration. She handed his treat back to him, and he let his fingertips graze her palm as he took it. Her hand was warm and soft, and as he glanced back up at her face, her red hair caught the light in such a way as to resemble a fiery halo.

"Are you an angel?" he blurted, immediately regretting it. Dread sank like a heavy stone to the pit of his stomach, chased by a heavy dose of humiliation.

Katarina let out a lighthearted laugh. "A what?"

Unable to meet her eyes, Micah answered in a voice so soft it was a wonder he could be heard at all. "An angel."

"No, little Micah, I'm not an angel." She giggled and tapped the tip of her finger on his nose. "Angels come from heaven. I'm not from heaven."

He wanted to tell her he thought she *was* from heaven, because she was too beautiful for earth. But he had already stuck his foot in his mouth once, so he kept quiet.

Neither spoke for a moment. Then Katarina pushed herself to her feet. "Will you save a dance for me later, little Micah?"

Surprised she would even ask, he looked up in startled amazement and nodded before he could stop himself. "Uh-huh."

Bending down, Katarina placed her hands on Micah's scrawny shoulders and kissed his cheek then pulled back with a conspiratorial smile. "I won't tell anyone that you snuck off with a treat as long as you promise to teach me how to use a bow and arrow, okay?"

All Micah could do was nod, his tongue tied in knots.

She laughed as if she realized her effect on him and thought it adorable. "Until our dance then, little Micah. Now, don't get caught ruining your dinner." She wagged a finger at him in farewell then turned and headed back into the courtyard.

Micah took another bite of the tart and watched her walk away, mesmerized by the gentle sway of her hips under her skirt.

After she had disappeared amid a crowd of adults, Micah looked down. Only one bite of tart remained: the one she had eaten from. Reverently, he raised the morsel to his mouth and slowly chewed as he placed his small palm over his cheek where she had kissed him. His body tingled and felt warm all over at the thought of her and the time they had just shared.

Eventually, he left his hiding place in the trees and joined his parents to eat. The food and drink were delicious, the music lively, and the celebration lasted well into the night. Micah got his dance with Katarina, and over the days and weeks that followed, his crush on her deepened.

Then the war erupted again, and his father left for the royal city, taking Micah with him to begin training for the king's guard. He met Malek there, and they became best friends, and then he met Tristan a short time later.

The years ticked by, but Micah never forgot Kat, even when he turned eighteen and ventured into the city with Malek and bedded his first female, a human named Mary. He spent a lot of time with Mary in the months that followed, and she taught him how to please a woman and be pleased, but he never felt for her the way he felt for Kat.

"Micah?"

Micah jolted from his memories and turned just as Sam entered the living room. She had put on a pair of peach-colored cotton panties and a pink, ribbed tank top.

She smiled sleepily when she saw him and rubbed her eyes. "Hey, what are you doing out here?"

He held his hand out to her, inviting her to join him by the window. "Just thinking."

"About . . .?" She slid her hand into his, and he pulled her against him, kissing her temple as she tucked her cheek against his shoulder and wrapped her arms around his waist.

"When I was younger . . . my childhood."

She let out a dubious snort. "You were a child?"

He grinned and pressed his lips against the top of her head. Her short, unruly hair caressed his face like short, silk ribbons. "Hard to believe, I know." He rubbed his nose over her scalp, inhaling her lilac scent. "It *was* a long time ago."

They stood in silence for a while, holding each other, staring out the window.

"What about Katarina? Were you thinking about her, too?" There was no blame, suspicion, or insecurity in Sam's tone, only curiosity.

He straightened and drew in a full breath. It wasn't that it made him uncomfortable to talk to Sam about Katarina. It just felt taboo. Kat was his past, Sam his future. Why mix the two?

"You never talk about her, Micah." Sam lifted her cheek from his shoulder and looked at him.

He gazed into her clover-green eyes, finding compassion and sincerity. And love. And strength.

Kat still haunted his memories in a way that felt unresolved. Then again, she'd been taken from him so abruptly, how could he ever find closure over her death? Maybe it *would* do him good to talk about her.

"You're a lot like she was," he said, brushing Sam's hair off her forehead with the tips of his fingers. "Spunky and strong."

She smiled. "Tell me about her. How did you meet? What was she like?" A twinkle sparkled in her eyes as she reinforced her hold on him, hugging him harder. "Tell me about your first kiss. The first time you made love."

He let out a snort. "Do you really don't want to know all that?"

"Sure. Why not?"

"I didn't think females liked hearing about the other females who came before them."

"I'm not like that. I want to hear. She was important to you, and that makes her important to me, because hearing you talk about what you had with her makes me feel closer to you."

"Are you sure?"

"Positive."

He searched her eyes without finding anything but love gazing back at him. Fine, he would tell her. He turned his attention to the window again. But he wasn't seeing the city. His vision went far beyond Chicago. Beyond the present.

"She was older than me, a good dancer . . . and she had this laugh that always made me think of angels singing."

Sam snuggled closer, and he felt her love seep into him as he continued.

He told her of the night of the celebration and of how he left with his father to train for the war, and then how he and his new friend, Malek, returned years later, all grown up.

"I was twenty-six, a far cry from the little boy I'd been when I left fourteen years earlier," he said, falling into the memory again. "I was a fully transitioned male."

As had occurred at the end of all the wars before, the vampires and drecks had reached a truce to end the fighting. A truce Micah had known would end sooner rather than later since the war never really seemed to come to an end, despite times of negotiated peace. To believe that permanent peace would result this time was naïve. Maybe the battle was over, but the war was sure to rage on.

But for now, all he wanted was to return home and see Kat again. To show her how much he'd grown. He was as tall as his father now, and his body had filled out, growing both broad and lean. Black scruff covered his cheeks and chin, and his hair had grown long and thick. Most importantly, he now knew how to please a female, and he wanted nothing more than to show Kat all he'd learned.

The moment he, Malek, and his father rode into the clearing just outside their village in the middle of the night, he began searching for her.

In a village inhabited mostly by vampires, nighttime was more active than day, so it didn't take long for word to spread that they had returned. Excited villagers spilled from their cottages and clogged the narrow cobbled road that curved its way through the village.

But none of them were who he wanted to see.

Then the air stirred. An energy called to him, and he turned away from a group of young maidens he vaguely remembered as little girls. He glanced to his left then pulled his mount to a stop as his mother rose from where she'd been shelling peas. Kat sat beside her.

When his eyes met hers, something inside him quivered. A

pulse of excitement stirred his heart, as if a wizard had cast a spell over him. He could tell she felt it, too. He could sense the quickening of her pulse, taste the scent of her aroused blood in the air.

He dismounted and rushed forward, his father on his heels.

"Mother!" He picked his mother up and hugged her before handing her off to his father amid tears and laughter.

Then he faced Kat, drinking in the soft curves of her face. When he'd left fourteen years ago, she'd stood three heads taller than he. Now he towered over her. She gazed at him from under her lashes.

"Little Micah?"

He grinned and closed the distance between them. "I'm not so little anymore."

Her face flushed as she demurely pressed her fingertips to the base of her neck. "No, I guess not."

Micah introduced Malek, and then his parents excused themselves and went home. It had been a long time since they'd seen each other, and Micah could tell by the gleam in their eyes they needed to be alone.

A group of villagers lit a bonfire in the courtyard, and before he knew it, a small feast had been prepared to celebrate his and his father's return.

But Micah didn't so much care about celebrating as he did spending time with Kat, and while Malek danced with every maiden in the village, Micah took Kat's hand and nodded toward the trees. "Come with me."

Her cheeks turned rosy as she stood and wrapped both her hands around just one of his. "Where are we going?"

He glanced at the rest of the villagers as they clapped and danced a ring around the bonfire, laughing and making toasts. Then he turned back to gaze into Kat's eyes. "All this . . . it's not for me. I want . . ." His gaze dropped to her plump, pink lips. "I want . . ."

"What?"

He dragged his eyes back to hers and tugged her toward him as he took a backward step toward the trees. "Just come with me."

Her eyes glittered in the firelight as she smiled and bit her bottom lip, and then she relented and allowed him to lead her away from the festivities and into the woods.

When he reached the tree where he'd fed her the tart fourteen years before, he stopped and pulled her to the ground as he sat with his back against the thick trunk.

She sat beside him on folded knees, facing him, and let out a breathy giggle. "Little Micah." She leaned forward and teased his trimmed beard with her fingernails. "I can't believe how much you've changed."

He snagged her hand before she could pull it away and held it within both of his. "You haven't changed at all." He lifted one palm to her face. With his fingertips, he brushed back her hair. "You're still as beautiful as I remember." He softly ran his fingers down her arm and over the back of her hand.

She shyly ducked her head. "Micah . . ."

His heart skipped at her modesty, and he chuckled as he pushed forward and lifted her hand to his lips. "You always knew I was infatuated with you, didn't you?" He kissed the backs of her fingers.

She squirmed but scooted closer, eyes downcast, shoulders forward as if shielding herself. "Yes." She spoke softly.

Her long auburn hair fell over her face again, and he pushed it back so he could watch her as he kissed her fingers. Her lashes fluttered then closed, her lips parting. Her shoulders rose as she drew in her breath.

He let his lips linger and play over her knuckles before drawing away and lowering her hand to his lap.

"In the years I've been gone," he said, "my affection for you has remained."

Her eyes flickered open, and she cast a daring, hopeful glance toward him. "It has?"

He nodded. "It's grown even stronger." He caressed her wrist and delicate forearm. "Not a day has gone by in fourteen years that I didn't think about you." He cupped her face in his palm. A palm that had grown in size and strength since she'd last seen him and had become rough from wielding a sword before his transition. Training for hours every day had taken its toll, and even though a transitioned adult couldn't develop calluses, an untransitioned youth could. And those calluses remained. But she didn't seem to mind as she bent her neck and pressed her cheek more firmly against his touch. "All I wanted was to return home so I could see you again."

She shyly bowed her head. "I always thought you were a special little boy, but I never imagined . . ." She shifted and shook her head uneasily then turned away.

He inched closer and leaned forward, bracing his arm over her legs, supporting his weight against the cool ground. "You never imagined what?"

Her throat worked as she swallowed. Then she met his gaze. "I never imagined you would grow up to be" — her gaze ranged his face then dropped to his chest — "to be so . . . "

"So what?"

"So handsome." She looked away as if embarrassed, which brought a wicked smile to Micah's lips.

"You find me handsome?"

She giggled and covered her face with her hands as she nodded.

"Why, Katarina, I do believe you're blushing."

She laughed and playfully slapped his arm. "Little Micah Black, stop teasing me."

"Teasing you? Me? I would never do such a thing."

Rolling her eyes at him, she huffed. "You've grown to be quite incorrigible, little Micah."

"Yes, but" — he trailed his index finger down her arm, silencing her soft laughter with a gasp — "I haven't forgotten the promise I made to you behind this very tree before I left for the king's city." He reached behind him and smacked his palm against the rough bark of the trunk.

She leaned toward him as if challenging him. "Oh, and what promise was that?"

He leaned in until they were almost nose to nose. She sucked in her breath and dropped her gaze to his mouth, but she didn't pull away.

"I believe I promised to teach you how to shoot a bow and arrow."

He stared into her eyes as she lifted her lashes and met his gaze, the flickering firelight reflecting off the flecks of gold in her green irises. "Yes, I remember."

"Do you still want to learn?"

She hesitated as hopeful anticipation lit in her expression. Then the corners of her eyes turned up in delight as she smiled. "Now? Tonight?"

He shook his head. "Tomorrow night."

A ghost of disappointment crossed her features before she brightened once more. "Where?"

"Meet me here just after sundown."

"Should I bring anything?"

He pressed forward and lightly brushed his lips over hers in a chaste promise. "Just you."

She appeared surprised but pleased that he'd kissed her, and her cheeks flamed rosy pink.

He led her back to the village, and with a secret glance between them, departed for home.

At sundown the next night, Micah slung his bow and quiver over his shoulder and passed through the village on his way to *their tree*, his heart beating a wild rhythm. He was going to be with Kat. Beautiful, magical Kat. The female he had pined for over half his life.

She was waiting for him beneath the forest canopy, pacing in the darkness, wearing a modest, moss-green kirtle that shimmered in the moonlight and accented her red hair. She reminded him of a woodland fairy, elegant and magical.

She stopped pacing the moment she saw him, and a relieved but nervous smile broke over her face. "Hi," she said breathlessly.

It took all his strength not to take her in his arms and cover her mouth with his, but he forced himself to remain an arm's length away, even as his gaze traveled over her alluring curves.

"Are you ready?" He reached for her hand.

She slid her fingers around his and nodded shyly.

"Then let's go."

As he led her through the forest, she clung to his hand and stayed close to his side.

The paths he'd used as a boy still existed, although the forest had thickened in places while thinning in others. But he could have traveled the terrain blindfolded, having spent endless childhood days and nights romping among the trees.

As they strolled hand in hand, they talked about the years he'd been away, how she passed her time reading and tending to the gardens, how homesick he'd been when he first arrived in the king's city, but how he'd grown into his own person among strangers who later became friends. But it all felt like small talk. Chatter meant to distract them both from the intense attraction growing between them with every step they took.

When they came to a shallow stream, he hoisted her into his arms without a thought.

"Micah!" She yelped and slapped her arms around his neck as he swept her feet out from under her and cradled her against him. "What are you doing?" She laughed as he started across the stream, carefully treading over a slippery path of rocks and boulders, which forced the water to gurgle as it rushed through the narrower passages.

"Isn't it obvious? I'm making sure you get across without getting your feet wet."

She glanced down at the water. "I've crossed streams before, Micah." Her eyes danced with amusement as she turned back toward him. "I'm sure I could have managed."

He stopped. "Would you like me to put you down then?" He pretended to loosen his hold.

She let out a squeal and clamped her arms more tightly around his neck, pressing more firmly against him.

"You're incorrigible, Micah Black!"

He chuckled and continued across. "I wouldn't be much of a gentlemale if I allowed you to get your hem wet, now would I?"

She sighed and settled into his arms as she flashed him a playfully wicked smirk. "I detest coddling."

"Then I'll be sure never to coddle you."

She rolled her eyes and let out a breathy laugh as he reached the opposite shore and set her down. "I may be a proper female, Micah, but that doesn't mean I'm a delicate flower."

His blood heated at her spirited rebelliousness. "Really now? You always seemed like a delicate flower to me when I was a boy."

She raised her chin and brushed her palms down the top of her skirt. "It might surprise you to know that you're not the only one who's changed in the past fourteen years. I'm not the same female I was when you left."

He drew in a slow, steadying breath, doing his best not to sweep her in for a blazing kiss right then and there. He liked this new, fiery Katarina. The sweetness he remembered from his youth remained, but now he saw a passionate side to her he'd never witnessed before.

"I can see that." He reached for her hand.

When she didn't immediately reach for his and instead crossed her arms in a faux, haughty show of impatience, he grinned and lowered his hand to his side as he arched one brow. "Fine. I won't *coddle* you." With an amused snort, he turned and started along the path again. "Follow me then."

She fell in step behind him then sped her paces to walk alongside him again, and even though she remained silent, Micah could feel her arousal. It clung to her like a wraith, ever present but invisible, its ethereal fingers stroking him and awakening a desire inside him he'd never known. He'd always found Kat beguiling, but now she was overwhelmingly irresistible.

. . . never knew he would grow up to stir my blood so wickedly.

Micah frowned and glanced down at her. He could swear he'd heard her voice, but he was certain she hadn't actually spoken. "Did you say something?"

She turned a quizzical expression on him. "No." Her cheeks flushed and she quickly averted her gaze back to the path in front of them.

His eyes . . . the way he looks at me . . . his gaze penetrates my soul as if he can see deep inside my heart. As if he can see how infatuated I've become with him.

Again, he heard her voice, but he was looking right at her. Her lips hadn't moved. No words came from her mouth. And yet . . .

Oh God, what's happening to me? He's only been home a day, and already I'm lost to desire and can't stop fantasizing what it would be like to . . .

Her voice inside his head cut off. That's when he realized he was hearing her thoughts. But he hadn't tried to see inside her mind. Her thoughts had magically materialized inside his head without him making any effort to probe for them.

That had never happened before, and he wasn't sure what to make of it. He glanced at her again, but no more of her words sprang to life inside his head. Not that it mattered. He'd heard enough to know what she was feeling for him. That she was as excited to be alone with him as he was with her.

He smiled to himself, and an instant later, her hand eased around his.

"I thought you weren't into coddling," he said, glancing down at their joined hands.

She flashed him a demure but heated glance. "I think I like it when you do it."

Breathing more easily than he had in over a decade, he secured her hand in his and, a few minutes later, led her into a clearing along a beach bordering the lake where he'd spent so much time fishing and swimming as a youth.

"You're going to show me how to shoot a bow and arrow here?" She shot him a dubious glance as she let go of his hand and meandered closer to the water.

"Do you doubt me?"

Her laughter flittered in the air like angelic chimes, stealing across the lake's still, glassy surface. "I don't think I know you well enough to know whether or not I should doubt you."

Taking his bow from over his shoulder, he pretended to be hurt. "I may have changed since you last saw me, Kat, but I'm still me. My sense of honesty has remained. Only my body has changed."

Well, a few other things had changed, too, such as his knowledge of a *female's* body. Of how a male and female gave each other pleasure. He had become quite skilled in the art of physical intimacy, all in anticipation of one day coming back to his Katarina. He hadn't wanted to make a fool of himself by fumbling ignorantly over her body, so he'd been quite the student under Mary's tutelage. And now, here he was, ready to show her all that he'd learned.

Kat tilted her head affectionately. "I'm only teasing, Micah. Of course I don't doubt you."

The breeze lifted her hair and wafted her floral scent in his direction, making his pulse race. God, he just wanted to touch her, feel her heat, taste her.

"Good. Then come here." He chucked his head in a come-here motion.

Her scent strengthened as she drew nearer, and enticing warmth raced down his spine, landing between his legs. Being this close to her was either going to drive him mad with desire or kill him. He withdrew an arrow from his quiver to keep his hands busy so he didn't grab her and take her to the ground.

"First, the stance." He turned his back to her to illustrate. She drew nearer and at an angle to peer over his shoulder at what he was doing. He pointed to a tree directly in front of his left shoulder. "See that tree?"

"Yes."

"That's what we're aiming for, so set your feet perpendicular to your sight line, which extends from you to the target." He planted his feet shoulder-width apart, parallel to one other.

"Like this?" she said.

He glanced behind him. She stood less than an arm's length away, her eyes gleaming in the scant light of the moon. He tore his gaze away from her lovely face to look at her feet, which peeked out from under the hem of her skirt. They weren't quite wide enough, but he would fix that later.

"That's good." He swiveled his head around to the tree again. "Now . . . stand up straight, rotate your chin so you're looking over your left shoulder, rotate your hips so they're tucked under, and push your chest, ribs, and shoulders downward."

She let out an exasperated laugh. "How do you ever get off a shot with all that you have to do before you've even nocked an arrow?"

His heart beat wildly at her amusement and the way it lit her face when he looked at her. "It becomes second nature after a while. I don't even think about it, anymore." Sort of like loving her had become second nature. He no longer thought about his love, he simply felt it. "Once you've done it enough, the right posture just happens." The same way his heart just happened to beat harder when she was near and ached when she wasn't.

"I certainly hope so." She shuffled her feet then glanced down at them as she got back in her stance. "Now what?"

He wanted to forget about teaching her how to shoot an arrow and shower her with kisses to learn if she tasted as sweet as she looked. Instead, he cleared his throat and turned back toward the tree. "Once you've found your stance, hold your arrow like this at the base." He demonstrated. "Then place the shaft against the side of the bow above the grip, rest the nock—the slender notch at the end—against the string, raise the bow, lift your right elbow to ear level, pull back, line up the shot, and then . . ." He released the arrow.

It whizzed toward the tree and pierced the trunk.

Lowering the bow, he turned toward Katarina. "Do you want to try?"

Her hands fluttered nervously. "There are so many steps to remember."

"It's not as bad as it sounds."

"You make it look so easy."

"I've had a lot of practice." He held the bow toward her and retrieved an arrow from his quiver. "You try."

Tentatively, she took the bow and arrow from him and eyed the tree. Then she ran through the steps in a hushed voice, as if she were talking to herself. "Feet parallel but perpendicular to the sight line, shoulders down, arrow against the side of the bow, elbow by my ear." She frowned and strained as she pulled back the string.

Her fingers slipped, the string snapped, and the arrow flew wide, tumbling through the air to land innocuously on the sand.

Laughing, Kat glanced up at him, face flushed. "I had no idea it would be so hard to pull back the string."

"It takes a bit of strength. Here, try again." He pulled out another arrow.

A playful look of defeat fell over her face. "I don't think I'm strong enough."

"I'll help." He stepped behind her, bending his head over her rear shoulder so their faces were side by side.

She took the arrow, got in her stance, nocked the arrow, and lifted her arms. Micah moved in close. So close the front of his body pressed against the back of hers.

She sucked in her breath and trembled slightly, but she kept her gaze aimed down the beach at the tree. "Is this right?"

He wanted to tell her how right it was to be this close to her. Her curves felt like they'd been made to fit against his strong angles, and her soft hair caressed the base of his neck and smelled like a field of wild flowers. He inched closer, and her rounded bottom welcomed his tightening groin. "It's perfect," he murmured.

Her eyes flicked toward him, and then her lashes fluttered as she looked away and gazed down the length of the arrow again.

Wrapping his right arm around her shoulders, he covered her hand with his, curling his fingers around the string, and helped steady the bow with his left hand. "Gently pull back," he said. "Like this." He drew back the string, and as he did, her body bent ever so slightly toward his, making their connection stronger.

Her heat, her fragrant scent, her soft firmness. He could barely form coherent thoughts. Blood rushed through his body, flooding his cock, needing to finally consummate the emotions that had started when he was a boy, grown alongside him as he matured, and now flooded him with desire beyond comprehension. Kat belonged to him, and he wanted nothing more than to plant his scent all over her body. To coat her with it inside and out.

He swayed into her, letting his nose dip into her hair. "When you're ready," he said, "let go."

Her body rose and fell heavily against him, lost to the same maddening flood of hormones rising to a fevered frenzy inside his own body. He could smell her arousal. He was drunk with it. Lost to its heady, all-consuming scent. She wanted him as badly as he wanted her.

She released the arrow, but he never saw where it landed. He didn't care. All that mattered was the gentle sighs breaking from her throat and the way she surrendered and let the weight of her body fall against him.

"Micah . . ."

"Sshhh." He took the bow and tossed it to the sand. His arms seemed to wrap around her torso of their own volition, his palms flattening against her slender stomach.

She laid the back of her head against his shoulder and turned her face toward the stars, eyes closed, lips seductively parted.

"Do you realize how long I've loved you, Katarina," he whispered, brushing his lips against her temple. Her soft hair caressed his face.

A wolf bayed at the moon in the distance as if mirroring the yearning in his own soul.

She moaned and shook her head.

His hand gently cupped the tender curve of her breast. "I've loved you from the moment I first set eyes on you. I knew even then that one day you'd be mine. That we would be together."

A fractured, abandoned groan broke from deep inside her throat as if she'd burst through an internal barrier. She turned to face him, burrowing in close, nestling herself within his embrace as she lifted her gaze to his. "I don't understand what's happening to me, but I need you in a way I've never needed anything." She searched his eyes, her gaze darting back and forth between them.

Primal lust shot through his body as he cradled her cheek. "What are you saying?"

Her mouth opened, but no words came. But words weren't necessary to communicate what she wanted. Her imploring gaze alone told him all he needed to know.

Make love to me. Please make love to me.

Her thoughts ghosted through his mind unbidden, and his engorged cock strained to give her exactly what her betraying thoughts desired.

"Do you want me to make love to you?" He pressed her toward the grassy edge of the beach.

She blinked drunkenly, her face softening with submission before she nodded. "Please . . ." She reached up and tugged on his cheek with her fingers. "Please, yes. I don't think I can go another night without feeling you inside me."

She needn't say more. He was hers. He would give her anything she requested. His body existed only to give hers pleasure. She already held his heart in her hands.

His mouth found hers, and she tasted as he expected. Sweet, like a field of honeysuckle. Her lips opened against his, and his tongue laved hers, so warm, so inviting. Her breath washed over his mouth as she sighed, and her trembling fingers left a trail of lightning strikes up his back as she helped him out of his clothes.

When she lay beneath him on the soft, cool grass, her naked body glowed with the enchantment of the full moon as the love he'd felt for so long finally circled back on him, flowing from her to him in a connection as old as time.

Katarina finally saw him as more than just a boy. In him, she saw a grown male. A virile male. And he would not disappoint as he laid claim to the one thing he'd coveted his whole life above all else.

And there, on that beach, he and Katarina had found each other for the first time. Within days, he had formed the mating link necessary for a male to produce young. Even so, he and Kat never had children. He hadn't been able to extend the Black bloodline through her womb.

As his words dried up—because what male wanted to talk about his shortcomings in the fertility department—he blinked and found himself once more in the present. He and Sam had moved to the couch, and now she sat silently beside him, her eyes glistening as if she were on the verge of tears. She probably was. She knew what came next. She knew of the tragedy that became of his life after Kat died.

He cleared his throat. "A few years later, the war began again." In the years that followed, both Kat and his parents had died—or so he'd thought. Now he knew his father had lived. Kat was still dead, perishing a few years after his mother, but, somehow, his father had survived.

He sighed, not giving voice to that memory. Not yet. He wasn't ready to face the truth about his father. "Then Kat was gone. My parents, too. I was left with no one. At least, that's what I thought."

Sam cocked her head, the short expanse of skin over her nose wrinkling. "That's what you thought? What do you mean?"

He groaned and slid his palm down his face as he steered his gaze briefly skyward before bringing it back down to her again. "I'll get to that later. I'm not ready to talk about it, yet."

Her eyes narrowed curiously, but she didn't push him.

"The point is, I thought I had no one. No family. No mate. No child. I possessed nothing to give me purpose, and I became a monster. I fell so far and had no regard for my own life. Honestly, I should have died a hundred times over by now. God knows I sought out death plenty enough, but it never took me. Somehow, I lived."

Sam touched his arm reassuringly but didn't say anything. She didn't have to. He could see in her thoughts how thankful she was he hadn't died, because without him, she'd likely be dead now, too. He had saved her from a terrible fate and given her a new lease on life.

The same as she'd done for him.

Last Christmas — barely over four months ago — he'd finally reached a point of despair so great that he'd decided to kill himself. Death wouldn't willingly take him, so he'd resolved to force its hand. That's why he had sought out Apostle the night he met Sam. He had been only minutes away from death when she found and saved him.

He lifted her hand to his lips and kissed her fingers. "If not for you, I'd be dead now."

"We saved each other."

He nodded, lacing his fingers between hers and tucking her hand against his body.

Sam truly was a lot like Kat. Both reminded him of angels, and while Kat had developed the sassy personality Sam had come prepackaged with, both never hesitated to call him on his shit. Then, of course, was the obvious similarity that neither Kat nor Sam had become pregnant during his calling.

Once more, the fear that he might be sterile throttled him.

Ronan might be the last hope of carrying on the Black name. At least *someone* could if he couldn't.

He didn't want to think about that. He wasn't ready to believe he would never create life. To concede he would never have children of his own felt like surrender. And Micah surrendered to nothing and no one. He wanted a son to raise to be a strong warrior like his father had raised him to be. He wanted a daughter to dote on, spoil, and guard against males who would take her innocence when she became old enough to date.

It hurt his heart to think he might never have that.

"So, Kat stole your virtue, did she?" It was just like Sam to provide a moment of levity at the exact moment he needed it.

He grinned. "More like I stole hers." Kat had been a virgin when he made love to her that night on the beach. "Mine had already been taken by then."

Her eyes flashed open wide. "Really now? You didn't mention *that.*"

He brushed his lips over hers then let them linger for a moment before pulling away. "There are still things you don't know about me, baby. And I do tend to take what I think belongs to me, even back then. But don't worry, Kat willingly gave me her virtue. And can you blame her? I mean, look at me. I'm a catch, don't you think?" He leaned back and presented himself, enjoying teasing her.

Sam's breathy laugh did to him the same thing Kat's always had. His heart beat harder and his blood warmed. Whenever she laughed, it felt like his soul opened to let in the light so it could dispel the darkness.

"You're such a guy." She rolled her eyes, pulling him back toward her, and tipped her forehead against his. "And no, I can't blame her. You *are* a catch. You're *my* catch."

"I love you so damn much." He cupped her cheek, rubbing his thumb back and forth.

He'd needed this tonight. He'd needed to feel her fortitude and lightheartedness so it could ground him. Sam was his foundation. She gave him balance and centered him when he felt like he was splintering into a hundred fragments.

He kissed her. "You make me feel things I never thought I would feel again. You warm me when I'm cold. You calm me when I'm upset. You laugh, and I feel like I'm a black hole turning back into a star." He pulled back and brushed her short blond hair off her forehead as he searched her face. "And when I'm a bomb about to detonate and destroy the entire city, you defuse me."

Her gaze drilled compassionately into his. "Is that what happened tonight?"

He recalled how close to the edge he'd been a couple of hours ago. Learning about this brother and his dad had nearly blown him to bits.

"Yes."

"Want to tell me about it?" She let go of him and stood.

Where did he begin? He pushed off the couch and followed her to the kitchen. "Sam, tonight was so many levels of fucked up I'm still struggling to make sense of what actually happened."

Sam opened the cupboard. "That's the thing about talking, baby. The more you do it, the clearer things become." She pushed jars of sauce and cans of soup aside. "Because I know you didn't call me over here tonight because you were reminiscing about Kat and your childhood." She gave him the side-eye as she reached into the back of the cupboard for the peanut butter. "The way you were with me tonight . . ."

He stood on the opposite side of the breakfast bar, resting his hands on the counter. "I know I was rough with you. I'm sorry."

She gave him her trademark stop-being-so-dramatic look as he took a seat on one of the barstools. "Micah, you weren't *that* rough."

He gestured toward her bruised wrists. "You have bruises and bite marks all over your body."

She let out a derisive snort as she snagged a spoon from the drawer. "In case you missed it, I came three times, and I flirted on the edge of a fourth for ten minutes — and would have come again if the first three hadn't been powerful enough to annihilate my orgasmic response. You obviously weren't rough enough to keep me from enjoying myself. And trust me, I would have told you to stop if you were hurting me." She eyed the brownish marks on her wrists. "In my opinion, these are stamps of ownership and badges of honor to be worn with pride." She swept around the counter and brushed her lips over his as she leaned provocatively into him. "They tell the world that I'm a well-pleasured woman with a badass boyfriend who knows how to do to me things mortal men can only dream about." She kissed him again then plopped her very fine ass on the barstool next to him, unscrewing the lid on the peanut butter jar and releasing the comforting scent of roasted peanuts. "So, spill it, Black. Tell me what had you so fucked up tonight that you needed to use me so mercilessly." She grinned and winked as she said it, dunking her spoon into peanut buttery goodness.

As she shoved the loaded spoon into her mouth, he took a deep breath then said, "I found out my dad's still alive."

Sam's hand jerked then went utterly still as her eyes flew open wide. "What?" she mumbled around a mouthful of peanut butter. "Your father is still alive? How did that happen?" Although that last bit came out sounding more like "Your fawder ith sdill alie? Ow did tha appen?"

Good thing he was fluent in peanut butter English, or he might not have been able to understand her.

"Fuck if I know. I'm still not one hundred percent certain this all isn't just a bizarre and totally fucked-up dream, because my father being alive is only a small piece of the fucked-uppery that got unloaded on me tonight. It's probably the easiest part to deal with, though."

She pulled the spoon out of her mouth and managed to swallow down enough peanut butter to speak clearly again. "If that's the easiest, I'm afraid to ask what the hard part of your evening was." Her tone held a touch of humor but remained serious.

He met her gaze and was thankful to find stalwart confidence staring back at him. That was his Sam. She faced everything — no matter how unbelievable — with enough strength and conviction for a platoon of Marines, even if she tried to inject a little humor to dull the pain.

And right now, he needed every ounce of humor and strength she could give him.

"I have a brother. Skeletor . . . Ronan . . . the guy who broke into this apartment . . ." He swept his gaze around the apartment's interior. "He's my brother."

The spoon dropped from Sam's hand, clanging once on the floor before flipping and skittering a few feet away. "Excuse me?"

"You heard me. That shithead who broke in is my brother. I've got a goddamn brother."

CHAPTER 9

IF ANYONE WERE TO WANDER THROUGH THE CEMETERY, they would shit themselves. Ronan sat atop a headstone, still wearing his skull mask. He looked like a demon — or maybe Death himself — waiting to harvest the souls of the newly deceased.

But he was just chillin'. Trying to screw his head back on straight after his encounter with the blonde with eyes as blue as Jamaican water. And the only place he could think of peaceful enough to go was the pyramid-shaped tomb inside Graceland Cemetery.

What did it say about him that the only place he could go for some peace and quiet was the local cemetery?

He stared at the small pyramid structure. This was the same tomb he'd broken into and used the ankh in only a few days ago, hoping to open a portal to another dimension, only to open a whole lot of nothing.

The earth had shuddered, a low hum had sounded, and it seemed as though he had found a way off the planet. Then everything just shut down. Stopped. Came to a screeching fucking halt.

It was the story of his life.

For as long as he could remember, any time it looked like something good was about to happen to him, something else came along and derailed it.

And the derailing had begun with the ripping apart of his perfect family when he was just a little boy.

He'd started out with a dad *and* a mom, and unlike now, his father had been happy. His father had smiled all the time. He had paid attention to what Ronan said. He had given him rides around the house on his shoulders and encouraged him to grow up big and strong.

Then there had been his mom. His mother had adored him, always playing with him, building blanket forts with him and taking him to the park after sundown to push him on the swings. She had read stories to him every night, made him homemade chicken soup when he didn't feel well, and baked mountains of cupcakes for his birthday parties. The house had always been filled with the comforting, fragrant aroma of her cooking.

Their small family hadn't been financially wealthy, but they'd been rich in love.

Ah, such happy times and fond memories.

Then everything had changed.

A strange male had come to the house one night after Ronan had heard his mom and dad arguing. The male had been tall, with light-brown hair, and dressed in a tailored suit. Possessive aggression as thick and heavy as a fog bank had rolled out of him, sending a chill through the air as he entered the foyer.

The moment the male saw Ronan's mother, he snatched her hand and pulled her against him like he owned her, scowling at his father.

Ronan would never forget what the male said next, before he whisked his mother away. "She is mine by law. I've mated her, and she's coming with me." Then the male's cold gaze turned toward Ronan. "The boy stays with you."

Despite his mother's protests and the way she cried, reaching for Ronan, the male dragged her away. Ronan never saw her again.

That was Ronan's first lesson in the king's law. The claim of a biologically mated male over a female always superseded the claim of an unmated male — and the son — who merely loved her. As if love were a choice. Something that could be prevented or turned off at will.

Love was a luxury for a male vampire, because a male in love knew that at any moment another male could come along and bond to his female. And if — and when — that happened, he was shit out of luck. No one would uphold his claim in the face of one based on biology.

Which was why it was a miracle Ronan had even been conceived. His father had never biologically mated his mother. He'd loved her, but that was all. Love hadn't been enough to keep her even though it had been enough to create him.

Now, instead of a miracle, Ronan felt like a curse. Because that's what his life had become after his mother was taken from him. Without fail, anything good turned to shit.

But as bad as Ronan suffered after she was gone, his father had suffered ten times worse.

There had been no more rides on his father's shoulders. No more words of encouragement. No more laughter. In their place came silence, solitude, anger, and resentment.

In many ways, Ronan became the adult the day his mother left. He had tended to his father, learned to cook, figured out how to do the laundry. He became the male of the house. For months, his father wouldn't even eat unless Ronan fed him. Wouldn't bathe unless Ronan did it for him.

For the first year, his father hadn't been much more than an empty shell, his eyes vacant and lost most of the time.

Only when he slept did he show any signs of life as nightmares consumed him, making him flail, shout, and curse. The words that escaped from his father during his night terrors painted a frightening picture. One filled with death, loss, and anguish. People his father had killed. The deaths of those close to him. The loss of a son named Micah and a mate named Isabel.

Ronan would lock his bedroom door at night and pull the blankets and pillows over his head, clutching a kitchen knife for fear his father would sleepwalk and tear into his room on a blind rampage, seeking to kill those in his nightmares and mistaking Ronan for the enemy in his unconscious state.

There were so many nights he cried himself to sleep listening to his father yell and sob at the horrors he relived in his dreams. Which was probably why his father began resisting sleep. Which then led to a sort of psychosis during waking hours, where he hallucinated, trading his night terrors for waking nightmares. Which led to angry outbursts about how Ronan should be more like his brother, Micah.

He came to hate hearing Micah's name, which eventually became a loathing for the male himself. *Why can't you be more like Micah?* His father would ask. Micah could shoot an arrow square between a boar's eyes at fifty meters. Micah could take on six drecks at once and defeat them all without breaking a sweat. Micah brought honor to the Black name. Micah this, Micah that. The perfect son, Micah.

Is it any wonder Ronan grew up to hate him?

So, yeah, Ronan hadn't exactly experienced an enviable childhood. When other kids his age were playing basketball and riding their bikes, he was paying the household bills and walking two miles to the store by himself to pick up groceries.

Oh, how he had yearned for a simple life. But that wasn't to be. Not then, not now, not ever.

Ronan's brow dug deep into his eyelids as his mouth fell open on a revelation. Money. There had always been enough money to cover the bills, despite their meager living conditions. Where had that money come from? And why had he never thought to ask that question before?

Well, shit, the answer was pretty obvious, wasn't it? Ronan had always been too busy staying out of his father's way, preparing for the next mentally unhinged tirade, and wishing he could be more like his unknown brother, Micah, because then maybe he could have helped his father return to the male he'd been before Mom left.

There hadn't been much room left to ask where the money came from. All that mattered was that every month, day in and day out, it was there.

He remembered the bank statements that came in the mail like clockwork. Since he didn't learn how to balance a checkbook until years later, he ripped open the envelope, scanned the statement for the remaining balance, stapled the pages together, and filed them away.

It wasn't until he was older that he started paying attention to the details, and even though every statement showed a deposit of five thousand dollars — and later, six thousand — he'd become so conditioned to simply stuffing the damn things in a file folder, he never stopped to think about where the deposits were coming from. Just that they kept coming.

He assumed at the time that his father had set up some kind of arrangement where money was deposited on a schedule, but now, years later, that explanation didn't hold water.

Someone had provided cash flow all those years to ensure he wasn't put out on the streets. Like a guardian angel or something.

But who?

Who would do that?

His mom? Had she secretly been funneling money to him and

his father after her new mate ripped her from their lives? Maybe. Maybe not. That douchebag in a suit hadn't looked like the type who would allow something like that. Then again, mates held a lot of power over their males, and she could have convinced him to keep Ronan and his father financed. Whatever. Maybe he would look into it. See what he could dig up. But if his mother was responsible for the mysterious deposits, he wasn't sure he wanted to see her. He was as angry at her as he was his dad. She could have fought harder to keep him, especially if she was the one who had sent the money.

So, yeah, his childhood had sucked in the worst fucking way. Devotion to caring for his father soon turned to resentment, and then to anger, and finally to rebellious loathing by the time he turned twenty.

Of course, by then, he was hanging out with the wrong crowd, stealing cars, getting a firsthand education in Beginner's Breaking and Entering, Advanced Chop Shop Etiquette, and honoring in How to Win in Hand-to-Hand Combat. All while learning how to evade human cops while adjusting to his maturing vampire body.

In the twenty-six years since, his resentment toward his father had only thickened, but at least he'd ditched the small-time thugs in favor of more elegant, as well as more philanthropic crimes.

The enchanting blonde had called him a hero.

He wasn't a hero.

He was the quintessential *anti*hero, overflowing with flaws and a horrific past. His skills fighting the enemy had been honed first by embracing a life of crime. Only after becoming disillusioned with thieving's lack of personal fulfillment had he turned toward fighting for a greater good.

That was about the time he met Alexis, not quite six years ago.

Alexis was a jack of all trades. Bounty hunter. Vigilante. Thief. Gun for hire if the price was right—and if the target was evil enough.

And let's not forget, she was an amateur surgeon and emergency care physician.

But what Alexis really loved to do was break up human trafficking rings. She had a nose for shitheads involved in the skin trade, and she took great joy in putting them out of business.

Her rules were simple. No children, no innocents. Everyone

else was fair game to fall inside the crosshairs of her gun's sight. The worse the criminal, the greater the target.

Most of the time she found her own targets and did society a freebie, but once in a while—just often enough to keep her bank accounts fat and her supplies stocked—she received contracted and paid work from an anonymous handler in exchange for protection. There were those she wanted to hide from, and her handler helped her stay off the grid, so it was a win-win as far as professional relationships went.

And now Ronan was her partner and protégé, thanks to being in the right place at the right time when she took out one of the human thugs Ronan used to hang with.

Talk about wake-up calls.

But hero? No. Not him. No way.

That didn't stop him from replaying how it felt when the blonde called him one, though. Warmth had flooded his chest, and in that moment, he wanted nothing more than to be the Tarzan to her Jane. To lift her in his arms, tuck her against him, and swing from vine to vine so far into the jungle no one would ever find them.

There, he would feed her, bring her water, wash her in a cool pool under a waterfall, and make love to her on a bed of palm fronds in his thatch hut. They would have children, and Ronan would prove he could be a better father to his young than his father had been to him.

Wait, what? Children? What the fuck was he thinking? He didn't need to be thinking about mating and children. God, no. That wasn't the path he wanted his life to take.

With a frustrated snarl, he stripped the mask from his head and tossed it to the side. It bounced and rolled, coming to rest facedown on the grass.

Raking his fingers through his hair, he tossed an angry glance over his shoulder at the pyramid tomb.

He was stuck here, in more ways than one. There would be no jungle hideaway just as there would be no portal opening to take him to another realm.

Although, now that he'd met the stunning blonde with sky-blue eyes, being stuck in the earth realm didn't feel quite like the prison sentence it had an hour ago. She intrigued and excited him. In the short while he'd known of her existence, she'd consumed his thoughts.

Who was she?

Why was she using cobalt?

What was she afraid of? And who?

The heartbreak and desperation he'd seen in her eyes as she begged him to save her had nearly broken his heart. A female like that . . . she should never feel threatened. She should never need to beg anyone to save her, because everyone who came in contact with her should feel instantly duty bound to keep her safe.

If she were Ronan's, he would protect her. He would —

What the hell? Why did he keep going down this path? He didn't need to think that way. He was not boyfriend material any more than he was father material. He wasn't a savior or a saint. And he wasn't her bodyguard or some kind of hero. He was a renegade. An outlaw.

A female as fine as she needed someone stable and safe, neither of which were him. A male like him could never be with a female like her. He wasn't worthy to look upon her, let alone touch her, whether intimately or casually.

He was a thief. She was a goddess. The two simply didn't go together.

But damn him if he didn't like the fantasy of her lips on his, her body wrapped within his arms, her hands touching him everywhere.

Everywhere.

Ah, but fantasies were the private inner workings of the mind wanting what the body couldn't have. Much like the freedom he'd lost when the ankh hadn't opened the pyramid tomb's portal last week.

He removed the ankh from his pocket and turned it over in his fingers, staring at it, knowing in his heart that if he kept searching, one day he would find the gate it opened. Then he would disappear and start over new wherever the portal took him. And he would take that beautiful female with him.

And that was yet another fantasy meant to taunt him, because he wouldn't be taking that beauty anywhere.

Knowing his luck, if he managed to open a portal, it would probably lead to a black hole and suck the life from him. But if she was with him, at least they would die together and be free of that which haunted them both.

Like Romeo and Juliet.

Only his life was anything but Shakespearean. As poetic as dying in the arms of such an angel sounded, he was more likely to die tragically alone and loveless than fulfilled in his heart.

But what was the harm in daydreaming that he really could be the hero her intoxicated mind had seen in him tonight? At least in fantasies he could be everything he wasn't in real life, and in his fantasies, he could be with her.

"Ronan?"

He jerked out of his reverie and lifted his head, surprised and a little troubled to find Rule, his mentor from the secret fight club, Grudge Match, standing beside the pyramid.

That was one more thing he could be pissed off at Micah about. The one thing he'd wanted for himself — to be a member of Grudge Match without any interference — was now a pipe dream. Like everything else, what was once a good thing was now ruined.

Micah and that bitch, Cordray, had somehow connected him to the fight club and shown up the other night. That had to have been how Micah found out where he lived. Had to have been how Micah had shown up at the house tonight to await his return.

What was he supposed to do now? He had exposed and brought shame on the club by being careless. No way would Rule and Digon allow him to remain a member.

Rule had recruited him into Grudge Match, trained him, and had become a father figure to him. Ronan couldn't say Rule was a friend, but his respect for the guy put Rule right up there with Muhammad Ali and George Foreman. His skills were superhuman. He moved with the grace of a tiger and the speed of a cheetah, and held black belts in every discipline. If he had anyone to look up to, it was Rule.

No one beat Rule in the octagon. No one. Ever. Fights he engaged in couldn't even be called fights, they ended so fast. That's how good he was.

Ronan stared up at the male. "What are you doing here?"

"We need to talk." Rule's grim expression sent a shiver down Ronan's spine.

Here we go.

No doubt, Rule had found out what he'd done and had come to expel him from the club. Not that Ronan was surprised. He had suspected he was out, but facing the reality upset him more than he wanted to admit.

"How did you find me?"

Rule continued toward him, his expression troubled. "It's a long story, one we don't have time for right now."

Ronan scoffed and glanced around the dark cemetery. "Actually, I seem to have all the time in the world." He looked away, not wanting to see the disappointment in Rule's eyes.

If only his circumstances were different. He'd lived a lifetime in Micah's shadow. For once, he wanted to be seen for who he really was, not for what his father wished he could have been. Not as the son his father had lost centuries ago and had longed for all Ronan's life. A son his father had now reconnected with, so what good did it do Ronan to continue hoping he could ever measure up? His father had what he wanted now. He had Micah. What more could Ronan offer him?

Rule hastily glanced over his shoulder as if checking to see if he'd been followed then turned, spied the ankh, and frowned. "What's that you've got there?" He asked the question as if he already knew the answer.

Ronan shoved the ankh back into his pocket. "Nothing. Just a trinket I found."

"Uh-huh." Rule crossed his arms, his voice betraying that he didn't buy Ronan's lie.

Ronan glanced away, in no mood to see yet another person he admired look at him like he was a failure.

Rule let out a turbulent exhale. One that sounded like it came with a mix of frustration, distraction, and impatience. "I just came from your house."

A chill raced down his back. He'd left Micah and his father at his house two hours ago. More than likely, his father was still there, awaiting his return. He could only imagine the conversation Rule had had with his dad.

"What were you doing at my house?" When Rule didn't answer right away, Ronan glanced up at him. "Well . . .?"

"I think you already know."

Anger simmered underneath the sharp-edged dread sending up goose bumps on his arms. Respect or not, he was fed the fuck up to fucking here with the shit he'd been through tonight.

Standing, he pushed into Rule's personal space. If he was out of the club, anyway, he was going to ensure he was *way* out.

"No, Rule, I don't know. How about you spell it out for me." If

Rule had been to his home, and was now looking at him like he should know what this little cemetery visit was about, he no doubt had gotten a rundown from good ol' Dad. God only knew what version of the story his father had given Rule, but it appeared as if Rule had taken his dad's version as gospel.

Rule simply stared at him, the only movement in his expression a tightening of the skin around his eyes.

"I'm waiting, Rule? What the hell were you doing at my home?"

Rule broke out of his statue impersonation and paced a few steps to the side as he glanced over his shoulder again. "First of all, you should know my real name isn't Rule. It's Rysk. Rysk the Second, to be exact." He said his real name like it was one Ronan should have heard before.

He hadn't. But . . . um . . . what the hell was this shit?

Rule had lied to him? Had been lying all along? What for?

He scowled, his anger pushing through the chilly layer of dread still coating his skin in gooseflesh. "You've been lying to me? All this time, you've been lying?"

Rule—Rysk—or whatever the hell his name was leveled him with a glance that sliced straight through the heart of him. "You mean like you're lying about the ankh in your pocket. I know it's not just a simple trinket, Ronan. I know what it's used for. And I know you're playing with fire. You have no idea how dangerous that thing is . . . what you've done by—"

"Fuck you, Rule . . . Rysk"—Ronan slashed his hand dismissively through the air—"or whatever your name is. You're in no position to preach to me about lying." If he had lied about his name, he'd probably lied about a whole lot of other shit, too. "I don't even know who you are, so how about you fuck off." He turned and paced away, his body trembling as he tried to regain control over his anger.

Was he destined to be disappointed by *everyone* in his life? Even those he thought he could trust? Was Alexis the next person who was going to let him down? He couldn't imagine she would, but he never thought Rule would end up being a liar, either.

"Ronan, don't make this harder than it already is. We *need* to talk. There are things you need to know. It's time you knew the truth."

Ronan whirled back around, not ready for friendly chitchat. "No, the time for me to know the truth was the moment we met.

When you told me your name. When you told me who you are."
He pushed his mentor. Hard. "You're all liars, aren't you? Every last goddamn one of you."

He spun on his heel again and began to march away from the tomb.

"Ronan, wait." Rysk came after him. "Would you fucking stop!" He grabbed Ronan's arm and forced him around to face him.

"Get your hands off me." Ronan yanked his arm free of Rysk's hold. He knew he couldn't take Rysk down if it came to fisticuffs, but it would feel great to land at least one punch, so the ensuing beatdown would be worth it.

"Then quit behaving like a juvenile delinquent and man up!"

Okay, sure, Ronan was only forty-six, which was still considered juvenile by vampire standards. Forty-six for a vampire was like sixteen or seventeen for a human. But, like a seventeen-year-old human trying to find adult footing and build a case that he was no longer a child, Ronan didn't appreciate Rysk's low blow.

"Fuck you, *Rysk*!" He whirled and began his had-it-up-to-here march through the cemetery again.

Then shit went sideways.

One minute he was upright and plowing away from Rysk like a linebacker returning to the huddle. The next he was facedown on the ground, tackled from behind, pain exploding through his bones as Rysk cranked his arms behind him and pinned the side of his face to the cold damp earth.

"Fuck *you*, Ronan." Rysk's voice came from so close to Ronan's ear, he felt the male's hot breath all the way past his eardrum to his nasal cavity. "You're in danger, asshole, and I'm trying to save your life!" Rysk's weight lifted off his back, and then he manhandled Ronan to his feet. "Now, are you going to shut the fuck up and listen to me, or are you going to keep mouthing off? Because if it's the latter, tell me now so I can knock your ass out and save us both a lot of time." He released Ronan's wrists and gave him an abrupt shove that felt like a wake-up call instead of aggression.

Ronan whirled and spit on the ground at Rysk's feet, unwilling to back down an inch. If Ronan had learned nothing else from his hard life, it was that you never showed weakness. "You're an asshole. I can't believe I actually looked up to you."

This had to be some kind of sick joke. A nightmare Ronan was beginning to fear he would never wake up from. First his father, then Micah, now Rule—Rysk, whatever. Were all the significant males in his life destined to be monumental, untrustworthy, cocksuckers?

"Believe what you want, but there's a reason we lied to you."

"We? So now it's *we*? Who's *we*? You and the Mickey Mouse Club?"

Rysk fisted Ronan's sweatshirt at the neck and jacked him up close and personal so they were nose to nose. "Stop being such a fucking goddamn diva! You're in danger!"

Ronan glared hard into the male's dark-blue eyes, seeing a stranger where he once saw a mentor. And that's what hurt the worst, knowing he'd lost someone he'd looked up to. Someone he'd seen as an example for the type of male he wanted to be.

"How do you expect me to believe anything you say after you lied to me?"

Rysk searched his eyes. "You're right. I did lie. We all did. But we did it to keep you safe."

Ronan took a step back. "Keep me safe?" He'd get back to who these "all" were in a minute. First, he'd punch holes in this idea Rysk had of how lies keep people safe.

"Yes."

"What a joke." He rubbed his wrists, avoiding Rysk's eyes.

"Why? Because people actually care enough about you to not want to see you die? Because they want to ensure your survival?"

Scowling, Ronan flicked his eyes quickly to Rysk's then looked away again. He hadn't thought of it that way. That there might be people looking out for him. Some of the fight blew out of him as he considered the possibility he'd never been as alone as he'd thought he was all his life. Then he considered who "we" were. Was his father included in that select group?

Not that it changed how Ronan felt about his dad.

Nope.

Not in the slightest.

He lifted his chin. "So, what's changed? You obviously don't need to keep me safe, anymore, or you'd still be lying. So, tell me. Why now? Why the sudden need for all this fucking *honesty*?"

He sounded like a petulant preteen even to his own ears, but goddamn it, he was done trying to be the bigger person. He was finished holding in his anger, having Alexis as his only outlet, and never being able to punish those who'd hurt him the most.

Rysk gritted his teeth and glanced side to side, scanning the darkness like he was looking for someone . . . or something. Then he met Ronan's gaze again. "Because you forced the issue. That's why. You confronted your brother. You made yourself known, which forced your father to reveal himself to save your life. And then you used that goddamn ankh and opened the portal, and now God only knows what's going to happen to—"

"I never opened the portal."

Rysk frowned at him like he was an idiot.

"It never opened," he repeated, holding his hands up, palms out, as if swearing his innocence.

"Ronan . . ." It was the singsong tone that said *you can't be that stupid.*

What was Rysk saying? That the portal opened and he never realized it? But if it had opened, how did he not know? There had been no indication that anything had opened. Nothing. Nada. The air hummed and vibrated. There had been a shimmering light. And then silence. No gates or tunnels had revealed themselves.

"Look," he said, scowling at Rysk as he paced a step to the side then back to the other, "nothing happened. I swear."

"The portal opened, Ro. Trust me. It opened."

Ronan's mouth fell open, but before he could speak, Rysk raked his hand through his so-brown-it-was-almost-black hair and said, "There's more."

"More?" Honestly, Ronan had had enough, but his curiosity wouldn't let this go. "Like what?"

"Like . . ." Rysk's eyes didn't just lock onto his, they bore into them, his whole face growing taut.

"Well . . .?"

Rysk took an ominous step closer, his expression grave. "Ronan, you're my grandson."

The scraps of fight that remained inside him left Ronan's body in a rush. His mouth fell open. Shock replaced anger. Denial replaced dread. He searched Rysk's face, seeking signs of deceit. He found none. "What are you talking about?"

His father had told him that the two of them and Micah were the last of the Black line. Had those been more lies? Or was Rysk the one who was lying now?

"You heard me," Rysk said. "You're my grandson." His gaze remained hard, but his face softened. "Actually, you're my great-great-great-grandson, but at a certain point, it's just easier to say grandson."

Ronan shook his head. This was all too sudden. "How can I believe you? My father told me we're the last. If that's true, how can you be my grandfather?"

Rysk blew out an exasperated breath and glanced impatiently behind him again. "Drake told you that because that's what *we* told him to tell you."

Here they went with the *we* again.

"Who the fuck is *we*?" This situation was growing more convoluted by the second.

Rysk bristled as if he'd caught a scent on the wind. "I'll tell you everything, but not here. We have to go. *Now*. They're coming." Rysk grabbed him by the arm and tried to push him in the opposite direction.

Ronan dug his heels in, resisting. "Who's coming?" He wasn't going anywhere with Rysk until this roller-coaster ride stopped. "Either you come clean right now, or I'm not going anywhere with you."

Rysk gripped his arm and began to usher him to the south before coming to an abrupt halt. Everything stopped. No movement. Not even a flinch. Rysk even appeared to stop breathing, his eyes focused on something over Ronan's shoulder. "Shit," he muttered under his breath. "We're too late."

Before Ronan could turn to see what had spooked his former mentor, a low, malicious, growl split the silence. Whatever made that noise was big. Bigger than a dog, for sure.

Then a creature unlike anything Ronan had ever seen stepped from the shadows behind Rysk. Black, on all fours, with glowing yellow-orange eyes. It snarled, bearing a mouthful of fangs dripping with venom. Another slinked in from the left, and two more from the right.

They were surrounded.

Surrounded by a pack of werewolves.

The night just got better and better.

CHAPTER 10

SAM REMAINED RAPT AS MICAH RELAYED THE EVENTS of the night. How he had gone to Ronan's home, ready to kill him, only for his father to come back from the dead to announce that Micah and Ronan were half brothers.

Surprise! Happy family reunion!

To her credit, Sam seemed to keep up and not go into a shocked stupor the way he had.

Throughout the recap, Sam listened intently, nibbling peanut butter, not interrupting until he was finished. Then, all she said was, "Wow."

Micah grinned. "Wow? I tell you my dad has come back from the dead and that I've got a brother, and the only word that comes to your mind is wow?"

She set down the peanut butter jar and pushed away from the counter. "What am I supposed to say?" She crossed the kitchen to the fridge. "What did *you* say when you found out?" She pulled out the carton of orange juice and snagged a glass from the cupboard.

He rose from the barstool. "I didn't say anything. I could barely think. My head was too fucked up to think." He entered the kitchen and smacked her ass as he passed her on his way to the fridge for a refreshment of his own. One that *wasn't* orange juice and contained alcohol. "But thanks to you, I'm once again able to form complete sentences and coherent thoughts."

"And . . .?" She filled her glass and handed him the carton as he opened the refrigerator.

"And what?" He returned the juice to the lower shelf on the door and pulled out a bottle of Corona.

He didn't drink alcohol often, and he drank beer even less, so he was obviously still off-kilter.

She used her glass to gesture side to side, making the bright-orange liquid slosh this way and that. "Have you accepted that your dad's still alive and you have a half brother . . . who happens to be a thief, by the way?"

"Um, no." He twisted off the bottle cap and tossed it in the trash as he took a quick swig. "I haven't accepted either, thank you very much."

She laughed as she took her seat back on the barstool and waited for him to round the counter and sit beside her again. "Ah, come on, I heard how you talked about Ronan just now. You're impressed with him. Admit it. He got into your home and evaded you, Trace, and Cordray for days until you finally tracked him down with Brak's help. Deep down, that tickles you silly, especially because you know he's family."

Micah took a swig of his beer as he stuck his finger in the open jar of peanut butter that still sat on the counter and dragged out a dollop on his fingertip, which he promptly sucked into his mouth "Okay, I'm impressed. He's got skills. I guess kick-assery runs in the family. But to learn my father has been alive all this time and didn't tell me?" He shook his head. "That shit hurts, baby." He took another sip of beer. "And I know there's more. I can feel it."

"Like what?"

"I have no idea. I just know whatever it is, it's big."

"How do you know?" She sipped her juice.

He flashed her an are-you-kidding-me glance. "Call it my sixth sense. After all, I haven't made it this far in life on my good looks alone."

Just then, a wave of energy touched his mind. It was the same static-like fuzziness that had hit him earlier, in the bedroom, while Sam was sleeping. He had assumed it was her dreams, but he couldn't use *that* excuse, anymore. Not with Sam sitting right beside him, wide awake. Something was trying to communicate with him. Or something invisible was in the apartment with them.

He stiffened, fell silent, and glanced around the apartment.

Sam set down her glass, immediately on alert. "What is it? What's wrong?"

He slowly placed his beer on the counter then stood. "We're not alone."

"What?" Sam leaped to her feet, her head turning this way and that as she peered into the shadows of the living room and down the hall to their bedroom.

"I felt it earlier," he said, prowling toward the hall, keeping his senses open.

The subtle wave of energy weakened but didn't disappear.

"What is it?" Sam crept up behind him.

Whatever was tapping his mind grew stronger.

"I don't know." He'd never experienced anything like this. There were no words to the thoughts. No direction. Just a haze of energy that ebbed and flowed, taunting him as if someone were playing a game.

"I swear to God, Cordray," he said to the shadows in the hallway, "if that's you and you found a way to fuck with my head, I don't care if you *are* Trace's mate. I'll kick your ass."

The swell of energy remained undiminished, growing stronger, almost like it had just awakened from a long sleep and was pulling the morning-stretch routine while considering its first cup of coffee.

Peeking into the bedroom, he reached behind him and gave Sam a gentle nudge. "Go back to the living room," he whispered.

"No."

"Sam, don't argue with me on this. Go back to the living room. I don't want to have to worry about you."

She sighed but relented, taking a step back as he pushed the bedroom door all the way open.

"Fine, but if I hear anything that sounds even remotely like war breaking out, I'm coming back in here."

"I'd prefer you didn't."

"Too bad." She gave him a stern look. "I'm as protective of you as you are of me."

Reluctantly, she retreated down the hall and disappeared around the corner, leaving him alone with whatever had been watching them.

He entered the bedroom and scanned the shadows. Nothing. No movement. No shadow figures. No foreign scents or sounds. Nothing felt out of place at all. Not in the bedroom, the walk-in closet, or the master bath.

But wait. The current he'd followed to the bedroom was gone. Well, not gone, but weaker, like it wasn't with him, anymore.

He swung his head toward the hall.

Sam!

It had followed her!

Bolting from the bedroom, he rushed to the living room, expecting to find Sam in some kind of ghostly choke hold with an invisible demon. All he found was Sam pacing by the window, nibbling on her thumbnail.

Her whole body jerked as she spun and faced him. "What? What was it? Did you find it?"

What the hell was going on? The static-like sensation was stronger here. And with each foot he closed between him and Sam, the white noise in his head grew louder.

"Micah . . .?" She took a hesitant step forward.

"It's you . . ." His gaze swept her from head to foot and back. "It's coming from you."

She froze, the whites of her eyes consuming the space between her eyelids. "What's coming from me?"

"The noise." He gave his head a tight shake, trying to quiet the murmur of energy caressing his mind. "Whatever is here, it's coming from you."

Sam swallowed so hard, he heard the gulp. "Am I okay? Am I sick? Is this something to do with Apostle's venom? Like a delayed reaction or something? Oh, my God." She looked down at herself.

The acidic scent of her fear made him want to take her in his arms and tell her everything was going to be okay, but he couldn't. Not yet. Not until he knew what was wrong with her and where this strange anomaly was coming from.

"Micah . . .?"

"Ssshhh." He circled her, scanning her systems. Had she been infected with some kind of parasite? A nanobot? Apostle had failed to kill her once before. Had he found a way to get to her that allowed him to go undetected. Had he hurt his precious Sam? So help him, if he had, Micah would spend the rest of his life hunting that fucker down and make him hurt, never killing him, always torturing, only to free him, give him a head start, and then continue the hunt.

"Micah . . .?" Sam whispered, her voice breaking as she trembled.

He shook free from his fantasy of vengeance and skimmed his palm over the back of her shoulders, trying to reassure her. "Try to stay calm, baby. I'm looking." He continued circling her, searching, reaching out with his senses, letting his intuition guide him.

As he stepped back around to the front, he looked her up and down then zeroed in on her stomach.

The breath burst from his throat as his mouth fell open.

No.

It couldn't possibly . . .

Could it?

"Micah . . .?" Sam's fingers twisted tightly around one another, and he could hear her pulse pounding hard and fast. "You need to talk to me here, because I'm really starting to freak the hell out."

"Ssshhh." He knelt in front of her, placed his hand on her belly, closed his eyes . . .

And smiled.

CHAPTER 11

Rʏsᴋ ʜᴇʟᴅ ʜɪs ʙʀᴇᴀᴛʜ as the werewolf behind Ronan took a menacing step toward them, followed by a deadly growl at his back. The three approaching from the sides hovered as if waiting for a sign to attack.

Damn it. He'd come here to get Ronan to safety, not put them both in danger. He should have knocked Ronan out when he had the chance and hauled his rebellious ass out of there. But he'd hoped to have enough time to convince his grandson to come on his own.

Looked like he'd made a terrible miscalculation.

"Don't let them bite you," he murmured to Ronan, barely moving his lips as he eyed the predators.

He could get them out of this, but he needed Ronan to follow his lead. Something he wasn't sure Ronan would do given how well their conversation had gone before the werewolves made an appearance.

"And how the hell do you suggest I do that?" Ronan hissed back, remaining still as his gaze skipped from left to right before jumping over Rysk's shoulder.

"Just . . . don't let it happen."

A werewolf bite wasn't fatal to a vampire, but it was hell to heal from. And Rysk knew that from firsthand experience. The most painful wound he'd ever endured had been a werewolf bite. They were nasty creatures with even nastier bacteria in their saliva and venom that made healing from a werewolf bite a long, uncomfortable process.

But Rysk hadn't kept himself alive for over four millennia without learning how to defend himself against all manner of beings, both human and paranormal. He had Argon to thank for that.

Argon had taken him all over the world so they could train with the best fighters from all cultures and disciplines, surviving by any means necessary so that one day they could rise up and take back what belonged to them. Their birthright.

After four thousand years of mastering one fighting discipline after another . . . after another, Rysk was probably one of the deadliest entities on the planet. He could slice clean through an adversary's torso with a longsword or gut them with a four-inch boot knife. He was an expert with all manner of blades, as well as with his body. He was a master in Krav Maga, kung fu, muay thai, Brazilian Jiu-Jitsu, and about a million other fighting styles. He could fight with a staff, a stick, a mace . . . you name it, he'd fought with it.

But he'd only fought werewolves once, a long time ago. That's when he'd been bitten. He'd fallen into a coma for days. To hear Argon tell the story, he'd almost died. But the vampire half of his genes had saved him. If he'd been a full-blooded dreck, he'd be six feet under right now.

Ronan's blood was purer, so he wouldn't grow as sick, but that didn't mean the wound wouldn't be a cakewalk.

Werewolf venom was one of the few things on earth that could knock a vampire on his ass and make him want to die, and Rysk had spent decades learning how to defend against another such attack if it ever occurred.

Too bad Ronan hadn't received that training, yet. His grandson would have to rely on his honed instincts.

He had what it took. He and Micah both did. The Black name carried some of the best fighters in the vampire race, and those inbred skills were what had kept Micah alive when, by all accounts, he should have died a long time ago.

Those same skills had kept Drake alive, too, albeit it in a more subtle way. Now, he prayed the talents passed from one generation to the next would give Ronan enough of an edge to make it out of this situation in one piece, because the only escape was through their fists, their legs, and their wits.

The double whammy where werewolves were concerned was that werewolves interfered with a vampire's ability to —

"I can't dematerialize," Ronan whispered, stealing the words from Rysk's thoughts.

Rysk's jaw clenched. "I know."

"Then how are we going to get out of this?"

Rysk stared hard into Ronan's eyes. "You've trained for this. What do you think Grudge Match has been doing all this time?"

Ronan blinked as his eyebrows crinkled. The lightbulb flickered to life in his eyes.

"That's right, Ronan. We've been training you. Grudge Match isn't just a way to pass time. It never was. We've been building an army. One dedicated to peace but not afraid to use force to obtain it. An army skilled to fight any opponent, whether human, vampire, dreck, mutant . . . or werewolf." He tried to convey all the confidence and devotion in his heart. Ronan was his family. His blood. The pride he felt for Ronan overshadowed all else in that moment. "You're good enough to beat them, Ro. Use their movements against them. Anticipate their attack then counter it."

For the first time in the last ten minutes, Ronan looked at him like he trusted him. "What do they want?"

Before he could answer, the werewolf behind him growled. He must have risen to his hind feet, because Ronan's gaze traveled upward as if tracking the beast's head. Rysk slowly glanced over his shoulder. The werewolf was over six feet tall, but couldn't stand straight. It remained bent forward, its front paws hanging in front of it for balance.

"The ankh," the werewolf said. "Give it to me." He voiced the words on a series of growls and took a crooked step forward as his pack mates did the same.

Rysk pressed his lips together, dropped his gaze to the pocket Ronan had stuffed the ankh in, and then met his gaze again. "When you used the ankh the other night, you sent out a beacon they were able to track to Chicago. To the ankh. To you."

"Then maybe I should give it to them if it means getting us out of here alive."

"No!" Rysk kept his voice to a whisper, but he couldn't prevent the urgency from adding bite to his rejection. "Whatever you do, you can't let them have it."

"Why not?"

"Because they'll use it to unleash hell on earth."

No doubt the werewolves were more aware of how to use the ankh than Ronan was. They would open a gate and bring in more of their kind. Criminals and murderers the lycans had relegated to slave status and exiled on some faraway prison planet to atone for their crimes.

Werewolves had once been lycans, but their crimes had been so heinous the lycans had cursed them, changing them into lesser beings through the magical powers they'd brought with them to this world. Werewolves were smaller than lycans, more aggressive, and traveled mostly on all fours, making it easy to differentiate them from their lycan keepers, who preferred to ambulate on two legs instead of four and were larger and more beautiful in every way.

As a physical comparison, werewolves were to lycans what coyotes were to wolves. Both were impressive, but there was something more majestic and awe-inspiring about wolves. Same with lycans. And they were more civilized.

Wait a second. Rysk glanced into the night sky. Something wasn't right.

There wasn't a full moon tonight. Instead, the sliver of a waxing crescent shone back at him.

Lycans could transition whenever they wanted, but werewolves couldn't. They required the full moon to catalyze the change. That was how the metaphysical laws of the supernatural worked.

Unless these weren't normal werewolves.

In which case, everything Rysk thought he knew about werewolves and lycans would do him about a shit's worth of good.

Any way Rysk sliced it, they were backed into a corner. One they would have to fight their way out of if it meant protecting not just themselves but the ankh.

"I'm going to give it to them," Ronan said, slipping his hand into his pocket.

"Ronan, no. You can't." Rysk gave a subtle shake of his head as his heart skipped then began pumping furiously. "You have no idea what will happen or the hell they'll rain down on earth." What was Ronan thinking? "Besides, they'll try to kill us, anyway. Whether you give them the ankh or not, we'll still have to fight our way out of this."

"Trust me." His grandson took a step back, his hand still in his pocket. He called to the werewolf behind Rysk, "I've got the ankh."

"Give it to me," the beast snarled.

"I want something in return."

"You're in no position to bargain, vampire."

Ronan shrugged cavalierly and exchanged glances with Rysk, his hand working inside his pocket. Then he glanced at the werewolf again. "We might not be able to kill all of you before you kill us, but we could take out at least three of you. Why risk it?"

The beast made a disgruntled but contemplative sound then fell silent as if thinking about Ronan's offer. It was a long moment before he spoke again. "Tell me your bargain."

"Let us go. That's it. I give you the ankh. You let us go. Everyone walks away."

Rysk had to give Ronan credit. Whatever game he was playing, he was doing so fearlessly, and with a level head, buying them time. Or maybe this was just dumb luck favored by rash stupidity, because Ronan's propensity was to act first and think later.

Rysk cautiously swept his gaze around the scene, seeking an escape route and marking the approaching werewolves as they stopped and deferred to who he assumed was their leader. When he turned his gaze back to Ronan, his hand was still working furiously in his pocket. What was he doing?

One of the other werewolves interjected. "Or we could just kill you, vampire, and take the ankh from your cold, dead fingers."

Ronan's hand suddenly froze, and a smirk twisted his lips. "Wrong answer." He yanked his hand from his pocket and shot it toward the werewolf behind Rysk. A pulse of energy bolted from the oscillator strapped to his palm.

Rysk whirled to see the werewolf behind him go airborne, flying feet over head.

That was his cue.

Springing to action, he engaged one of the other werewolves before it could swipe Ronan's head off, meeting it in a blur of movement. His booted foot connected with the wolf's throat, knocking it to the ground as Ronan's oscillator split the air and torpedoed two more of their attackers.

"Ro! Look out!"

Ronan ducked and fell into a body roll just in time to miss getting julienned by a paw full of daggerlike claws. He was on his feet in a flash, using his oscillator and a blade he'd pulled from one of the holsters hidden by his dark clothing, keeping three of the wolves at bay.

But Rysk had his own problems to worry about as the other two came for him.

Digging deep into his skill set, he countered their every move, his fists and feet flying with graceful speed, landing on his targets with deadly precision.

Fur flew, blood sprayed, and in short order, he and Ronan had gained the upper hand. Crimson trails dribbled from the beasts' fangs and fur, and it looked like the worst of the fight was over.

"Ronan! Go!" Rysk turned, grabbed Ronan's forearm, and jerked him away from the fight. "Run!"

Thank God Ronan didn't try to be a hero. He spun and, together, they sprinted for the fence. Three of the werewolves recovered immediately and gave chase, followed quickly by the other two.

"If we can get far enough away from them, we can dematerialize," he shouted to Ronan.

Ro nodded, pumping his arms and legs hard to put distance between him and their enemy.

But the werebeasts were too fast. They caught up to them at a massive gargoyle tombstone marked by the name Grimm. How was that for irony?

Looked like they were going to have to fight their way free, because trying to get away on foot wasn't going to happen.

Just as he and Ronan spun and reengaged the five werewolves, a blue-green light shimmered from the area around the pyramid-shaped mausoleum they'd left behind, warping the air. A bright light flashed as Rysk fell to his back, overwhelmed by his adversary, his hands buried in a mass of dark, bristly fur as he strained and tried to kick off his attacker. Venom dripped from its fangs and splattered on his cheek.

Heavy footfalls echoed on the ground, and then the werewolf was lifted off him as if the creature had been plucked like a weed from a flower garden. The wolf whined then yelped. Once, twice. The third yip cut off with the sound of snapping bone.

Rysk jumped to his feet in time to see a white-kilted lycan toss the dead werewolf to the side as if it were nothing more than dirty clothes. The carcass crashed into a marble headstone, cracking it. More bones snapped, and the werewolf landed on the grass in a heap of twisted flesh before transforming back into its human form.

The lycan towered over him at nearly ten feet tall on his hind legs, straighter than his werewolf counterpart. His physique rippled powerfully beneath a layer of black fur, his shoulders wide, waist tapered, abdominals like stacked bricks under a sparse smattering of coarse hair. A cartouche hung from a heavy gold chain around his thick neck.

For a prolonged moment, the lycan stared down at him, its eyes like black holes. Then it turned away to monitor the fight as another tombstone broke in half and toppled to the ground with the force of another werewolf's skull being cracked against it.

Two more linen-kilted lycans — one with sandy-brown coloring and a long mane down the back of its neck, and the other as black as pitch — dispatched the remaining four werewolves easily enough, snapping their necks or ripping out their hearts. In less than twenty seconds, five lifeless human forms lay on the ground, covered in blood.

Where was Ronan?

Rysk searched the darkness for his grandson. "Ronan?" He limped around the headstones. "Ronan!"

"I'm here. I'm okay." Ronan pushed himself to his feet from behind a gravestone and rested his hands on top of it as he caught his breath. "I'm goo—" His voice cut off when he saw the three enormous lycans advancing toward them. "There's more?" He straightened and stared. "Shit, these three are huge." He inhaled deeply as if preparing to fight then exhaled as he lifted his arms and waved his fingers in a *come-on* motion. "Okay then, bring it."

But Ronan looked like he was in no shape to take on anything but a bowl of cereal. His grandson's shoulders slumped forward, and his skin had taken on a greyish pallor. The fight had depleted him more than he seemed ready to admit.

The air shimmered as the lycans shifted into their human forms. Even dropping their beastly personas, each was over six and a half feet tall.

The linen kilts covered them from waist to midthigh, and each wore a gold cartouche, no doubt their version of military dog tags. No pun intended. Cartouches were simply their way of identifying themselves. It had always been so, all the way back to Ancient Egyptian times, when humans had worshipped them as gods.

"Rameses," Rysk said, immediately recognizing the male in the lead as the brother of the lycan *imeut*, or leader, Memnon.

Rameses regarded him through the same inky-black eyes that had studied him a moment ago in his lycan state. He stood proudly, shoulders squared, chest out, but not like he was *trying* to appear intimidating. He just was. Rameses's posture seemed as effortless as his demeanor, as if the air held him upright because he willed it to do so. In this moment, the world belonged to Rameses, and all who resided there existed because he allowed them to.

He and Memnon always carried themselves this way. They suffered no one, and all suffered them. But of the two, Rameses was the more forgiving. Rysk didn't want to think about how differently this encounter could have gone had Memnon shown up instead.

Without a word, Rameses turned away from Rysk, his gaze landing almost indifferently on Ronan. "The ankh." His voice was so deep it was almost an echo. "It belongs to us."

His expression gave nothing away. No anger, no benevolence. No malice nor amnesty. The placid facade could have been hiding caged fury he could unleash so swiftly you would never see your death coming, or it could have been a veil for immeasurable gratitude for keeping the ankh safe all this time. After all, the ankh's rightful place was with the lycans. They had created the portals, and, consequently, the keys to open them.

Which was something Micah nor Ronan could have known since Memnon and Rameses had decided eons ago to withdraw from vampire lands and take their secrets with them. The only place anyone could find record of the ankhs now was in the king's archives.

Or from Argon and Rysk. Argon had told him all about the ankhs and how they opened gateways between worlds and dimensions.

Which was how Drake had learned about the ankh's power.

And, of course, Drake then relayed the information to Ronan during one of his night terrors and subsequent waking outbursts, also revealing the ankh's whereabouts. That he'd given it to Micah.

Which was why Ronan had stolen the damn thing then tried to use it like a damn bloody fool.

And now, here they were, all their secrets spilling like coins from a broken piggy bank.

He met his grandson's eyes. God, Ronan looked exhausted. "It's okay, Ro. You can give it to him. It belongs to them."

Rysk didn't fear much in this world, and he had no reason to fear Rameses or his two companions, because vampires and lycans had never been enemies. Strained allies, perhaps. Uneasy cohabitants on the same continent, yes. But never enemies. Still, Rysk feared them. The lycan race could make the staunchest, most revered ally if they chose to align their cause with yours, or they could spell certain doom if they decided your existence endangered the planet or the human race. After all, that was why they were here. To protect the planet and humanity from the dark forces lurking in the shadowy places of the universe.

The question was, which Rameses had he and Ronan crossed tonight? The benevolent one? Or the unforgiving one?

Ronan hesitated, warily eyeing the lycans. Dark circles shadowed his eyes. The evening had taken too much out of his grandson. He needed to get Ronan home, and after a much-needed rest, Rysk could formally introduce him to Argon, the dreck Ronan had come to know only as Digon, the founder of Grudge Match, and explain the truth he had yet to reveal about their bloodline.

But first, he needed Ronan to give up the ankh. Ronan needed to let go of whatever reason had motivated him to take it in the first place.

Rysk nodded tightly. "Go ahead, Ro, give it to them."

Weaving forward and back on his feet, Ronan slid his hand in his pocket. "I don't . . . I'm not feeling so goo. . ."

Then shit went south. Way south.

As Ronan weakly pulled the ankh from his pocket, blood trickled from under his sleeve and down his hand.

"He's been bitten." The other black-haired lycan rushed forward, catching Ronan under his arms as he went bobblehead and nosedived into unconsciousness.

"Ronan!" Rysk rushed toward his grandson.

Rameses's hand shot out, and the ankh flew from Ronan's hand to his as if pulled by a magnet. "Priest, our clothes. Get them." His commands snapped out of him like staccato notes as he secured the ankh in his fist. "Dain, give the boy to Rysk."

The blond male with hair from here to Sunday nodded curtly and disappeared in a shimmer of light as the black-haired lycan hoisted Ronan into Rysk's arms.

Ronan was out cold, the color rapidly draining from his face.

Blood coated the sleeve of his black hoodie. So much blood.

Rysk shoved up the sleeve and gasped. A dozen festering puncture marks marred Ronan's forearm. Shit. This was bad. Ronan-could-die bad, being that he had no idea what kind of werewolves they'd come up against that could transition without a full moon. The fact that Ronan was bottoming out faster than a draining barrel didn't reassure him.

The puncture marks were already swelling with infection, oozing and bright red. He'd never seen a worse werewolf bite, or one that grew so ugly so quickly, but Ro probably hadn't even felt it with the adrenaline blasting through his veins.

The air shimmered again and the lycan Rameses had referred to as Priest reappeared holding a large leather duffel. Rameses's expression gave nothing away. Was Rameses going to order Ronan's death? Save him? Abandon him?

Rameses took a step toward Rysk. "Take the boy to AKM." He reached behind him as if waiting for Priest to hand him his dinner jacket.

Priest placed a silver-grey pullover in his hand. Rameses flicked it so it unfolded, and then held it in front of him as if getting dressed in a cemetery was as normal as wearing a cowboy hat in Texas. "We'll clean this mess up and meet you there. Go." No critical rush invaded his voice. No sense of excitement. Just straightforward matter-of-fact calmness.

But Rysk sensed the urgency coming from the trio even if he couldn't see or hear it.

Dain shifted back into his lycan form and began gathering the bodies as Rameses and Priest got dressed.

Speechless, Rysk could only watch, feeling as though he were in a parallel reality. How could Rameses, Dain, and Priest be so calm when his grandson's life was hanging in the balance?

Rameses placed his hand on Rysk's shoulder.

Rysk lifted his gaze and looked into irises so dark they seemed like pits.

"You must hurry to your healers. We will meet you there and do what we can to help." For the first time since he appeared in the cemetery, Rameses allowed a hint of emotion to pass over his face. A shadow of compassion displayed in the microscopic lift of the corners of his mouth. That was probably as much of a smile as anyone would ever get out of Rameses. "You must go now. We'll be right behind you." Rameses squeezed his shoulder, lowered his chin, and then turned away, grabbed one of the fallen werewolves by its head of human hair, and dragged it back to the pyramid mausoleum without another word. Dain and Priest were already there waiting for him.

Rysk shifted his hold on Ronan, stared after Rameses for a moment, and then connected with his grandson's aura. As he dematerialized, he saw the blue-green light shimmer around the pyramid.

Cleaning up the mess. That's what Rameses had said. In other words, they were disposing of the bodies. Probably sending them back to the prison planet they'd come from. Either that, or they were dumping them into the middle of empty space.

One mess down. A shitload more to go.

Starting with making sure Ronan made it through the night alive.

CHAPTER 12

MICAH SHIFTED HIS PALM ON SAM'S STOMACH and held his breath.

Oh my God.

This couldn't be happening.

But there was no denying it.

The strange buzz of energy he was feeling. It was coming from inside her. Coming from inside her belly. It was—

"Why are you crying?" Sam placed her hand over his. "Am I . . .? Is it . . .? Is there something wrong with me?"

Was he crying?

He swiped his fingers under his eyes. They came away wet. "Nothing's wrong."

"Am I okay?" Desperate worry edged her words.

He bent forward, kissed her stomach, and stretched his gaze up her body to her glorious, beautiful, enchanting face. "You're more than okay, baby. You're pregnant."

For a second, she looked back at him like he'd just spewed gibberish in a foreign language she couldn't understand. Then her mouth fell open as her eyebrows shot up in her forehead.

"I'm *pregnant*?" Her head cranked down, and she stared at her stomach like it was going to grow a mouth and start talking to her. "Are you sure? Really? How . . .? I thought—"

"That I couldn't get you pregnant without a calling? Yeah, that's what I thought, too."

But there was no denying it. She was carrying his young. That's where the odd white noise had come from.

He blinked, bent forward again, placed both hands on either side of her abdomen, and kissed the smooth expanse of skin right below her belly button. "I hear you," he whispered. Then he looked up, meeting Sam's glistening eyes. "I hear them."

She covered her mouth with her fingertips as a tear dropped off her lashes. "*Them?* As in . . .?"

He nodded and tipped his forehead against her stomach. "Twins. You're carrying twins." His voice was but a whisper. "*My* twins. *My* young. *My* babies." God, it felt good to say that.

He forced himself to breathe slowly, calmly, despite the stinging in the backs of his eyes.

Pregnant. His precious Sam was pregnant.

He'd thought for so long that children were never going to happen for him. So long, in fact, that he had assumed he must be sterile. But no. He wasn't shooting blanks. He'd gotten his mate pregnant without a calling, and that was as far from shooting blanks as a male could get.

Hallelujah.

Take that, Lakota! Oh, he of the powerful sperm who could get a female pregnant just by looking at her.

Everything else Micah had learned tonight faded like fog in the morning sun. His thieving brother. His living father. The ankh that Ronan had stolen from him. None of that mattered anymore. All that mattered was that Sam was carrying his babies.

Babies! Because as sure as he lived and breathed, Sam most definitely carried not just one child, but two.

He felt them both.

Overwhelmed with emotion, he wrapped his arms around her waist as he pressed kisses over her stomach. "My mate, my children." Moisture licked his eyes as more tears welled and dropped to his cheeks.

No longer was he the odd man out. Over the past several months, he'd watched his friends announce their own coming bundles of joy. Tristan, Io, and Malek were all going to be fathers, and now that Trace had mated Cordray, he would likely join the father-to-be club sooner rather than later, especially since he was on the verge of his calling.

Now, Micah could be the one to walk into the room full of proud fertilization factories and proclaim that, yes, he was going to be a father, too.

Tremendous relief engulfed him, and he tipped his forehead against her stomach as if in prayer as he squeezed his eyes closed and let his tears slide down his cheeks.

Sam's fingers smoothed into his hair and cradled his head against her.

"You're going to be a father." She spoke softly, reverently.

She knew how much he'd wanted this.

Lifting his gaze to hers, he blinked through the film of moisture blurring his vision to find her smiling down at him. Her own tears dripped from her softly pointed chin.

"And you're going to be a mother," he said.

The corners of her mouth lifted as she nodded, the smile expanding over her face and brightening her eyes.

"I had begun to think this would never happen." He slowly rose to his feet.

"Why?"

He studied her shimmering eyes. "Because of Kat. Because I was never able to get her pregnant. And because you didn't get pregnant when I had my calling. I thought . . . maybe I was the problem."

Her eyebrows scrunched into a compassionate furrow as she tilted her head. "Oh, Micah." She caressed his face. He dipped his cheek into her palm and closed his eyes. "You should have talked to me."

"I didn't want to worry you." He kissed her palm and placed his hand over her belly again so he could feel the twin life forces stirring inside her. "But now I don't have to. What I thought might never happen has."

She giggled and glanced down at her stomach again as she covered his hand with hers. "I'm going to be a mother?" Her words lilted like a question, but he could see in her mind that she felt more a sense a wonder than disbelief.

"Yes, baby. You're going to be a mother. A wonderful mother."

His mind shot to what they'd done earlier . . . how rough he'd been with her. She wore the evidence of his harshness all over her body. The bite marks where he took her blood. The bruises on her wrists where he'd restrained her, and between her legs where his body had slammed hard and repeatedly against hers.

Recoiling, he took a quick step back and inspected her. "Oh, my God, Sam. Look what I did to you. I hurt you."

"Huh?" Bewilderment replaced wonder in her expression. "What are you talking about?"

"This!" He lifted her hands and glared at the bruises around her wrists then stared pointedly at the lingering signs of the bite marks he'd left on her neck and the parts of her breasts that weren't covered by her tank top.

He had taken blood from her when she needed it most. When his unborn young needed her at her strongest.

"What?" She looked at him like he was crazy. "A little bruising?"

"It's not a little. You look like you were in battle."

She laughed, reaching for his hands even as he continued inspecting her. "Calm down. I'm fine. Really."

She couldn't know what she was talking about. This was his responsibility. He needed to protect her, keep her safe, ensure no harm came to her.

Shaking his head, he pulled her into his arms and tucked her against him. "I promise to take better care of you. I promise not to hurt you like that again."

"Whoa!" She shoved out of his hold and planted her fists on her hips. "Are we back to that?" She cocked her head. "I already told you. You didn't hurt me. I'm fine. I'm better than fine."

"You're pregnant, and—"

"And I'm not going to break like a dry twig, Micah. I'm a tough bitch. I can handle you, no matter how rough you get."

"As the male, it's my duty to—"

"Yeah, yeah." She rolled her eyes and crossed her arms. "It's your duty to take care of me and keep me safe and dote all over me now that I'm your baby mama." She squared him up in her sights. "Micah Black, I don't need to be handled like I'm made of paper-thin glass. If we're going to have kids together, we need to get that straight right now, because I can assure you, if you start treating me with kid gloves, it will hurt me more than anything you've ever done to me in bed."

He took in her determined, stalwart expression. Sam *was* a tough female who could dish it out as well as take it. She had moxie and verve, and she thrived on her independence and her ability to roll with the punches. It was why he'd mated her, because he needed a female who could stand up to his overbearing personality and not wilt when he sank into one of his moods. Her strength was what had drawn him to her in the first place. Maybe he needed to have a little more faith in that.

"Come here," he said, opening his arms, wanting to feel her again, needing that physical connection.

She stiffened her shoulders and raised her chin. "Do you understand how important this is to me, Micah? Do you get how important it is for me to know you don't see me as weak? Because if you don't—"

"I do, baby. I get it." He stepped toward her, arms still out. "I'm sorry. I'm just feeling a little overprotective at the moment. This is all new to me. I've never had young, and I got caught up in the excitement." He slid his palms over her hips. "But give me some leeway. It's in a male vampire's nature to tend to his pregnant mate."

She uncrossed her arms and gently pressed her palms to his chest as if she wasn't quite ready to forgive him. "Then tend to me, but don't coddle me."

His thoughts jumped to Kat. *I detest coddling.* That's what she'd said to him that night. Now Sam was warning him not to coddle her, either. The two most important females he'd ever welcomed into the most intimate corners of his life were alike in so many ways. Maybe they weren't one in the same, but they were certainly spiritual twins.

"Why are you smiling like that, Black?" she said, arching one eyebrow as she fought back a smile of her own. Her hands smoothed up his chest to his shoulders.

Shaking his head, he tightened his grip on her hips and tugged her closer. "I'm just happy. You make me happy."

She allowed the smile to blossom over her face as she acquiesced and leaned into his body. "Good answer."

"Are you sure I didn't hurt you. Are you sure you're okay?"

She sighed and angled her head to one side. "Yes. I'm fine. You don't need to give me a blood transfusion or anything."

"Funny." Lacing his fingers over her rump, he pulled her against him as he flicked his gaze to the kitchen. "You hungry?"

"A little. I just had that peanut butter, but I could eat. Why?"

"Because it's kind of an honor for a female to eat from her male's hand, especially when she's pregnant."

"This is going to be a thing with you, isn't it?" She brushed her mouth gently over his.

He licked her taste from his lips. "Yep."

One delicate brow raised into a shallow arc as her eyes twinkled. "Okay, fine. I'll let you feed me . . . on one condition."

Oh, how he adored her, always negotiating her will into his.

"Anything."

She stepped into him and ran her hands down his arms. "You have to let me take a few bites on my own, too."

The embers in his soul began to smolder again as heat rose within his body. "Then I will feed you" — he leaned in and kissed the curve at the base of her neck — "and then I'm going to make love to you" — he crossed to the other side of her neck and kissed her there — "and then I'm going to bathe you" — he kissed her nose — "and then I'm going to hold you while you sleep." He planted a chaste but burning kiss on her lips then broke away and pulled a plate from the cabinet.

"You are, are you?" She leaned her hip against the counter, watching him.

He nodded. "I most definitely am." He gathered cheese, crackers, a small bunch of purple grapes, and a knife, piling it all on the plate before taking her hand and leading her to the bedroom.

"And you don't think this is coddling?"

He pushed open the bedroom door with his foot. "Absolutely not."

She resisted the smile pulling at her mouth. "Then what do you call it?"

"I call this 'Micah milking the newfound knowledge he's going to be a father to its fullest extent, because his little soldiers are as badass as *he* is to get you pregnant without a calling.' That's what I call it."

She laughed and let him pull her to the middle of the bed, where they sat cross-legged, facing each other. He rested the plate between his knees and picked up the block of cheese in one hand and the knife in the other as she opened the paper sleeve filled with buttery Keebler goodness.

"How am I going to survive the next nine months with you?" she said, giggling as he cut off a piece of cheese and held it out to her.

She leaned forward and parted her lips, taking the nibble of cheese into her mouth. A sensation like butterflies taking flight erupted inside his chest at the way her tongue swirled around the tip of his finger. Her teeth grazed his skin as she slowly pulled away then moved on to his index finger.

The breath blew out of his lungs, and he let out a quiet groan.

"How am I going to survive the next nine *seconds* with you performing fellatio on my fingers?"

She giggled seductively, inching closer as she plucked a grape and popped it in her mouth. "I call this 'Me milking your overactive hormones to *their* fullest, because I'm an opportunist who knows how to push your buttons to get what I want.' What do you think of that?"

He sliced off another bite of cheese and leaned closer as he held it in front of her. "Wicked female. Taking advantage of me like that."

She took the morsel of food into her mouth, briefly letting her lips close around the tips of his fingers before easing away. "You bet your pants I'm taking advantage of you." She ate another bite, took the knife and cheese from him, moved the plate to the nightstand, and then scooted closer until her knees rested on top of his. Her hand slid up the inside of his thigh to his erection. "Especially when you're so much fun to take advantage of."

Resting his hands on her hips, he glanced at the abandoned plate. "I thought you were hungry."

"I am." Lifting onto her knees, she maneuvered onto his lap, eyeing his mouth. "I'm *very* hungry." Her hand eased inside the waist of his pants, and her palm glided down the length of his cock before wrapping around the base.

Lying back, he pulled her down on top of him. "Mmm, then maybe I should feed you."

Her supple curves molded perfectly against him as she freed his erection.

Reaching down, he helped her push his pants off then removed her panties.

Hours ago, he'd needed hard fucking. Punishing sex. He'd needed to take, take, and take some more to drive out the shock and confusion that had resulted from earlier events.

Now, none of that mattered.

Sam was pregnant. He wasn't sterile. He had new priorities that had nothing to do with his father and brother.

There was nothing he couldn't overcome now that he'd achieved what all male vampires aspired to once they've taken a mate.

As Sam's lips found his, he closed his eyes and let out a relieved exhale, pulling her against him, one arm wrapped around her shoulders, the other locked against her lower back. His mouth fused with hers, and his tongue slid past her lips. He gently rocked his hips between her legs, desiring the friction but in no hurry to bury himself inside her.

Earlier, he couldn't claim her fast enough nor hard enough. Now he wanted to take his time. Taste her inch by inch. Feel every ripple of her body. Worship her.

The creation of life was a miracle in itself, but to carry that life? To nurture it as it grew and became another living being? That was truly miraculous. Truly divine.

She was his goddess, and he her faithful subject.

"You're shaking," she whispered, pushing up on her arms.

He opened his eyes as a tear broke free and rolled down the side of his face.

She ran her thumb down the tear's trail and searched his face. "Micah?"

He cradled her cheek then stroked his fingers down her face. "I love you. I love you so damn much." His heart broke open at the way her green eyes sparkled, her expression softening. "There's nothing I wouldn't do for you. Nothing I wouldn't do for our children." He was changing. With each moment that passed, he was becoming a new version of himself, and he had no idea when the transition would end or who and what he would be when it was over.

She kissed him. "I love you, too."

They stared into each other's eyes for the longest time, their bodies gently rocked against each another. He still hadn't entered her, but it didn't matter. Feeling her slick core glide up and down his length was more provocative than being inside her, especially as her breathing intensified.

She wrapped her fingers around his, clutching them tight, and pressed his hands to the pillow on either side of his head. Her exhales morphed into moans, each growing higher pitched than the last. Her hips rocked harder, forward and back, dragging her clit over the full length of him, all the way to the head, before driving down to the base again.

He lay beneath her, fascinated by the way she took what she wanted and restrained him. By the way her eyes drifted closed before she forced them open again to stare into his, as if she took her desire by stealing it from his gaze. As if eye contact alone propelled her rising arousal to its climax yet kept her from launching skyward as her orgasm crested.

Crying out his name, she threw her head back then forward. Her grip crushed his hands, pushing them hard against the bed, and her body fell into violent tremors.

That's when the primal warrior inside him broke free.

In one fluid motion, he had her on her back, still in the throes of her orgasm as he drove into her, a relentless barbarian, unleashed and abandoned.

"Micah . . . Micah . . . God, yes . . . MICAH!" She came again, driving her blunt nails into his back.

His body seized, his hips convulsed, and a keening, sated growl roared from his throat as he emptied inside her.

In the afterglow, both of them breathing hard, arms locked around each other, his cock still twitching every few seconds within her slick heat, an overwhelming sense of gratitude washed through him. Gratitude and peace. The priorities in his life had shifted. For a thousand years, he'd known only one life. Now, a whole new existence had opened to him.

Sam and his unborn children were his life now. They were his heart.

With his arms still around her and his face buried in her soft hair, he inhaled deeply and saw a new path for his life.

"I'm done," he murmured.

Her fingertips skimmed up his spine. "Mmmm, I know. So am I. And it was incredible."

He pushed up on his arms and stared into her eyes. "No. I mean, I'm quitting my job. No more AKM."

Her eyebrows scrunched. "You're quitting your job? Why?"

"It's time. Time for something else."

"Like what?"

But he had no idea. He just knew he couldn't go on being a grunt enforcer.

He lowered himself over her again, resting his weight on his elbows. He gave a little shrug. "Maybe I'll just stay home, make love to you all day, and make babies, now that I know I don't need a calling to get the job done."

"If you stayed home all day, you'd drive me nuts."

"Good nuts?"

"No, the bad kind."

"I've got a pair of good nuts with your name all over them."

"You're not hearing me, Micah."

The concerns she was voicing inside her mind told him everything he needed to know about what she thought of his sudden desire to quit his job. She was worried he was jumping too quickly without thinking things through. She was concerned he would grow restless and frustrated if he wasn't out on the streets, tracking down drecks and kicking criminals' asses.

Maybe she was right. Maybe not.

More than anything, she feared he would become bored and, in an effort to keep himself entertained, try to interfere too much in the groove she'd created for herself and settled into as his mate. She had things she wanted to do without him. Things she needed to do to maintain her identity. Her independence was important to her, and if he was around all the time, she was afraid she'd feel suffocated.

Honestly, part of him worried about all those things and more, but he just couldn't see enforcing as a viable career option, anymore. Too many rules. Too many restrictions. It felt like for every step AKM took forward, they were knocked back three by the loosely worded terms of the truce. If they were going to make a real difference and put an end to cobalt distribution and the slow chipping away at the vampire race the drecks were getting away with, they needed a new approach. One that didn't bind their hands. One that gave them a fair shake against the drecks' new tactics, including those perpetrated by Bishop. Because everyone knew Bishop worked for Premier Royce. That he, in fact, had Royce's blessing.

"I'll figure something out," he said, resting his body weight on his elbows. "Right now, I just want to love you full time."

"That sounds dangerously like coddling."

"It's just for a little while, then I'll find something else. A new job." He chuckled. "Maybe I'll take up music and tour the club scene with Ari."

"Oh, I'm sure he'd *love* that."

"Hey, we get along now. It's not like how it used to be between us."

"Yeah, well, I doubt Ari is looking to become a duet with anyone other than Severin."

Micah rolled to his back, pulling Sam against him. "Then I'll get a normal job."

A lightness filled his soul. He was daring to be something else. Someone else. All his life, he'd been a warrior of one kind or another, but now he was eyeing a future as a family man. Maybe he could get a regular job. Something that didn't put him in harm's way every night. Didn't he owe that to his unborn children? Sam? Himself?

"Like what?" she asked.

"I don't know. Accounting maybe?"

She laughed. "I can just see you the first time your accounts don't balance." She mimicked taking out a knife and stabbing something with it over and over. "Damn fucking numbers! Balance, little shits! Goddamn stupid . . ." she trailed off on a series of garbled curses of discontent that sounded like miniature roars.

He shrugged. "Okay, so maybe not accounting."

She laughed. "You could become a hairdresser." She ran her fingers through his hair.

"That's Aiden's job."

Aiden was one of the youngest children from Cordray's shelter, but despite being only three years old, she had mad skills when it came to braiding his hair.

"Yeah, that kid's got talent." Sam brushed her fingers through his hair.

"For a toddler."

Sam rolled her head and looked at him like he'd missed something. "Baby, she's got talent for a seasoned Hollywood stylist for the superstars. I swear that girl is going to grow up to be the most in-demand hairdresser in the world. People will probably pay her to travel to London or Tokyo just to do their hair."

Micah laughed then sighed as Sam settled against him again. "Well, I'll think of something to do. Something *normal*."

But would a normal job make him happy?

Honestly happy?

He craved action. He needed the adventure and mental sharpness that came with hunting drug dealers, vagrant drecks and vampires, and the occasional mutant. Normal might not cut it.

He dismissed the troubling thought. His happiness didn't

matter as much as becoming a father. He didn't want to leave Sam without a mate and his kids without a dad if something were to happen to him.

"Micah, you know you're not cut out for normal work," Sam said, giving voice to the concerns rumbling through his own thoughts.

"I could be."

She laughed and propped herself on her elbow. "You're a fighter. You won't be happy unless you're out there fighting."

"You don't know that. I could change. People change all the time."

Sam drew in her breath to reply, but the doorbell interrupted her, followed by a loud, urgent knock.

"Who the fuck?" Micah growled up at the ceiling out of frustration. He was trying to have a serious conversation with his mate, for Christ's sake. "Go away!"

These untimely interruptions were one thing he wouldn't miss once he officially quit his job.

The knocking came again, more insistent.

He had liked it better when the apartment had been a secret hideaway no one at AKM but Tristan knew about. Now every fool and their uncle knew he lived there. At least when he wasn't at the house in the burbs.

Sam scurried out of bed and started pulling on her clothes. "You'd better answer it. It sounds important."

"This"—he gestured between her and him—"is important." He pushed himself off the bed and reached for his clothes. "That"—he pointed in the direction of the front door then began tugging on his pants —"is a nuisance. It's why I want out of my job. I can't even spend a night with my mate—the most important night of my life—without being interrupted."

She smoothed out her hair. "I know, I know, and we'll discuss it. And I'll support whatever decision you make, but right now, you still have a job to do."

Pounding came from the front door again, even more insistent than before.

"Jesus! I'm coming! Lay off the fucking door!" He stormed out of the room as Sam followed.

Whoever had come to throw water on his love fire had better have a good reason for being there, because they'd just landed on his boot-up-the-ass list.

Flinging the door open, he frowned and took a step back. Severin stood in the hall with Micah's dad and that dreck who ran Grudge Match, Digon, behind him.

"What's going on?" he said to Severin, eyeing the other two.

Severin appeared stuck between bewildered and pissed off. "I could ask you the same question." He glanced over his shoulder at the two males standing behind him. Clearly, Sev had gotten the lowdown on Daddy-O and was just as confused by Digon's presence as Micah.

"It's your brother," his father said, his expression grim.

Micah's sixth sense lit up. "Ronan? What about him? What's happened to him?" He might not feel all warm and fuzzy about his father or his brother right now, but Ronan was family, and blood ran thick in Micah's world. Nothing bad had better have happened to Ronan now that he'd only just learned of his existence.

"You need to come quickly," Digon said.

"What are you even doing here?" Micah asked him.

Digon sighed and gestured toward the elevators. "That's not important right now. You need to come with us. Something has happened."

"I'll determine what is and isn't important, fuck you very much."

"Micah . . ." Sev took his arm, and Micah picked up all kinds of grave thoughts from the guy. Something about an attack, venom, blood, and Ronan in excruciating pain.

"Somebody had better tell me what the fuck is going on. Right now. I'm seriously not in the mood for games."

Severin drew in close and lowered his voice. "Your brother? Ronan? That Skeletor guy . . .?" Sev's blue eyes lasered in on Micah's to let him know he knew the truth about his newfound family issues. "He got bitten by a werewolf."

"So?" Vampires couldn't die from werewolf bites.

"This apparently wasn't a normal werewolf," Digon said.

That caught his attention. "How so?"

"We're still trying to figure it out, but it's not looking good."

Cold gooseflesh prickled Micah's body at the grave expression on his father's face. "What do you mean, it's not looking good?"

His father sighed, and concerned lines furrowed his face, which sent stabs of dread up and down Micah's spine.

"Micah . . . it's bad. Real bad." He frowned and cleared his throat. "Ronan could die."

"From a werewolf bite!" This had to be a bad joke.

Digon placed his hand reassuringly on his dad's shoulder. "Like we said, Micah, they weren't normal werewolves."

Well, shit. This night just couldn't stop raining on his parade.

CHAPTER 13

KING BAIN SAT ACROSS FROM HIS TWO TOP LIAISONS inside the headquarters of AKM, growing more impatient by the moment. When he arrived there, for personal reasons having nothing to do with ruling the race, he hadn't expected to find Ulrich and Gregos huddled in discussion in one of the corridors. And he certainly hadn't expected to be corralled into a private audience once they saw him.

Then he learned that Ulrich's daughter, Persephone, had been brought in from a cobalt overdose, which explained Ulrich's presence, but not Gregos's.

And now he was in an increasingly heated back and forth with Ulrich in the AKM conference room regarding what he was doing about the accelerating cobalt problem.

As emotions boiled over into impropriety, Ulrich pounded his fist on the oval table between them as he shot forward in his seat. "Not enough is being done about cobalt, Bain! *You're* not doing anything to put an end to this crisis! I want action! I want justice! For my daughter and my family!"

Gregos Savakis cautiously placed his hand over Ulrich's forearm. "He is just upset about his daughter, Your Highness. He means no *disrespect*." Gregos sent a cutting glare toward Ulrich. One that seemed more personal than professional.

King Bain glanced from Gregos to Ulrich and back, a niggle of unease prickling the hairs on the back of his neck. He couldn't put his finger on what was wrong, but something wasn't right between these two. They'd been exchanging private glances throughout this entire conversation, and the secret language they seemed fluent in made Bain increasingly suspicious.

He definitely needed to get to the bottom of whatever was

going on between them, but for now, he would let it stand. He had other more important issues to attend to in the foreseeable future. Issues that, if things went the way he hoped, would get around to uncovering whatever might be going on behind the scenes with Gregos and Ulrich, anyway, so why rush?

For now, he would address the greater threat. That of a werewolf bite that was more potent to a vampire than any werewolf bite he had ever seen. Because if some new race of werewolf had evolved to threaten them, that was a more imminent threat than cobalt.

Micah's half brother, Ronan, was at this very moment fighting for his life, and Bain wanted desperately to end this tiresome discussion so he could get an update from the doctor overseeing the efforts to keep Ronan alive.

He turned his attention back to Ulrich. "I will overlook your tone under the circumstances, Ulrich, but it would behoove you to remember who you're talking to."

Yes, Ulrich's emotions were high. Persephone had overdosed. Bain remembered his own emotional upheaval during Miriam's cobalt addiction. An addiction she still fought every day. Thank God she had Io to help her through the cravings and phantom withdrawal. And thank God he'd woken his ass up to his part in sending her to those death dealers in the first place. Otherwise, it might have been Miriam in a hospital bed from an overdose instead of Persephone.

Bain hadn't even realized Miriam's best friend, Persephone, was back on the blue shit. The last he heard, she'd been in rehab and doing well. Now here she was, back on cobalt, and from Ulrich's recounting of the situation, she'd almost died tonight. Still might. From the sound of things, it was bad.

If not for Ronan, she wouldn't even have a chance. She'd already be dead. Micah's brother had saved her.

And now he himself was fighting for his life.

From a fucking werewolf bite.

What in the hell were werewolves doing in Chicago?

That's the issue he wanted to be getting to the bottom of right now. That was why he was here. Well, it was *one* of the reasons, but he would keep his personal motivations to himself for now. In time, all would be revealed.

The point was, he didn't have time to hear about Persephone's cobalt habit, especially when her reasons for using the shit were sitting right in front of him.

Gregos and Ulrich had tried to force a mating on her with Gregos's son, Arion. Ari would have made a fine mate for Persephone, but he had already taken a mate. Severin. That hadn't sat well with Ulrich. It hadn't gone over well with Gregos, either, who refused to acknowledge Severin as his son's mate on the basis that theirs was an unnatural union. To compound the matter, Ulrich was furious Bain wouldn't enforce the arranged pairing between his daughter and Arion.

But that hadn't stopped Ulrich from seeking out a more suitable mate for his daughter. And he'd put Bain's son, Colin, at the top of his wish list. Ulrich had made numerous inquiries, each increasing in demand, seeking an audience between Colin and Persephone and an agreement that they would be joined as mates.

A severely inappropriate overstep on Ulrich's part. One that broached on dissension and insurrection, but one that was meant as a hard shove. The insinuation was that since Bain's law to protect biological matings had taken Persephone's arranged mate away from her, then he should give his son—the prince—in exchange.

A ballsy, bully move. And foolish. A move that would backfire if Ulrich didn't tread more carefully.

For all Bain cared, Ulrich could send him a hundred requests to arrange a pairing between Colin and Persephone. The answer would forever be no. He had no intention of giving Ulrich that kind of royal access. Besides, he had learned his lesson with his daughter, Miriam. Never again would he interfere in the mating habits of his children.

He had never planned to pair Miriam to a male who hadn't biologically mated her, but he had paraded eligible males in front of her relentlessly in search of one who would strike up a bonded claim. And when that claim came from the most unlikely source—the playboy enforcer, Io—he had resisted. Almost to his and Miriam's detriment. She had almost died because of his opposition to Io's mating bond to his daughter.

Never again. Now that he'd had time to see Miriam with Io and vice versa, he knew that male was the best thing that had ever happened to his daughter, despite Io's womanizing past. Io didn't so much as look at another female's *shadow*, anymore. He adored Miriam, and she treasured him. To see them together was like watching the living definition of true love.

It was proof enough that biology knew best, and from now on, Bain wouldn't meddle with its decisiveness. He didn't care whether a mating was heterosexual, homosexual, made between a vampire and a human, or whether the mating involved more than two people. His laws on the matter were clear. As long as the mating link was borne of biology, it was sacrosanct. He would honor all biological matings over any pairings that were engineered by outdated practices, such as those inherent to the wealthy, aristocratic families who preferred arranged unions to biological ones.

Such families believed they knew better than biology who was suited to whom. They wished to serve pedigree, not the survival of the race. Only those proven by wealth, political position, and social status were good enough to mate with their children.

Those families never learned. They still tried to manipulate bloodlines to their desires, even risking the extinction of their line by forcing a pairing that would never produce young.

And once a family got it in their heads that it was time to mate off their female progeny, they were relentless in the pursuit of an acceptable male.

Case in point, it had only been two months since Persephone's failed joining with Arion Savakis.

Two months.

And Ulrich had been shopping her around like a broodmare at auction for weeks. Almost immediately after the pairing with Arion fell apart, he was putting out feelers, searching for a suitable replacement. He hadn't even given her time to mourn before putting her back on the market. Hadn't given her time to process what had happened. For God's sake, give the young female a moment to catch her breath.

And Bain knew his son wasn't the only male Ulrich had been making inquiries about. He'd approached several families but had narrowed the choices down to the prince and Otto Chastain's son, Cecil. The Chastain line was wealthy beyond imagining, but they were useless.

Otto was a pompous, loathsome vampire, and his son was just as incompetent. No female would choose him of her own volition.

Pairing him with Persephone was lunacy.

Bain had no doubt her father's meddling had been key in driving her back to cobalt. Yet Ulrich sat in front of him, fuming, his face filled with blood, insisting that Bain do more to fight the insurgency of blue death that was driving a knife into the heart of their people when he should have been paying attention to what his daughter was trying to tell him through her self-destructive behavior. But, as usual, he saw only what he wanted to see and refused to admit he might actually be the cause of Persephone's drug addiction.

Persephone deserved to find what Miriam had found. Miri was undeniably happy now, her own cobalt addiction, which Bain had shamefully taken responsibility for, was rapidly fading into the past, thanks to Io. Miriam had a new lease on life, and Bain owed everything to Io for saving her.

If only there were something Bain could do to save Persephone the same way. It was blatantly obvious to Bain that she didn't want the life Ulrich insisted on forcing her to accept, but her father was too damn deaf to hear her pleas for help, even when she was screaming at the top of her lungs.

But Bain had no grounds to interfere. Until another male biologically mated her, there was nothing Bain could do.

"Why is she doing this to me?" Ulrich said, dropping his face into his hands.

Bain shook his head. "She's doing it to herself. The question you should be asking yourself, Ulrich, is what reason she has to self-medicate to the point of almost dying."

Ulrich slammed his palms on the table and shot out of his seat, leaning across the expanse of polished wood. "I know what you're getting at, Bain!"

"Ulrich . . ." Gregos blanched as he reached for Ulrich's arm.

"No, Gregos!" Ulrich whipped his arm away, launching himself from the table. He paced aggressively, taking abrupt, angry breaths. "I will be heard on this!" He jabbed his finger into the air in front of him.

Bain remained seated, eyes narrowed, body taut. If Ulrich so much as flinched his direction, he would subdue him so fast, the idiot wouldn't know what hit him until after his ass shot out his mouth.

Bain might have been royalty, but he was expertly trained in self-defense and could more than hold his own in a fight. He'd seen his share of battles during the war and took credit for hundreds of kills. If Ulrich moved on him, it would be the last move he made.

"What's on your mind, Ulrich?"

Ulrich spun to face him. "Your inability to put an end to this poison killing our people! Your lack of support when I petitioned you to dissolve Arion and Severin's mating so Arion could honor the arrangement Gregos and I made for him to mate my daughter! Your continued refusal to give me an audience to discuss an alliance between Persephone and the prince." He seethed, his face red. Then he sealed his fate. "Your *complete inadequacy* as the *ruler* of our *people!*"

Bain blasted out of his chair and was on Ulrich in an instant, capturing Ulrich by the neck, wrapping his massive hand around the thick column supporting Ulrich's head before the other male could escape. He lifted him off the floor Darth Vader-style until they were nose to nose.

Ulrich clawed at Bain's hand, struggling to breathe. Gregos shrunk toward the exit like a cowardly snake.

"I have maintained my patience with you beyond what others would deem reasonable, Ulrich," he hissed. "You know the laws regarding mating. Laws my father put into effect that I have no reason to alter, nor do I wish to, because to rescind them would be a death sentence.

"I will not condemn the males of our race to mania or death for losing what is biologically theirs to possess. I will not allow our race to turn back to a time when we lost males by the hundreds — the *thousands* even, to the edge of certain *extinction*. Do you know how perilously low our male population fell not even two thousand years ago? If we had remained on that course, any who survived would now be under dreck rule. I will not see our race regress. I will not allow our males to suffer or die because the females their bodies chose were already bound to another through arranged couplings.

"You know this, and you know my position, and yet you insulted me and insolently wasted my time with your useless petition to dissolve a mating deemed honorable by the laws of my court.

"You insulted me further by seeking an arrangement between

your daughter and my son, breaking the chain of protocol that should have prevented you from making such a request of your king in the first place. Especially when I know you are working on a separate arrangement to mate your daughter with that insolent half-wit, Cecil.

"You continue to insult me now, and I would be within my rights to snap your neck and impale your head in front of my home as a lesson to others who would think to insult me and my sovereignty as you have. If not for the undue attention such an act would bring upon our race by human law enforcement, you would be dead by now, so mind your tone with me from this day forward, Ulrich, or I will follow through on my threat. As for remaining in my employ as a liaison, consider yourself demoted to civilian, your rank stripped. I will give you only one warning. The next time you force me to discuss this topic with you will result in your last breath."

Ulrich continued to thrash, attempting to free himself, but Bain was just getting started.

"As for your daughter." Bain squeezed Ulrich's throat a little tighter. "Persephone doesn't want an arranged pairing, you egotistical ass. That's why she's using cobalt. That's why she's trying to kill herself on that shit. Because she doesn't want to be saddled with a male whose greatest love is himself and whose second greatest love is his family's money.

"But you're so obsessed with the idiocy of ensuring strong bloodlines that you fail to see the simple truth to your own daughter's unhappiness. To the very truth that she's using cobalt to rid herself of *your* foolishness.

"Yet you dare to question how I'm handling the cobalt problem. Have you no brain inside that skull of yours? Have you not paid attention during our council meetings? Punishing drecks for dealing cobalt is not within my jurisdiction. That is Premier Royce's responsibility. If you want to deal with the cobalt issue in your own home, I suggest you look to yourself. Because it is you, not I, who is the answer to your problems, Ulrich."

Gregos cleared his throat as he took a hesitant step forward. "Meaning no disrespect, Your Highness, b-but" —his whole body trembled as he swallowed—"couldn't Premier Royce's lack of attention to this matter be considered" —he pressed his lips into a thin line—"a violation of the treaty?"

Bain narrowed his eyes on Gregos, coming to a sudden realization. "Are you saying you want war?" He turned his gaze on Ulrich.

Ulrich and Gregos had been meeting with high-ranking members of vampire society in recent weeks. During the daily briefings Bain held with his liaisons, they'd hinted of restlessness within the community. He often noticed the two of them exchanging knowing glances — the same glances he'd become wary of only a moment ago — during those same meetings.

Awareness gripped him by the balls. He couldn't say with certainty that Gregos and Ulrich had been unifying the people against him and, thus, staging a coup. He couldn't even say that they were stirring the civilians into thinking war was in their best interests. But his instincts told him they were up to something that could jeopardize the entire vampire race. He needed to tread carefully with these two and find a way to look into the intrigues they were orchestrating behind his back at the earliest opportunity.

Gregos attempted to speak again. "Your Highne — "

Bain dropped Ulrich to his feet. "Get out."

Ulrich fell into a coughing fit, bent forward, clutching his throat.

Gregos frowned nervously. "But, sire — "

"I said get out." Bain glared at him then shot daggers at Ulrich. "I will not entertain this conversation further."

One thing had become clear in the last thirty seconds. They were plotting against him, he just didn't know how deep or far their disloyalty and deviations ran, or how forked their tongues were.

But he had a plan. One he intended to unveil tonight. One that would reveal their treachery if any was to be found.

He could put it off no longer. It was time to take precautions.

Time to tell Micah the truth.

Time for Micah to fill the role he'd been meant to fill.

No, *born* to fill.

And then he would get to the bottom of the treason apparently going on right under his nose.

CHAPTER 14

WHEN MICAH BURST THROUGH THE DOORS leading into AKM's medical unit, it was clear the shit was hitting the fan. The place was a hornet's nest, everyone scurrying to and fro, doctors barking orders to nurses who tried their best to keep up. Medical equipment beeped and whistled. A shrill alarm sounded.

Surely this wasn't all for Ronan. It was a werewolf bite. Yes, getting bitten by a werewolf was a shit bag of fun even on a good day, and, sure, from what he'd been told, the beast that had bitten Ronan was allegedly some kind of Frankenwolf, but Ronan should at least be stabilizing by now. Hell, how bad could a lowly werewolf bite be?

"What the fuck's going on?" he said to no one in particular.

No one replied.

Micah grabbed the arm of a passing doctor. "Is he okay? Is Ronan okay?"

The grim look the doc gave him said it all. The situation wasn't good. "We're doing everything we can, but we're having difficulty stabilizing him." The doc freed his arm. "I'm sorry, I have to get back." He hurried off like he was being chased by a school of bloodthirsty piranha.

It was a fucking werewolf bite! Why couldn't they stabilize him?

Maybe a better question was what kind of abnormal werewolf created this much chaos?

He spied Brak in the corner, hunched over in a chair, his pallor a sickening grey. A waste can sat beside him.

Dodging aids and nurses, he hurried to Brak's side and knelt in front of him.

"Brak, what's going on? What's happening to Ronan?"

With Brak's nifty healing powers, he'd joined the medical

staff to assist in situations that required more than standard care. Situations that were more like life and death and needed a special brand of deep healing. For Brak to have been brought over from the new facility meant shit was critical, especially if the staff were still running around with this much urgency *after* Brak had performed his healing magic.

Brak lifted his head and peered through the long brown strands of his sweat-soaked hair. If not for all that hair, he would have looked exactly like his brother, Trace.

When he spoke, his voice sounded as weak as he looked. "I've never seen anything like it." He closed his eyes and went utterly still as if holding back his gag reflex. After several seconds, he peeled his lids open and let out a long exhale. "Whatever bit him wasn't natural, Micah."

"What do you mean, not natural?"

He shook his head, keeping the movement small. "That venom was man-made."

"Micah!"

He glanced over his shoulder as the doctor he'd spoken to a moment ago approached, his expression grave.

"What is it?"

"We need blood," the doc said. "Can you —"

"Absolutely. Sure. Just give me a sec." He turned back to Brak and squeezed his shoulder. "Thank you for trying."

Brak nodded tightly and looked like he was about to lose his cookies as Micah stood.

He joined the doctor, who directed him into a chair on the far side of the room. A nurse rushed forward with a tray of blood-drawing paraphernalia as he rolled up his sleeve.

Things moved too fast for him to ask questions. The doctor rattled off some instructions to the nurse as she nodded and wrapped an elastic band around his biceps and tapped the crook of his arm for a vein. Then the doctor was gone and his blood was being sucked through a slender tube into a plastic bag.

"Take as much as you need," he said, watching the red fluid drain out of him.

A few hours ago, he wasn't sure whether he wanted to kill Ronan or welcome him into the family. Now, he was ready to give half his own blood to save the fucker. If that didn't speak volumes about how his feelings had changed where his brother was concerned, he didn't know what did. Still, he didn't have to like the little shit to want to save his life.

"This will suffice for now," the nurse said, checking the bag.

A flash of black hair and a black shirt caught his eye from the other side of the room. His father paced outside what Micah assumed was the room where Ronan was being treated. A giant pane of glass was all that separated father from son. Micah couldn't see much going on inside, but the look on his dad's face said it all. The sitch was going from bad to worse, and it was ripping his father to pieces.

Whoa. Who were the two imposing males with coal-black hair milling around on the periphery? The ones as tall as skyscrapers who looked like they owned the place?

The one with the goatee looked familiar. Micah was sure he'd met him before, but where?

He sniffed, filtering through the smells of blood, vomit, astringent, and surgical soap until he isolated their scents.

Lycans.

That's where he's seen goatee boy before. It had been a long time ago, soon after arriving in North America, when he was part of an escort guarding King Bain the First while meeting with the lycans regarding territorial boundaries.

What was the guy's name again? Ramey? Rammstein? Rainman? No, Rameses. Like the pharaoh. And he wasn't just any lycan. He was the brother to their *imeut*. That was what the lycans called their leader. If he remembered correctly, the title of *imeut* had something to do with the Ancient Egyptian god, Anubis. Lycans were allegedly descendants of Anubis, so the title made sense.

Rameses was second-in-command only to his brother, Memnon, and oh, what a joy Memnon was. He never smiled, never showed compassion, never allowed emotion of any kind into his expression.

Micah felt sorry for any female unfortunate enough to get stuck in the same bed with the guy. He probably fucked like a bulldozer. Or a ram. And not the animal kind. Micah was talking about the kind of ram that medieval armies had used to bust down the barred gates of castles and fortresses.

He could almost see it. Memnon probably climbed on top of the woman, shoved her legs apart, and impaled her before slamming into her a few times—just enough to get off, because efficiency seemed to be Memnon's thing—and even before his cock stopped twitching, he dismounted and left the poor female wondering what in the hell just happened as he showered then returned to his golden throne. Or wherever he went when he was acting as commander in chief over the lycan race.

Memnon's sexual habits aside, Chicago wasn't lycan territory. So, what the fuck was Rameses and his black-haired sidekick, *Pretty Boy*, doing here?

The nurse finished drawing his blood and slapped a bandage on his arm before hurrying off with her bounty.

Rolling his sleeve down, Micah stood and meandered closer to where his father and the two lycans stared intently through the window at what was going on inside the room where he assumed Ronan was being treated. As he stepped around the nurses' station and carts of equipment, more of the room's interior broke into his field of vision. He saw the silver footrail of the bed first, then the white sheets covering what he assumed were Ronan's feet and legs.

And then . . .

What the fuck?

Another lycan, a behemoth with a mane of sandy-blond hair longer and prettier than Severin's, stood with his eyes closed and his hands extended over Ronan's body like he was some kind of shaman.

Micah had seen it all tonight. Dead vampires who came back to life. A brother he never knew he had. A set of twins growing inside his mate's belly even though he hadn't had a calling. And now . . . some lycan with a hair-band complex was going medicine man on his brother.

Micah just hoped Twisted Sister didn't end up giving his bro a lobotomy.

PRIEST HEARD THE COMMOTION GOING ON AROUND HIM, the doctors and nurses bringing in blood, blood, more blood, transfusing Ronan while he continued planting ancient healing energy directly from the goddess Sekhmet herself into the vampire's body.

Frantic voices shouted instructions, nurses called for more

blood, and bodies bumped into Priest as the activity reached a fever pitch. But Priest remained focused on the task at hand, his body and mind in a more or less meditative state, homed in on Ronan like the vampire was the only other living being within a square mile.

Priest's left hand hovered horizontally over Ronan's torso. In his right hand, he held his gold cartouche. Its gold chain coiled around and between his fingers.

Gold held tremendous value to the lycans because of its transformative powers and ability to conduct spiritual energy. They used it to heal, to bring their brethren out of hibernation, to open the portals between worlds and cities. To the lycans, gold was the difference between life and death, peace and war, justice and corruption. Without gold, they would be lost, which was why they hoarded any they could get their hands on.

He had known what he would find inside Ronan before he started the healing process. But he hadn't expected the damage to be so prolific. The motley werewolf's venom was more corrosive to vampires than he and the others had assumed it would be.

This wasn't by accident. This wasn't some random beast whose venom coincidentally did more harm to vampires than old werewolf venom did.

This was a weapon. One designed specifically to target vampires.

In their never-ending quest to hunt down the werewolves and eradicate them from this realm, Priest and his lycan brothers had recently begun to notice a change in their behavior and physiology. Not in all werewolves, mind you, but there was a new breed of werewolf infiltrating the hierarchy of paranormal beings that called earth their home.

There were lycans, vampires, drecks, and werewolves, among other lesser beings like fairy creatures and benign shifters who tended to do more good than bad, but this new class of werewolf didn't fit in with anything they were familiar with. They could shift without a full moon. They were more cunning than their lupine cousins. Their venom was as corrosive as battery acid, and it worked quickly, spreading and infecting its victim with the speed of a lightning strike.

These werewolves were not of a natural order. They were creations.

Someone had made these beasts.

The lycans needed Hunter more than ever now. Hunter would be a tremendous asset in tracking and destroying these abominations. These motleys. None of his brethren could hold a candle to Hunter's tracking abilities and slaying skills.

And now he was back. Returned to earth by the curious and troubled mind of the vampire prostrated beneath his healing hands.

No doubt Ronan hadn't a clue what he'd done by opening the gate. From what little he, Rameses, and Dain had overheard through the portal before activating the gateway, Ronan didn't even know he'd opened it. He thought the ankh — the key — had failed. Only because he had no idea how the gates worked.

He and the others had a good chuckle at the conversation between Ronan and Rysk, waiting for them to depart before coming through, but then the werewolves had shown up, and it had become clear they couldn't keep their arrival in Chicago a secret. They had to pass through the gateway, not necessarily to save the vampires, but to kill the beasts.

After millennia of hunting and killing the escaped werewolves, lycans were hardwired not to let even one get away. It was their bound duty to kill them. They had sworn an oath to both Osiris and Anubis that they would remain and hunt the werebeasts to the very last one. To rid this realm of their poison. Their sickness.

The problem with werewolves was that they bred quickly, and in a myriad of ways. They could infect a human with the sickness through a bite. Or a male werewolf in human form could mate with a human female and produce a werewolf child. Or a female werewolf could lay with a human male. Of course, the child would be latent until it reached adulthood and went through its first change.

This was an even bigger problem because lycans couldn't detect werewolves until their first shift. That's why such an effort was made to identify the offspring of known werewolves. Tracking and eliminating offspring during their first shift accounted for at least a fourth of the lycans' kills.

And now they had these engineered motleys to contend with.

Which was why Memnon needed to cease Hunter's exile. Immediately. Before they fell even further behind.

Yes, what Hunter had done was bad. Mating a vampire when

it could result in an abomination was verboten, but this was no time to sit your star quarterback on the sidelines. They needed Hunter in the field, doing what Hunter did best, even if Memnon cast him from the clan. Having Hunter in this realm as an outcast was better than relegating him to some prison planet where he couldn't do any good at all.

Priest sensed Dain and Rameses felt the same way, but even Ram, as Memnon's blooded brother, held little persuasion over their *imeut*. And trying to withhold the knowledge that Hunter was back in the earth realm wasn't an option. Memnon would know. He would see it in their thoughts. Which meant they had no choice but to tell Memnon the truth and hope they could persuade him to allow Hunter to stay, given these new developments.

New developments that caused Priest to think forming an alliance with the vampires was the best course of action. Something else he sensed Rameses agreed with him on.

He directed more healing energy into Ronan's blood, gradually siphoning out the poison.

Vampires were crucial to maintaining the balance among the paranormal beings on earth. Without them, drecks would run rampant, and then the lycans would have two direct enemies, with no buffer to offer protection. And since Priest held little doubt these new motley werewolves were creations of that psychotic dreck, Bishop, it wasn't a stretch to imagine Bishop also possessed long-term ambitions to do to the lycans what he was perpetuating against the vampires. Bishop had already dealt the sin eaters a heavy blow with cobalt, and now he piled on the hurt even further with his deadly motleys.

What would Bishop have in store for the lycans when the vampires were no longer a threat?

Priest didn't want his brethren to be caught on their heels. It was time to be proactive and make a change. A lot of changes. Their survival depended on it.

He only hoped Memnon agreed once he was awakened and briefed.

Because if he didn't, Priest might have to make hard decisions he would rather not make.

Remain loyal to his brothers? Or join Hunter and create a new path?

CHAPTER 15

MICAH JOINED THE TWO LYCANS AND HIS FATHER outside the window of Ronan's room, his stomach knotting as he watched Ronan writhe in obvious pain.

His brother. That was his brother in there.

"What's he doing to him?" He gestured toward the blond lycan just as Digon and his Grudge Match sidekick, Rule, exited an examination room a few doors down.

Rule appeared worse for the wear and strung tighter than a crossbow. He'd been patched up from what looked like one hell of a fight, and contusions darkened both cheeks and one eye.

Without turning toward him, Rameses answered his question in a deep, no-frills voice, "Priest is healing your kin."

"Kin?" How did Rameses know Ronan was his brother?

Rameses's gaze slid to his. "Is he not a vampire?"

Okay, so maybe this was a general term lycans used regarding vampires. "Yes, but—"

"Then he is your kin." Rameses remained unaffected, facing the action in Ronan's room once more.

What a dick. But it wasn't worth getting into a battle of words while Ronan was fighting for his life. Instead, Micah made a mental note to revisit this with Rameses later.

Digon and Rule joined them, remaining a safe distance away, as if they knew tensions were high and didn't want to spark an explosion. Rule's clothes were splattered with blood and covered in dirt and grass stains. One sleeve was shredded. The other had been ripped clean off. Blood-soaked bandages covered his arms and neck. From the clawlike rips across the front of his shirt, it was a good bet his stomach was bandaged, too.

Rule huddled to the side with Digon, near his father, whispering quietly, exchanging glances with his dad in a way that made it clear they knew one other. A moment later, his father joined them, and it didn't take a body language expert to know good ol' Dad didn't just know Rule, but Digon, too. And he knew them well.

Very well.

They looked more like three best friends who'd known one another long enough to know who among them wore boxers, briefs, or went commando.

Okay, so maybe that came off sounding too homosexual. Micah knew his dad didn't swing that way, and while Digon and Rule were elegant enough to give the impression they were into male-on-male action, there was something about both of them that screamed heterosexual. He'd noticed both of them eyeing the females of Grudge Match during the one and only visit he'd made to the fight club only a few days ago. Gay males didn't get that special gleam in their eyes when they were checking out females. But hetero males did, even if they had every intention of keeping their hands off the goods.

So maybe another way of putting this would be to say that it was a good bet Digon and Rule knew his dad's full, painful history, and he knew theirs. Micah couldn't pick up anything but a black void from inside their heads, but he couldn't ignore the gut feeling that the trio had known one another a long fucking time.

And he wasn't sure what to think about that.

But he didn't have long to ponder the sitch as the double doors swung open and King Bain strode in.

And there it was, the trifecta of bizarro to put *The Twilight Zone* cap on the evening.

"Micah," Bain said in greeting before eyeing the rest of the crowd gathered outside Ronan's room.

Interestingly enough, Bain didn't appear surprised or taken aback to find a dreck, three lycans, and his father among the crowd. In fact, he nodded privately to each in turn.

"Your Highness? What are you doing here?"

It seemed a pretty far stretch that the king of the race, who was notoriously private and reclusive, would leave his home and come to AKM to check in on the condition of a civilian. And, to Bain, that's what Ronan was. A cat burglar, yes, but a civilian. And, well, Micah's brother. But, surely, that wasn't reason enough to bring Bain out of his fortified royal home.

Without answering the question, Bain spied the bandage on the inside of Micah's elbow then snapped his fingers in the direction of the nurses' station. "Take my blood, too." His heavy voice boomed, drawing the attention of everyone within twenty feet.

A shocked nurse nearly dropped a tray of vials and syringes as she tripped over her own feet when she saw the king. "Yes, sire." She nodded, bowed, nodded awkwardly again, then hurried to collect what was needed to draw another bag of blood.

Bain dropped into a nearby seat and started rolling up his sleeve to reveal his massive arm.

Trying again, Micah asked, "Sire, what are you doing here?"

Bain cast him a sidelong glance. "Once Ronan stabilizes, you and I need to talk. I'll give you answers then." He nodded toward the buzz of activity in Ronan's room. "How is he?"

"Actually, he's *not* stabilizing."

"Shit."

The nurse rushed over and got to work drawing the king's blood, sticking his arm. The clear plastic bag hanging beside him began to fill.

Micah lowered his voice and chucked his chin toward Rameses and the other dark-haired lycan standing off to the side. "What are they doing here?"

Bain studied the lycans. "They killed the werewolves that attacked Rysk and Ronan."

"Who the hell is Rysk?" Micah didn't know anyone named Rysk.

It felt like the world had turned upside down while he'd been finding out he was going to be a father, and now he was playing serious catch-up.

Bain sighed as if he'd realized he shouldn't have said anything. "Rysk is Rule. Rule is Rysk's alias."

Micah glanced toward the male he knew only as Rule. The guy had never given Micah the warm and fuzzies, and this surprising switcheroo with his name gave Micah one more reason not to like him.

"Why the hell does that asshole need an alias?"

Bain pinched the bridge of his nose. "It's a long story."

"I'm not going anywhere."

"I'll tell you later."

"With all due respect, sire, what aren't you telling me?" Micah didn't like this keeping-him-in-the-dark feeling one bit.

Bain dropped his hand to the arm of the chair as the nurse finished drawing his blood and slapped on a bandage. "Drop it, Micah. It's been a long fucking night, and I'm about to throw my royal titles in your face if you don't shut the hell up."

Micah took a deep breath and sighed as he bowed his head. "My apologies. It's been a long night for me, too."

He glanced at his father again, who was still speaking in hushed tones with Digon and Rule — er, Rysk. Jesus, it was getting hard to keep all the players straight, but it did beg the question of whether or not his father knew Rule's true identity. Given how chummy the three seemed to be with one another, Micah had a feeling his father knew the truth and a whole lot more.

"I know it has," Bain said, rising. "And it's only going to get longer. But first, let's see what we can find out about your brother. We'll discuss the rest once we know he's out of danger."

Micah didn't even question how Bain knew Ronan was his brother. Right now, he felt like a visitor in an alternate reality, so he was going to stick with being an observer more than a participant. Maybe that would shed light on what everyone else around here seemed to know already.

In reluctantly dutiful observation mode, he followed but hung back as Bain joined the others.

"Rameses." Bain extended his hand to the lycan.

"Bain." Rameses shook his hand. "It's good to see you again. I only wish it were under better circumstances."

The necessary royal formalities were exchanged, but all Micah wanted was for them to get past all the hoity-toity bullshit and talk shop. He loathed wasting time, and that's what all this *"How's the queen?" "Fine. How's your brother?" "He's in hibernation now." "Oh, that's nice."* was. It was all Micah could do not to grab Rameses by the scruff and demand he tell them why he was there and what had happened to his brother.

"This is Dain." Rameses introduced the other black-haired male then nodded toward the imposing blond performing whatever voodoo magic he specialized in on Ronan. "That's Priest. He's our healer. He will ensure your kin pulls through."

There was that term again. Micah almost mouthed off about how just because they were all vampires, that didn't automatically make them kin, but before he could, Bain turned toward him and gestured.

"This is Micah Black, my strongest enforcer."

Rameses faced him, and Micah found himself gazing into the darkest set of eyes he'd ever seen. So dark they were like black holes. Not even a shred of light or emotion stared back at him. No color, no fear, no anger, no discontent. Only an astute sense of observation that dissected him and made him feel like he was under the lens of a microscope.

"Micah Black," Rameses said. "It's been a long time."

My God, were they going to dance this politically correct waltz all night?

"It has." Micah remained wary, keeping his distance.

Rameses blinked, and one corner of his mouth ticked subtly upward. "We have found much amusement in following your exploits."

Was Rameses making fun of him or just stating a fact? It was hard to tell. But if the latter, how the hell would Rameses have learned anything about what Micah had been up to? And why would he find his "exploits" amusing?

"We?"

"Memnon and me. Tales of your achievements in battle have made it to our territory for centuries. You are quite an accomplished warrior."

Yeah, well, flattery would get Rameses absolutely fucking nowhere. Micah didn't like the guy, didn't trust him, and wanted to get this meet-and-greet over so Rameses and *his* kin would return to their corner of the continent sooner rather than later.

"Funny, I've never heard anything about you." That wasn't exactly true, but it wasn't like Rameses could read his mind to learn the truth. Lycans couldn't read vampires' minds.

"Micah . . ." Bain's tone held a warning for him to behave.

One of Rameses's black eyebrows rose a fraction as he eyed Micah. Then he turned back to Bain as if dismissing him. "We should talk."

"About?"

"This." Rameses chucked his head toward Ronan. "The werewolves that attacked him. The ankh." That sharp eyebrow arched toward Micah again. "The ankh is ours. It was taken from us a long time ago."

Micah frowned. He knew nothing about how his father came in possession of the ankh. "You can talk to my father about that shit. I was just told to protect it."

"A task you failed at. And now look what's happened." He gestured toward Ronan.

"Fuck you, dog." This politically correct conversation had just escalated into something aggressive, because Rameses had just grated on Micah's last remaining unfrayed nerve.

"Micah!" King Bain grabbed his arm and pushed him back before he could take a swing at Rameses.

Before anything further could be said, a shriek rang out from Ronan's room.

Micah shot around to find Priest's fangs sinking deep into Ronan's wrist. The lycan wasn't fully wolfed out, but he definitely didn't look fully human anymore, either.

Rage erupted inside Micah. Pure, unadulterated rage. That was his brother in there.

"What are you doing to him?" He shot forward, ready to rip Priest's head off and shred him limb from limb.

"Micah, no!" Bain's hold on his arm strengthened, cutting off the circulation.

"He's killing him!" Micah twisted his arm from Bain's hold and made a dash for Ronan's room as doctors and nurses scattered to get out of his way.

He was a fraction of a second away from leaping through the door and clocking Priest across his chiseled jaw when, out of nowhere, a thick arm fired out and snatched him from his I'm-going-to-kill-him trajectory.

Micah spun to find Rameses's black eyes staring him down like calderas from twin volcanos.

"Priest is helping him." Rameses's deep, calm voice didn't mesh with the extraordinary strength restraining him. Strength Micah couldn't break free from.

Talk about a blow to his ego.

Another bloodcurdling shriek rent the air as Rameses dragged him from the doorway.

"You call that helping?" Micah gestured toward his brother and tugged against Rameses's hold.

Rameses tossed him against the far wall like he weighed no more than a notebook. "Let Priest do his work. He's using his venom to kill that of the werewolf who bit him."

Micah's gaze shot back through the glass panes separating him from his brother, remembering how he'd used his own venom to kill Apostle's after he bit Sam. The experience had been excruciating for Sam, but even more so for Micah to have to stand by helplessly and watch her suffer.

He felt the same way now.

But this was a werewolf bite. Sure, a werewolf bite did more damage to a vampire than a dreck bite, but vampires didn't die from that shit. Ronan's superior vampire genes shouldn't need the venom of a lycan to help him fend off werewolf venom.

"What about my venom?" he asked. He would much rather give his brother his own venom than watch a lycan do it.

"It won't help." Rameses kept a watchful eye on Micah, ready to stop him if he made another move to interfere. "Not for this."

There was something ominous in Rameses's tone.

"What do you mean? Not for this?"

Rameses glanced from him to Bain. "We should talk privately."

Not waiting for an invitation, Micah followed Bain and Rameses into the empty hallway. No one argued with him, probably because they knew it would be pointless. He was going to hear what Rameses had to say, whether the lycan liked it or not.

"What's going on?" he asked once the doors to the medical unit closed behind them. "Why isn't Ronan getting better? He shouldn't be suffering this much from a werewolf bite." Okay, fine, he would still be suffering, but not to the point of needing lycan venom. Not so much that their doctors couldn't ease his pain and stabilize him.

"They weren't regular werewolves," Rameses said.

"So I've been told. So, what in the hell are they? And why did they go after Ronan?"

Rameses held up his hand, palm out, as if telling him he would answer all his questions but didn't want them rapid-fired at him. "They found Ronan because he used the ankh to open the portal housed in the mausoleum at the cemetery. The moment he did that, he sent out a signal that served as a homing beacon, alerting every lycan and werewolf on the continent to its presence. He's lucky we showed up when we did or both of your kin would be dead now."

Enough was enough. "Cut the kin crap."

Rameses tilted his head. "Isn't Ronan your brother?"

"Yes, but . . . wait, how do you know that?"

"We know a lot of things."

"Apparently."

"Micah," Bain interrupted, "cut it out." To Rameses, he said, "You still haven't told us what they are, Rameses. These creatures that attacked Rysk and Ronan."

Rameses glanced from Bain to Micah and back again as if he knew he was about to drop a bomb. "They are your new worst enemy."

CHAPTER 16

Sam stood over the pile of freshly folded clothes in the laundry room, her hand on her belly and a smile on her face. She was going to be a mom. In nine months, give or take, because she had no idea how long she'd been pregnant, she would be washing pastel-colored Onesies and tiny socks no bigger than her ear. She would be up in the middle of the night breastfeeding, changing diapers, and suffering from the exhaustion that comes with being a new parent.

And she couldn't wait.

At least her increased appetite made sense now, as well as all the weird foods she'd been craving, such as salmon and scrambled eggs, cold lobster and hash browns, bread and butter pickle and peanut butter sandwiches. With vampire young inside her, she just hoped she wouldn't start craving blood like that girl in the movies about the sparkling vampires.

Sighing contentedly, she started the next load of laundry then shut off the light and made her way upstairs to check on Cordray's kids. It was just after two in the morning, so she still had a few hours of quiet to wrap her mind around the news that she was pregnant before her house became a symphony of children looking for breakfast and preparing for school.

The orphans Cordray looked after had been through so much in the past few days—the fire that destroyed their home, losing everything they owned, being uprooted in the middle of the night and shuttled to a strange place to live with people they didn't know.

All things considered, they had adjusted remarkably well. Sometimes children were more resilient than adults. They bounced back so quickly from tragedy. But that didn't mean they wouldn't carry the psychological effects of the fire for years to come.

She peered into the room Aiden and Null shared. The toddler twins were inseparable, even in sleep. They were snuggled against each other in the center of the full-sized bed.

Somewhere inside Sam's brain, a maternal valve had clicked on the moment Trace and Cordray had shown up with the children in tow, especially when she saw Aiden and Null, the youngest of the bunch. All the kids had been bleary-eyed and confused, and she had felt the need right away to care for them like they were her own. Now, she couldn't shut off her motherly instincts.

She placed her hand over her belly. Soon enough, those instincts would come in handy with her own children.

Children. Plural.

Because she was going to have twins. She still couldn't believe it.

She smiled and looked down at her stomach. "Be nice to each other in there," she whispered. "And be nice to me, too. I've never had a baby."

She opened the bedroom door wider and quietly approached the bed. Aiden had a choke hold on her Pooh Bear, which Sam had tossed in the washing machine to clean off all the soot from the fire. Now Pooh was back to his spritely canary yellow, and his vest was once again bright red.

Sam smiled at Aiden's and Null's cherubic faces. They looked like tiny Cupids, with plump, rosy cheeks and golden ringlets swirling over their foreheads.

Null had fallen asleep sucking his thumb, which Cordray said he did when he was stressed. Sam gently pulled his thumb out of his mouth and brushed her palm over his blond curls. Poor little guy. He put on a resilient front during the day, but he couldn't hide how vulnerable he felt when he slept.

She straightened and affectionately gazed down at them. They were so small, still shaky on their feet when they tried to run, with tiny hands that felt so fragile folded inside hers.

With their fair coloring and blond hair, they easily could have been her own kids, but she doubted she and Micah would ever produce children that looked like her. Micah dominated in every facet of life. Why would producing a child be any different? No doubt their kids would come out with hair the color of coal and eyes shaded midnight blue.

And you know what? That was fine with her. As long as they had ten fingers, ten toes, and were healthy, she would take them however they came, little bitty vampire fangs and all. Although, she understood the fangs came later, as they went through their transition from juvenile to adult.

Talk about going through puberty.

She pressed her palm to her belly again, imagining how it would feel as they grew inside her. Like their father, would they rob her of rest as they grew from pea-sized clumps of cells to fully formed fetuses? Not that she was complaining about her life with Micah. She loved how he took care of her without being too overbearing — most of the time. And she loved how he mentally challenged her, and how they fit together so perfectly in every way.

She loved him, period. In fact, she wasn't sure love was a strong enough word for how she felt about Micah, but what was stronger than love? Adoration? Reverence? Worship? She giggled to herself. She could definitely say that her feelings didn't fall in line with worship. Micah might have enjoyed that, but saying she worshipped him took her feelings a bit too far. No woman should ever worship a man — male, whatever. In fact, to hear Micah talk, it was the male who worshipped the female in this supernatural world of vampires and shapeshifters.

This life was certainly beyond anything she had ever seen for herself as a child, but now that she was living it, she couldn't imagine any other future.

She pressed light kisses to Aiden's and Null's chubby cheeks then quietly left the room.

As she approached the room Panya and Faith shared, she heard a muffled sniffle.

She eased the door open and peered inside. Faith was sound asleep, but Panya was sitting up in bed, hugging her knees to her chest as she gently rocked forward and back. She raised her face, and Sam saw tears glistening on her cheeks.

"What's wrong?" Sam whispered, hurrying to her side. "Are you okay?"

Panya brushed her fingers over her face, wiping away her tears as she shook her head. "I had a bad dream. Fire was everywhere." She held her arms straight out in front of her, looking down at them as if they were covered in flames. "It was all over me, on my arms, melting my clothes to my skin . . ." She started crying again, and Faith stirred and rolled over.

Now that she was closer, Sam could see that Panya was drenched with sweat. Her pajamas clung to her body, and perspiration slicked her neck and forehead. Her long lashes were clumped with tears.

"Come on, let's go downstairs." Sam gestured toward the door. "I'll get you a change of clothes, and we can watch a movie. I'll make you a cup of cocoa. Do you like marshmallows?" If she talked about something else, maybe Panya would stop thinking about her nightmare.

Panya hesitated then nodded.

"Okay then. It's a date." She held out her hand, and Panya slipped hers inside it.

A moment later, Sam quietly shut the door and led Panya down the stairs to the kitchen.

The TV was on in the living room, with the sound turned low. A Harrison Ford movie was just coming on. You couldn't go wrong with Harrison Ford.

Sam pointed to the plateful of remaining chocolate chip cookies she and Panya had baked that afternoon. "Have a cookie. I'll be right back with dry clothes."

In the laundry room, Sam rummaged through the piles of folded clothes Brenna, Mya, she, and Cordray had pulled together to replace those lost in the fire. Sam had spent the better part of the afternoon and evening washing them. Mya put off sleep for over twenty-four hours, lending a hand with the washing and folding before finally collapsing in an exhausted heap around nine o'clock, leaving Sam to continue the fight on her own until Micah called. And there was still a lot of washing to do before it was finished.

She found a pair of sweats and an oversized T-shirt and hustled back to the kitchen.

Panya was sitting at the counter picking bites of cookie off with her fingers.

Sam set the folded clothes on the counter. "You can change in the bathroom while I start the cocoa."

Panya set the uneaten half of her cookie on a napkin and slid off the barstool as she scooped the clothes into her arms. Then she quietly slinked away in the direction of the bathroom as if she wanted to remain as invisible as possible.

What was Panya's story? Where had she come from? And how had she found her way to Cordray's shelter?

She reminded Sam of a fawn who'd been abandoned by her mother, or maybe a small dog who'd been left behind by its owner when the family moved. She just seemed so lost and unsure, as if she expected to be kicked out of the nest again and again and would never find her place in the world.

Sam knew how it felt to be lost. After leaving her ex, she'd been scared and uncertain, too. Not just about where to go and how to survive while she was on the run, but about everything. For months, she'd been suspicious of everyone she met, mistrustful even of a good Samaritan politely holding the door open for her. There was always this abnormal fear that the person offering her a smile or a helping hand would chloroform her the moment she turned her back, load her in the trunk of a car, and then whisk her back to Steve.

To be honest, she still wasn't over her fear. Micah had removed all memory of her from Steve's mind when he'd tracked her down in January, but she still couldn't stop looking over her shoulder when she was out in public. Her heart still hitched in fear when she saw a black Mercedes, even if it wasn't the exact model Steve used to drive. The Mercedes logo alone was enough to dump adrenaline into her system.

In time, she was sure to move past her fear, just as Panya would get past hers. But the fact they both seemed to be victims in one way or another created a bond between them. Sam would do whatever she could to help Panya find herself, and maybe in the process, she could get one step closer to eradicating her own demons.

A couple of minutes later, Panya came out of the bathroom holding her sweat-soaked pajamas as Sam was putting the milk back in the fridge. "Where do you want me to put these?"

Sam was tempted to take them herself, but she wanted Panya to feel like this was her home, too, rather than a temporary stop, so she pointed down the back hall extending off the kitchen. "The laundry room is down that way. You can toss them in the hamper in there, and I'll add them to the next load I put in."

Panya pattered off while Sam spooned cocoa mix into two mugs.

When Panya returned to the kitchen, she sat back down and began nibbling on her cookie again.

"So, how old are you?" Sam said. She and Panya had baked cookies and brownies all afternoon, but she hadn't thought to ask her age.

Panya stared at her cookie. "Sixteen."

"Ah, sweet sixteen." Sam stirred the milk so it didn't scald. "That's a great age."

Panya shrugged one shoulder as she popped a bite of cookie in her mouth. "Yeah, I guess."

"Aren't you excited about being sixteen?" Sam pulled a bag of mini marshmallows from the cupboard. "I know I was ecstatic when I turned sixteen."

Another one-shouldered shrug. "It's all right."

Sam tore open the bag, plunged her hand in to nab a handful of puffy sweetness, and extended the bag toward Panya. Her eyes twinkled briefly as she perked up. After considering the bag of marshmallows for a moment, she gingerly reached her hand into the bag and pulled out a few.

"You can take more if you want," Sam said.

"Are you sure?"

Sam shook the bag encouragingly. "Absolutely."

Panya smiled weakly and grabbed a small handful then popped a couple in her mouth as Sam set the bag on the counter and checked the milk.

"Cordray doesn't like us to eat from the bag like this," Panya said.

"Well, I don't mind, and since you're in my house, we'll go by my rules. Cordray doesn't have to know. How's that sound?"

"Okay." Panya grinned and grabbed a few more marshmallows from the bag. "So, are you a full-blooded vampire, or are you a mixed-blood like Cordray and Trace?" Her eyes twinkled when she said Trace's name.

Cordray had previously told Sam that the older kids knew who and what they were, but that the younger ones—Faith, Null, and Aiden—hadn't gone through *the talk*, yet. Humans had the birds-and-the-bees talk, vampires had the you're-going-to-change-into-a-creature-of-the-night talk. Humans definitely came out on the easier end of *that* comparison.

"Neither." Sam dipped the tip of her finger into the milk. It was warm, but not quite hot enough for cocoa. "I'm what vampires call a davala."

"What's that?" Panya grabbed another cookie from the platter.

Sam turned and leaned against the counter, trying to recall how Micah had described what a davala was. "The way I understand it, a davala is a female who was once human, but a male vampire mated her and used his venom to make her immortal."

Panya's eyes brightened. "You were once a human?" Her awed expression amused Sam.

"Up until January of this year. That's when Micah and I met, and he mated me."

After the nightmare Panya had just had, Sam didn't think now was the right time to explain that she'd almost been killed by Apostle, which was what forced Micah to change her in the first place. And Panya certainly didn't need to know how painful the ordeal had been.

"Wow! That was, like, only a few months ago."

"I guess you could say I'm still kind of like a newborn when it comes to all this vampire stuff."

"That is so cool." Panya seemed genuinely impressed that she was in the presence of someone who had once been human.

Sam checked the milk again. It was perfect. "You know, before Micah, I didn't even know vampires existed." She slowly poured the steaming milk into their mugs, stirring so the cocoa mix wouldn't clump. "When did you find out you were a vampire?"

Panya stuffed her hand into the marshmallow bag as she frowned and wrinkled her nose. "Cordray told me about five years ago."

"Hey, what's with the sour face?" She set one of the mugs in front of Panya and tossed in a bunch of marshmallows, which floated on top and began melting into a gooey layer. "Aren't you happy about being a vampire?" She added marshmallows to her own mug.

"It's gross," Panya said, her face screwing into a Mr. Yuk expression. "You have to suck people's blood. Just . . . ew! That's so nasty."

"Oh, I doubt you'll think that way once you're older." She knew from what Micah had told her that vampires underwent a major transformation into adulthood during their late teens and early twenties. In a few years, Panya's body would begin changing. She would gradually become intolerant of the sun, start craving blood, develop her abilities to dematerialize, read minds, and strip memories from humans she fed from. She wouldn't be able to stop the change from happening any more than a teenaged human girl could stop her period.

"I don't want to be a vampire." Panya pouted into her mug of cocoa.

Sam rounded the counter and rested her arm around Panya's shoulders. "Well, how about we have another cookie" — she snatched a pair of cookies from the plate — "drink cocoa, watch a movie, and not think about vampires or anything else for the rest of night, hmm? What do you say to that?"

Panya's mouth twisted into a meager smile. Then she looked over Sam's shoulder toward the living room. "Can we watch *Godzilla*?" Her eyebrows lifted hopefully.

Sam pulled back and narrowed her eyes on the teenager. "Old school or new?"

"The one with Aaron Taylor-Johnson." She smiled dreamily. "He's so hot."

And there was the typical teenager Sam had been hoping to find. One who talked about boys, painted her fingernails funky colors, and experimented with too much makeup and hair products.

"Don't you think he's hot?" Panya said, grabbing one of the cookies from Sam's hand and following her into the living room.

"Absolutely. Did you see him in *Savages*? He was even better looking in that movie. His hair was longer, and he was just so *yummy*." Good thing Micah wasn't around. His ego would never entertain the notion that she could be completely in love with him but still find another man attractive.

"I haven't seen that one." Panya dropped onto the couch and tucked her legs underneath her.

Sam knelt in front of their collection of Blu-rays, which were organized alphabetically by movie title, and snagged the one for *Godzilla*. "Well then, that gives us something to watch another night then, doesn't it?"

Panya smiled. "We'll save it for my next nightmare. At least that way I'll have something to look forward to."

Sam laughed. "No more nightmares." She popped the Blu-ray in and started it up. "We can do a movie night without all that drama." She joined Panya and settled in beside her at the other end of the couch as the movie started playing. "You know, you're going to make some lucky male very happy watching movies like this."

Her brown eyes brightened. "A male like Trace?"

"Ummm . . ." Apparently there was more to that previous twinkle in Panya's eye than Sam had originally thought.

"Oh, I know he's with Cordray," Panya continued, "but he's hot. If I could find a guy like that, I could die a happy girl."

"If you find a guy like that, you'll be happy you *can't* die."

Panya's eyebrows scrunched over her nose. "I, uh . . ."

"You never thought of being a vampire that way, did you? Being immortal?"

Panya's face shaded pink as she looked down. "No, I guess not."

"So maybe being a vampire isn't such a bad thing, huh? I mean, I've only been living inside this world a few months, and I've already seen that males of the vampire persuasion are some of the sexiest things on the planet. Wouldn't it be nice to spend eternity with a guy like that? Especially knowing his body chose yours over all others? That's pretty powerful, don't you think?"

Panya offered her a weak smile and took a bite of cookie. "Knowing my luck, I'll never find a guy like that. Who would want *me*?"

Sam gazed compassionately at the plain girl sitting across from her. Panya wasn't outlandishly pretty. Her hair was brown, her eyes were brown, she had pale skin, and her chest was more or less flat. She was what Sam would have called a late bloomer by human standards. The scraggly grey duckling who would one day grow into a beautiful swan.

Just like Sam had been. At sixteen, Sam had looked more like a boy than a girl, but two years later, her contours had molded into those of a young woman who became the top earner at Suzy Q's, where she danced nights and weekends before joining the Army when she was nineteen.

She folded her legs underneath her and reached across the couch to brush her fingers over Panya's hair, tucking it behind her ear. "A lot can happen between now and the end of your transition, Panya. Your body will change. It will fill out, and boys will start looking at you differently." She dipped her head to the side and squeezed Panya's hand. "And you'll start looking at boys differently, too. They'll still be hot, but your idea of what's hot and what's not will change. You'll also start considering what kind of father a male will be. What kind of mate he will make." She'd almost said husband, but changed it at the last second to the vampire term, mate. "And then there's *that*."

"What?"

"The whole mating thing. Vampires take mates. They don't get married like humans do. The way I understand it, mating is stronger, and it's dictated by the male. It won't matter what you look like. Once your mate finds you, he'll mate you, and the match will be perfection. The way it's been described to me, there's nothing more magical or more powerful than when a male vampire finds his mate and forms a bond with her. I have a feeling that when your mate finds you, you'll wonder what you ever saw in Trace."

Panya regarded her for a moment. "But what if nobody mates me? I mean, what if I'm this freak of nature who never finds my mate?"

Sam squeezed her hand. "You can't think that way. You just have to know he's out there, somewhere, and he's waiting to find you, too, when the time is right. Eventually, your paths will cross, and your life will be forever changed for the better."

Panya smiled tightly but didn't appear convinced.

"Come on" —Sam pointed to the TV—"let's watch the movie. You've got plenty of time before you have to worry about all that grown-up stuff."

Sam felt for Panya. She really did. It was hard being a kid these days, let alone a vampire kid. Panya didn't just have to deal with all the normal teenage angst all kids went through, but all the baggage that came with being a vampire, too. Sam could only imagine the identity crisis young vampires went through, but from what she could tell, they all adjusted eventually.

All the vampires she'd met thus far appeared comfortable with who and what they were. Even Trace. The fact that he was a vampire never seemed to be the source of Trace's problems. And now that he had mated Cordray, it was like he was a brand-new person. That much was already clear, and they'd only been officially mated a few days.

She and Panya watched the movie and sipped their cocoa in

silence. After thirty minutes, Panya's eyes grew heavy. Another ten minutes later, she'd fallen asleep.

Sam carefully eased herself off the couch so as not to wake her, grabbed a throw blanket from one of the drawers under the large, square coffee table, and pulled it up over Panya's body. Then she quietly grabbed their empty mugs and returned to the kitchen.

She still had at least a couple of hours before she could expect Micah to come home, and there was still a ton of laundry to wash. She might as well get to it.

CHAPTER 17

"HE'S STABLE."

Everyone turned as Priest pushed open the double doors and stepped into the hall.

Micah was still recovering from what Rameses had just said about werewolves being their new worst enemy, but at least now he didn't have to worry about his brother.

Given the drawn, gaunt nature of Priest's face, it looked like the lycan had paid a heavy price to ensure Ronan's recovery. The front of his shirt was soaked with sweat, and he staggered once before catching himself and leaning his back against the wall.

Micah had to admit that seeing how weak Priest was made that blond-tressed lycan's stock value rise. Priest hadn't been obligated to help Ronan, but he had chosen to, anyway. And that went a long way toward making Micah see him and the other lycans with a little more respect.

Priest rubbed his mammoth hands up and down his face and looked up at the ceiling before closing his eyes. "Praise be to Osiris, but that nearly killed me." His tired, deep voice cracked as if he'd just awakened from a week-long nap.

"The werewolf venom in the boy's veins?" Rameses asked, still showing next to no emotion in those black holes he called eyes.

Micah considered telling Rameses that Ronan wasn't a boy but figured it wouldn't make any difference, so he snapped a lid on his snarky retort. Yes, that crackling sound was hell freezing over.

Priest took a heavy breath. "Gone."

"You killed all of it?"

"Yes." Priest's eyes peeled open. "But it's worse than we thought."

Micah and Bain both perked up.

"Worse?" Bain said. "What do you mean?"

Rameses turned away from Priest to address Bain. "We've been monitoring the dreck known as Bishop for a long time. Until recently, he resided in our territory." He gave Bain a pointed look. "As you know."

Bain tilted his head in deference, his face flushing. "Yes. We tracked him there and conducted a raid of his facility."

Rameses studied them both for a long moment. "You should have contacted us before entering our territory."

"My apologies, but the situation was rather dire. Speed was of the essence, and the situation was . . . personal." Bain's face pinched tightly. Thinking about Miriam's abduction no doubt troubled him.

"Yes, I know your daughter was involved, as were the lives of many vampires."

Maybe Bain felt obligated to dance this political waltz with Rameses, but Micah didn't. He turned angrily toward Rameses.

"Don't you think *you* should have contacted *us*? If you knew about Bishop and what he was doing—killing vampires as some form of fucked-up science fair project or recreational activity—don't you think that was something we should have been made aware of?"

"Micah . . ." Bain slowly reached toward him as if he were prepared to hold Micah back if he lunged for Rameses's throat.

Rameses appeared unfazed. "We had been monitoring *Bishop*," he clarified. "We had only recently become aware of what his residence was being used for. We were going to take care of it on our own. We were planning our attack even as your people invaded and rescued his test subjects. Some of them, anyway."

Micah frowned. "*Some* of them?"

"Yes." A flicker of annoyance passed over Rameses's face. "He took his most prized subjects and brought them here when he moved back into your territory."

"And you didn't think to warn us?"

"We're warning you now."

Micah pointedly glanced in the direction of his unconscious brother. "A little late, don't you think?"

Rameses's expression remained smooth and even as he glanced between Micah and Bain. Then he drew in a deep breath and slowly blew it out.

Micah wasn't sure if Rameses was about to go all lycan apeshit on his ass or if he was actually going to admit he'd made a mistake.

"You're right, we should have warned you sooner." Rameses seemed to stand a little taller, as if by boosting his physical appearance, he could save face.

"I bet that was hard to say," Micah said.

Rameses's black eyes slid to him. "You have no idea."

There wasn't much that lycans disdained more than admitting they were wrong and that vampires were right. As equal as they claimed their two races to be, lycans possessed one helluva superiority complex that put them at the top of the food chain.

To Bain, Rameses said, "Truthfully, we had hoped to track him down and contain the situation quietly, eliminating the threat before anyone knew of its existence."

"In other words," Bain said, "you were planning to secretly enter our territory without alerting us to your presence, as well."

"Yes."

"Touché."

The two males stared at each other, neither moving. Then Bain grinned, and a glimpse of respect and humor crossed Rameses's features, even though not a single muscle moved.

Micah wouldn't exactly call it a lovefest, but at least an icebreaker.

"So," Micah said, impatient with their royal do-si-do, "what are these favorite test subjects of Bishop's? The ones you had hoped to eliminate without our knowledge?"

Rameses took two measured steps to the side. "They are genetically enhanced werewolves. We call them motleys."

"Motleys?" Micah scoffed. When Micah thought of the word motley, he saw dancing jesters in a king's court. That or Mötley Crüe. "Sounds like a stupid name to me," he said to Bain under his breath.

"Micah . . ." Bain sighed and shook his head as he briefly dropped his gaze to the floor. He looked like he'd given up trying to muzzle Micah but wished he could.

Rameses tilted his head at Micah. It was the first sign of impatience he had let slip past his stony veneer. "We have called them a lot of things. Super werewolves, bastard werewolves . . . then one of our brothers called them 'mottled werewolves' a few months ago. That led to motley weres, and now we just call them motleys." He stared Micah down. "Does that answer your inane question?"

If only Micah could slap that guy. Instead, he plastered on a gooey smile. "Yes, thanks for the history lesson."

"Micah, please show some respect to our guests," Bain said.

"I'm just—"

"You're just being you. I know." Bain held up his hand before Micah could reply. "Rameses is not our enemy, so how about you be a little more welcoming."

Micah held up his hands in surrender. "Fine." He crossed his arms and raised an eyebrow to Rameses. "Please . . . do continue. I promise to keep my editorial commentary to myself."

At least Bain wouldn't have to put up with his mouth much longer. As soon as he got the chance, he would let Bain know of his decision to quit AKM. Sayonara! It was family man for him from now on.

"How generous of you." Rameses regarded him a moment longer then continued. "These *motleys* were once regular werewolves. Bishop captured them, conducted his demented experiments, changed them." His tone fell ominously as shadows crossed his eyes. "But what Bishop didn't know was that someone else had beaten him to the punch."

A bottomless pit opened inside Micah's stomach, and a cold chill ran up his back. He had a bad feeling about where this was going. "What do you mean?"

"Your friend Searcy . . ."

An aggressive jolt shot through Micah as he exchanged troubled glances with Bain. "What about him?"

"He had already created an army of motleys."

"How do you know this?" Bain asked.

Rameses hesitated. "Because we've been killing them for over a year."

Had Micah really heard that right? "A year?"

"Yes, and Searcy's motleys are stronger than Bishop's." Rameses let that sink in for a second. "We think the ones we killed early on were simply test subjects used to see how much work needed to be done to make them battle ready and willing to take orders from a vampire. But now . . . the tests appear to be concluded. The motleys we encountered tonight were stronger than any we've ever come up against. Not strong enough to defeat *us*, but certainly strong enough to defeat you. It seems Searcy and Bishop have joined forces and shared their knowledge with each other, because Bishop's motleys are now as strong as Searcy's."

"How can you tell which belong to whom?" Micah asked.

Rameses tapped his nose. "By scent. Bishop's creations carry the scent of expensive tobacco. Searcy's don't." Rameses made a point to glance toward Ronan's room. "But both are deadly to vampires, and you will not be able to destroy them without our help."

Bain crossed his arms, opening his stance. He looked both imposing and pissed off. "What are you saying, Rameses?"

"I'm saying it's time we discussed a more formal, militarized alliance."

"What does Memnon think of that?"

"Since Memnon is currently in hibernation, he can't render an opinion, but I think I can safely say he won't like it. It's not a secret that his opinion of your race is more soured than mine."

Bain made a derisive sound. "Yeah, I think it's safe to say that."

"Don't take it personally. He doesn't hold a high opinion of any bipedal species that isn't lycan. But he will eventually see the benefits of an alliance between our races. Vampires and lycans are both committed to saving humanity. Yours from the drecks, ours from the werewolves. Now that our common enemies are working together — because we know, as do you, that Bishop is in league with not just Searcy but Premier Royce, even if they deny the alliance and try to hide it — it's time we form a counterstrategy. If they manage to destroy the vampire race, we know where they'll strike next."

"They'll go after the lycans." Micah was beginning to sense his days as an enforcer might not be over after all. Not with the enemy growing stronger.

"Precisely." Rameses returned his focus to Bain. "The time for putting aside our territorial borders and joining forces is upon us. Memnon might resist at first, but I know my brother. He will see the wisdom of this plan. Fighting alongside one another will make us stronger. We will teach you what we know about these motleys, and all we ask in return is that you share your knowledge with us, as well."

"I think we can manage that." Bain cast Micah a pointed glance. "Can't we, Micah?"

Micah studied Rameses. He was an emotionless bastard, and his black eyes looked like something out of *Jeepers Creepers*, but he could put aside his personal feelings for the greater good of the vampire race, especially if it meant keeping Sam and his unborn young safe.

He shrugged, glancing from Rameses back to Bain. "I can play nice with the lupines."

Besides, Rameses and his lycan Furbies were the least of his problems. The greater problem was that shit was happening in his world he'd never been aware of. "Super werewolves" were threatening all that he loved. Motleys, as Rameses called them. And they'd been created by that bastard, Searcy. And here he'd hoped they'd seen the last of that prick when they chopped off his son's hand and maimed his female fuck buddy, Lorena. Wishful thinking.

If Searcy was still hanging around, and he'd built an army of motley wolves with the power to kill vampires, there could be only one reason. He intended to declare war on King Bain and overtake the throne.

And wouldn't that work right into the drecks' hands. If Searcy and Premier Royce had formed their own alliance and had this *super army* at their disposal, that gave them the upper hand. And upper hands were hard to overcome when you were caught with your pants down and your hand around your pecker, which was exactly where the vampire race was right now. Joining with the lycans, who seemed to be more aware of what was happening, leveled the playing field.

The vampires been weakened by cobalt addiction. Royce had strung Bain along, pretending to be working with him, when he'd been working with the enemy all along. Now, thanks to both Searcy's and Bishop's experiments, the drecks had an army of venomous werewolves ready to finish the job cobalt had started.

Micah couldn't let that happen. He couldn't let his race be wiped out. He had children to protect now. And a mate. And friends he would fight to the death for.

This wasn't how he thought the rest of his evening would go. He wanted to get out of enforcing and enjoy the life of a family man, but he couldn't deny he'd been born to fight. He'd always been a warrior. He would always *be* a warrior. He couldn't take some safe, pencil-pushing job now that he knew what was at stake.

"I fear our respective worlds are about to be severely challenged." Bain took a step toward Rameses. "I've sensed unrest and disruption closing in from all sides for months." Bain gave Rameses a crooked grin and uncrossed his arms, holding out his hand. "So, yes, I would be honored to fight alongside you and your brothers, Rameses. I think we'll be much more powerful as a united front than as individual armies battling the same enemy."

Rameses clasped Bain's hand. "The honor is ours. Consider this my word that we will fight alongside you and yours. I will take responsibility for getting Memnon on board when he awakens."

"Better you than me."

With a soft chuff, Rameses released Bain's hand. "God Osiris help me, Memnon will not be pleased, but there is more at stake now. An alliance must be struck if we are to do the job we were placed here to do and survive. All of humanity depends upon our success."

And so it began. The new war. Micah had known peace would last only so long. It always did. The war between the vampires and the drecks was neverending. It just changed faces every time it surged back to life.

And, once again in only a few hours, Micah's whole world shifted.

How many more times would it shift before dawn? Because he knew there was more to come.

Hadn't Bain told him they needed to talk after Ronan stabilized? Well, Ronan was stable. Time to see what else the night had in store for him.

He just hoped his mind wouldn't be completely blown when the dust settled.

CHAPTER 18

ULRICH MATERIALIZED BEHIND GREGOS'S HOME. He needed to return to AKM to check in on Persephone, but not until he and Gregos had come to an accord.

Bain had gone too far. The time to move was now.

He scanned the empty landscape then turned his gaze back toward the sprawling structure in front of him.

Much like his own house, the Savakis manor wasn't so much a house as it was a palace. Two stories, a full attic with dormers, and a finished basement. At least ten thousand square feet in total, made even more impressive by the multilevel patio and deck that extended the length of the home and descended toward a pond whose surface was like glass and black as oil as it reflected the predawn sky.

Moving swiftly, Ulrich approached the wall of sliding windows along the back of the home as Gregos hurried forward and opened the way in, holding his finger over his lips.

"To my office," Gregos said softly, sliding the door closed as silently as a whisper.

The two males were quick of foot and quiet as mice as they journeyed to the den in the back of the house, but as soon as the heavy wooden doors latched behind them, Ulrich could hold back no longer.

"This is preposterous!" he said, fisting his hands and pacing. "You saw what he did to me tonight." He pulled his collar aside to reveal the bruises King Bain had left on his neck. "He's out of control."

Gregos poured them a pair of drinks. Expensive bourbon from the look of it.

"To be true, you did provoke him." Gregos handed him a glass.

"Only because he wouldn't listen and refuses to do anything to solve this mockery Royce is making of us."

"Still, you shouldn't have raised your voice."

Ulrich threw back his drink and helped himself to another. "Whose side are you on, Gregos? Don't tell me you're getting cold feet."

"My feet are fine. My point is you could have ruined our plans. Your outburst—"

"Was fully warranted!"

"Ulrich!" Gregos whisper-yelled, rushing to the door. "Keep your voice down." He peeked out then quietly latched the door again.

Ulrich tossed back his second shot of bourbon and slammed the base of the glass on the desk. "This has gone on long enough. If Bain will do nothing about Premier Royce and the cobalt infesting the streets and infecting our children, then I say it's time we move with our plan."

Gregos joined him by the desk again. "What I was about to say a moment ago is that I think your outburst tipped off the king. He knows we're up to something."

"Then we must move quickly."

"Or . . . we pull back and hold our aces until we have a better opportunity."

Ulrich wouldn't let this chance pass them by. He was out for blood and would entertain none other than a move to usurp Bain's throne now. "There will be no better opportunity. If Bain knows we're planning against him, then the faster we move, the better."

Gregos sighed and swirled his glass, making the tawny liquid spin. He kept his eyes downcast.

Ulrich refilled his glass, carefully setting the bottle down as he weighed his words. "Gregos, you know we can't wait any longer. King Bain must be stopped. Look what he did to our children. Your son . . . my daughter. Arion and Persephone would be mated and setting up their home now if not for his progressive, meddling laws. He is destroying our values . . . our *traditions*."

Gregos met his eyes, his jaw tight and chin lifted, his gaze twitchy but unwavering. With a trembling hand, he lifted his glass and gulped down the contents then set the empty crystal tumbler on the polished walnut surface of his desk as he wiped his palm over his mouth.

Gregos had reason to be nervous. What they were doing was treason. If they were caught, they would be put to death. But they'd both known when they began talking about overthrowing the king in hushed whispers almost three months ago that their plotting didn't come without risks. They'd known all along this would be dangerous.

But they had the support of at least half the aristocrats. Many of them felt Bain's laws against arranged pairings violated their rights and put their wealth at risk. Nobody in the wealthy class wanted to see a commoner — or, God forbid, a lower class vampire — infiltrate their ranks . . . a pauper's son mated to one of their daughters, or a whorish female mated to one of their sons. Or, God forbid, another unnatural homosexual union like Arion had with Severin.

What a travesty. An abomination really.

The shame Gregos must have felt at his son mating another male was surely a heavy burden to bear.

Which explained why Gregos had disowned Arion and removed him from his bloodline's records, thus alleviating any chance Arion would inherit Gregos's estate someday.

"Gregos . . .?" Ulrich prompted, stepping closer. "What say you, my friend? Can I count on you to help me bring proper values and traditions back to our race?"

Gregos poured himself another shaky glass of bourbon, the bottle rattling against the rim of the glass as his hand trembled tightly. Then he raised his drink and gave an abrupt nod. His hand still shook, making the tawny liquid shiver, but his gaze was steady. "Aye, you can count on me, old friend. I am with you."

Ulrich raised his own glass and clinked it to Gregos's. "Then let us toast to our success . . . and to the end of Bain's reign."

CHAPTER 19

Alexis pulled the homemade lasagna from the oven and checked the time.

Again.

There were still a couple of hours before dawn, but Ronan should have been back by now.

Whenever they made plans to spend the day together, he never stayed away for long, especially when he had her Kawasaki. Not only did he respect her boundaries where her motorcycle was concerned, but they both treasured the escape of physical pleasure too much to resist the temptation. The promise of sex was like opening the gates to an amusement park. Neither was getting it elsewhere, and it had been weeks since they'd been together, their tryst earlier this evening notwithstanding.

In Alexis's opinion, they didn't have sex enough.

No, he wasn't her mate, and no, she didn't want him to be her mate. She wasn't even in love with him.

But praise be to God, Ronan knew how to fuck her just the way she liked.

In that way, their partnership was perfect.

But it wasn't all play and no work. They made a great team in the field. He didn't get in her way when they hunted bounties, and he made the perfect backdoor man during a hit. And when they needed medical supplies, they could be in and out of a pharmacy undetected in less than three minutes, coming away with twice what she could snatch by herself.

But when the work was done, the play began.

And, oh, how they played.

He fondled her breasts, sucked and nibbled her nipples, and spanked her without getting too rough. Best of all, he tied her up and indulged her rescue fantasies, pretending to rescue her from her make-believe incarceration, getting her so hot she sometimes came just from being untied.

Of course, sometimes her fantasies took her down a darker path. One where she wanted him to pretend to be her captor, and she was his hostage. The thrill she got when they performed this way was just as exciting and just as explosive as when they played rescue games, only in a more sinister way.

Sometimes, she felt as though she were trying to rewrite the horrors of her childhood through her fantasies so she didn't see herself as a victim. By taking control in her fantasies and playing them out with Ronan, she found a certain amount of reconciliation with the past. No longer was she the scared little girl paralyzed by fear. Instead, she became the aggressor, taking what she wanted and turning her captor into her savior when he realized he adored her so much he could no longer keep her restrained. All her fantasies ended by having her bindings removed.

The only problem with letting her fantasies follow this course was that Ronan was not her prince. She couldn't even call him her savior. He was a means to an end. A reasonable facsimile. A stand-in for the real thing.

And that was just fine by her. She didn't need the real thing. She'd survived on her own for over one hundred years. She could survive on her own a hundred more and then some.

But who knew the abuse she had suffered as a child would manifest in adulthood as a sexual fantasy so powerful she could get off without being touched.

She went to the front door and glanced through the peephole. Nothing. No Ronan. No Kawasaki. Only his Jeep, still sitting at the curb like a dog waiting for its owner to return.

She paced into the sitting room, pushed the opaque curtains aside, and scanned up and down the street. Still nothing. No sign of him anywhere.

Returning to the door, she disengaged the series of locks and deadbolts securing her home then stepped onto the porch. There was a slight chill in the air, but otherwise, it was a comfortable night. Inhaling, she sought for any sign of Ronan on the breeze.

All she picked up was the stench of urine from a nearby alley and a hint of fresh-brewed coffee from her neighbor's brownstone. Her neighbor was an older human female who was up by four every morning, rain, snow, or shine. She was actually awake early today. Bad dream, perhaps?

Passing one last glance up and down the street, she went back inside and returned to the kitchen, where she took a sip from the glass of wine she'd poured for herself while waiting on the lasagna to bake. It was a lovely cabernet. Rich and full. It would pair well with the hardy Italian dish.

She sat on a barstool.

She tapped her fingernail on her wineglass.

She glanced at the clock.

"Fuck it."

Hopping up, she covered the casserole dish of lasagna with foil and shoved it into the fridge. Then she twisted her long hair into a ponytail, tucked it under a black knit skullcap, and grabbed her gun, a spare clip, her jacket, and keys.

In a flash, she was out the door and locking up. The next moment, she ducked into the shadows on the side of her porch and dematerialized, following the trail Ronan had left hours ago.

It was easy to track him, not only because of the scent of blood his bullet wound left behind, but because they fed from each other. It was easier to track someone you'd fed from than it was to track someone you hadn't, and vice versa.

She homed in on the South Side. Ronan had been itching for a fight, and the South Side was where you went when you were looking one. And like any other adolescent male vampire, Ronan had a lot of angst to work out.

If only a vampire aged more like a human. Human adolescence ended between nineteen and twenty-five. In comparison, a vampire's adolescence could, on rare occasions, continue past the age of fifty. In his late forties, Ronan was a perfect example of that.

But here was the catch: By eighteen, a vampire looked more or less like they would as a "mature adult." Their body would continue to age through their transition, which usually ended by the age of twenty-six — *usually*, because there were always exceptions — but at eighteen, a juvenile vampire could do almost everything a mature vampire could do. They could have sex. Feed. Take a mate. Have young. Their dematerializing and memory-altering skills might still lack, but that was about it.

And nothing said "babes raising babes" like a twenty-year-old vampire with a child. It happened. Not often, but it did.

That would never be Ronan, though. The guy was more averse to taking a mate than she was. Mostly because of what had happened with his parents. His father was a fucked-up mess of a male still suffering over the loss of his *true* mate, and his mother had been ripped away from him when *her* true mate had found her. So, yeah, there weren't a lot of happy family memories for Ronan to emulate. And not much of a foundation to build on. A father who was emotionally bankrupt and mentally fractured half the time, and a mother he hadn't seen since he was a little boy.

Was it any wonder Ronan acted like a rebellious teenager?

Within seconds, Alexis ghosted into an alley and found her Kawasaki. Just in time, too. A pair of hoodlums had spied her ride and were prowling in for a closer look, all "Whoooooeeey! Would you look at that."

She materialized between them and the motorcycle, her gun already drawn.

Anywhere else, pulling a gun would have been overkill, but not on Chicago's South Side. Here, pulling a gun was how you said hello to strangers, especially when they were eyeing your property like they wanted to have sex with it. People killed for a whole lot less than a motorcycle on the South Side, where you could get shot just for your shoes.

The two lowlifes stopped and blinked, their mouths falling open. They were probably trying to decide whether she was real or a hallucinogenic product of whatever narcotic they'd swallowed, smoked, or injected.

"Sorry, boys, this ride's taken." She cocked her Glock and put the laser sight between the eyes of the one on the left. The one who had flinched like he was thinking about doing something stupid, like trying to disarm her or maybe pulling his own gun. Nope, not gonna happen. If he so much as twitched like he was going for a weapon, she would blow a hole in him. "I think you understand."

"You don't think we can take you?" the one on the right said.

"Nope."

He raised one eyebrow, leering as his gaze passed over her body. "There's two of us, baby, and only one of you."

"It wouldn't be a fair fight even if there were six of you. Trust me, I can shoot both of you dead before you can even wrap your amateur hand around the pistol you've got tucked somewhere inside those ridiculously loose jeans hanging off your ass." It was her turn to raise an eyebrow, challenging Mr. Dipshit to make a move.

For a long moment, they stared each other down, neither backing off. Then the guy on the right took a slow backward step.

"Yeah, okay. It's your ride, baby. We were just watching it for you." He shoved his friend's arm. "Right, Spider?"

Spider? Really? That was the best nickname he could come up with?

"Yeah, yeah. We was just watchin' it for ya."

She nodded and waved them away. "Well, I'm here now. Go guard someone else's ride."

She kept her gun trained on them while fishing her keys from her pocket with her other hand. Then she deactivated the net pod, slung her leg over the seat, and fired her up.

Only then did she lower her gun and tuck it into the back waist of her jeans.

Cranking the throttle and the brake, she swung the Kawasaki around as the engine whined, the back wheel spinning and throwing up gravel and white smoke. Then she gunned it, leaving Dumb and Dumber in the alley scratching their balls.

She picked up Ronan's trail again, followed it to a warehouse where she found two freshly dumped bodies, then tracked around to the side of the building where the smell of drecks and cobalt wrinkled her nose. A dead dreck lay crumpled on the dirty, wet pavement.

Yep, Ronan had definitely been there.

But where was he now?

Investigating, she picked up the scent of another vampire. A female. One high on cobalt and in distress. Her scent mixed with Ronan's, which meant only one thing. He'd been a good little Boy Scout and taken her somewhere for help.

And where does one vampire take another who's suffering from a cobalt overdose?

That's right. The only place that *could* help. AKM.

Jesus.

She really didn't need to show her face around AKM for a baker's dozen of reasons, but if she was going to find out what had happened to Ronan, she would have to bite the bullet and at least follow Ronan's trail there.

After racing home, she changed into clothes a little more appropriate for a common civilian, slicked her hair into a tight spiral, and pulled on one of her wigs. Then she rolled her eyes — because why in the hell was she doing this? — said a quick prayer that nobody would recognize her from a WANTED poster or by scent, and poofed to the shadows of AKM's rear parking lot.

She wasn't actually a criminal, but her profession sometimes put her in opposition with the king's enforcers and their mission, and she didn't want to risk bumping into anyone who might have picked up her scent from a kill or could otherwise identify her. Given her surroundings, it would be best to keep herself as invisible as possible.

Checking herself to make sure her disguise was in place, she started around the building.

Only to be accosted by a hooded, shadowy figure that leaped from the shadows only a few feet from the front of the building.

So much for staying invisible.

Her back slammed into the brick wall, and a heavy hand landed over her mouth.

But Alexis was not just some pansy-assed pretty face. She was a fighter. Her training had gotten her out of tighter situations than this, and if she kept her wits and struck back swiftly — *before* her attacker could completely incapacitate her — she'd get out of this one.

She slammed her forearm against her attacker's, trying to dislodge his hold. When that didn't work, she shot her other hand out and struck whoever the guy was in the chest.

A deep, masculine *oomph!* was music to her ears as his hand fell away and he took a staggering step backward.

Seizing the opportunity, Alexis turned to bolt, only for that same heavy hand to cage her wrist in a hold so strong, she'd be lucky to get away without any broken bones.

"Alexis, stop. It's me." The male thrust back his hood.

Everything stopped. She knew that scarred face. She knew it well.

"Hunter?"

What was he doing back? Hunter had been exiled twenty years ago, right before —

"Is she still alive?" he asked.

She. Her sister. Annalise.

This wasn't a conversation to have here, especially when she hadn't been prepared for it.

"Hunter, maybe we should—"

His grip tightened, making her wince. "Is she still alive?" The desperation in his face tightened the jagged scar that ran from above his right eyebrow, over the bridge of his nose, and down his left cheek to curl and come to an end at the corner of his mouth.

Bowing her head, she closed her eyes. Why did he have to be here? Why now?

"No," she murmured. "Annalise is dead. I'm sorry."

A choked noise broke from his throat, and his grip weakened, his hand eventually falling away from her wrist as he stumbled backward until his back hit the wall of the building next door to the one that housed AKM.

"Dead? My beloved . . ." He didn't so much as fall to the ground as his body folded in on itself and sank with the pull of gravity until his butt kissed the pavement. "She's gone? My Annalise . . . my heart . . . she's gone?" His eyes lifted to hers, glistening against the light coming from a nearby streetlamp. "How? What happened?"

"Hunter . . ."

"Please . . ."

He looked so defeated. So . . . broken. They'd been close once. A long time ago, when Annalise had still been alive. "I'm so sorry, Hunter."

"Alexis, please tell me . . . how did she die? Was it . . ." His slashing eyebrows dug toward the bridge of his nose as his jaw tensed. "It wasn't my brothers, was it? It wasn't Memnon and—"

"No."

"Then how?"

She knelt beside him and gently placed her hand on his arm. "Annalise died in childbirth, Hunter."

His expression twisted into one of agony. "Childbirth? My son? He killed her?"

Of course he would know his child was a son. Like vampires, lycans could sense the sex of their unborn children.

She moved closer and took his hand inside both of hers. "My sister loved you. When you were sent away, it broke her heart." She squeezed his hand as his fingers curled tightly around hers. "I did what I could, but it wasn't enough."

He lowered his head and raked his free hand through his thick black hair. Forward and back, forward and back, until it stuck out in all directions. Tears fell from his chin, landing on his black cargo pants, where they soaked into the fabric.

All she could do was watch. This was her sister's lover. No, Hunter was more than that. He'd been her mate, as far as vampires and lycans could mate one another. And she had died because he'd been taken from her.

Yes, he was a lycan and she'd been a vampire, but they had loved each other in the most magical, truest way, despite the aggressive resistance of her family and his brothers. No one had wanted them to be together, but they had persisted, defying them all.

Which had led to Hunter's eventual exile and, ultimately, to Annalise's death.

"What are you doing back here, Hunter?" she asked gently. "Did your brothers let you return?"

He shook his head, but Alexis didn't know if he was answering her question or still in denial over her sister's death.

"Hunter . . .?"

He dropped his hands to his knees and looked up. A glimmer of hope shone in his eyes. "My son. What of my son?"

Oh, God. She'd known he would ask, but that didn't make answering any easier. She needed to tread lightly and choose her words carefully.

"Alexis?" His gaze drilled into hers, begging for good news. "My son. Did he survive?"

She couldn't tell him the truth. Not only because she'd sworn secrecy to her sister, but because too much was at stake, the danger too great if the truth came out. Not only did she have to worry about Hunter's brothers, but her own family. No one had wanted the baby to survive but her, Annalise, and Hunter, and nothing had changed. Twenty years might have passed, but to her family — and, most certainly, the lycans — that wouldn't matter. She hated lying, especially to Hunter, who she had always liked, but telling the truth wasn't an option.

"I'm sorry, Hunter . . ." It wasn't *really* a lie, because she *was* sorry, but that didn't do anything to make her feel any better, because she knew he would take her somber apology as an admission of his son's death.

Fresh tears puddled on his lower rims, and his strong brow

twisted with anguish. "He didn't . . .? My son is . . .?"

Seeing his pain nearly undid her. The backs of her eyes stung, and she had to blink and look away. When he dropped his forehead to his thick forearm and began sobbing, she nearly cracked.

"Oh, Hunter, I'm so, so sorry."

If only she could tell him the truth, but that would put them all in jeopardy. She needed to remain strong. For the sake of the innocent, she needed to keep her vow of secrecy.

After a couple of minutes, Hunter straightened and wiped his face as he pulled himself together and clamored to his feet, keeping one hand on the wall behind him as if to catch himself should his knees give out.

She pushed to her feet, too, ready to catch him should his emotions overtake him again.

Once he was upright and stable, he drew in a deep inhale, squared his shoulders, and blew it out. "Thank you, Alexis. Thank you for telling me." Another deep breath, and then another. He appeared to be piecing himself back together with each pump of his lungs.

"I wish I had happier news."

"No, I needed to know the truth. I will mourn them, and then I will move on." Bitter determination wrapped around his words. Bitterness at his brothers, no doubt, who had forced him to leave Annalise. He knew as well as she did that if he'd been allowed to stay, she would still be alive and their family intact.

She wanted to invite him to visit her when he was finished mourning, but she held her tongue. It was best they not see each other again. If he came to her, she might slip and tell him the truth. And if that happened, all hell would break loose.

The less she knew about Hunter and his whereabouts, the better, and vice versa.

Then the thought occurred to her . . . Hunter was here. At AKM. And he didn't know the fate of his own son. So then, why was he there?

"Did you follow me here?" she asked.

"No," he said without hesitation. "I followed my brothers."

The air blasted out of her. "Your b-brothers?" Her gaze darted to the building.

Shit, shit, *shit*!

His face hardened as he wiped away the remnants of his tears with his palm. "Rameses, Dain, and Priest. They're here, and I must speak to them."

"What are *they* doing here?" Please, God, please don't let them figure out the secret.

"They are here for a vampire who was bitten by a werewolf."

Ronan! She knew without Hunter having to say it that the werewolf's victim was Ronan.

Her heart began racing. "Did he have dark hair? Was he dressed all in black?" No wonder Ronan never returned.

"Yes."

A chill rippled through her body. "Oh, God."

"He's a friend of yours?"

"Yes."

"Then I have detained you too long." He backed away.

She was already making a break for the front of the building. "I'm so sorry, Hunter, but I . . . I need to—"

"Thank you for telling me about Annalise," he said dismissively. Then his eyes flashed, and he turned and disappeared into the shadows as if he'd never been there.

Part of her ached for him. For the pain he was surely feeling at such a weighty loss. She paid the empty darkness a moment of deference before turning and rushing toward AKM's entrance, barely pulling herself together before reaching the door.

The encounter with Hunter troubled her, but she had greater things to worry about, such as seeing Ronan and making sure he was okay. Maybe they weren't mates, and maybe they weren't exactly what you'd call lovers, but she cared about him. Hell, he was her best friend.

Calming herself, she forced herself not to rush inside and demand to see him. She needed an excuse for being there. Something that wouldn't give her away. What did she know about AKM that she could use to get her back to the medical ward?

Blood. That was her way in. They always needed donations of vampire blood.

Tugging the door open, she stepped inside.

The female behind the desk glanced up. "May I help you?"

Here went nothing.

"Does AKM still take blood donations?"

The female's eyes opened a little wider as if she were pleased to see her. "Yes, we do. Are you here to donate?"

"Yes."

The receptionist picked up her phone and punched in a series of numbers.

Alexis noted that the female had a bandage on her arm where one would be if she'd recently given blood herself.

"We've transferred that task to our new facility," the female said as she brought the receiver to her ear, "but we brought in a couple of emergencies tonight, and I know they need blood back there, and" — she straightened and directed her attention to the phone — "yes, this is the front desk. Tell the doctor I'm sending someone back to make a blood donation. Yes. Uh-huh. Right away." She hung up and buzzed open the double doors to the left. "Go on back. Just follow the signs to the trauma center. Normally someone would come up to get you, but they're all pretty busy back there."

That had been easier than she thought. No security check or anything. Then again, there were probably enough vampires in the building to sniff out danger if it entered unchecked.

Alexis tried to remain calm as she passed into the hallway that led into the heart of AKM.

Speaking of hearts, hers was beating at twice the normal rate. Not because of what had happened with Hunter, and not because she was afraid of needles. The very real threat of incarceration inside King Bain's dungeon had a way of spiking her adrenaline. She didn't always operate on the legal side of the law, but that was the cost of taking care of those who couldn't take care of themselves.

Once the double doors closed behind her, her pace picked up. Bulletin boards and notices lined the walls, but she didn't notice any WANTED posters with her face on them. That was a good sign. As she traveled farther and realized how vacant the building was, she picked up her pace again. She was practically jogging as she spied a sign for the trauma center that directed her down a hall to the right.

Less than ten seconds later, she pushed through the doors of the trauma unit.

The doctors and nurses didn't seem to be running in crisis mode, but tension filled the air, as if at any moment a buzzer would go off and send everyone into a fit of emergency rescue.

"Are you the one here to donate blood?" a nurse asked.

She nodded, searching for Ronan but trying to *look* like she wasn't searching. But it was hard pretending to be nonchalant when your heart was beating hard enough to break through your rib cage.

"The receptionist made it sound like there was some kind of emergency back here," Alexis said.

The nurse let out a soft laugh and pointed her in the direction of an examination room off to the side. "You should have seen it thirty minutes ago."

Just as Alexis began to follow the nurse to the exam room, she caught sight of three towering lycans on the other side of the room. The blond one appeared a bit grey and green around the gills. Rameses, Dain, and Priest. Hunter's brothers.

She quickly ducked her head and hurried into the room on the nurse's heels.

"What happened thirty minutes ago?" she asked as the nurse closed the door.

"Werewolf bite victim was brought in. And before that, an overdose." The other female prepped her arm. "It's been a crazy night."

"Sounds like it." Her foot tapped nervously.

"Afraid of needles?" the nurse asked.

"No." She immediately stilled her foot.

Her arm was banded, the needle inserted, and the blood bag began to fill.

The silence was too much for her. She needed to find out what had happened to Ronan.

"I didn't think werewolf bites were dangerous to vampires."

"This obviously wasn't a normal werewolf."

"How so?"

The nurse shook her head as she checked the bag. "I guess it was genetically modified. The venom was pretty deadly."

"Deadly?" She swallowed. "Did the vampire die?"

"Almost. It was touch and go for a while, but he pulled through. One of those lycans out there helped heal him. But he's in for a loooong recovery."

Thank God Alexis had gotten a Chatty Cathy nurse. If only everyone she tried to get information out of was as forthcoming.

"How long?"

"Weeks? Months? I don't know. We've never seen anything like this. All I know is that he's in a lot of pain, so we've sedated him."

This was horrible, but thank God Ronan was alive.

The nurse finished drawing her blood then bandaged her up. "Okay, you're all set. Thanks for coming in. Our blood supply is running pretty low after the night we just had, so this really helps." She lifted the clear plastic bag of blood.

Alexis stood and glanced around. She couldn't leave just yet. Not until she saw Ronan with her own eyes. And maybe one of their *other* patients. One who seemed to be in a lot more danger now than he'd been twenty-four hours ago, especially with Hunter's brethren there.

"Um, do you have a ladies' room I can use?"

"Sure, I'll take you."

The nurse led her out of the exam room. She kept her face hidden as she passed the lycans, but her eyes remained alert, glancing back and forth, searching for her best friend. Within seconds, she found pay dirt.

As the nurse took her past a set of rooms, she saw Ronan in one of them, lying like a corpse under layers of blankets, eyes closed, face gaunt, his skin almost translucent. It looked like he'd lost twenty pounds in the last few hours. Jesus! What had that werewolf venom done to him?

"Here you go." The nurse opened a door marked for females and flipped on the light switch. "I'll wait for you over there."

Thanks.

She went inside and locked the door. Okay, so she'd found Ronan and satisfied her curiosity that he was at least safe, even if he looked like death. Now she needed to find the other patient currently in AKM's care that she was personally attached to. The patient she'd been sworn to protect but had let get captured by Bishop's lackeys, anyway. A mistake she would never forgive herself for, considering what had been done to him.

First, she needed to convince the nurse to let her stay in the medical unit just a little longer. She cranked on the cold water and splashed some on her face then lightly blotted it dry before pressing her hands against the damp paper towel for several seconds. Just long enough for her hands to feel cool and damp.

After waiting a little longer, she opened the door and took a shaky step out, pressing her hand to her forehead.

The nurse rushed forward. "Are you okay?"

"Yes, yes, I think so. Just a little woozy." She made it a point to touch the nurse's hand so she could feel how "clammy" she was. "I think I just need something to eat. I haven't eaten in hours, and then giving blood, you know . . ."

The nurse nodded and guided her to a chair. "Sit here. I'll get you some juice and crackers." She hurried off.

Alexis glanced around. The lycans were still gathered on the other side of the room, chatting quietly to one another, not paying her a bit of attention.

She peeked into the room nearest her. Empty. The next one was occupied, but she couldn't see by whom, even though the main area of the trauma unit was arranged in a large circle, probably so the nurses at the station in the center could keep an eye on every patient.

Her gaze traveled to the next room, and she leaned forward in her chair as she sniffed the air.

"Here you go." The nurse appeared in front of her, holding a bottle of orange juice and a package of cheese crackers.

Alexis quickly leaned back, pressing her fingers to her forehead as if she were woozy.

"Thank you." She took the offered refreshments and unscrewed the lid on the juice.

The nurse patted her on the shoulder. "Take your time. When you're ready, just call me over and I'll escort you out. My name's Jan, by the way."

She ripped open the package of crackers and pulled out one of the little round sandwiches. "Thanks, Jan. I should be fine in a few minutes. Don't let me keep you."

Jan hurried off, leaving Alexis alone. As she nibbled on her crackers, she tipped her head to the side and peered into the room three doors down.

There was a doctor in the way of her seeing the patient's face, checking the bags of fluid hanging by the bed.

Come on, move.

She swallowed more juice and started on another cracker.

The female doctor remained at the bedside. It looked like she was taking the patient's pulse or maybe listening to his breathing. As she grabbed the blood pressure cuff that hung on the wall, a nurse joined her. From what she could pick up of their conversation, it sounded as though the doc wanted some of the patient's blood drawn.

Several irritatingly long moments later, the doctor removed the cuff from the patient's arm, folded it, and stuffed it back in its station on the wall next to the bed. Then she made a quick notation on her tablet and left the room, finally revealing what Alexis assumed all along.

The patient was Achilles.

Or, rather, Savill. That's what the human couple who had adopted him named him.

But to her, he would always be Achilles.

Her sister's son.

Hunter's son.

The most important secret she'd ever possessed.

She glanced back at the lycans still huddled in discussion.

If they figured out what lay less than fifteen feet away from them and made a move for her nephew, this trauma unit wouldn't just have three more patients. It would have three DOAs.

She had failed to protect Achilles once. She would not fail a second time.

CHAPTER 20

Drake Black stepped quietly into Ronan's room.

Dr. Snow stood at his bedside, checking his vitals. His sallow skin looked thin as paper. Blue veinlike tracks ran up and down every inch of exposed skin like rivers on a map. Bite marks marred both arms where Priest had bitten him at least a dozen times.

Through it all, Drake had been able to do nothing more than watch and pray to whatever God answered a vampire's prayers to save his son. Both of his sons. Because Micah was being just as uncompromising as Ronan.

Micah had refused to hear him out earlier. To hear nothing of Drake's explanation for why he had never let Micah know he was alive. Before Drake could get out more than a couple of sentences, Micah had bolted without so much as a backward glance.

And the anger! The fumes of animosity that had come off Micah had been like those from a gasoline can, ready to ignite if sparked.

Drake had hoped for a warmer reception from Micah, the son he'd been so proud of both as a child and now as an adult. He'd obviously misjudged the situation, but that didn't mean Drake shouldn't try again. And he would keep trying until Micah heard him out.

A long time ago, Drake had been a male of strength and honor. But that male had died with Isabel. He had died with his entire village. It was only dumb luck that had allowed him to survive, but once he realized everyone he'd loved and watched over his whole life had perished or fled to start a new life elsewhere, all he'd wanted was to die, too. And he would have if Argon and Rysk hadn't saved him.

Saved.

Such a subjective term.

They had saved his physical body, but his mind and soul had already been fragmenting into a living death state. His heart beat. His lungs processed oxygen. His organs still functioned. But could this really be considered living? This wraith he'd become who wasn't even half the male he used to be? He had failed everyone he loved, especially his own children.

Look at Ronan. Ronan resented him. Maybe he even hated him. All because Drake had never been able to forget the past and forgive himself for abandoning Micah.

But that didn't mean he didn't love Ronan. He loved him more than his own life. Ronan was the only reason he hadn't killed himself and ended his misery years ago. But every time he tried to tell him he loved him, the words came out wrong. Every time he tried to show him how much he cared, he ended up behaving like a bastard. It's like he wasn't in control of his faculties. Not his thoughts, his words, or his actions.

But he refused to stop trying. Someday he would get it right. Someday his mind would fuse back together again, with all the right pieces where they belonged, and he would be able to convey all he'd failed at for the last thirty-six years, since Ronan's mother left.

He stepped farther into the room and placed his hands on the rail at the foot of Ronan's bed. "How is he?"

Dr. Snow glanced up, her index and middle fingers pressed against the underside of Ronan's wrist. "He's sedated," she said quietly. "As soon as Priest gave us the word his blood was clean, we tranquilized him so he could sleep off the pain." She offered a compassionate smile. "He'll be fine . . . eventually." She let go of Ronan's wrist and gently placed his arm over his stomach before pulling a blanket over him. "You should get some rest, too. He won't be awake for hours and won't be in any shape to receive visitors for a while."

"I'd rather stay." He eyed the cushioned chair in the corner.

Dr. Snow gave him what he imagined was her patented, placating-doctor smile then nodded. "Okay." She tucked her iPad into the crook of her arm. "Once we know he's completely out of the woods, we'll move him to the new facility to begin rehabilitation. He's suffered temporary nerve damage and will need help adjusting as the nerves heal. You can stay with him in one of the suites there. I'm sure he'd like that."

"Doubt it," said a familiar male voice from the door.

Drake turned just as Micah strolled into the room then stopped and crossed his arms. "I doubt Ronan would appreciate either of us offering him a helping hand. Right, Dad?"

Dr. Snow gave them both a confused frown, as if she wasn't sure whether Micah was joking or serious but felt it best not to ask. "If you need anything, I'll be right outside." She quickly left the room.

Silent stares passed between father and son.

Finally, Micah broke eye contact and crossed to the side of Ronan's bed. "How is he?"

"Stable. Recovering. Sedated so he doesn't feel any pain."

"Lucky him." Micah spoke under his breath but just loudly enough—and sarcastically enough—for Drake to receive the message he was sending loud and clear.

"Son—"

"Cut the son crap, Dad."

"What do you want from me, Micah?"

Micah's head jerked up, his gaze slicing clean through him. "Honestly, I don't know. I really don't. I don't get why you lied to me all this time, letting me think you were dead. My last memory of you was of you lying halfway inside our cottage, blood pouring from stab wounds all over your body. I thought you were dead. With what I thought was your last breath, you told me to take the box and guard its contents with my life. And then I assumed you died and have lived with that horrible knowledge all my life. The knowledge that I couldn't save you. That you died, leaving me as the last of our bloodline, with nothing but the contents of that box to remember you by."

The box was what Drake had called the small wooden chest that had contained everything of value to their family, including a gold crest, gemstones, and faded scrolls detailing the specifics — but not all of them — of his, Isabel's, and Micah's births. It had also contained the ankh he'd found during the last war prior to his "death," while Micah had been training in the king's city.

Drake knew the ankh's purpose. He'd always known, because his father had taught him, and *his* father had taught *him*, and so on up the family tree, in the same manner Drake had intended to teach Micah when the time was right.

His mistake had been in thinking they *had* time. Time to find a way to return the ankh to the lycans. Time to talk about their family tree. Time to share all the secrets passed down through each generation of their family. If only he'd possessed the foresight to see what was to come, he would have shared his knowledge with Micah sooner.

But then the attack on their village had occurred, and all that time he thought he had ran out. At that point, all he'd had time to do was tell Micah to take the box and guard its contents, especially the ankh, with his life.

And then he had fallen unconscious, certain he would die.

As Micah continued unloading verbal vomit on him, Drake pulled himself from the past and caught back up midsentence. " . . .save myself and Kat. You told me to look after the survivors. But it wasn't your last breath, was it? You lived. And you never came to find me. You never thought to let me know you'd survived. You let me think you were dead. Do you know how much I suffered after you died? When I'd lost both you *and* Mom?"

"Son—"

"No, Dad." Micah held up his hand. "You lost the right to call me your son when you let me believe you were dead."

Micah's words cut through his heart with surgical precision, but he swallowed his pain and took the lashing he deserved. The choices he'd made hadn't been easy. In fact, many had been made *for* him, both by Argon and Rysk, as well as by the suffering that gnawed and devoured him in turns. He'd been kept in a coma-like suspension for much of the time between the loss of his old life and the discovery of the new, when he met Ronan's mother. Only then did Argon and Rysk step aside to let him return to a more or less independent way of life. But they were never far away, always keeping an eye on him.

Then, after Ronan's mom was gone, he fell back into suffering, just not as deeply as before. Otherwise, Rysk would have stepped in and put him under to raise Ronan himself.

Drake stayed just aware enough to prevent being put back into a coma, but at no time had he been in the right frame of mind to consider finding Micah.

But what should he have done? He was a male caught deep inside suffering's grasp, enduring the loss of a bonded mate, as well as the loss of a female he'd fallen in love with but not bonded to. Most males in his situation would have died long ago. And yet, somehow, Drake survived.

Why?

To what end?

He couldn't be fortunate enough to find another mate, so why did fate keep him alive?

"I'm sorry, Micah. I truly am, but I can't go back and undo what's been done. But I can try to explain if you'll let me."

"*Can* you?" The words bit back at Drake with the force of a cobra bite. "Can you really explain, Dad? Because from where I'm sitting, none of this makes a damn bit of sense."

Drake lowered his gaze. He had much to atone for. "Honestly, I don't know, son — Micah. Sometimes, I don't know if I have the strength to even *understand* what happened to me, let alone explain it." He lifted his gaze to Micah's, surprised to find a sliver of compassion in those navy blue eyes that were so like his own. "But I can sure as hell try. I owe you that." He turned his gaze to Ronan's motionless form, which had needles and tubes coming out both arms and an oxygen tube taped under his nose. "I owe both of you that."

MICAH STARED IN DUMBFOUNDED SILENCE at the male in front of him. The male he hadn't seen in so long it was just easier to say it had been a millennium. The male he'd once looked up to as larger than life but now, despite his physique being only slightly thinner than what he remembered, appeared half as tall and frailer than a blade of drought-weary grass.

Something had taken a heavy toll on his father.

He blinked, and in the split second his eyes were closed, he once again saw his father how he'd been that final day. It was the last memory he had of him, lying just inside the threshold of their home, blood spilling from his wounds.

He'd never found his father's body. He'd assumed the sun had claimed him. Now he knew the truth.

In less than six hours, Micah had gone from being the last surviving member of his bloodline to having a brother and finding out his father was alive. He was no longer the last hope to carry on the family name, and a certain amount of relief came with that knowledge.

But he still had so many questions. He hadn't been ready to hear the answers earlier, which was why he'd bolted only moments after Ronan did. Seeing his father had shocked him too much, and not in a good way. But now he was ready.

"What happened to Mom?"

His father's eyebrows pulled inward as if just thinking about Micah's mom hurt him. "You know what happened to her, Micah. She died. She was trying to protect—" He winced and blinked several times. With emotion choking his voice, he continued. "Your mom tried to protect me after I'd been injured." He squeezed his eyes shut then blinked back tears as he opened them again. "She should have fled when I told her to. She'd still be alive if she had."

Micah gave him a moment then asked, "How did *you* survive? I didn't think there was any way you were going to live when I left you."

His dad dragged a thick inhale through his nose as he wiped his palm down his face. "I came to. Must have been only minutes after you'd left. The sun was about to rise. I saw your mom. I wanted to help her, but I couldn't. She was already gone. I couldn't feel her life force inside me, anymore. Her spirit had already left her body." He blinked several times and pressed his lips together, shifting uncomfortably. "Somehow, I managed to drag myself farther into the hut. Into the shadows." He cut off and cleared his throat, obviously still tormented by the guilt and sorrow he'd felt that day. "I couldn't save your mother," he said softly, bowing his head. "I couldn't save her." His whispered words broke with grief.

He sounded like he was talking more to himself than to Micah, chastising himself, facing his guilt but unable to look it in the eye. "I should have let myself die for failing her, but I didn't. I was too selfish to join her in death, and not a day passes that I don't wish— at least once—that I could go back, drag myself to her body, and hold her one last time as I let the sun consume us both, together."

It was as hard to hear the account of his mother's death as it obviously was for his father to tell it. It was equally hard to hear his father talk of his desire to go back in time and die with her.

"She died, Micah." His dad's voice was barely a whisper. "And a piece of me died with her. A very large piece." He shook his bowed head. "I'm nothing but a coward."

"A coward?" Why the hell would his dad think that?

The other male's eyes briefly met his before falling away again. "If I were really as courageous as I thought I was, I would have died with her. Only a coward saves himself while his mate burns to dust under the sun's light."

Finally, Micah understood. The vacancy in his father's eyes. His absence all these years. The pain. The tormented suffering. The mental wasteland that became not just *where* you lived but *how*. Micah knew that life all too well, because he'd walked a million miles in those shoes after Kat died. Hadn't his father walked those same miles? Was still walking them?

Micah had Sam. He'd found his salvation. From the looks of it, his father hadn't, despite having a second son. Part of him had assumed his father had taken another mate, but maybe he'd assumed wrong. Had his father taken another mate only to lose her, too? If so, it was a miracle his father was still alive.

Maybe he could cut his father some slack, because Micah knew better than anyone how irrational and insane a male vampire could be after losing his mate.

"No, Dad. You're not a coward." His father lifted his gaze and met Micah's. Somewhere behind those eyes was the powerful male he'd all but worshipped as a child. "Only the bravest and most courageous male forces himself to live after losing a mate."

His father said nothing in reply, just nodded in consideration, and then looked away again. Micah could almost feel the shame billowing out of him.

For several long, tragically silent moments, nothing was said. Micah wasn't exactly sure where to go from here, and his dad seemed in no rush to say more. But wasn't that how Micah had been during his own suffering? Silent, brooding, secretive?

Rebellious?

Micah shifted uneasily and forced back his own remorse as he glanced down at his brother.

Ronan wouldn't be here today if his father had died. It still felt odd to think he had a brother when he'd spent his entire life believing he was an only child. And if his father had let himself die, that's exactly what Micah would have been. An only child.

As angry as he was at his dad for keeping his survival a secret, he was grateful to learn he had family. A dysfunctional family, but that was better than no family at all.

Ronan had the same black hair as he and his father. The same strong jaw and angular eyes. He even had the same full lips. The only feature of Ronan's that hadn't come from the Black bloodline was his eye color. Slate blue. Otherwise, the three of them could pass for brothers, not a father and two sons born from different mothers.

"Who is Ronan's mother?" Micah kept his gaze on his brother, finally seeing him for the first time. Really seeing him.

When his father didn't answer, Micah turned away from Ronan, frowning when he saw that his dad wore a vacant expression, his eyes watery and glazed over.

"Dad?"

He blinked and looked at Micah. "I'm sorry, what?"

"Ronan's mother? Who was she?"

His father looked around as if he'd forgotten where he was. He blinked a few more times and scrubbed his palms up and down his face as he cleared his throat. "Ronan's mother?" He dropped his hands to his sides and looked at Micah as if he hadn't understood the question.

"Yes. Is she human? Vampire?"

"Oh, uh . . ." He cleared his throat again and paced to the opposite side of Ronan's bed, where he placed his hands on the rail as if he needed the support. "She was a vampire. A full-blood."

"Where is she?"

His father shrugged and glanced casually toward the door. "I assume she's with her mate."

Micah's brain slammed on the brakes. "Whoa, wait. What?" He raised his hand, palm out.

His dad shoved himself away from Ronan's bed. "She wasn't my mate, isn't my mate, and will never *be* my mate."

"Are you saying you never had a calling with her?"

Creating a child without a calling was like trying to find your way through a maze wearing a blindfold and soundproof headphones. You might eventually find your way out, but it would be a whole lot easier to find your way if you could see and hear.

And didn't the aristocrats who were in arranged matings experience their own share of miracles when it came to bearing young? It was rare without a calling, but once in a while, a young was conceived.

Looked like he and his father at least had that in common. They'd both found their way through the procreation labyrinth despite their handicaps.

"Are you sure you want to talk about this, Micah? I know what happened with Kat. I know —"

Micah cut him off. "Just answer my question. Did you have a calling with Ronan's mother or not?" He didn't want to talk about Kat or how he'd been unable to produce young with her. He was with Sam now, and she was carrying his children. That was where his heart was. As much as he'd loved Kat, she was in his past. He would always love her, and he would have loved having a child with her so a part of her could have lived on, but that's not how things worked out. No sense dwelling.

His father frowned in the way Micah remembered him doing when he was frustrated. "No, I didn't."

What was with the short, clipped response? Micah couldn't tell if his father was angry, resentful, uncomfortable, or just filled with regret over giving that part of himself to a female who wasn't Micah's mother. Or maybe his father had been whoring himself after Mom's death? Sleeping indiscriminately with any female willing to spread her legs. Had Ronan's mother been just one of many one-night fucks? If so, it was no wonder he was so angry.

"Who was she to you if she wasn't your mate?" Micah couldn't hold back the accusatory bite in his voice.

"Look, Micah, after your mother died, I was fucked up." His father tossed a perturbed frown at him. "You of all people should know what that's like. You lost Kat. You suffered. I know you did." His gaze fell to the floor. "I suffered, too. Bad. So how about you ease up on the attitude."

"Fine, whatever." Micah paced to the side and grabbed a bottle of water from a shelf. He twisted off the cap just so he could expend a fraction of the nervous energy curdling under his skin.

He didn't like the idea of his father with another female, especially if she meant nothing to him. That disgraced his mother's memory more than if his father's relationship with Ronan's mom had been pure.

Or maybe hearing his father talk about his mother's death and how it affected him was too strong of a reminder of how bad his own suffering had been after Kat's death. A suffering that had lasted until he met Sam.

No male wanted to remember such depraved sorrow. The kind that splits your soul into two halves. One half that hurt beyond description because it remembered how good life used to be, and one half that felt like acid because all it wanted was to die, die, die . . . please let me die.

There was nothing good in the suffering. The only hope came from remembering how good life *used* to be, but sometimes that wasn't enough to prevent a male from letting death take him. Consequently, it wasn't unusual for a male in suffering to die.

His father retreated to the far wall then turned to face him. "I was in a bad place, Micah. I was ravaged by guilt. I didn't understand why I lived when your mother died. I was ashamed because I didn't die with her. I tried to make sense of her death and my survival, but I couldn't." He paced across the room, rubbing his hands together as if his own nervous energy was getting the better of him. "Then again, there's no making sense of death . . . why it takes one person and leaves another to suffer the loss. All you can do is accept it and move on, but for us, accepting death isn't so easy, is it?" He turned his navy blue eyes on Micah, and a sense of knowing shone from their depths. Wherever his father had been for the past nine hundred years, he'd seen a lot of darkness and lived through a lot of hell. Was probably still living through it.

Micah shook his head, knowing exactly where his dad was coming from. "No, it's not."

The ghost of suffering a male endured after losing a mate was like adhesive residue left behind on the bottom of a vase after the price tag was removed. It still coated a part of your soul, even though it no longer hurt and could no longer be seen. But just knowing it was there was enough to strike fear in a male's heart, because no male who had experienced suffering wanted to go through that kind of pain again.

Which was why Micah would sacrifice his own life to save Sam's if it ever came to that. He wouldn't want to go on living if he lost her.

His father returned to the far wall and placed his hand on the back of a cushioned chair. His head was bowed, and his short, thick hair was mussed as if he'd run his hands through it a few hundred times in the last six hours. His other hand clenched into a fist as if he were reining himself in so he didn't explode.

For several seconds, he didn't speak. Then he took a deep breath and blew it out. "I still haven't accepted your mother's death, Micah. I'm not sure I ever will. But I've come to terms with it." He turned around. "Savannah helped me do at least that much."

"Savannah?"

"Ronan's mother." A tremulous but gentle smile turned up the corners of his father's mouth. "He got the grey in his eyes from her."

"And he got the blue from you?"

His father nodded. "Yes, but he got so much more from me than just the blue in his eyes. My fire. My passion. My rebellious nature." His gaze traveled proudly to Ronan's still form. "My stubbornness."

The qualities his father had just ticked off were all qualities Micah saw in himself, as well. He was beginning to understand why he and Ronan butted heads as easily as they did. They probably always would. They were similar creatures, and when like faced like, one was bound to rub the other the wrong way.

His father's smile broadened as his shoulders squared. "Ronan is his father's son, I'll give him that. Even if my own fire and passion are gone."

"It's not gone, Dad."

His father looked up at him as if surprised by Micah's gentle tone. "It *feels* gone."

Micah shook his head. "No. Only dimmed. It's there, and someday, when the time is right, it will flame back to life, and you'll be your old self again. You'll be the hero I always saw in you as a kid. The hero I wanted to be when I grew up."

A beat of silence passed between them as Micah's words sank in.

"I've failed him." His father glanced at Ronan. "I've failed you both."

"You didn't fail me, Dad," Micah said. "I turned out all right."

"You have, but what of Ronan." His father's sad eyes swept up Ronan's motionless form. "I haven't been the kind of parent Ronan needed. He needed the hero I was for you, but I couldn't be that for him. I couldn't even be my own hero, so how could I be his?" He sighed then turned his gaze to Micah's. "And I allowed you to think I was dead. That's not very heroic or courageous, is it?"

"Yeah, well . . ." Micah was still angry about that, but not as angry as he had been a few hours ago. "I'll get over it. And, you'll see, Ronan will eventually get over it, too."

They stood in silence for a while, watching Ronan as he slept. Okay, so it was more like he was passed out cold from heavy meds.

"Why didn't his mother raise him?" Micah asked.

His father shrugged as if in surrender. "Another male mated her after Ronan was born. I met her about fifty years ago, in the late 1960s. She was a full-blood vampire living in Louisiana at the time. There's a pretty large vampire community in Louisiana, and for a while, those I was traveling with took up residency there." He scrubbed his hand over his face. "I'll be honest, Micah. I was extremely messed up until I met Savannah. The people who were taking care of me often had to take turns guarding me to ensure I didn't try to kill myself or do something equally stupid. I was kept in an induced coma more often than not, but when I was awake, I was more like a ghost than a living being. When I was lucid, they had to force me to eat. Sometimes they even had to force me to feed. Most of the time, I held little regard for my own survival, and I struggled with taking blood from someone who wasn't your mother. But they forced me. Their will to keep me alive was stronger than my own. I'm grateful for their protection and efforts now, but at the time, I was a fucked-up mess. That's why I never came to find you. Most of the time, I could barely think about anything beyond surviving through the next minute."

Bad memories of Micah's own trip through the wastelands of suffering popped into his mind again, and he took an aggressive gulp of water to force down the lump in his throat.

"At any rate," his father continued, "I met Savannah, and suddenly the world wasn't such a dark place. She was the proverbial breath of fresh air so many people speak of, and I quickly became addicted to her smile and her laughter. We began spending time together, and we fell in love. I didn't mate her, but I definitely loved her.

"A few years later, we were surprised to discover she was pregnant. I hadn't experienced a calling, so this came as a shock to us both. A welcome one, but still a surprise. Then Ronan was born, and things were great for a while. I was actually happy again. I hadn't been happy in such long time that it felt a little strange, but then I got used to it, and life began to feel normal. Then the worst thing that could've happened did." He frowned then sadly bowed his head. "Another male mated her. Ronan was still just a little boy, and his mother was taken from him."

The way his father scowled and bit out his words made the reason for Ronan's paternal upbringing clearer.

Sometimes when a vampire mated a female who already had children with another male, he rejected the children and forbade his mate from bringing them into their union. This meant the father of the young usually had to become a single parent, or, if the father was already dead, the young was sent to an orphanage, while the mother was whisked away to begin a new life and family with her mate.

In Micah's opinion, such situations were ten levels of cruel and fucked up. He would never force a mother to abandon her children on his account, and neither would his father, but it was obvious by the disgruntled expression on his father's face that Savannah's mate clearly hadn't shared their opinion.

"He should have been raised by his mother," his father said of Ronan. "She would have done a much better job than I, but that's not the way it was meant to be. So I took Ronan and started a new life with him. By then, with Savannah's help, I was no longer a threat to myself, and Ronan gave me purpose, but getting through the days was still hard. The first year was the hardest. The people looking after me stayed away, though. They were never far, and there were times I feared they would take Ronan away from me, because sometimes I struggled just to get out of bed, but they never took him. They kept their distance, letting me find my own way back, but by then, I'd already fucked up Ronan's life so badly we hardly had any kind of relationship.

"I struggled to provide the emotional support he needed, because there was still a part of me that was suffering, too, no matter how small that part was. And maybe I bragged about you too much when he and I had disagreements." His brow furrowed as he bowed his head almost shamefully. "Maybe I talked about you and glorified you too much . . . told him how much I missed you . . . how you were the perfect son any father would be proud to call his own."

Micah swallowed past the lump that formed in his throat,

understanding not just the source of Ronan's resentment, but also how deeply his father's love ran. "If you missed me so much, why didn't you ever come and find me?"

"Like I said, I was lucky just to get through the days, Micah. Until I found Savannah, I hardly knew day from night. I honestly didn't even consider it. That's how ravenous my pain and suffering were. Anguish ate at me every day. The weeks blurred into months, and those blurred into years. To be honest, I was shocked to learn how much time had passed when Savannah brought me out of my living corpse."

Irrational anger began to rise inside Micah's heart again, fed more by the latent grief he'd suppressed for centuries than his outrage at being kept in the dark all this time. "But what about then, Dad? What about after you met Savannah? After you came back into yourself and were no longer caught inside suffering's grasp? Why didn't you come and find me and tell me you were alive then?"

His father's face twisted into an expression of apologetic misery. "I couldn't."

Micah took a step back. His annoyance, fury, heartache, and sorrow bubbled up inside him like he was a boiling pot over a fire pit. "Couldn't? You *couldn't*? Do you know how much I suffered, Dad? Did you know what I was going through?"

The guilt that shone back at him when his father lifted his face was all the answer Micah needed.

"You knew. You knew how close to death I was and how important it could have been for me to know you were still alive. And yet you felt no compulsion whatsoever to contact me? To tell me you were alive and that I had a brother?"

"That's not what I said." His father stepped around the bed toward him, but Micah didn't want anywhere near him right now and stormed to the other side of the room. His father blew out an exasperated exhale. "Don't put words in my mouth, Micah. I never said I felt no compulsion to contact you. I wanted to contact you every single goddamn day."

"Then why didn't you?"

His jaw clenched. "Because I couldn't," he said again.

"What the fuck does that mean? You *couldn't*? What? Was someone forcing you not to see me?"

His father's scowl deepened, but so did the air of guilt hanging over him.

Micah reared back as it dawned on him that it hadn't been his father's choice. Someone else had kept him from reaching out.

"That's it, isn't it? You let someone force you not to come to me?" Who would do such a thing?

His father held up his hands in a calm-down gesture. "Not exactly."

"Then what? What aren't you telling me?"

"I wasn't *forced* to stay away, son, but I was told I shouldn't see you. I was told it could put us all in danger."

"Us? All? Who are you talking about?" He marched left then right, feeling caged in. He needed to escape before life as he knew it changed yet again, because he got the feeling his father was about to blow his mind for about the hundredth time tonight. That whatever his father was hiding would rock him to the core.

His dad tracked him, drawing closer, hands held up almost pleadingly. "Micah, this is a lot bigger than just you and me. There's a lot you don't know. Things about our family. Things I never got the chance to tell you. Things that could get a lot of people hurt or killed."

Micah spun toward his father. "What people?" He was one decibel away from shouting. "Who the fuck told you not to contact me?"

"I did." The air stirred with Digon's presence a split second before he stepped into the room. His weird sidekick, Rule — oh, that's right, *Rysk* — entered behind him. Both wore earnest, wary expressions.

Micah scowled at Digon then looked at his dad before turning his focus back to the dreck. "You did? You told my father not to contact me?"

"Yes."

Micah's gaze swung angrily toward his father. "Is this who watched over you? Is Digon the one who looked after you while you were in the suffering?" Micah didn't know what hurt more, that his father hadn't reached out to let him know he was still alive or that he had allowed a dreck to be his protector instead of seeking out Micah to fulfill that role.

"Micah, you don't understand—"

"You're right, I don't."

Digon shimmered briefly before shifting into his blue-skinned dreck form. "It had been for the best that he remain hidden, Micah.

That the world thought he was dead."

Micah bristled. He had been in enough dreck altercations to know they shifted to blue for two reasons. Either they were in full-on attack mode or they wanted to demonstrate peaceful intentions by openly revealing themselves. How was that for duality?

Micah got in Digon's blue-tinted face. "What right did you have to manipulate my father? To keep him from his own son?"

"Micah, calm down." Rysk tried to push between them.

Micah shoved him aside. "This doesn't concern you, so fuck off."

"You're wrong. This does concern me." Rysk's tone was benevolent but assertive. Then he glanced sideways at Digon, as if deferring to Digon's lead, although Micah sensed Rysk was bursting at the seams to say more.

"It concerns *all* of us." King Bain's booming voice broke through the mounting tension in the room, and all eyes turned toward the king as he strode into the small, getting-more-cramped-by-the-second space.

Bain's crisp, blue eyes scanned the room, landing on each person's face long enough to convey that there would be no more talk of this matter in the open.

And that sat about as well with Micah as a dagger up the ass. He scanned the faces around the room. "Someone had better tell me what the fuck is going on here and fast, because I'm—"

"Micah." King Bain's firm voice was as effective as a slap on the face.

Micah spun, ready to square off with his king, when he pulled up and snapped his mouth closed. Something in Bain's grave expression silenced him. Both heaviness and duty shadowed Bain's eyes. Whatever he had on his mind wasn't something he looked forward to revealing, but he appeared ready to unburden himself anyway.

"Come with me." Bain walked toward the door.

"Where?"

Bain stopped and glanced over his shoulder, but he didn't make eye contact. "To my home."

Micah exchanged looks with his father, who remained stoic and silent. From his aware expression, he seemed to know what this was about. They all did.

All of them but him.

Anticipation prickled the hairs on the back of Micah's neck. He had known there would be more, but something about the way the energy shifted in the room made his stomach clench.

First he had learned that Ronan was his brother. Then he learned his father was still alive. Then—surprise!—Sam was pregnant. Next came the news that Ronan had been bitten by a werewolf, and not just any werewolf, because then he learned from the lycans—welcome to Chicago!—that mutant werewolves known as motleys had been created with the purpose of murdering the vampire race. That had led to making an alliance with the lycans, who now stood nearby, watching the unfolding drama curiously.

And for the *coup de grâce*, King Bain was inviting Micah back to his home.

Bain never allowed anyone into his home except on special occasions, which were few and far between.

It appeared there was at least one more kick-in-the-nuts awaiting him before dawn.

Bain headed for the exit, walking as if he fully expected Micah to join him.

Call him a glutton for punishment, but Micah had to know what remained unsaid. He knew it would probably shatter his reality even further, but he wasn't one to slowly peel off a Band-Aid. He ripped it off to get past the pain faster. If a little skin came off in the process, oh well. It would heal.

Without another word to his father, Micah followed Bain out of the room. "Why are we going to your home?"

"Because what you need to see is there."

"And what do I need to see?"

"Your family tree."

Micah nearly stumbled over his own feet as he threw his gaze back in the direction of Ronan's recovery room. His father had told them their family tree had been destroyed. That no record of it existed. That all Micah had of his lineage was the details of his own birth, and the births of his mother and father. Another lie, perhaps?

"Why do *you* have my family tree?" His mouth was so dry that his tongue felt thick as balled-up cotton and stuck to the roof of his mouth.

Bain stopped and faced him, his gaze penetrating Micah's. "Because I'm on it."

CHAPTER 21

AFTER WATCHING MICAH LEAVE WITH BAIN, Rameses turned his attention back to Priest, who had gone from being able to stand on his own two feet to resting on his haunches against the wall, his head down. His whole body shivered so violently his bones rattled. He was getting worse, not better. They should have left earlier. They would have if they'd known Priest's strength would be this slow to return and that he would only get worse the longer they remained away from the compound.

He pulled a blanket from a nearby stack, unfolded it, and draped it around Priest's quaking form before kneeling in front of him.

"You need rest, my brother." He placed his hand on Priest's shoulder. The other male was burning with fever.

"I'll b-be f-fine." Priest clutched the blanket to him, but his bright-blue eyes remained laser-focused.

Rameses squeezed Priest's arm. "You could be on your deathbed and still tell me you're fine, my friend."

Priest smirked proudly and let out a throaty chuckle, which set off a wave of violent tremors throughout his body. His teeth chattered so loudly they sounded like a woodpecker knocking on a tree stump.

"Is there anything I can do to help?"

Rameses peered up to find the female doctor who had been tending to Ronan standing over them. Her name tag revealed her name to be Dr. Cora Snow, and worry tugged at her expression.

He was impressed. Here they were, lycans infringing upon vampire territory, and this vampire *doctress* was more compassionate than resentful. So sympathetic to their plight, in fact, that she wished to ease Priest's suffering.

Rameses rose to his full height. Once standing, he had to angle his head down to meet Dr. Snow's eyes. She was a good foot and a half shorter than he. "Thank you, but there is nothing your medicine can do for him. We must return to our home, where he can heal."

Priest would require a week, if not two, in Osiris's chamber to recover from his efforts to save Ronan's life.

Dr. Snow offered a friendly smile. "How about a bottle of water? He sweat out a lot of fluids in there." She pointed toward Ronan's room. "He has to be dehydrated. Getting fluids in him could go a long way to making him feel better."

Rameses liked this vampire. She was smart, assertive, warmhearted, and didn't treat them like diseased vermin the way some vampires did. In fact, she seemed not to fear them at all, even though he could fit three of her inside one of him.

He offered her a smile. A rarity, to be sure. "Water would be good."

She smiled back, and what do you know? He couldn't see her fangs. "I'll be right back."

His eyes followed her appreciatively then stopped on the patient in one of the other rooms as she disappeared around the corner. The patient was a young male. Approximately twenty years old. His features were familiar. The boy sort of resembled . . .

His smile faded.

No, it couldn't be.

But the age seemed right.

There had been rumors Hunter had created a child with the female vampire who had been his ruin. Could this boy be Hunter's son?

Rameses took a step closer and drew in a deep inhale. He had to know if this was Hunter's progeny. Much could be at stake if it was. He inhaled again then gasped.

Blessed be to Osiris, it *was* Hunter's son.

Memnon would not be pleased. They had tried to corroborate the rumors of a child ever since Hunter's banishment, but had been unsuccessful. Which meant someone had helped hide the boy. And anyone who was protecting him likely knew who he was, who his father was, and what would happen to him if he were ever discovered.

And now Hunter was back, which upped the stakes even more.

Rameses had felt Hunter come through the portal when Ronan activated it. Not that Rameses would mind having Hunter's superior tracking skills back with the family, especially given the motleys now wreaking havoc, but Memnon's decision was final. Hunter had been warned that if he ever found a way to return to earth, the family would hunt him down and kill him for his betrayal.

This put Rameses in a hard spot. Memnon was the true leader of their race. Their *imeut*. Rameses only led the families when Memnon hibernated in Osiris's Sleep, as he did now. But Memnon's fifty-year sleep was about to be cut short. With the situation as dire as it was, he would have to wake Memnon sooner rather than later. For that matter, *all* the lycans who slept Osiris's Sleep would have to be awakened.

War was upon them, and every able-bodied soldier would be needed.

"Turn around and walk away."

Rameses turned toward the quiet voice directed at him from a few feet away. "Excuse me." He studied the female seated nearby. She held a bottle of orange juice in one hand and a cheese-and-cracker sandwich in the other.

"The boy isn't your concern," she said quietly, her lethal gaze locked on him from beneath a head of cropped brown hair that was obviously a wig.

"Friend of yours?"

"You could say that." Her tone held a warning. She would strike if he took one more step toward the boy's room.

Whoever she was, she sure was protective of Hunter's son. Perhaps she was the one who had kept him hidden all this time. Or maybe she was one of those vampires who, unlike Dr. Snow, held a loathing for lycans.

He forced a pleasant smile to disarm her then took a step back. "My apologies. I was simply curious about what had happened to him."

"You don't need to know."

Everything inside him tightened at her rudeness. "Of course." He spun and returned to the others, bristling.

"What is it?" Dain asked.

Rameses flicked his eyes in the direction of the boy's room. *It's his son.*

Whose? Dain carefully peered around him.

Rameses tilted his head. *Hunter's.*

Dain's brown eyes went cold then focused hard on the boy as he inhaled. *Are you sure?*

Yes. And the female sitting by the nurses' station is very protective of him.

The one wearing the wig?

Yes.

Dain turned his attention to the room where Hunter's son lay, inhaled deeply, then held his breath, processing the scent coming off the young male. Then his eyes slid to Rameses's. *Shit, it is his son. Either that or a long-lost relative.*

Priest's mental voice joined his and Dain's. *Memnon is going to shit scarabs.*

Priest, are you well enough to travel? Rameses asked through their mental link.

Yes.

Then we must leave. Now.

Dr. Snow returned with three bottles of water and handed one to Priest. "Here you go."

Priest opened one of the bottles and guzzled it in one long swallow as he rose shakily on wobbly legs.

"Whoa, hold on there." The doctor reached for him, attempting to steady him. "Maybe you should lie down."

"We must be leaving." Rameses reached for the other two bottles of water.

Dr. Snow frowned. "Leaving?" She looked at Priest, who was struggling to remain upright. "Look at him. He can barely stand. You can't leave."

Rameses liked the fire and compassion in this doctor.

"Then we will carry him if that pleases you."

"Nobody will c-carry me," Priest said, his voice breaking over his words. "I will l-leave on my own two f-feet." He rebelliously cast the blanket aside as if to prove his point.

Rameses handed him another bottle of water, which he downed in three massive gulps.

"See, he's fine." Rameses handed the third bottle back to Dr. Snow.

Priest reached out and took it back.

She arched her brow and gave the three of them a stern,

dubious glare as Priest guzzled the third and final bottle. "Fine. I can't stop you from leaving, but the next time I see you, I'd better not have reason to say I told you so."

Rameses cocked his head to the side. "You assume there will be a next time."

"Oh, I have a feeling there will be a lot of next times, given what I overheard between you and our king."

She was referring to the new alliance between the vampires and lycans. No doubt with the two races fighting alongside one another, many of their paths would cross again.

"Well, until then, Dr. Cora Snow, thank you for your refreshing company."

She scoffed. "Refreshing my ass."

Rameses almost laughed. Almost. Like Memnon, he was a master at keeping his emotions hidden to the outside world. In their compound, not so much. That was where he and Memnon were the most different.

Memnon was a stone wall no matter where he was. If not for their mental link, he would never know if Memnon was pleased, angry, happy, or ready to rip off the heads of his enemies.

Rameses was the same way when he was in the field. But in the comfort of home, Rameses let down his guard and relaxed. He laughed and even told jokes at home. But not here.

"Thank you for the water," Priest said, taking an unsteady step toward the exit as Dain drifted alongside him.

The doctor watched Dain and Priest slowly make their way through her trauma unit then turned toward Rameses. "Take good care of him. He saved our asses tonight. Without him, Ronan would have died."

"I will personally escort him to our healing chamber the moment we arrive back at our compound. I will not allow him to return to his duties until he is fully healed. Will that satisfy you?"

Dr. Snow looked from him to Priest and back again. "Not really, but I guess that's the best I can expect." She grabbed a file off the nurses' station, along with a rack of vials filled with Ronan's blood. "We'll begin running tests on this. I'll make sure the results get forwarded to you." She began to walk away.

"Do you require my contact information?" He followed her, prepared to provide his requisite phone number and email address.

She stopped and gave him an aloof look. "I'll send them through the king's people. I'm sure they know how to reach you."

Rameses fished a card from his pocket. "I would prefer you contact me directly." He extended the card toward her. "It will be quicker that way."

She took the card and slipped it into the file with an indifferent shrug. "As long as the king has no objection, I'll copy you on the reports."

"I would appreciate it." He took a step backward then gave a tight bow. "Thank you, Doctor. I look forward to hearing from you." He straightened, spun, and followed Dain and Priest out the door of the medical unit.

"We must hurry," he said to his brothers as they began winding their way through the halls toward the exit. "There's much to do."

Once outside AKM, they made haste to the cemetery, back to the pyramid mausoleum and the gateway that would take them home.

Dain was in the process of unlocking the outer door when a large, shadowy figure leaped from a nearby tree, tackling Rameses.

A mountainous shoulder rammed into his chest, nearly toppling him over as he released Priest and staggered backward. In his weakened state, Priest's knees gave out, and he tumbled to the ground, as helpless as a kitten in a bull fight.

Reacting with lightning reflexes, Rameses dug in his heels as his old friend, Hunter, barreled into him again. Sod churned and rolled underfoot as he wrestled with Hunter, who grappled for the duffel flung over Rameses's shoulder.

"My ankh! Where is it?" Hunter yanked so hard on the duffel that Rameses shot forward, slamming into him.

Dain abandoned unlocking the mausoleum and leaped into the fray, snagging Hunter by the shoulders and wrenching him into a choke hold.

But Hunter was more skilled than Rameses and Dain combined, quickly dispatching Dain to fly feet over head and land on his stomach with a guttural grunt several feet away.

"Give it to me!" Hunter fisted the duffel and pulled with such ferocity that the nylon strap gave, ripping from the side of the bag.

This wasn't a fight they could win, so when Dain clambered to his feet and was about to reengage, Rameses held up his hand.

"No, Dain. Stay back. Let him take it."

Hunter had been born into a family of trackers, all of whom were now dead. Hunter was the last.

Well, not the last. He had a son, didn't he? Surprise, surprise. A half-breed who could come down with the sickness in a blaze of gruesome destruction before he ever got a chance to track so much as rat.

"Where is it?" Hunter snarled as he fished through the duffel bag.

A moment later, he pulled out his hand, the ankh in his grasp, and flung the bag aside.

Dain caught it, eyes alert, body tight, as if he were ready to go back to the hand-to-hand at a split-second's notice.

The three of them exchanged glances, lungs pumping hard from the exertion, silence stretching like poisonous gas between them.

Hunter eyed them warily as he took a backward step, as if he wanted to ensure they wouldn't follow him.

"You can run, Hunter," Rameses said, "but Memnon will find you."

Hunter's top lip pulled back as he growled. Then he spit on the ground. "Memnon can *try* to find me, but he won't. You and I both know it. He can fuck himself for what he did to me." His black eyes swept over the three of them. Rameses, Dain, and then Priest. "For what you *all* did to me. You knew it was wrong, and yet you let him do it, anyway. Not one of you stood up for me when I've caught every one of your backs at least once. I've saved all your lives, and yet, you let Memnon take mine away from me."

An uncomfortable pit opened inside Rameses's gut. Guilt made a cruel mistress, and Rameses carried his share of it, especially where Hunter was concerned.

Rameses hadn't agreed with the punishment Memnon had leveled on Hunter, but he was not the *imeut*. Memnon was. Rameses's power only went so far. His brother made the law and ordered its enforcement, and Rameses had no doubt Memnon would issue a kill-on-sight order once he learned Hunter had returned.

The question was, would his lycan brothers follow the command. Hunter had been a beloved warrior. A *strong* warrior. The strongest among them. His tracking skills were unparalleled, and he was unrivaled when it came to kills. His banishment had been a tremendous loss, and it was an even greater one now.

They needed Hunter, now more than ever with motleys replacing common werewolves.

They'd seen too much pain and loss in their lifetimes. Too many lovers taken away from them. Too many mates. One in particular. Memnon's. It's why he was the way he was, because when she died, a little piece of each of the lycans had died as Memnon mourned. He *still* mourned, but he would never admit it. He would rather channel his mourning into something cold, dark, and sterile.

But that one death had been enough for them all to know the pain of loss. A pain Hunter had lived firsthand for the past twenty years and would continue to live as soon as he knew his Annalise was gone from this earth to dwell in the other world.

"What is done is done, Hunter."

"Fuck you, Rameses."

His brow hardened as he stared Hunter down. "Where are you going to go?"

Hunter held up his ankh. "I can go anywhere I please."

"You can't go *home*."

Home. The dimension they'd all come from so long ago it almost felt like a dream. The one place none of them could return to until the threat on earth was destroyed. And now that they had the motleys to contend with, they would never be allowed to go home.

Hunter's jaw clenched. "Oh, I can go home." He said it like he had it all figured out. Like he had formulated a devious plan that not even Memnon, with all his foresight and wisdom, would consider.

"If you do, they will kill you. And if they don't, they will strip you of your ankh and send you back here to our doorstep, bound in chains, and then Memnon will kill you. Either way, you'll be dead."

"I'm already dead."

The quiet proclamation came with such calm it stunned Rameses. He recoiled and snapped his jaw closed.

"What d-do you mean?" Priest asked.

Rameses turned to find that Priest had managed to pull himself to his feet, but his skin held the deathly pallor of an overcast sky.

"My beloved . . ." Hunter's voice took on a reverent tone. "My Annalise . . . she's no longer of this world."

The fact that Hunter knew of Annalise's death came as a surprise. How had Hunter learned of her death already? He hadn't been back long enough to have made the trip to Louisiana, track down her family, learn the truth, and return to Chicago. Besides, Annalise's family despised Hunter. They never would have talked to him about her death. Kill him? Yes. Inform him of Annalise's fate? Not a chance in hell.

Hunter's scarred face turned away, but not before Rameses saw the pain and sadness flicker through his dark-brown eyes. "She is dead," he said softly, "and so is my son. My son . . ." His voice took on a faraway quality, as if he were considering all that he had lost, and then he pulled himself back into the present and lifted his gaze defiantly to Rameses's. "I only wish to mourn them, and then I will release myself from life to join my beloveds in death."

He didn't know. Hunter had no idea his son was still alive.

What to do with this knowledge? If he told Hunter the truth, he would be enabling the banished male to remain on earth, where, despite Hunter's defiant remarks to the contrary, Memnon *would* hunt him down, find him, and kill him. But if Rameses said nothing and let Hunter believe his son was, in fact, dead, Hunter would take his own life.

Either way, the outcome was unacceptable.

He needed to buy time. Once he told Memnon about the motleys and the accord he'd struck with the vampires, he might have a chance of convincing Memnon that welcoming Hunter back into the family was a good thing. That the twenty years of banishment was enough punishment. At the very least, they could keep Hunter here but banish him from the family. Surely, Memnon would see how vital Hunter was now. With new enemies breaking into the fray, they needed Hunter more than ever, and even if he had no contact with the family, Hunter would still hunt werewolves. It was in his blood.

Rameses was still contemplating what to do about the situation when Priest said, "Tell him, Rameses."

A flash of heat shot through Rameses's body. Priest was only two steps removed from the role of *imeut*, but that didn't give him the right to speak out of turn. He met Priest's gaze with an angry look he was certain could turn mortals to stone.

Priest remained composed and determined. "Tell him, or I will."

"Tell me what?" Hunter glanced between them, bristling.

"Priest, this is neither the time nor the pla —"

"Your s-son is alive," Priest said to Hunter with a sickly shiver. His color was worse than before.

Silence.

Not even a breath sputtered out among them.

Then the top blew everywhere all at once.

"Priest!" Rameses admonished the fair-haired lycan and started toward him just as Hunter rushed forward, caught him like a viper, and put him in a choke hold.

"You knew my son was alive?" Hunter hoisted Rameses off the ground.

Dain lunged forward, grabbing the scarred lycan. "Let him go, Hunter!"

But Hunter wasn't having any of that. "You knew?" he yelled. "You knew and didn't tell me?"

Rameses scraped and grasped at Hunter's fist, trying to free himself, but Hunter had him dead to rights.

"Hunter!" Dain's voice growled ominously. He was on the verge of the change that would shift him from man to beast. "Let him go! Now!"

Rameses didn't need Dain to save him. He called on his lycan form while using the special powers granted to him by royal birthright to block Hunter from doing the same.

Fabric ripped, shredding into ribbons as his body swiftly metamorphosed into ten feet of pure, pissed-off lycan. Hunter lost his grasp then stumbled backward as Rameses rose sharply above him, fangs bared.

Do not ever *put your hands on me!* He pushed forward.

Not one to shrink away from a beast who could fillet him in less than thirty seconds, Hunter pushed out his chest and sneered. *I'm not afraid of you.*

That's your problem, not mine.

Why didn't you tell me about my son?

Because telling you wasn't that simple.

Hunter barked out a caustic laugh. "Not that simple? Are you fucking kidding me?" He glanced toward Dain and Priest then back to Rameses.

I only just discovered him an hour ago. We haven't had time to fully investigate. What if he ends up not being your son? What then?
Highly unlikely. The boy at AKM held Hunter's scent. He resembled him in coloring and facial features, even though he had yet to go through the change. Still, there was the slimmest chance that, upon closer analysis, the boy wouldn't turn out to be who Rameses and the others thought he was. He could end up being some other mixed-blood creature who only smelled like Hunter. Again, not likely, but who the hell knew with all the shit popping up in the supernatural world recently?

Hunter frowned as if he hadn't considered that. Then he glanced at Priest. "How certain are you that he's my son?"

Priest paid a deferential look at Rameses then addressed Hunter. "He's yours. I am certain of it."

Damn Priest. Rameses knew he meant well, but this was not his call to make. The two of them would have words when Priest was better, and Rameses would remind him of his place within the clan.

Rameses took a menacing step toward Hunter. *And now your plan is to remain here, isn't it? Because of your son.*

Hunter squared his shoulders, his jaw set, eyes determined. *Yes.*
Fool.
And that puts your life – and his – in danger. Memnon will kill you both.

Not if I kill him first.

Rameses's hackles went up. This was his brother they were talking about. The *imeut.* Royalty and leader of their people. Memnon wasn't perfect, and he had his problems, but simply thinking about killing him was a crime.

That would be a death sentence.

Hunter glared at him. *I will do whatever it takes to protect my son, even if that means killing the* imeut. His gaze swept the group. *Even if it means killing all of you.*

You would damn the human race to the werebeasts? Because it wasn't just werewolves they fought now, but motleys and Osiris only knew what other creatures that were being cooked up in Bishop's lab.

You and I both know Memnon cares not for the humans.

Ever since the humans turned on the lycans and killed his beloved, Memnon had taken a more hostile attitude toward them.

But he still abided by his oath to Anubis. They all did.

That may be true, Hunter, but he honors his pledge to protect him, and he will kill you to continue doing so.

Then let him kill me if he can.

They were at a stalemate. Rameses knew Hunter well enough to know that he wouldn't give an inch. And neither would Memnon if Rameses couldn't convince him they needed Hunter.

I don't want to see you die, Hunter.

Then change Memnon's mind.

Easier said than done.

You'd better find a way, or it's war between us.

One against an entire race seemed like severely uneven odds, but Hunter was not to be underestimated. He was skilled enough to make good on his promise and kill them all. It would take time, but Hunter was as patient as he was lethal. If he had to wait fifty years to take down every last one of them, he would.

Hunter –

"This conversation is over." Hunter turned away from Rameses to address Priest. "Where is he? Where is my son?"

Priest hesitated as if he finally understood it wasn't his place to speak, but it was too late for that. The damage had been done.

"He's at AKM," Priest said.

"AKM?" Hunter scowled, his gaze slowly dropping to the ground as if he were playing back a memory.

Rameses concentrated on his human form and shifted back. "He's in their medical unit." He ripped what remained of his shirt and pants from his body. He cared not if anyone saw him naked.

Hunter's head shot up. "Medical unit?"

When he, Dain, and Priest simply stared back at him, Hunter continued, his voice panicked. "Is he okay?"

Rameses recalled the bandage wrapped around the boy's torso. He had looked fragile. Too fragile. Thin, gaunt, deathly still. A feeding tube had been taped over his mouth, and an oxygen tube under his nose.

"Truthfully, no. When I saw him, he looked quite ill."

Concern and worry flashed over Hunter's expression, and he began to pace. "What's wrong with him?"

"That I do not know." He thought of Dr. Snow. She was impressive as far as doctors go, even if she was a vampire. "But he is getting the best possible care."

Dain looked at him like he was talking foolishness, and maybe he was. But he had to try to persuade Hunter from going wrecking ball on AKM just to get to his son. That wouldn't bode well for the new alliance he'd struck tonight with the vampires.

Hunter continued pacing, grumbling under his breath in angry murmurs. Rameses could just barely make out what he was saying. "She lied to me. She was there, and she lied to me."

Could *she* be the female Rameses had encountered outside the boy's room?

"Hunter." Rameses stepped forward and dropped his hand on Hunter's shoulder.

Hunter jerked around and grabbed Rameses's wrist before calming himself and letting him go. Whoever *she* was, whether the female who had warned him away from Hunter's son's room was her or not, she had better prepare, because Hunter looked like he was about to go on a warpath.

Rameses slowly drew his hand away, careful not to make any sudden movements.

"Let the doctors do their job," he said. "He needs medical care right now. If you tear in there and take him, he could die."

Hunter recoiled from the word. Rameses hoped that meant he understood and wouldn't try to be a hero.

Rameses backed away then gestured for Dain to open the mausoleum.

"Let the vampires heal your son, Hunter. I will buy you time with Memnon, and I give you my word that I will try to persuade him to recuse you from the remainder of your punishment. But don't expect any miracles."

Hunter nodded, but his gaze remained vacant, as if he'd returned to running whatever memory he'd been obsessing over a moment ago through his mind.

Rameses silently directed Dain and Priest inside the mausoleum, ready to return to the compound. Priest was still too weak to take more than two or three steps without assistance, so Dain propped himself under Priest's arm and shouldered him inside.

Hunter wouldn't follow them. Rameses was certain of that. But it was best not to chance it. Hunter didn't appear to be himself.

"I'll be in touch, Hunter," Rameses said, stepping into the mausoleum. "Just don't do anything stupid before then."

Hunter didn't even acknowledge him.

"Did you hear me?"

Hunter was murmuring to himself again, his demeanor growing more and more agitated, an increasing edge rising in his voice.

"The bitch lied to me," he snarled.

Then, without another word, Hunter spun on his heel and bolted into the cemetery's depths, disappearing into the shadows.

"What the fuck was that about?" Dain asked.

Rameses shook his head, gazing in the direction Hunter had gone. "I'm not sure, but I have a feeling that female vampire who warned me away from his son's room is going to be getting a visit." He turned and bobbed his head toward the keyhole. "It's not our problem. Take us home."

Dain passed Priest off to Rameses then crossed the small interior to the corner. "What are you going to tell Memnon?" He slipped his ankh inside the hole and stood back.

Rameses held onto Priest with one arm and pulled the door shut with the other. "I'm going to tell him the truth. He'll find out, anyway."

The portal opened, and they returned to their compound out west in a shimmering flash of light, appearing in the pyramid room.

"That'll go over well," Dain said, without missing a beat.

"I'll handle it." Rameses hooked his arm around Priest, who was growing weaker by the second now that the excitement was over, and started down the grand, gilded hall toward the healing chamber. He was still naked as a jaybird except for the cartouche hanging from a gold chain around his neck.

Dawn would be upon them in a few hours, and there was much to do before they woke Memnon.

"Dain, assemble the families," he called over his shoulder.

"What should I tell them?"

"Tell them we're going to wake their kin and that we're pulling Memnon out of Osiris's Sleep." He shuffled Priest a little farther down the hall then added, "And tell them to prepare for war."

Because whether the war came from Hunter, the motleys, the drecks, or all of the above, a war was coming.

CHAPTER 22

MICAH SAT ACROSS FROM KING BAIN in the back of his limousine as it pulled up to the royal mansion. A uniformed servant standing at the side of the drive stepped forward and opened the door then stood aside to allow them out.

He stared up at the royal mansion, but his mind was still obsessing over what King Bain had said to him less than fifteen minutes ago.

Because I'm on it.

Bain was on his family tree?

What did that mean? Surely, that was code for something else, because if Micah and King Bain were on the same family tree, that would mean . . .

Micah didn't want to take that thought to its natural conclusion.

King Bain had said nothing further on the drive here, instead taking the opportunity to read his emails and text messages. A king's job was never done, but Micah got the impression Bain was biding his time. That he wasn't in any rush to spill the details about his hospital room confession and was, in fact, not looking forward to it any more than Micah was.

Micah wordlessly followed Bain up the steps to the imposing double doors, which had to be at least ten feet tall and made of thick slabs of wood not easily breeched by an enemy. Once inside, they passed through the main foyer with its twenty-foot-domed ceiling and enough splendor for the queen of England. They were greeted by gold walls, hand-carved tables, and matching floral arrangements that perfumed the vestibule.

Bain strolled past it all as if he'd seen it a million times and no longer registered just how grand his home was.

"This way." Bain directed him out of the foyer and into the main hall that split the home into two equal halves. The wide passage from the front of the building to the back reminded him of the inside of a giant cathedral, with intricate murals painted on the arched ceilings and priceless works of art lining both walls. Their heavy footsteps echoed in the large, open space.

Toward the end of the hall, Bain veered them to the right, into another hall—this one narrower—with large picture windows overlooking a sprawling lawn dotted with trees. It was still dark, but he could see that the property extended down a sloping hill to a line of trees in the distance. Beyond, the lights of the city illuminated the night sky.

The next stop was a well-appointed study with hand-carved mahogany wainscoting. A polished Elizabethan hutch sat along the near wall, holding a silver tray set with expensive bourbon and crystal tumblers. Victorian-era furniture was strategically placed throughout the room.

Then there was the desk. The size of a baby elephant and stained a rich, deep, cherry brown, King Bain's desk matched the mammoth leather chair behind it and presented an imposing air of power and sophistication. This wasn't just his office. It was his throne room.

"Care for a drink?" Bain flipped over two tumblers and lifted the bourbon.

"Sure." Micah had a feeling he was going to need it.

Bain handed him a glass and took a drink from his own.

"So," Bain said, "I guess the past couple of days have been a little rough."

"You could say that."

"How's Sam holding up?"

"Better than I am." It didn't feel like the right time to announce she was pregnant.

Bain nodded and took another drink. "Good. That's good." He seemed distracted, as if he were intentionally putting off the reason for bringing Micah here.

Micah downed his shot of bourbon and helped himself to another glass. "With all due respect, sire, it's been a long night. It'll be dawn soon, and I really want to be home with my mate when the sun rises." He swallowed his second shot of bourbon and poured another. "So, can we get to whatever it is you want to talk to me about?"

Bain swirled the bourbon in his own glass as he regarded Micah out of the corner of his eye. Then he smiled and strolled toward his desk. "I remember the first time I met you." Bain's voice held a paternal note. "I didn't know much about you except that you were young and had already risen to the top of my father's guard. You had quite the reputation as a lethal warrior even then." He chuckled. "He admired you, you know. My father. Dare I say he was even proud of you. The way he spoke of you often made me think of you as a brother and not just my mentor."

Bain the First had employed Micah to train his son, and given King Bain's wry tone, Micah was beginning to question if there was a greater reason for his assignment to train the young prince — at the time — than he'd been aware of.

Bain took another drink. "Then my father told me the truth about who you were."

The rough edges on Micah's nerves tingled with impatience.

"And, now, it's time for *me* to tell *you*." Bain approached a pedestal that held what appeared to be a large, ancient book. "There's something here I want you to see, Micah."

Micah's skin prickled as a chill ran down his spine. The book was open, the dull, yellowish pages lightly wrinkled, as if they'd seen their share of the elements and were lucky to still be in one piece. Elegant cursive writing in black ink covered the page. It was the kind of writing one would associate with historic records.

Undeniably curious, he stepped closer, trying hard not to stare at the tome but unable to take his eyes off it.

"What is it?" Tension filled his shoulders, and he realized he was holding his breath. He already knew what was on that page. He just wasn't sure he was ready to face it.

He was faintly aware that Bain was watching him. He tore his gaze from the book as he stopped in front of the pedestal. When he met the king's eyes, he found warm benevolence gazing back at him.

"This is your family tree," Bain said.

Even though he'd already known that's what the book contained, Micah nearly dropped his drink as his eyes shot once more to the leather-bound book.

His gaze devoured the page whole, unable to focus on any one name for the excitement blasting through his veins. This was his lineage. All of it. If he could just focus long enough to tame his eagerness, he'd be able to see the names of his ancestors.

After being told their family records had been destroyed, he'd never dared to hope he would one day learn the truth. It wasn't as if he could go to Ancestry.com, plug in his information, and get a dozen little leaves tracing his origin. It was a pretty good bet Ancestry.com didn't contain vampire records. But here he was, only inches away from all the answers about where he'd come from. Answers he would now be able to relay to his own children someday when they were old enough.

"Breathe, Micah." Bain rested his large hand on Micah's shoulder and gave him a gentle shake.

He sucked in a breath and blew it out, leaning closer. "I'm just . . ." The decorative letters began to come into focus, forming names. "I thought all my family's records were gone."

"No. They've always been in my possession."

Most of the names were unfamiliar to Micah. Only a few were ones his father had shared with him, such as the name of his grandfather.

Then a name on a side branch caught Micah's eye.

He bent forward, blinked, and looked up at Bain, pointing to the name on the page. "What's this?"

Bain followed where the tip of Micah's index finger rested lightly on the page. "That's me. That's *my* name, Micah."

Micah turned his gaze back to the page and followed the bloodlines.

Bain the Second.

Bain's name extended up through Bain the First to a male named Ryland, whose brother had been—

Wait a second.

"Is that . . .?" He took a closer look. "Does that say 'Rysk'?"

Bain's eyes never left him. Micah could feel the king watching him like a hawk would a field mouse. "Yes."

"As in . . .?" Micah thought back to Digon's buddy. The guy he thought was named Rule but just found out tonight was really named Rysk.

Bain spoke quietly as he began to explain, pointing to the various names as he ticked them off. "My ancestor, Ryland, was the brother of Rysk the First, who was the father of Rysk the Second."

Micah couldn't put words to the question trying to make its

way from his brain to his mouth. All he could do was stare at Bain with his mouth hanging open.

"Micah, Rysk the Second is the male who was with Ronan tonight. The male who is *friends* with your father. But, as you can see, they're not really friends. Rysk is your father's great-great-grandfather."

Micah dropped his gaze back to the family tree and followed the generations from Rysk's name down to his then back up, searching for anything to explain how his name had gotten there, ensuring this wasn't a crazy mistake. It wasn't. His line flowed directly to Rysk the Second, up to Rysk the First, and on up to King Cato himself.

"Are you telling me Rysk is my . . ." He counted the generations from his name to Rysk's. "My great-great-*great*-grandfather? That King Cato was my—"

He couldn't choke out the words. Micah descended from the very first king of the vampire race.

Bain took a cautious step toward him, as if he wasn't sure what to expect from Micah's reaction. The king appeared just as ready to defend himself as he was to catch Micah if his knees buckled.

"That's right." Bain spoke slowly. "He's your ancestor." Then his features tightened. "And so is Digon. But that's not *his* real name, either." He turned back one page in the book, revealing another family tree. "Digon's real name is Argon. He's been using Digon as an alias to keep his true identity a secret."

This wasn't happening. This couldn't be happening.

Digon—or Argon—was a dreck. A full-blooded dreck. If Argon was Micah's ancestor, that meant . . .

"I have dreck blood in me?"

Fiery heat erupted in his chest, and his hands clenched into fists. The one thing he despised the most—drecks—and his body contained dreck blood. He wasn't sure if he was going to throw up or destroy something.

"Yes, Micah." Bain remained close, but not too close.

This couldn't be true. He couldn't have dreck blood in him. That would mean . . . oh God, he wasn't a pure blood after all. He was a mixed-blood, and the worst possible kind. The kind that could get him ostracized by his peers.

Like Severin, he had to hold this new truth tight to his vest, because there were assholes who would surely *love* to use this knowledge to destroy him. Apostle, for one. And just about everyone he had ever roughed up, locked away, or otherwise insulted.

What if this got out? Would it put Sam and his unborn children in jeopardy? Would they all suffer because of this?

Panic flooded him as the walls closed in. The room suddenly felt far too small.

"Micah . . ." Bain came toward him, but he appeared to move in slow motion.

Micah had already had a hell of a night. His emotions had been played like Ping-Pong balls in a Chinese tournament for the better part of eight hours, and he'd run the length of the scale, from livid to furious to happy to elated and back again. And back once more.

And now he worried about the safety of his mate and children.

He'd reached his limit.

Done. Finito. Wave the checkered flag. *Adios, muchachos.*

Lights out.

Micah stumbled backward, teetered as blackness pushed in from the edges of his vision, which swam with milky white orbs.

"Micah!"

He listed to the side, staggered, and then his vision poofed out on him entirely as gravity pulled him down. The back of his head slammed against the arm of a nearby settee, casting him sideways. He rolled onto his stomach, his bourbon puddling on the floor and his nose mashed against a very expensive — and very gawdy — tapestry rug.

Well, fuck. There went his man card.

CHAPTER 23

THE MEDICAL WARD HAD FINALLY GROWN QUIET. Bain and Micah had left, the lycans were gone, and Argon and Rysk hovered near the nurses' station, readying to depart.

It was just Drake with Ronan in his room.

"I'm sorry I screwed things up so badly between us," Drake whispered, placing his hand on Ronan's. "You deserved better than an ancient male too fucked in the head from his own suffering to be a proper father to you."

He stood beside Ronan for a while, not speaking, eyes closed, just holding his son's hand. He was too weary even to pray.

A knock on the door a few minutes later jarred him back to life.

He looked up to find Argon standing at the threshold. "Rysk and I are taking our leave for the day."

"Fine."

Argon remained. Obviously, he had more to say.

"You should come with us."

Drake shook his head. "No."

Argon sighed as if he were trying to reason with a two-year-old. "Drake, you need to rest."

"This is my son. I'm not leaving."

Argon glanced between father and son then gave a reluctant nod. "Perhaps just knowing you're here will give Ronan a bit of comfort."

Drake snorted. "Not likely, given his animosity toward me."

Argon tilted his head sympathetically. "Then why stay?"

"Because it gives *me* comfort."

Argon's expression softened into one of sad understanding. "I see. Well . . ." He gave a nod of farewell. "Rysk and I will return this evening and see you then. We have much planning to do and need to start soon."

Drake nodded and lifted his hand in a half-assed wave goodbye.

After they left, he pulled the cushioned chair to the side of Ronan's bed, settled into it, and watched his son sleep.

His son.

A son he barely knew.

A son who hated him.

But a son he loved more than life itself.

MICAH SAT ON THE COUCH, an ice pack on his head. Servants worked to clean up the last of his spilled drink, and the pack of smelling salts they'd used to rouse him lay abandoned on the corner of the table.

"Drink this." Bain thrust a glass of water toward him.

He took the glass and drained the contents. He still felt on the verge of passing out again, but he willed himself to stay conscious. He really needed this night to end so the rollercoaster ride could stop.

"How do you feel?" Bain sat down beside him.

"That's a stupid question. How do you think I feel?" He was beyond caring that he was talking to the king. Then again, Bain wasn't just his king. He was Micah's cousin. A distant cousin, but family. He was entitled to speak informally to family, wasn't he?

Bain waited for the servants to leave his study and close the door behind them before speaking again.

"I know it's all a bit overwhelming, Micah, but you need to know your history, and we've run out of time for me to feed this to you bite by bite." The king pulled the book containing his family tree into his lap, angling it so Micah could see it better.

"Get that goddamn thing away from me." Micah looked away from it.

"There's more, Micah, and you—"

"More?" Micah tossed him an incredulous look. "You mean my life hasn't been fucked up enough tonight, so why not fuck it up some more?" Then Bain's words registered, bringing him to a standstill, and he cast a wary sidelong glance toward his cousin.

"What do you mean, we've run out of time?"

Bain held up his hand, beseeching him for patience. "First things first, and then I'll get to that." He opened the book back to Argon's family tree. "So, let me explain our history, starting with Argon and Cato. Argon was the first ruler of the drecks. He was best friends with our ancestor, King Cato, the first king of the vampires. Back then, our two races got along."

Micah sensed this was going to be a long story, so he settled in, holding the ice pack against the back of his head and keeping his mouth shut.

"Argon had a daughter named Abrial, who was promised to Teo, the son of a wealthy dreck in Argon's inner circle. Unfortunately, Cato's son, Rysk the First, formed a mating bond to Abrial. King Cato pleaded with Argon to dissolve the arrangement between Abrial and Teo so that Rysk the First could claim his rightful mate, but Argon refused.

"You see, Argon was in a bad position. If he broke his promise to Teo's family, they would have decried his leadership and led a coup against him. That's how powerful Teo's family was. Probably one of the most powerful families of the dreck race. But by honoring his promise to Teo's family and denying Cato, Argon stacked the cards against himself on *all* fronts.

"Denied his mate, Rysk the First fell into an agonizing suffering. He was locked away and would have certainly died, but his suffering gave him tremendous strength, and he broke free of his confinement and fled to Abrial. His intent was to claim her and make her his mate." Bain raised his index finger and pointedly angled his head for emphasis. "Oh, and I should add that Abrial wanted this. She was as much in love with Rysk as he was with her."

Micah shrugged. "Then what was the problem?"

"Teo. He didn't care that Abrial didn't love him. All that mattered to him and his family was that she was the premier's daughter. She was royalty, and taking her as a mate gained him significant power among their people.

"He also knew that if Abrial and Rysk were to mate—a prince to a princess, as it were—that eventually the dreck race would fall under vampire rule."

Rule. Interesting that Rysk the First's son, Rysk the Second, had chosen the name Rule as his alias.

Micah set aside the ice pack and rubbed the bump on the back of his noggin. "I think I'm beginning to understand the source of the problem between our two races."

Bain held up his hand. "Just wait. It gets worse. Upon finding Abrial locked away like a prisoner in Argon's palace, Rysk ghosted in, rematerialized, and was about to steal her away when Teo showed up, armed and ready to kill Rysk to keep Abrial from escaping. A fight ensued, blood was drawn, and Rysk killed Teo. Then he stole Abrial away and satisfied the urgings of his calling."

"Good for him," Micah muttered.

"Not exactly." Bain kept his gaze on the tome as if he could read their history from its pages. "Teo's family demanded both retribution and retaliation. They wanted the couple hunted down and Rysk put to death. The situation grew even more dire as Argon found himself trapped between duty and friendship. Argon and Cato tried to find a diplomatic solution, but before they could, one of the hunting parties Teo's father sent out found the mated pair and killed Rysk.

"Furious at the betrayal, and mourning the loss of his son, Cato ceased talks with Argon and sent an army to destroy what remained of Teo's family in retaliation for killing his son, which he construed as an act of war. He kidnapped Abrial, refusing to release her until his grandson was born.

"Rysk the Second's birth seemed to calm things for a while between our two races, but Argon's sons continued to pressure him, mounting growing dissent against his continued alliance with Cato and the vampires, given all that had transpired.

"Eventually, the drecks overthrew Argon and inducted his oldest son, Tauno, as their new premier, sending Argon into exile, where he watched the growing conflict from a distance.

"Once Rysk the Second was born, Cato took custody of him, which sent Abrial into such despair she took her own life. A month later, all-out war erupted between the two races. A war that continues to play out today."

Micah looked at Bain like there had to be more. That this war had to be about more than a love triangle gone wrong. "Are you telling me this war started because a dreck and a vampire loved each other?"

Bain shrugged one shoulder. "I guess that's one way of looking at it."

"Jesus, that's fucked up."

The two sat in silence for a moment, and then realization began to sink in, which led to understanding, and finally to awareness. Micah raked his hands through his hair then flung his arms forward. Not only did he carry dreck blood in his veins, but *royal* dreck blood. And not only did he carry royal *dreck* blood, but royal *vampire* blood, as well.

Which meant . . .

He bowed his head and cursed under his breath.

He was royalty. He was motherfucking, goddamn royalty. Not just on the dreck side, but on the vampire side, too.

This was shit news, because Micah wasn't one for royal entitlements and hoity-toity social dinners where you had to pretend to be polite and play by a set of ball-crushing etiquette rules. And a suit? Forget about it. Micah didn't do suits. There were only a handful of people he would don a suit for, and a room full of fake-ass well-to-do vampires who put more clout in material wealth than personal substance didn't make the list.

Still, now that he knew the truth of his lineage, factors of his own life were beginning to make more sense. He wasn't a pure blood as he'd always thought. He was a mixed-blood. An extremely diluted mixed-blood, since it looked like the rest of his line was pure, but even a diluted mixed-blood could possess special abilities, such as the one that allowed him to see the thoughts of those around him without trying to infiltrate their minds. And now he knew why he could create young without having a calling. It was his dreck blood that had made him fertile and created the twins growing inside Sam's belly this very second.

Micah recalled something Bain had said to him last month. He'd said he'd grown impatient and was ready for Micah to fill the role he'd always been meant to fill. Exactly what role was that? Prince? Duke? King-in-Training? Micah sure as hell wanted nothing to do with such aristocratic titles, nor the responsibilities they entailed.

Two hours ago, he might have been ready to stop enforcing and try on a normal job, but this wasn't what he'd had in mind. The idea of sitting behind a desk all day rankled his nerves and made his skin itch.

The truth was, he was good at enforcing. He was a skilled killer and could track down the filthiest of criminals night after night without question. He just couldn't take all the risk with no reward, anymore. There were too many rules enforcers had to follow, and many of those rules ran counter to others. And more inane rules were added every couple of months, thanks to Premier Royce's incessant whining.

At least now they knew what all his bitching had been about? Diversion.

The point was, working as an enforcer wasn't fulfilling, anymore. There were too many asses that needed to be kissed and dicks to be sucked to get anything done. Every night felt more like a bend-over-and-take-it-up-the-ass than any kind of progress in the ongoing enforcement of the peace that seemed to be slipping away at an accelerating rate between the vampires and drecks.

Who wanted to keep doing a job that set you back at the starting line — or even farther and farther behind it — each night you geared up and hit the streets?

Only one thing was worse. Becoming a politician. And that's exactly what a royal title would make him.

Nothing sucked a male's nut sack more deeply into a vacuum than pushing a pencil into his hand and making him glad-hand other politicians. Micah was too fond of his balls to lose them to such a fate, so if King Bain wanted him to wear the royal insignia and be a figurehead for peaceful negotiations, he could stuff that shit up his ass.

Put Micah into a room with a dreck like Premier Royce, and peaceful was the last adjective anyone would use to describe the encounter. He would just as soon give Royce a nose job with the heel of his boot than pretend that fucker was concerned with keeping up good race relations with vampires.

If it was one thing Micah was sure of, it was that Royce had his hand in every bad situation affecting vampires, from cobalt to Bishop's lab experiments to the damage done to that half-lycan youth, Savill, who was still recovering inside the AKM trauma unit. That poor kid had been cut open from neck to groin like a frog cadaver in high school biology class.

So yeah, Micah had seen too much blood and death in the streets to keep a level head in any kind of royal capacity.

As Micah stewed over what this new information meant for his future, Bain continued going through their family tree, explaining their history and pointing out key relationships.

"Premier Royce descended from Tauno's line. He and those of Teo's family who survived Cato's attack ended up forming tight alliances that have endured even to today. So tight, in fact, that members of Teo's family could almost be *part* of the ruling family." Bain dragged his finger down the page and stopped on three names.

Micah peered closer, a fresh wave of shock hitting him at what he saw. "Bishop, Apostle, and Deacon?"

"Teo would have been their great-great-great-uncle."

So many of the questions Micah had asked himself for so long now found answers. The reason why Premier Royce never punished Bishop for the obvious crimes he'd committed in breach of the truce was because, to Royce, Bishop was as close to family as you could get without actually sharing genes. And Apostle's hatred of vampires had obviously been passed down from four generations of animosity before him.

How ironic that Apostle was the dreck Micah had sought out to end his life before he met Sam. That was some fucked-up karmic voodoo right there.

"If you knew who I was — that I was your cousin, royalty, and all that shit — why didn't you or anyone interfere when I tried to get myself killed last winter?"

"Someone was about to step in when Sam showed up and saved you, instead. And your friend Trace was there, too. My people would have only interfered if it looked like there were no other options. We didn't think you would actually go through with it."

Micah gave a dubious snort. "You underestimated me then."

"And yet, here you are. Alive and well."

Micah couldn't argue with that.

"How did Rysk the Second come to be with Argon if Argon was in exile?"

The grin that spread over Bain's face was one of admiration. He obviously held a lot of respect for Argon.

"Just because Argon was in exile didn't mean he remained there. He kept watch. He stood vigil over what was happening to his people. He followed them. And he kept tabs on his grandson. During one particularly bloody battle, he stole into Cato's palace and rescued Rysk from certain death. He was still just a boy, and Argon took him to safety and protected him. Everyone thought Rysk had died, and Argon knew making people believe that he *had* died was for the best. He knew that if anyone, whether vampire or dreck, learned that the son of Rysk the First and Abrial was alive, he would be a target. No one wanted to see a bastard mixed-blood rise to the role of ruler over both races, and that was Rysk's destiny."

Micah was beginning to get a bad feeling about what all this meant for his own future and that of Sam and his unborn children.

He glanced down at the list of names between his and Rysk's. "And what of all these descendants?"

Bain couldn't hide the grim worry that overtook his face. "Dead."

"How?"

"Until recently, they've been under royal protection, but someone has learned who they are and where to find them. One by one, the families are being slaughtered."

"My grandfather? Durin?"

Bain sadly closed his eyes and gave a single nod. "He was found dead just a few weeks ago. The only ones who remain are Argon, Rysk, your father, your brother, you, and your uncle Rory."

"My uncle is still alive?" This was too much. Micah's entire world had blown wide open in less than eight hours, and if his spill into unconsciousness a while ago was any indication, his plate was already too full to process anything else.

"Yes, he's alive. We're bringing him here. He'll be safer in Chicago now that the secret's out that Rysk's line lives."

Looked like Micah could expect to have one, big, not-so-happy family reunion in Chicago soon. Not that he wasn't looking forward to seeing his uncle Rory, but they weren't exactly meeting again under the best of circumstances. Their ancestors were being murdered, mutant werewolves—*motleys*—were hunting them down, and it looked like the drecks and Dacians were in league with one another to wage a new kind of war.

Maybe to humans it was just another day in the big city, but to Micah, it felt more like the end of the world.

"How are they finding us?" he asked.

"My bet is there's a mole inside AKM or even on my staff. Someone who's able to find the information and feed it back to Royce and Searcy."

Strange that Micah knew just about everyone at AKM and had never caught a random thought that would give away a traitorous mole. That didn't mean someone couldn't hide his or her thoughts from him, though. People who knew of his mindreading talents could mask their thoughts the same way Argon's female cohort, Sonia, did.

"What are you doing to sniff out the mole?"

Bain settled back on the couch, the book still open in his lap. "There's a countermole inside AKM working to find the leak."

"Who?"

"Sonia."

"Argon's Sonia?" Speak of the devil. "I've never seen her around—"

"You know her better as Eva."

"Eva?" No way. The mousy file clerk whose wardrobe seemed more appropriate for an I-Love-the-Eighties revival was actually the fiery-spirited Sonia?

Eva hardly said a word to anyone, held herself like she was trying to leave the smallest possible carbon footprint known to mankind, and seemed unable to look anyone in the eye.

That was the exact opposite of the female he'd come to know as Sonia, who was brash, sassy, and looked you so hard in the eye you thought she could see straight down to the contents in your stomach. He had to give it to that female, she'd created one helluva disguise.

"But Sonia is a dreck."

"A *friendly* dreck," Bain emphasized. "And she's a master at masking her scent, among other things. Her father was a brilliant scientist who wanted nothing of Royce's new war, so Royce had him killed. What he neglected to realize was that Sonia is even more brilliant and cunning than her father. She's taken his research and inventions and made them better. We're fortunate to have her on our side."

Shifting gears, Micah asked, "How long have you known Argon was alive?"

"Not long." Bain sighed. "Oh, I'd heard rumors that he was alive, and since his body was never found, there were plenty of rumors to go around, but until he reached out to me a few days ago, I had assumed like everyone else that he'd perished."

"Reached out?"

"He asked for a meeting."

"And you agreed?" King Bain was what some would call

excessively cautious. To meet with a dreck who claimed to be the first ruler of his race without more than just his word seemed like a risk Bain wouldn't normally take. "Why?"

"He knew things only Argon would have known. And I sent someone to vet him. Someone I could trust to see inside his thoughts and decipher the truth. I told him it was the only way I'd meet with him."

"Who'd you send? Cordray?" Because everyone knew how tight she was with the king.

Bain grinned. "I sent Tristan."

"Tristan? But I thought he was still on house arrest."

Bain shrugged indifferently. "I'm the king. I can occasionally bend the rules if I deem it necessary to the survival of the race. And since I'm the one who ordered him on house arrest, I'm the one who can end it."

Micah cocked his head and gave his cousin a crooked grin. "Which begs the question, *have* you ended Tristan's house arrest?"

"I think the real question you're asking is whether you're still in charge of his team."

"Maybe."

If Tristan was back on duty, it threw Micah's role inside AKM into the realm of the unknown. If he was no longer in charge, would he go back to being a grunt? He didn't want that. He'd gotten a taste of leadership, and he'd liked it. He was good at it.

One thing was certain. His dream of becoming a stay-at-home dad wasn't going to happen. Not because he couldn't force the issue and retire, but because with so much happening with Bishop, Searcy, the motleys, and their new alliance with the lycans, the race needed him to stay and fight. And, really, would he be able to chillax at home with his feet propped up on the ottoman and a beer in his hand when he knew the enemy was closing in, and when an assassin was hunting down his family line? Hell, no. He'd be on high alert twenty-four seven. His home would become a fort, and he would guard the doors and windows day and night, ready for an invasion. Which would drive Sam bonkers. She would end up *begging* him to return to AKM.

Bain leaned back into the corner of the couch, eyeing Micah as he spread his arms over the back of the cushions. "I have other plans for you, Micah."

This sounded juicy. "What other plans?"

"We'll get to that. Just know that I carefully vetted Argon, as well as Rysk and Sonia, before meeting with him. Not only did Tristan go through their minds and confirm everything Argon said as true, but I also had their blood tested. Both Argon's and Rysk's. Rysk is who he says he is. He's our ancestor. Half his genes matched my line, and half matched Argon's."

That settled that. You couldn't argue with a DNA test.

"It was Argon and Rysk who saved your father," Bain added.

"Yes, he told me that they watched over him."

"No, I mean, on the day your mother died. Argon and Rysk were the ones to find your father and keep him alive. From what they told me, Drake was in bad shape. He'd lost a lot of blood, as well as the will to live. Rysk forced your father to drink from him. They remained with him all day, keeping him from walking into the sun to end his life, and then fled with him to safety the following night. They almost lost him numerous times, because your dad wanted nothing but to die, but they eventually convinced him he had reason to live."

Micah sat in stunned silence. His father hadn't told him that part. That Argon and Rysk had been there.

"What were they doing in our village?"

"They tracked the dreck raiding party there, expecting the worst, that they'd lost both you and Drake. Thankfully, that didn't happen."

Micah thought about his mother and bowed his head. "A lot of other good people were lost that day, though."

"I know." Bain placed his hand on Micah's shoulder. "Your mother was one of them. I'm sorry."

Micah bit back his sadness before breathing in a full breath and straightening.

Bain released him. "I wasn't even aware Drake survived. See?" He pointed to a notation in the family tree, showing Drake as being deceased. "Looks like I'll have to update my records. I'll need to add Ronan, as well."

Micah reached over and tapped his own name. Sam's had already been added beside it. "You'll want to add two slots below my name, too."

"Oh?" Bain's brow rose in a severe, surprised arch. "Is Samantha . . .?"

For the first time since this conversation started, Micah

smiled as feelings of love and awe rose inside him. His chest and shoulders lifted proudly. "She's pregnant. Twins."

Bain chuckled and hoisted the book of records off his lap and plopped it onto Micah's as he rose from the couch. "You've always been an overachiever, Micah." He clapped him on the shoulder. "You've waited a long time to become a father, old friend."

No truer words had ever been spoken. "So long I was beginning to think it would never happen."

Bain grinned. "We must celebrate this good news." He crossed to his bar and opened one of the cabinets, then pulled out what looked like a very old bottle of brandy. "When did you find out?"

"Actually, I just found out a few hours ago."

Bain poured brandy into two snifters. He returned to the couch and handed one to Micah, lifting his in a toast. "To strong bloodlines and continuing the Black name. Congratulations, *cousin*."

Micah clinked his glass to Bain's then drank.

As Micah lowered his glass, his gaze fell back to his family tree. He browsed through the myriad of names as Bain took his seat beside him once more.

"We're family, Micah," Bain said. "And while the knowledge of our family connection was a coveted secret meant to protect you, it's time for the truth to come out so you can take your rightful place among our race."

His rightful place? There was that term again. A sinking feeling swallowed up his insides and plummeted toward his feet. He couldn't do the royal thing. He wouldn't. That was Bain's realm. Micah's was elsewhere.

"What place is that?" He wasn't sure he was ready for the answer. Then again, would he ever be ready? Might as well keep ripping off Band-Aids until he had no skin left.

Bain raised his hand. "We'll get to that. We're not quite finished here, yet."

Micah's gaze scanned the cursive swirls that filled the page. "You mean there's more?" He couldn't imagine any more family secrets existed after all he'd already been told.

Bain nodded toward the book. "Take another look."

Frowning, Micah ran his gaze over the names. What was it Bain wanted him to see? He ran through the names of his line twice, finding nothing extraordinary.

"I don't understand. I'm not finding —"

"Not at your line," Bain said. "Look at mine."

Micah turned his attention back to King Bain the First and followed the line down. Ryland, Bain the First, Bain the Second . . .

Wait, what?

He scanned back up. There was a branch off to the side of Bain the First's name.

His head shot up, eyes wide.

The dead calm of Bain's demeanor slammed into Micah like a sword slicing through bone.

"Is this right?"

Bain tilted his head, one brow arching. "Recorded by my own hand from that of my father's."

He glanced back down at the book and blinked in disbelief at Cordray's name beside Bain's. But her name lay under the name of a female who hadn't been Bain the First's queen.

"Your father had an affair?" Micah refused to believe it.

How was this even possible? Bain the First had sired young with two females? Had both been mates? Or, like him, had Bain the First been able to father a child without experiencing a calling? If so, which offspring was from his true mate, and which was a miracle?

"He never mated my mother," Bain said quietly, answering Micah's unasked question. "He mated Cordray's mother. She was a human. My mother was of an arranged pairing meant to give my father a queen, but his true mate gave him a daughter. Cordray."

It all made sense. How Cordray could speak to Bain so casually. How she openly disagreed with him. How she called him Bain in public when no one else could.

Family.

If Cordray was Bain's half sister, that meant she was Micah's . . .

This had to be some kind of sick joke. Medusa? Satan's mistress? She was part of the family, too? He didn't want to believe it, but there it was, scrawled in elegant black ink, her name in the family tree, right next to Bain's.

His father coming back from the dead he could take. Finding out that Ronan was his half brother? Yeah, he could handle that, too. He could even accept that he had dreck blood in him, because he knew in his heart that was how he'd been able to sire the young growing inside Sam's belly. And finding out he was of royal blood, both dreck *and* vampire? He had already begun to assimilate that knowledge, as well. After all, you didn't live the life Micah had lived without learning to adapt to shocking news quickly. But *Cousin Cordray?* He just couldn't bring himself to embrace that idea.

"Kind of makes you feel all warm and fuzzy inside, doesn't it?"

Micah's gaze swung around to find Cordray leaning against the doorframe, arms crossed, her dark-red lips knotted in a shit-eating smirk.

"Honestly, it makes me want to vomit."

"And ruin this glorious antique Aubusson rug?" She waved her arm in a dramatic arc toward the huge rectangular layer of carpet on the floor. "And I was so hoping you'd name your firstborn after me."

"Don't count on it."

"I heard Skeletor ended up being your brother." She pushed away from the door and sauntered into the room. "And here I thought you and *I* had problems."

"We do have problems. And from the looks of things here" — Micah gestured toward the book — "Skeletor is part of *your* family, too."

"Yeah, yeah." She approached Bain's desk. "I was almost pissed about that. Then I considered how entertaining it will be to watch you deal with him, and it filled my little black heart with joy."

"I bet it did."

"Besides, he's directly related to you. I barely share genes with him. *And* you."

"Lucky me."

Bain finally stepped in. "Knock it off, you two." He faced Micah. "Cordray *is* my half sister, Micah," Bain said, rising from his seat. "*And* your cousin, so try to get along." He glanced between them. "I know the two of you have a history, but her heart is pure."

Micah snorted. "Yeah, as pure as arsenic."

"Aw, you do care." Cordray plopped her ass on the edge of Bain's desk, swinging one long, latex-clad leg over the other.

Bain shook his head in exasperation, approaching Cordray. "What have you got for me?"

She pulled what looked like a microSD card from a pocket in

her leather jacket, which had a huge embroidered sugar skull on the back. "This is it."

Bain took the card. "I'm actually surprised to see you here."

"Why?" She swung her leg forward and back, making the latex crackle and creak as it rubbed together.

"Shouldn't you be with Trace? I assume he'll be entering his calling soon, and you don't want to be far when he does. He might destroy the city to get to you."

"I'm on my way to him now, but I figured I had time to drop this off first."

Micah pointed to the small card. "What is that?"

"A report from Sonia."

Micah glanced up. "You know about her?"

"I just learned who she is yesterday."

Bain turned the small disk over in his large fingers. "Did she tell you if she found something?"

"Based on what she said when she gave me the card, I'd say she found the mother lode."

"Why? What did she say?" Bain asked.

"She said, and I'm paraphrasing, of course, 'There's enough evidence here that not even God could talk his way out of being guilty.' I have a feeling she's been very thorough."

"Great. I'll start going through the files as soon as I'm done here." He set the SD card next to his blotter.

Cordray hopped off the desk then slithered up beside Micah and sat down next to him, peeking over his shoulder at the family tree. "I'll admit, I was as revolted as you are when Bain told me you and I were cousins."

Micah gave her the side-eye. "Doubtful."

She pretended she hadn't heard him. "I was like, 'No. Micah's a major ass. I could never be related to such a wanker.'" She smirked.

"So, you didn't know?" Part of him had considered that she'd known the truth all this time and had hidden it from him.

"Nope. Not until yesterday." She gave a subtle shake of her head and sighed as she sat back and crossed her legs, making all that latex crackle again. She casually stretched her arm over the back of the couch behind him. "Honestly, I'm still trying to get used to the idea, but I've realized it could be a lot worse. At least my line doesn't contain dreck blood."

"Cordray . . ." Bain's tone held an edge of warning.

She smiled sweetly. Too sweetly. "I'm only kidding. Micah knows I'm only teasing him, don't you, cousin?"

Micah glared at her. "Please tell me I'm not going to have to put up with you at family dinners from now on."

She issued an amused snort. "Oh, come on, where's your sense of humor. After all, we're *distant* cousins. As in *way* distant. So distant that—by human definitions—we could legally get married."

The thought made him want to gag. "If that's supposed to make me feel better, we need to work on your bedside manner."

She shrugged flippantly. "Just sayin'."

"Don't you have a new mate you should be fucking?" How did Trace even put up with her?

She pushed herself off the couch. "As a matter of fact, I do. Bain." She nodded in farewell as she swept past him. When she reached the door, she stopped and looked over her shoulder at Micah. "See you soon, *cousin*." She laughed then breezed out the door.

When she was gone, Micah met Bain's gaze with enough irritation to cause a rash. "I may have to kill your sister."

Bain grinned. "I often think the same thing."

"I'm being serious."

Cordray was enjoying the newfound familial link between them a little too much.

Bain waved his hand dismissively in Cordray's direction. "Give her time. You'll see she's a solid ally. She's my most trusted advisor for a reason. No bullshit. No games—at least when it comes to official business. She might ruffle feathers, but she shoots straight." He harrumphed. "And she is Trace's mate, so you're going to have to get used to her sooner or later."

"I'd prefer never." He closed the book and stood, extending it toward Bain. "Is there anything else in here I need to know?"

"No."

"Then get it away from me. It's done enough damage for one night." As Bain took the book from him, he snagged his brandy snifter from the table and paced to the window. God, it felt good to get that book out of his hands.

Bain chuckled then quickly sobered as he set the book back on its pedestal. The ensuing silence felt like pending doom.

"We have one more thing to discuss." Bain placed a Plexiglas cover over the book and locked it.

"Just one. Are you sure?" Could the avalanche of shit that had been dumped on him tonight finally be coming to an end?

"Yes, just one, and then you can leave."

Micah checked the time. Dawn would be upon them soon, and he wanted to return home to Sam. Especially now, when it seemed his decision to quit his job as an enforcer wasn't going to be as easy as he thought.

Bain made his way behind his desk and pushed back his throne-like chair. Before he sat, he gestured toward the wing chairs on the opposite side. "Have a seat, Micah."

"I think I'd rather stand." Sitting felt too official. Too much like Jesus being led to the cross so his hands and feet could be nailed down.

Micah didn't do being nailed down. Or crosses. Or any of that sacrificial shit.

Bain didn't respond for a moment then offered a pinched smile. "Very well." He lowered himself into his massive leather chair with all the dignity expected of a king, which made Micah feel even more like a lamb led to slaughter.

The role you were meant to fill.

The words lilted through his mind again. The words Bain had said to him weeks ago. Words that had haunted Micah ever since. Now, as Bain's austere gaze fell upon him, he could almost hear him saying those same words now.

I have other plans for you, Micah. Wasn't that what Bain had told him a few minutes ago?

Bain laced his fingers together and rested his hands on his desk's polished surface. "Now that you know your bloodline extends all the way back to King Cato, we need to discuss your future, and I'm not going to pull any punches." He squared Micah in his sights. "I want you to be crown regent."

The snifter nearly slipped from Micah's hand. Okay, so maybe he should have taken that seat Bain had offered.

He took a hasty drink, spilling some of the brandy down his chin. He quickly lowered the glass and wiped his mouth. A chill rippled down his back. "Crown regent? As in . . ."

"As in, I want you to rule in my place if anything should ever happen to me. Your line hails from King Cato's eldest son. Rysk was older than my forefather, Ryland. By rights, your line should have sat on the throne for the past four thousand years, not mine. Naming you my regent is perfectly acceptable."

"But . . ." He eyed the chair, which was looking more and more inviting by the second. "What about Colin. Your son should be the one—"

"He's not old enough." Bain rocked his head back and forth. "Let me clarify. He's not *experienced* enough. I plan to correct that with your help, but he isn't ready to rule a kingdom."

"Then Miriam. What about her?" His ass finally found its way to the chair, seemingly of its own free will.

"She's able," Bain said thoughtfully, "and one day she'll make a fine queen if it comes to that, but she's still recovering from her addiction and not yet mature enough to take the throne. Remember, Micah, she and I only just began to mend fences with each other. It will take some time for us to be able to work together so that I can show her what it means to be sovereign over our people and teach her everything she needs to know. But all that's academic. She's about to start a family. She has no interest in ruling."

Micah wanted to tell Bain he had no interest in ruling, either, but he didn't think that would hold the same sway as Miriam's lack of interest.

Micah's gaze dropped to his lap. Surely someone else was more suited to be regent than he was. "What about Rysk?"

Bain shook his head. "He's half dreck. Naming him crown regent under the current political climate would create chaos and potentially lead to civil war. The vampire race needs to be strong now, not divided under a king many of our people wouldn't trust."

"Then my father. He's higher in the royal line than I am."

"He's not up to the task, still lost to suffering. You know that. No offense, and I commend him for the Herculean effort it must have taken for him to stay alive in the face of such tremendous loss, but how is he supposed to lead a race when he struggles just to get through each day?"

Micah searched his mind. "Cordray. What about her. She's your sister. She—"

"No." Bain's firm tone broached no argument. "No one can know she and I are related, Micah, or it will cast doubt over my entire reign."

"But you had nothing to do with her becoming your sister?"

"It won't matter. The truth will cast a shadow over my father's reign, which will in turn cast doubt over me and weaken our race."

"Then my uncle Rory. Surely, he—"

"No."

"Why not?"

"Because the people wouldn't look favorably on his new profession."

"Which is . . .?"

Bain offered him a tight smile. "He cooks the books for crime syndicates and plays mercenary in his spare time. He's become a bit of an opportunist to maintain his cover and expend his aggression and frustration over losing a child." He rocked back in his chair and steepled his fingers under his chin.

"He's mated?"

Bain shook his head. "No."

Aahhh, so this was another case of the Black line's handy-dandy dreck genes producing offspring without a calling.

"Is he still with the female who gave him a child?"

"No. She was human, and since she wasn't his mate, he wasn't allowed to change her." Bain gave him a hard look that spoke volumes about how Uncle Rory felt toward Bain for not allowing him to make the human female his davala.

"He's not exactly happy with you, is he?" Micah asked.

"I'd say that's an understatement." Bain's mouth twisted into a frustrated smirk. "I imagine he wouldn't mind adding me as his latest victim on his hit list."

"I see."

Bain rocked forward again. "Yeah, well, the point is, once word got out about his profession—and it *would* get out—the people would never accept him as their ruler."

"Yeah, I get that." Way to go, Uncle Rory. A mercenary. He was really putting those Black family skills to good use. It was just unfortunate that his family had endured so much suffering. Him, his dad, Ronan, and now Uncle Rory. They were a genetic saga of tragedy.

"Besides," Bain said, "no one knows Rory. He's pretty far off the radar. You, on the other hand, have been in my employ your whole life. The people know you. They respect—and *fear*—you. And never underestimate the power of fear. It can do wonders to keep otherwise rebellious civilians in line."

Bain pulled in a cumbersome breath then blew it out on a heavy sigh. "As much as I don't want to put this on your shoulders, Micah, it's you or no one. Our people need a regent, especially now, with all that's going on with our enemies. And you are more than up to the task.

"Since you mated Sam, you've become even stronger than you were in your youth. And since you took over for Tristan, you've exceeded all my expectations for the type of leader you will become. Micah, you truly are cut of the same cloth as our forefathers . . . of the kings who came before us. With you as regent, I have no doubt our race would be in good hands should it come to you stepping into my shoes.

"You're able to make sound decisions on the fly, and you aren't influenced by greed or lobbyists who have their own political interests in mind. You can say no without a shred of guilt and see through false veils meant to make you question your decisions. With you, there are no questions. You do what needs to be done for the greater good of the people, and you don't let anything interfere with that. You're levelheaded, intelligent, ruthless when you need to be, compassionate when warranted, and judicious. Those are the qualities needed of a king."

King.

The word fell like a wrecking ball being released from its chain. Boom! The weight of it shook the room, leaving an echoing silence in its wake.

"But I have dreck blood in me."

"Only a negligible amount. Not enough for it to be obvious. And no one outside you, me, Cordray, your father, your uncle, Rysk, and Argon know the truth. We'll bring Ronan into the fold once he's recovered from tonight's attack."

Micah wasn't so sure informing Ronan of their dreck lineage was a good idea. Since Ronan didn't feel any warm fuzzies for Micah, he might accidentally-on-purpose leak the don't-ask-don't-tell about dreck blood in their family tree, which would halt any ideas of Micah filling in as king.

But the alternative of leaving Ronan in the dark wasn't acceptable, either. He'd suffered enough. Ro needed to know who he was and where he came from. Micah just had to have faith Ronan would do the right thing if and when push came to shove.

"What about Sam?" he asked. "I can't hide this from her."

"She should know the truth, too, Micah. She's your mate, and I don't expect you to hide something this significant from her."

An overwhelming sense of responsibility fell over Micah. What Bain was asking of him would alter his entire life. If he chose to accept the appointment of crown regent, he would be thrown under a spotlight. He would have to become more engaged with Bain and his politics. Forget taking a regular job. He would become more embroiled in the affairs of vampires and their protection than he'd ever been.

"Would I be expected to change residences?" He imagined a gated home with greater security and guards posted at the exits, as well as patrolling the grounds.

"I would prefer it. You would be safer, as well as closer." A contemplative look crossed Bain's face. "And given the other aspect of this role I'd like to discuss with you, I think you'll find a new residence could be more suitable." He said it as if he already had a property in mind.

"What other aspect?" He should have known "one more thing" wouldn't be as simple as that.

Bain pushed forward in his chair, growing even more serious, as well as more passionate. "I want you to head a new team at AKM."

Micah's mouth fell open. Naming him crown regent he could understand. He possessed royal blood. But leading a new team of enforcers? Wouldn't that just be more of the same. Same old rules. Same hands being tied. Micah didn't know if he had it in him, especially when he'd decided to quit for the very reasons he was now concerned about.

"Actually, I should clarify" — Bain pushed out of his chair — "this team would *not* be part of AKM." He came around to the front of his desk and leaned against the edge where Cordray had sat a few minutes ago.

Now Micah was intrigued. "Not part of AKM?"

"No. The team I want you to lead would be a highly specialized black ops team."

"Black ops? You mean—"

"One that *doesn't* follow the rules." Bain's weighty gaze held his as if silently asking if Micah understood what he meant by not following the rules. "Among other things."

"Are you saying you want this team to operate *outside* the

terms of the truce?"

Bain gave him a small half smile of affirmation. "I know Royce isn't lifting a finger to help fight the cobalt issue because he secretly has a hand in it. The way I see it, if he's going to subvert the terms of peace between our two races, the best countermeasure is for me to do the same."

This was what Micah wanted. The freedom to do whatever it took to bring down the forces working to destroy their people. No rules binding his hands. Nothing to prevent him from enacting his own brand of justice against repeat offenders. Drecks who had been arrested over and over only to be back out on the street in weeks, dealing their blue poison to vampires who would overdose and lose their lives to an addiction manufactured by Royce and Bishop in an effort to chip away the vampire race's power.

The possibilities and opportunities to actually make a difference were limitless, and Micah couldn't deny his excitement.

In a blink, Bain's offer had changed his entire outlook.

"How far outside the terms of the truce would I be allowed to act?" he asked.

"As far as is necessary."

"And you would turn a blind eye?"

Bain settled his joined hands in his lap and tilted his head in a way that made Micah think he was more of a conspiring partner, not the king. "You'll have complete autonomy over the team and its activities. All I ask is that you report directly to me and keep me informed of the team's operations so I'm not caught off guard when Royce comes at me with accusations and complaints of bloodshed against his people."

"And when he does . . .?"

A sickly-sweet smile spread over Bain's mouth. "I'll inform him I have no knowledge of any such attacks and will promise to put my best men into investigating his claims, just as he's done to me."

"You would lie?"

"In a heartbeat."

Micah could get used to this new side of King Bain. "And by best men, I assume you're referring to — "

"You and this new team you will create."

Micah was liking this idea more and more. "In other words, you won't look into his claims at all."

"Exactly." Bain crossed one ankle over the other and gripped the edge of his desk on either side of his hips. "Micah, I want a team that can strike at the heart of both Searcy's and Royce's undertakings. If they're building a genetically modified werewolf army, I want to counterstrike against them. Hard." He lifted one hand, curling it into a fist as determination burned in his eyes. "I want to hit the heart of those bastards without them seeing it coming. Do you think you can do that?"

Could he do that? That was like asking if a bear could bite off the head of a salmon in one chomp.

"I have no doubt."

Bain nodded approvingly. "You'll be free to use whatever means necessary, but I want no ties back to me."

"How would you suggest I do that?" The simple fact he was even asking the question was enough to alert Micah that his acceptance of this new opportunity was a foregone conclusion. He hadn't even agreed to take the job, and yet he had.

Bain eyed him the way a hunter eyes a deer when it enters a clearing. "You'll come up with something. You always do." He pushed off his desk and rounded it, returning to his chair. The leather wheezed as he dropped his weight into it. "And I want you to put tabs on my liaisons. Particularly Ulrich Fenton and Gregos Savakis."

"Ari's father?"

"Yes."

"Why?"

Bain's jaw worked like he was clenching and unclenching it. "Call it a hunch, but they're up to something. I need to know what."

"Do you think they're conspiring against you?"

Bain's eyes met his, and Micah could see the answer in his gaze before Bain said, "Yes."

Whoa. Arion's father was under suspicion for treason. That was some heavy shit.

"Do you think Arion's involved?" Highly unlikely, but the question warranted asking.

Bain shook his head decisively. "No. Gregos disowned Ari. He wouldn't have done that if Ari were involved." He tipped his head contemplatively as one corner of his mouth turned up. "Maybe Ari wouldn't mind giving *us* a hand."

That wasn't a bad idea. "I'll look into it."

Silence fell over them as Micah mulled over all that Bain had asked of him. Crown regent? Leader of a new black ops team? Spy? These were big decisions. Ones he didn't want to make until he'd talked to Sam. She needed to have a voice in this, especially now that she was pregnant and he'd told her he wanted to quit his job to be a full-time family guy.

But that had been before Bain had offered him the greatest gift on earth. The ability to do his job without having to worry about the rules. Not that Micah would abuse that power, but it would be nice to kick off the shackles and face the enemy on an even playing field for once. He felt like he'd been doing his job with one hand tied behind his back and one leg in a brace for decades.

"Would you build the team or would I?" Micah asked.

"You will, but I would like some input."

In other words, Bain wanted Cordray on the team. Fine. She had talents he could use, just as long as she understood who was in charge.

"I'm assuming you'll bankroll anything I need to get the team operational?"

"Yes."

"Complete autonomy?"

Bain issued him a slow, sincere nod. "One hundred percent. I will not interfere beyond providing input I think could help."

"And the lycans?"

"What about them?"

"Would my team be expected to work with them?"

Bain took a moment to consider his answer. "Yes. With the new information we were given tonight, I think your team would make the perfect point of contact for them. It might even be wise to consider adding a lycan or two to the team, as long as Memnon approves."

Micah curled his lip.

Bain held up his hand, nodding patiently. "I know, Micah. You don't like them. But I can tell you respect what they did tonight . . . saving your brother's life. Focus on that. They're our allies now, and they did us a solid. If we've added mutant werewolves to our list of enemies, having a couple of lycans around could be beneficial, especially for training purposes. I just want you to consider it."

Bain made good points. He would take that into consideration when — *if* — he decided to accept Bain's offer. It was pretty much a foregone conclusion he would, but Sam needed to give her stamp of approval first.

"When do you need an answer?" he asked.

"When can you give me one?"

Once he got home, he would pull Sam aside. He didn't think it would take long to get her on board. One thing he could always count on from her was support.

"Tomorrow night?"

"I'll look forward to hearing from you then." Bain grabbed a notecard bearing the royal seal and quickly jotted down a pair of phone numbers. "This is my direct line. Only my liaisons use this, but now you can, too." He pointed to his other number. "This is my residence. No one but my family and closest friends have this number."

Micah tucked the card into his back pocket. "You have friends?"

Bain gave him an eat-shit grin and stood. "A couple."

Micah joined him and followed him out.

When they reached the main entrance of the mansion, Bain held out his hand.

Micah clasped it with his own.

Then Bain pulled him into a one-armed hug, patted him on the back, gave one final squeeze, and released him. "Welcome to the family, Micah."

Family. The word held new meaning for him now.

He'd learned a lot tonight. Some of it troubled him, such as the knowledge that he possessed dreck blood and that ancestors he'd never known had been killed before he could even learn of their existence. Some of what he'd learned tonight even sickened him, such as learning Cordray was his — *ew!* — cousin. And some of it excited him. That's where the creation of the new black ops team came in.

It would take him a while to fully process his new reality, but two things were certain. He was no longer alone, and his life would never be the same.

CHAPTER 24

THE LAST THIRTY MINUTES BEFORE DAWN was Sam's favorite time of night. Well, morning. But it was still dark, so it felt like night.

She often took this time to meditate, read, or just enjoy a hot cup of tea on the patio while she listened to the heavy silence before the birds started singing for a new day.

That's where she was now, relaxing in her favorite cushioned lounger, a steaming mug of cocoa in her hand and a letter from AKM's medical department resting in her lap. After Panya woke up and returned to her bedroom about an hour ago, Sam had finally gotten around to opening the previous day's mail. But if she'd known this letter had been waiting for her, she would have opened it hours ago.

Lifting the letter, she smiled proudly as she read the introduction.

Congratulations! You've been accepted into AKM's Nursing Program.

Without telling Micah, she'd submitted her application on a whim about a month ago. As a former Army medic, she'd hoped they would see enough potential to give her a chance, but, honestly, she hadn't been confident. After all, she was a human. Well, not exactly a human, anymore, but she definitely wasn't a vampire. The job she'd applied for involved providing medical assistance to vampires. The biology was bound to be at least a little different.

Against all odds, she'd been contacted for a phone interview a couple of weeks ago. That had gone well enough that she'd been asked to interview with someone named Cora Snow. Dr. Cora Snow.

She had met the doctor in a small café downtown one night while Micah was working.

"So, you're Micah's mate?" Dr. Snow had said.

"Yes." Sam hadn't been sure if being Micah's mate was an asset or a detriment.

"Micah and I seem to be running into each other in the trauma ward a lot lately." The doctor let out a quiet laugh as she stirred creamer into her coffee, smiling fondly. "You know, he's really turned around in the last few months." Her indigo blue eyes pointedly met Sam's. "Since about the time he mated you."

In other words, the good doctor gave Sam credit for Micah's new state of mind and behavior.

"I hear he used to be a lot . . . *different*." That was putting it mildly. To hear Trace and the others — including Micah — talk about what he was like before she came along was like listening to tales of a completely different person. One hellbent on self-destruction and taking everyone around him down with him.

"He's better now, thanks to you." The doctor sipped her coffee.

"I'm still learning about the whole vampire mating thing, but I guess when a male takes a mate, it does something to him."

Dr. Snow laughed. "You can say that again. It does a whole *lot* of something, but sometimes I think mated male vampires are worse than human females when it comes to hormonal issues." She raised her hand. "No offense."

"None taken. As a former human, I know full well how bad hormonal peaks and valleys can be."

"Multiply that by a hundred, and you'll have a mated male vampire. They're such divas."

They had laughed about that, because Sam couldn't deny that Micah could be a handful when it came to going all me-Tarzan-you-Jane on her. And his calling. Just . . . she'd never experienced anything like that as a human. That shit was for real. So, yeah, she could believe human female hormones had nothing on the hormones of a mated male vampire.

After a couple more minutes of small talk, Dr. Snow had asked her a few questions about her experience and training and had seemed impressed, but Sam honestly hadn't thought she would make the cut.

She glanced down at the letter, which had been signed by Dr. Snow herself. Looked like she'd been wrong about not having a chance.

Now came the hard part. Telling Micah.

She knew she shouldn't have kept her application a secret from him. It's a miracle he never saw it in her thoughts, but she tried not to think about it around him. Not that she feared his reaction. This was just something she'd wanted to do on her own.

Sometimes, she missed certain aspects of her human life. She'd always been so self-sufficient. She adored her life with Micah, but there were times when she wanted to be more involved. More active. She'd always been a fighter, and sitting at home made her restless. She felt like she should be doing more. Making use of her medical background seemed like the perfect solution.

She just didn't know how Micah would take it, especially now that he no longer wanted to work at AKM.

"Hey."

Speak of the devil.

She set the letter back in her lap and held her hand out to her mate as he leaned out the sliding patio door. "Hey, baby. I was starting to worry you wouldn't make it home before dawn."

In the last few minutes, the eastern horizon had turned from black to dark blue, and a few birds had started to chirp and whistle their greeting to the coming day.

Micah took her hand, leaned in, and kissed her. His lips were tight, reserved. He was holding something back.

"What's wrong?"

"Nothing."

"Liar."

One corner of his mouth lifted, and then he glanced down at the letter. "What's that?"

She let go of him and dropped her hand onto the sheet of paper, fingers splayed to cover it. "Nothing."

A dark chuckle rumbled from deep inside his throat, and he gently pulled the paper out from under her hand. "Liar."

"Micah . . ." She reached for the letter, but he pulled it away.

"From AKM. The medical department." He gave her a knowing smirk, making her frown.

Maybe he had seen inside her thoughts, after all.

"You knew, didn't you?"

His gaze slid left to right as he read her acceptance letter. "Yes."

"Why didn't you say anything?"

"Because you didn't want me to."

"But . . . aren't you angry."

His strong brow bowed inward. "Angry? Why?"

"Because I did this without talking to you first. Without asking you."

"Shit, no, I'm not angry. I'm proud as hell." He set the letter on the patio table then crouched beside her and layered his palm over her stomach. "You don't have to get my permission to follow your heart."

She had a feeling she could expect his hand on her belly a lot over the next nine months. "You sure?" She placed her hand over his.

"Absolutely." He kissed her again. This time his lips softened, tasting her more deeply.

He motioned to join her on the lounge chair, and she shifted to the side to make room. His arm fell around her shoulders then folded her against him as he gazed up at the stars that were beginning to wink out one by one.

There was something different about him. Something calm yet tense. He reminded her of someone taking his last look around before being locked away for the rest of his life. It was like he wanted to remember everything just as it was in that moment. The stars, the sky, the trees, how a gentle breeze lifted the ends of his hair. Her. How she felt in his arms.

She could sense he had something to tell her, but she knew better than to ask. He would get to whatever it was in his own time.

Instead, she curled against him and laid her cheek on his chest. Together, they listened as more birds awoke and broke into morning song, ready to greet the sun. Within minutes, a few distant chirps turned into a symphony.

"This is nice," he murmured.

"Mm-hm." She closed her eyes and listened to the *thump-thump* of his heart. The beat was steady and calm, heavy in its strength. He was so much calmer than he'd been a few hours ago.

Sounds of life emerged from inside the house. Brenna and Mya were awake, preparing to get the older children off to school. In one week, that would change. School would let out for summer, which meant until the new dorms were built, the house would be a hive of children's activity seven days a week, from dawn to dusk.

Micah kissed the top of her head. "Let's go inside," he whispered. "I need to talk to you about something."

"I know you do."

"I know you know." He smiled at her as he helped her off the lounge chair and grabbed her letter off the table. "I can't hide anything from you."

"Does that bother you?"

He took her hand. "Nope."

"Why not?" She couldn't help teasing him just a little.

He stopped just outside the door and pulled her to him. "Because we're partners. You're my life. You're as much a part of me as my own flesh and blood. How can I keep secrets from something that's a part of me?"

She pulled the letter from his fingers. "But I kept a secret from you."

He grinned. "Trust me. You didn't."

She laughed softly. "Have I mentioned that I hate your mind-reading abilities."

"Once or twice." He reached for the door handle. "Now, come on, we have a lot to discuss."

This sounded serious. Given the grim set of his brow, she wasn't sure if she should be nervous, scared, or excited. A little of all three? With Micah, anything was possible.

She greeted Brenna and Mya and gave them a quick rundown about Panya's nightmare as Micah stole a few pieces of bacon and some toast off a platter.

The two females assured her everything was under control and wished her and Micah good night, and then Sam grabbed a handful of bacon and toast for herself and followed Micah downstairs. He was quiet. Too quiet.

Something else must have happened tonight. Something big. Bigger than finding out Ronan was his brother and his father was still alive.

Once in their bedroom, she stuffed the last bite of toast in her mouth and dusted bacon crumbs off her fingers then pulled open the dresser drawer that held the tank tops and boy shorts she used as pajamas while Micah stripped and made for the bathroom.

"Just let me take a quick shower. Then we'll talk."

"Okay."

Normally, he would ask her to join him, but she got the feeling he wanted the extra time to get his thoughts together before he told her whatever it was he needed to say. Besides, she'd already showered an hour ago, before she took her reprieve on the patio.

While she waited for Micah, she changed into a pair of red boy shorts and a pink tank top then rubbed lotion up and down her legs and arms. Then she climbed into bed and waited for Micah to join her.

She didn't have to wait long. Two minutes later, he shut off the shower. Less than a minute after that, he reentered the bedroom naked as the day he was born. God, could that man — *male* — rock a birthday suit. Just . . . damn!

But he wasn't oozing let's-fuck-like-rabbits-for-the-next-hour like he usually did. Tonight, he was all business. The grim set of his brow and the tension in his jaw made it clear he was worried about her reaction to what he was about to tell her.

Sam hugged her knees to her chest as he pulled on a pair of black flannel pants and a black T-shirt.

"The suspense is killing me," she said, trying to sound light-hearted amid all the strained silence shooting out of him.

"I'm sorry." He released a thick exhale and painted a stiff smile on his face as he shut off the light on the dresser. The only light remaining came from the small lamp on her nightstand. "It's just been a long fucking night." He brushed his palms down his face. "A lot of shit got thrown at me after I left you at the apartment."

"I'm starting to get that impression."

He approached the foot of the bed, climbed over the low footboard, and crawled up the mattress. He pushed her knees apart, slid his torso between them as she settled back against a mound of pillows, wrapped his arms around her, and laid his head on her stomach. "But now I'm here. I'm with you" — he lifted his head, pushed up her tank top to expose her belly, and planted a tender kiss just below her navel — "and with my babies." He kissed her stomach again, right next to the scar left over from her human life, a reminder of the hell she'd lived through to get here. "Can you hear me in there?" His whiskers brushed her skin.

She combed back his hair with her fingers, smiling at the way he stared at her stomach as if he could see the twin babies growing inside her.

What could she expect from carrying a vampire's young? Was it harder than carrying a human baby? Would the morning sickness be more ruthless? She'd heard Micah talk about how sick Tristan's mate, Josie, got during the first trimester of her pregnancy. Tristan had even taken a leave of absence from AKM to tend to her, it was so bad. Could Sam expect the same?

"God, I can't wait to meet you." He kissed her tummy again then placed his palm over her belly and fell still.

She knew he could feel them through their energy. No doubt, he was monitoring them to make sure there was nothing wrong.

"Can you tell what sex they are?" she asked, holding still.

He moved his hand a little to the right then closed his eyes. When he opened them, he smiled. "Yes."

"And?"

"Are you sure you want to know? You don't want to be surprised?"

"I want to know." Were they having two girls? Two boys?

"One's a boy and one's a girl."

Even better. "Really?"

"Yes."

"How can you tell?"

"A boy's energy resonates at a lower frequency than a girl's. I feel both."

"How sure are you?"

"Ninety-nine point nine percent."

Okay, so they were definitely having a boy and a girl.

"Can you tell how long I've been pregnant?"

He pressed his hand against her belly again and closed his eyes. "Maybe three weeks."

Not even a month. She tried to think back and come up with when she conceived, but it was impossible. She and Micah had a lot of sex. Almost every day. He was damn near insatiable. Then again, so was she.

His eyes slowly opened before he nestled against her again, wrapping his arms around her and pressing his cheek to her stomach. "I love you. I love you so damn much."

"I love you, too." She played her fingers through his hair, letting her nails gently scratch his scalp.

Perfect moments like this—sublime, peaceful, and time-stopping calm—were rare with Micah. There always seemed to be something happening. Some crisis that needed his attention. Fires that destroyed dormitories, for example, thrusting them into emergency mode to ensure everyone was safe and had a roof over their heads. She loved the excitement and diversity, but she loved this side of her mate even more. The side he didn't get to show her nearly enough, but which she knew existed even when he was kicking ass and taking names.

She allowed the transcendent moment to go on for a couple more minutes then said, "So, what is it you need to talk to me about, baby?"

After all, perfect flashes in time aren't meant to last. They're meant to grant the recipient a greater appreciation for the good times when they happen.

He sighed, kissed her belly one last time, and pushed himself away from her body. "I liked what you thought just now. About perfect moments."

She was too at peace to be angry at him for peeking inside her mind again. "You did, huh?"

He settled beside her, reclining against a mountain of pillows, and wrapped his hand around hers. "We don't get these moments nearly often enough."

"No, we don't." Why did she feel like this had something to do with what he wanted to talk to her about?

He inhaled deeply and released his breath in a long, heavy exhale as he squeezed her hand. "You know what I told you earlier? About quitting my job?"

She bit her bottom lip. She hadn't yet decided how she felt about that. On one hand, she liked the idea of him being around more. On the other, she worried he would just get in her way out of boredom. And now that she was going to be working at AKM as a nurse, him quitting his job wasn't really going to give them more time together, anyway.

"What about it?"

He lifted her hand onto his lap and encased it with both of his. "There's been a change in plans."

CHAPTER 25

"You're what?" One second, Sam was reclining against the pillows beside him. The next, she was sitting on her knees, facing him. She'd moved so fast, if Micah had blinked, he would have missed it.

"I'm King Bain's cousin."

Her eyes popped wide, those dainty brows encroaching on her hairline. "His *cousin*?"

He'd known this would blow Sam's mind. "Yep."

"What are you saying? That you're royalty?" Her green eyes were wide and full of questions as she stared at him like he'd just told her he'd grown a sixth toe on each foot.

He had to admit, the whole royalty thing was still a shock to him, too.

"That's what I'm saying, yes. I'm of royal blood." Was that ever weird to say out loud. "My bloodline extends all the way up to the first king of our race, King Cato. I'm descended from one of his sons, a male named Rysk. King Bain is descended from Rysk's brother, Ryland. That makes us cousins."

"Cousins." Sam relaxed on her haunches and dropped her dismayed gaze to the bed. "Holy shit." The words came out as a whisper.

"There's more."

"More?"

Hadn't he spent the entire night thinking the same thing?

"Hard to believe, I know, but yes."

Her eyes locked onto his, but it was as if she were only half aware. As if her brain had locked onto *I'm royalty* and couldn't quite shift to the next gear.

"I need you to focus, baby." He took her hands and shook her arms.

She gave him an agitated nod. "I'm focused. I promise. I'm just . . . okay, wow. Royalty. Yeah. But really, I'm focused."

He went on to explain about Rysk the Second and Argon. How he was related to them, as well, and that Argon was the rightful leader of the drecks, which meant Micah carried not just royal vampire blood, but also royal dreck blood. How Bain wanted him to be crown regent. No detail was spared.

He revealed all that he'd learned about his father's "death." About why his father had been sequestered all this time. About how his ancestors were being systematically murdered in an effort to kill the line that linked him back to both sides of the war.

The more Micah divulged, the more stunned Sam became.

An hour later, he quieted. He held both her hands in his, and from the thoughts coursing through her mind, she was processing everything he'd told her faster than he had, quickly coming to terms with it.

"You okay?" he asked.

She blinked and nodded then shifted position, crossing her legs and settling in beside him, facing him. "I'm starting to understand why you came home in such a stupor."

"Like I said, I got hit with a lot of shit tonight."

"You can say that again." She shook her head and breathed out. "Is there anything else?"

"Just one more thing."

"Ah, Jesus. You saved the best for last, didn't you?"

He shrugged. "It all depends on how you look at it."

"Well, hit me. I'm not going to let this conversation end until I've heard everything."

That's what he liked about Sam. She was a rip-the-Band-Aid-off kind of person, too.

"King Bain wants me to head up a covert black ops team."

Her slender eyebrows popped high into her forehead. "Black ops?"

He nodded, careful not to read too much into the surprised worry rocketing through her thoughts.

"What exactly does that mean? What would you be doing?"

He told her about Bain's plan.

"Sounds dangerous."

"No more dangerous than what I'm doing now. Only I won't be

hampered by stupid rules that actually put me in greater jeopardy than if I didn't have to follow them."

Sam scooted off the bed and began pacing. "What you're saying about hitting Searcy, Bishop, and Royce where it hurts . . .? Can't that be construed as an act of war?"

He hopped off the bed and secured her hands in his, stopping her worried movement. "War is already upon us, Sam."

"What do you mean?"

"Haven't you heard everything I just told you? The Dacians and the drecks have formed an alliance. They've built an army. They're intentionally weakening the vampire race, putting us in harm's way. They're already preparing for war. And there's only one reason for someone to prepare for a war during a time of peace. They plan on starting one."

Her shoulders fell as the air rushed out of her. "War? This is seriously coming to war?"

He stroked his thumbs over the backs of her hands. "It's been this way for hundreds of years. Thousands. Long periods of war have been broken by shorter periods of peace. This is the longest peacetime we've ever experienced, but whether we like it or not, war is coming."

"And this black ops team is meant to hasten that?"

"Not if I can help it." He let go of her hands and raked his fingers through his hair. "I'd like to think we might be able to hold it off, or at least buy us some time to prepare. By joining with the lycans and making some precision hits to cripple their operation, we could considerably push back their timetable. Maybe even put off an attack indefinitely. I don't know." It was his turn to pace. "I know it's risky, but it's no riskier than being an enforcer. And if I can put together the right team and find a way to hit the drecks where it hurts for maximum impact, our kids might have a chance to grow up in a world where they don't have to think about this godforsaken war."

Sam grabbed his arm and pulled him around to face her. She searched his face, her eyes full of respect and admiration. And love. There was most definitely love in her eyes. Her hands wrapped around his reassuringly. And in the same way he'd calmed her only moments ago, she calmed him.

"Do you want to do this?" she asked.

"It's a lot of responsibility." The fate of the entire race could depend on how well he built and ran his team.

She sighed and squeezed his hands, giving him a pointedly impatient grin. "Do you want this?" she asked again, emphasizing each word for maximum impact.

He stared into her eyes, knowing whatever answer he gave, she would support it. That was his Sam. Stalwart. A rock. Unshakeable and determined, even for him.

"Do you?" she asked again, speaking more quietly and giving him a little nod.

He shifted his hold on her hands and pulled her closer. "Yes. I do."

"Then do it." Her eyes sparkled.

"But you're worried for my safety."

"Baby, I'm always worried for your safety."

"Yeah, but you're more worried than usual."

"That's only because I don't know what to expect, yet." She let out an abrupt breath. "And I think part of my concern is that I don't want our kids to have to live in a world torn by war."

"War is inevitable."

"It doesn't have to be."

He let go of her hands and pulled her into his arms. "I know, and maybe now we can create permanent peace."

"Do you really think that's possible?"

He released her and shrugged. "I don't know. Maybe. Everything just feels different this time. With the lycans joining us. With Argon revealing himself after all this time." He pulled her back to the bed and sat down on the edge. "It feels like everything's coming full circle."

"Maybe it is."

He looked at her. She was smiling at him in the way that always made him feel like the luckiest male in the world.

"War or no war," she said, "this is what you've been wanting, right? A way to do your job without all the rules getting in the way?"

She'd had to listen to him bitch about being hog-tied by the terms of the truce ever since he'd mated her. Of course she knew what running his own team meant. To be granted free rein over how ops ran. Never having to answer to anyone but himself. He was a kid set loose inside a toy store with a limitless credit card. He could have anything he wanted.

"Yes."

Sam sat back down on the bed. "So, you're going to accept?"

He joined her. "I wanted us to decide together."

Sam inched closer and reverently wrapped her hand around his, letting her fingers slide firmly between his, instilling him with the feeling that she was handing the power completely over to him. "I think you should do it."

"Even though I told you earlier I was going to quit?"

Her head tilted to one side. "I didn't actually believe you'd quit, Micah. You need the action too much."

He turned to face her, pulling his legs up onto the bed. "If I take this on, it could mean longer hours—"

"Not necessarily." She mimicked his body language, turning to face him, too. "You'll be in charge. And black ops missions can usually be pulled off in less time than a full shift walking the streets, right? I mean, if they're anything like human military ops, you'll have weeks of planning and recon followed by a few hours of execution."

This was another thing he liked about Sam. With her military background, she could speak his language.

"Okay, but my job *will* be more dangerous. You were right about that."

"It was dangerous before. Now you'll be able to minimize the risk by planning for every contingency *outside* the normal rules of engagement you've had to follow as an enforcer. You'll have more options to protect yourself."

"But—"

"Micah, just do it. Quit trying to talk yourself out of it when I know the idea of running your own black ops team has got to curl your toes."

"What about you and the babies?"

"What about us?"

"You're my responsibility. It's my duty to look after you."

She sighed and nodded patiently. "I know, I know." Her voice took on a caveman-like quality. "You, big bad male. Me, weak female. You take care of me."

"I'm not that bad."

The look she gave him could have frozen water. "Really?"

He rolled his eyes at the image of him she'd painted as some kind of modern-day Tarzan. "I don't think of you as weak."

"Oh, I know, but sometimes I think I need to remind you that I did manage to take care of myself for almost thirty years before I met you."

"Technically, your parents took care of you until you were eighteen."

"Well, technically, I took care of myself. No disrespect to my parents, because they were great parents, but I was always independent, taking no shit from anyone."

Images of a young and feisty Sam danced provocatively through his mind.

He shifted closer, his knees touching hers. "That was then, this is now. And as a mated male vampire, I'm supposed to protect my mate and my children."

She patted her stomach. "We'll be fine." She dropped her hands to his knees and rubbed up and down his thighs encouragingly. "Accept the job, baby. You know you want to, and, honestly, you were made for it. It's the perfect job for you."

Despite the worry still haunting her mind, Sam was giving him the green light. She wasn't going to let her fears rob him of this opportunity. If he wanted to accept Bain's offer, she wasn't going to put up any roadblocks to stop him.

"What if we have to move?" he asked, recalling what Bain had said about relocating.

"Fine."

"What if I told you a security detail would be assigned to you at all times?"

She huffed as if she hadn't thought of that, but then said, "I'll get used to it."

"And what if something happens to Bain and I have to fill the role of king?"

A coquettish, lopsided grin curled her lips. She leaned toward him until her face was only a few inches from his. "Would you make me kneel before you?"

Desire began a slow churn in his groin. "Only if you wanted to."

She bit her bottom lip and trailed one finger down the center of chest. "King Micah. I like how that sounds."

"Don't let it go to your head," he teased, enjoying her seduction. "I'm just the understudy. I'm not the king and may never be. In fact, I hope it never comes to that."

Her hand trailed lower, stoking embers into flames beneath his skin, until she reached the waist of his pants. Her palm flattened against his cock and firmly rubbed down and back up before her fingers curled loosely around his shaft through the flannel.

Blood doubled its efforts, racing to his growing erection like firemen rushing to a burning building.

"You'll always be *my* king."

"Is that so?"

"Yes." She crawled closer and brushed her lips over his, reinforcing the friction down below.

Her soft lips left simmering kisses down the side of his neck then back up to his ear, where her tongue flicked his earlobe right before she caught it with her teeth.

"You're taking all this better than I thought you would." He caressed the backs of her thighs as she climbed onto his lap.

She released his ear and rose up over him, hands on his shoulders, and circled her hips, making him grow even harder. "Maybe I'm channeling my fear into something more productive." She giggled and rotated her hips against him again. "And maybe power turns me on."

He grinned and shook his head, sinking down until he was flat on his back. "You're too humble."

She laughed and rocked her hips forward. A flash of heat zinged down his back and burst inside his groin. His grip on her thighs tightened as he rolled his hips against her, increasing the contact.

Her laughter cut off abruptly, giving way to an aroused sigh as she dropped her hands to his chest and arched her back, rocking against him more forcefully.

No more talking. No more rehashing the night's events. Now was the time to love his female and feel her body give way to his. She was his foundation. No matter the challenges he faced outside these four walls, he could always come back to her and find his center.

Without her, he would be nothing. He wouldn't be where he was now. She was his power. She was the strength that made him the male he was. With her, nothing was out of reach. He could accept anything life threw at him as long as Sam was by his side.

She quickly stripped out of her shorts and tank top as he shoved off his pants, and then she sank down on him and paid him the kind of fealty any good king deserved from his queen.

CHAPTER 26

Soft skin. Ronan had never felt such soft skin. And he'd never felt silkier hair flowing between his fingers or looked into bluer, kinder eyes.

Where am I?

It didn't matter as long as she kept touching him and he could keep touching her.

Her.

He didn't even know her name, but he knew her face. He knew her heart. And she knew his.

Her body rolled against him as she tasted his lips. God, she was the sweetest female he'd ever laid eyes on. Who was she? Where had she come from? Her fingers locked around his, and she held down his hands as she took her pleasure from him.

She wore flowing pale-blue robes that cascaded all around them, lifted as if on a breeze.

Everything was white. Soft white bedding beneath them, white walls, white sky outside the white-framed window.

"I choose you," she whispered.

It was an odd thing to say, but here, in this white room with its angelically white walls, it sounded perfect. He knew exactly what those words meant, even though he couldn't put that meaning into words of his own.

"I choose you, too." He pulled her mouth to his and kissed her. Deep, thoroughly, feeling the connection all the way to his soul.

She felt it, too. He could feel everything happening inside her just as if it were happening to him.

This was right. As she sighed and rocked her hips more insistently against him, they both knew how right this was.

"I never thought I'd find you," she whispered, her breath warm and urgent against his skin.

"I didn't think I *wanted* to find you." He'd never seen a more beautiful creature. One who stole his breath, his heart, and his body with only one look.

"Don't let them take me."

"No one will take you."

"I'm scared." Even as tears formed in her eyes, her body quickened.

"I won't let them hurt you." In this place, he had no idea who "they" were, and yet, he did. He just couldn't see their names. Only their faces.

She gasped, grinding herself against him harder, faster, with a sense of desperation.

He felt her pleasure rise alongside his, but hers was all he cared about.

"Stay with me," she begged.

"I'm here."

"Don't let them take me."

"I won't."

"Pleeeaase!"

A blast of white light exploded from within her as she came in a powerful rush. And then she was gone. Her weight lifted off him as if stolen away.

He could see her, but he could no longer hear her. No longer feel her. Someone was dragging her away from him. She was screaming. A scream without sound. She reached for him, but he couldn't move. He couldn't go after her. He wasn't keeping his promise. He'd told her he wouldn't let them take her, but they were, and he couldn't stop them.

"No!"

Her mouth opened in a soundless scream as she strained to free herself, but she couldn't wrench herself out of their grasp. She was being pulled farther and farther away into a black tunnel that spread its impenetrable darkness into the room. The walls, the bed, the space outside the window . . . all of it turned into an inky well of black as it swallowed her like a pool of oily quicksand.

"HELP ME!" Her scream finally broke through the thickness, and it was the most agonizing thing he'd ever heard.

His heart shattered. Outrage rose inside him like a volcanic eruption.

He would find her. He would save her. And when he did, he would kill those who had stolen her from him.

Kill them!

He jolted awake, breathing hard, covered in sweat, eyes darting around the room.

Where was he? Just like in his dream, there was a lot of white here. White and chrome. And monitors. And beeping. He had tubes and wires hooked up to him, and a bag of clear fluid hung from a tall stand beside the bed.

Was he in the hospital?

How the hell had he gotten here?

He tried to sit up and was met with a shit-ton of no-fucking-way-*that's*-happening as pain lanced every muscle in his body.

Holy hell! Had he been run over by a pack of Hell's Angels and couldn't remember?

That's when the evening started coming back to him. The cemetery. Rule. No . . . Rysk. His name was Rysk. The werewolves. The bite on his arm. He tried to lift his arm but immediately abandoned the idea as he let out a strangled, anguished grunt at what felt like a thousand needles stabbing up and down from shoulder to wrist and back again. Talk about acupuncture from hell. Satan himself was putting in *these* needles. All at once. And his limbs were like one-ton sacks of lava. Hot, heavy, and hard to move without a forklift.

"Ah, you're awake."

Unable to move much else than his eyes, Ronan looked toward the female voice to find a doctor with short blond hair walking toward him, wearing the kind of smile all doctors wear when they're about to deliver bad news.

"Where am I?" His voice sounded the way the rest of him felt, coming out in a string of croaks that served as syllables.

"AKM." The doctor checked his IV and studied what he assumed were monitors behind him.

"What happened to me?"

"You were bitten by a werewolf." The doctor pulled her stethoscope from around her neck and popped the ear pieces into her ears with the expert swiftness of someone who'd performed the task a million times. "A genetically altered werewolf," she added as she pressed the scope to his chest.

Her name tag read Dr. Snow.

He closed his eyes, wanting nothing more than to go back to sleep and dream about the beautiful blonde some more. But with pain ranging up and down his body like an electric current being woven into a web by radioactive spiders, sleep wasn't something he could look forward to anytime soon.

"How do you feel?" Dr. Snow grabbed a blood pressure cuff from somewhere to the side.

"Like shit."

She laughed as she carefully wrapped the cuff around his arm and began pumping air into it. "Can you be a little more specific?"

He sighed, and even that hurt. "There's pain everywhere. All over my body. Nothing doesn't hurt."

She stopped pumping, listened with her scope for a few seconds, and then released the cuff. "I can increase your painkillers for the next twenty-four hours to see if that helps." She made a note on her iPad.

Painkillers would be awesome. As in, better-than-bacon awesome. And nothing was better than bacon.

"I can't move, either. Everything feels heavy." Abstract fear briefly iced his blood. "I'm not paralyzed, am I?" But that didn't make sense. Why would he be feeling pain if he were paralyzed.

She shook her head. "Your nervous system has been traumatized, but you're not paralyzed. One of the lycans who saved you had to use his own venom to kill that of the werewolf. What you're feeling is partly the result of the war that raged throughout your body as the lycan venom neutralized the werewolf venom. You'll be able to move again in time. We're going to start you on physical therapy as soon as you're no longer in so much pain. That should speed things along so you're back on your feet again in no time." She glanced to the side and smiled. "Well, look who just woke up."

Ronan couldn't see who she was looking at, but as he inhaled again, his whole body went rigid as he identified the other person in the room by scent.

His father.

"I was just checking his vitals," Dr. Snow said to him.

His father came into view, his dark eyes sleepy but concerned. "Is he okay?"

The doctor smiled and tucked her iPad under her arm. "He's stable." She turned to Ronan. "I'll leave you two to visit."

"I'd rather you didn't," Ronan said.

She just smiled again and lowered her gaze. Before she could say anything further, a nurse poked her head into the room. "Doctor, we have an emergency."

Ronan caught the sounds of rushed movement outside his room. Equipment and personnel raced to whatever was happening.

The doctor paid them a hasty farewell and raced out of the room, barking an order to someone to bring him pain medicine before disappearing from view.

As the commotion continued outside, silence stretched like poisonous gas between he and his father. Ronan refused to look at him. He didn't want to see the disappointment staring back at him. Didn't want to face the scrutiny and criticism he was sure his dad wanted to unload on him. *You shouldn't have taken the ankh. You shouldn't have stolen it from Micah and tried to use it. This is all your fault. You wouldn't be in this condition if you hadn't acted out like a spoiled ten-year-old. If only you could be more like Micah. He never would have done something so foolish. So destructive.*

Ronan closed his eyes, trying to block out the pain that had nothing to do with World War III taking place in his organs. This pain hurt twice as much and cut ten times deeper.

You'd think after all this time, he'd be immune to it, but you never really grew immune to being dismissed and cast aside. You just learned how to channel and twist the pain in a new direction.

"Go ahead and say it," he said, keeping his eyes closed. "Tell me how bad of a fuckup I am and get it over with."

His dad remained silent.

"Come on, Dad, I know you think I'm a failure. I know you resent that I'll never live up to Micah's name and that you wish I'd never been born and—"

"I don't think *that*." His father's hand wrapped around his, jarring Ronan's eyes open to find his father standing right beside him, staring down at him with nothing but love and compassion.

Ronan frowned. His father had never looked at him that way.

"You're the only thing that kept me going all these years, Ronan. I know it didn't always feel like that, but you've given me purpose again, and I couldn't be prouder of you."

All the years of criticism and hurtful words rushed back to him, emboldening his anger. "You sure could have fooled me."

"I was in a bad place, Ro. In a lot of ways, I still am. Without your mother, and still suffering the loss of Isabel, I made a lot of mistakes. I couldn't be the kind of parent you deserved, and I fumbled my way along, trying to say and do the right things but never quite able to get the words to come out right." His father frowned and looked away. "You were never the fuckup, Ronan. I was." Their gazes met again. "I was the fuckup. *I* failed *you*, not the other way around. You could never fail me. You honor me just by existing."

Ronan wasn't sure what to say. This was a side of his father he'd never seen. A side he'd longed for throughout his childhood. A side he'd needed for so long he'd stopped hoping for its existence long ago.

But he was an adult now. The time for a caring father who was proud of him was over.

"It's too late for apologies."

"It's never too late for apologies," a voice said from the side.

Ronan followed his father's gaze to the door as Rysk entered the room. Rysk, a.k.a. Rule — a.k.a. lying sack of shit.

Rysk approached the bed. "Don't let your resentment prevent you from letting your father in, Ronan. What happened isn't his fault."

Liar.

The word rose unbidden inside Ronan's mind. Rysk had lied to him, too. About his name. About who he was. Where did the lies stop?

"How would you know?" This was just what he needed right now, a tag team of disappointing father figures to irritate the holy living shit out of him while he already felt like someone had taken a meat tenderizer to him.

"Because I was part of it," Rysk said. "I was part of the reason why you were kept in the dark."

Ronan scowled at Rysk then at his father. His dad and Rysk knew each other, and not because they'd just met. The unspoken awareness passing between them bespoke a familiarity that extended far beyond only a couple of days. They'd always known each other. Seeing them together proved it.

"Who the fuck *are* you?" If only he could move, he'd deck the fucker and storm out of there, to never look back.

"I already told you. I'm your grandfather."

Ronan's thoughts shot back to the cemetery. *You're my great-great-great grandson.* He'd thought Rysk had been joking. That he'd been playing some kind of sick mindfuck on him.

"You were serious?" Where was the doctor with his painkillers? He just wanted to go back to sleep. Or maybe he was asleep now and the dream he'd had about the beautiful blonde had been reality.

It didn't matter. He didn't want to hear this. Any of it. And, yet . . . he did. He wanted to belong to something bigger than himself. He wanted to believe he had a family. He just couldn't accept that this was the family he'd been born into.

"Ronan," his father said, touching his hand again.

Ronan yanked it away, immediately crying out as pain exploded up and down his arm, rippling out to the rest of his body.

His father and Rysk jumped away from the bed.

"What's going on in here?" A nurse rushed into the room, carrying a small bag of fluid. Most likely morphine.

Ah, relief. Relief that would not only get rid of the pain, but would also put him back to sleep where he could be with the beautiful blonde.

Every muscle in his body twitched from the overstimulation, which sent even more stabs of agony through him.

The nurse shoved past Rysk, who backed even farther away, and thrust the bag onto one of the hooks on the IV stand. Moving like quicksilver, she hooked the bag up to his IV then started a slow drip.

Within seconds, the drug broke into his system, calming the spasms, dulling the physical torment to a subtle ache. Just as he began to sink into a blissed-out stupor where he didn't care about anything but the sweet sensation of nothingness, he heard the nurse tell his dad and Rysk that maybe it was time they left. That way he could get some rest.

His dad argued, but the nurse insisted.

Through blurry vision, he watched as his dad gathered his things, gave him one last, sad look, and lumbered out of the room. Rysk followed.

At last, he was alone.

Now he just needed to return to his dreams and find the female.
The female who took him away from his shit life and gave him a
better one. The female who needed him to save her. The female he
vowed to save even if it killed him.

The female he had chosen.

But for what?

He didn't know. But whatever he'd chosen her for, it felt
important.

Like the difference between life and death.

PERSEPHONE'S EYES SHOT OPEN AS HER BODY ARCHED violently off the
bed. Searing pain ricocheted inside her chest. When she collapsed
back on the bed, she didn't so much gasp for air as she gulped in
heaving vacuum-like draws for oxygen. She felt like she'd been
underwater?

"We have a heartbeat!" someone shouted.

A heartbeat? Surely, they weren't talking about her.

Paddles were drawn away from her exposed chest, and hands
worked all around her, touching, examining, probing.

"Pulse is erratic. She could still crash again."

"Hold."

The paddles remained over her, but didn't touch her skin.

Within a few seconds, the pain in her chest began to subside,
and her breathing evened out, although the room faded from light
to dark a couple of times, as if she were on the verge of falling
unconscious.

Something cold pressed against her chest.

"Her pulse is stabilizing."

She blinked through the milky haze clouding her eyes as
people blurred in and out of her vision.

"Okay, clear the room. She's back." The female voice beside her
sounded relieved.

Scratchy cloth covered her exposed breasts, and most of the
people hovering nearby began to disappear. A few remained, and
as her vision slowly came back into focus, she realized she was in
a hospital room. These people were doctors and nurses.

A female with short blond hair leaned over her. Fingers pried
her eyelids open, and a bright penlight swung left to right, then

right to left, briefly blinding her. Her arms were lifted. Monitors beeped. Nurses scurried in with equipment and bags of fluid. But Persephone got the sense that whatever excitement had just occurred was pretty much over.

"We thought we lost you," the blond doctor said, wearing a relieved smile as she straightened and stuffed her penlight in the breast pocket of her white coat.

"Hu-what?" Persephone blinked against the too-bright lights shining down on her.

The doctor adjusted the sheets and blankets over her. "Your heart stopped. We had to shock you. I'm Dr. Snow. You're at AKM."

Her heart had stopped? The haze in her mind was gradually clearing. "Are you saying . . .? Did I die?" She lazily rubbed her palm up and down her arm. God, she itched all over.

"For about two minutes." The doctor checked the monitors as more nurses left the room, taking the crash cart with them.

Persephone watched them leave, taking her freedom with them. They'd stolen the only reprieve available to her. She wanted to scream at them. To flail her way out of the tubes taped to her arms and dripping lifesaving medicine into her so she could attack them for doing this to her. She'd been so close, and they'd screwed it all up.

Instead, she swallowed her tears and stared down at her too-pale hands. Her vision was still blurry, and the mother of all headaches was setting up shop behind her eyes, but she didn't care. All that mattered was that she'd been within arm's length of true freedom and had lost it. Again.

Now she was back where her life was nothing more than a stage show. Where she was nothing more than a commodity to be sold to the highest bidder. Where she had to endure her father's obsession with pairing her up with a "suitable mate" instead of letting biology take its course.

Yes, she was lonely. Yes, she wanted a mate. Yes, she desired to have what Miriam had found with Io.

There's nothing like it, Seph! All those times we sat and fantasized about what it would feel like to find a true mate don't even begin to describe how it really feels. You have to convince your father to let your biological mate find you. You just have to!

But there had been no convincing her father. He refused to

listen to her pleas and told her she would be paired with a suitable male by the end of summer, end of story. It was now the end of May, and he'd already found the male he intended to sell her off to. No money would change hands, but as far as Persephone was concerned, her heart was the commodity being bartered, and her body would be sold into sexual slavery.

She didn't want a male who hadn't biologically mated her. She wanted what Miriam had. She wanted the supernatural sex, the intimate bond, the magical dynamic that had taken Miriam's and Io's hearts and melded them into one. One biologically mated, inseparable, no-one-will-ever-come-between-us heart.

She had no interest in Cecil, the male her father had chosen for her. In fact, Cecil disgusted her. He was too thin, with oily hair, and his hands were clammy. And all he ever talked about was money. How much money he had, how much money he invested, how much money he spent, how much money he expected to make this year. He was such a bore. There was no way she could endure a lifetime of him touching her with his cold, damp hands, let alone sticking his penis inside her.

Death would be a better option.

And she'd almost had it. Forever sleep had been within her grasp twice tonight, and both times she'd been saved. Once by the good doctor, and once by . . .

Him.

The male in the mask.

Her heart skipped a beat.

She'd seen his face. Only for a moment, but it had been long enough for her to know she'd never seen a more glorious male. He'd had the most beautiful eyes, the color of a storm breaking apart to reveal a dusky blue sky. And his features! Strong, dark, intense.

She'd dreamed about him, too. When she'd been dead. She'd been with him. He had touched her. They had kissed, and it had felt so real, as if he'd really been there.

She lightly touched her lips, remembering how his had felt on hers.

But he hadn't really been there, had he. It had all been a dream. A fantasy she had been taking with her into the afterlife, before the doctor and her team of nurses had brought her back from both the fantasy and the pearly gates.

She was doomed to the reality that she had to live another day, another week, another month in this hell. It didn't matter how many days she had left. She would find freedom another way. Somehow, someday soon, she would manage to succeed. No one could save her. She'd already decided to die, and nothing would change her mind.

"Hey, what's wrong?" Dr. Snow stepped up to the bedside, her head tilted curiously.

Persephone realized she was crying. She smeared the tears from under her eyes. "Why didn't you just let me die?"

The doctor recoiled as if she couldn't believe what she'd heard. "It's my job to *save* people, not let them die."

Persephone sniffled and swallowed past the lump in her throat. "You should have. Let me die, I mean." She swiped tears off her cheeks again.

The doctor drew nearer and took her hand. "Persephone . . .?"

She couldn't look at the older female.

"Persephone, look at me."

She finally brought her gaze up to the doctor's.

Dr. Snow squeezed her hand. "You have so much to live for, Persephone."

"No, I don't."

The doctor's eyebrows pinched together. "Sure you do. Your family. Your dreams."

Persephone let out a caustic laugh that could have corroded copper. "I have no dreams." Her father had stolen them all.

"Everyone has dreams, Persephone. Even you. You just have to find them."

"Why? What's the point? He'll just take them all away from me again."

"Who will?"

Before Persephone could answer, her father's booming voice ruptured the tender mood settling between her and the doctor.

"Where is my daughter! Why haven't I heard anything, yet?"

Persephone cringed, and heaviness settled over her as she met Dr. Snow's gaze again. "Him."

CHAPTER 27

MICAH'S EYES BLINKED OPEN to the sound of the shower turning on. Sam wasn't in bed with him.

He rolled to check the digital clock on his nightstand. It was almost eight o'clock. At night. Damn. He'd slept all day. He never did that. Then again, last night had drained him both physically and emotionally. He had needed the recovery time.

Apparently, Sam had, too, if she was just waking up.

Stealing into their large master bath, he managed to relieve his bladder and rinse his mouth with Listerine without Sam seeing him then quietly opened the shower door and snuck in behind her.

"Good morning."

She jumped then relaxed before leaning against him. "Good morning." She tilted her head back so he could kiss her.

As he did, he saw her engagement ring sitting on the shelf in the corner.

He picked it up. "This should be on your finger."

She took it from him and gently set it back on the shelf. "Not when I'm showering. The soap dulls the shine."

"We can always have it polished."

She shrugged. "I know, but I like keeping it as shiny as I can."

He took her lilac-scented shampoo from her and poured some in his hand. "Turn around."

With an impatient sigh, she did as he asked. He rubbed his hands together, spreading the shampoo between them, and then began gently massaging it into her hair.

"This wouldn't be you coddling me, would it?" she asked, tilting her head into his hands.

"Sshh, female."

"Micah—"

His hands bunched into loose fists, pulling her hair. "Sh. Just enjoy it."

Her shoulders relaxed as she gave into him without another word. He rubbed her scalp, working the shampoo into her hair. Dollops of suds fell to the shower floor, and the air filled with the fragrance of lilacs.

"I love that scent," he said.

"My shampoo?"

"Mmm, yes. It reminds me of the first time I saw you."

"You mean the night I saved your ass."

He chuckled and guided her into the falling water to rinse away the suds. "I thought you were an angel." He'd told her this before, but he never tired of remembering. "An angel sent to save me." He scrubbed soap up and down her arms. "And you did. In more ways than one."

After he washed and rinsed her, he picked up the engagement ring again and held it out in front of him as he lifted her left hand.

After sliding the ring back on her finger, he brought her hand to his mouth and kissed it, right over the ring. His lips brushed against the diamond. "There. Back where it belongs."

She smiled and gazed down at the ring as he released her hand. "And it's still shiny."

He slid his arms loosely around her waist, planting a chaste kiss on her lips.

They stood like that for a few seconds, letting the water shower over them.

When he'd given her that ring, he'd promised he would marry her. She'd told him she wanted a human wedding, and he'd vowed he would give her one, even though it held no bearing on how he felt about her as his mate. After all, once a male vampire found his mate, not much could separate them. There was no such thing as divorce among vampires.

Oh sure, arranged pairings could still be dissolved by royal decree, but for someone like him, who had formed a biological link to his mate, there would be no such dissolution. He and Sam were bound to each other forever.

"Why do you want a human wedding when you're not human anymore? When there's absolutely no chance I'll ever want to leave you?" He wasn't questioning her, only her reasons.

In only a few months, he'd come to know Sam in a way no one had *ever* known her. Not just because he could see inside her mind and piece together her past to discover who she was at her core because of what he found there, but because they were connected in a way that went beyond the physical.

Theirs was a spiritual connection. One that defied logic and felt preordained by a higher power.

Even so, some things about her were beyond his comprehension. Particularly, her reasons for doing and wanting some of the things she did. Like the nursing position. He fully supported her in her choice, but she'd wanted to go after the job on her own, without telling him. Her independence was important to her even as she coveted her relationship to him.

He could make assumptions and educated guesses about why she behaved this way based on what he knew about her, but sometimes hearing her own words, spoken straight from her heart, was the only way for him to be sure.

She shrugged. "It's just something I've always wanted. You know, the white dress, the standing before God, friends, and family and declaring that this is the man—or male, in your case—I've chosen to spend the rest of my life with. I want that with you. The ceremony. The reception. The cake. The honeymoon. I want to do it right for once."

She'd been married before. To that jackhole Steve. He could see in her thoughts that she was thinking about their wedding day. How it had been planned hastily before her deployment to the Middle East. How she hadn't even had time to buy a proper dress and order a cake. They'd run off to Vegas and said, "I do" in some little Elvis chapel. They didn't even have time for a real honeymoon. They'd spent the night of their wedding in a cheap Vegas hotel room.

That's where Micah disengaged from her memories. He didn't need to see what Steve had done to her on their wedding night.

Not that it mattered now. She hated Steve. She didn't want to think about those days any more than he wanted her to think about them. She regretted everything about her relationship with that asswipe.

"Your wedding to Steve was a mistake, Sam." He wasn't asking or trying to point out the obvious. He was simply paraphrasing what he saw in her thoughts.

"I know, but . . ." She let out a quiet sigh. "I got it all wrong with Steve. We rushed into it. I didn't really know him — obviously." She gave voice to everything he'd seen in her mind. "We ran off to Vegas and had a shotgun wedding that really didn't mean anything. We had no friends with us to witness the ceremony. My parents weren't there. I didn't even have a proper wedding dress." She issued a tender snort. "It's not that I need a huge wedding that takes months to plan or the perfect dress with a mile-long train. I just . . ."

He plucked the words from her mind. "You just want to do it right this time. You want the fantasy wedding all human women dream about."

She nodded and swept her wet hair off her forehead. It stood up in blond peaks for a moment before starting to fall again as water droplets weighed it down. "I *do* want to do it right. I want to stand in front of our friends, dressed in white, holding a proper bouquet, and take real vows." A gentle smile touched her mouth. "Vows that mean as much to me as they do to you. Vows from the heart, you know?"

"And you also want to wash Steve completely out of your past."

Her gaze penetrated his. "Yes."

"Why?"

She drew in an agitated breath. "Because I don't like how it feels knowing I messed up so badly with him. Maybe it doesn't make sense, but in my head, marrying you would wash the slate clean and erase that whole horrible time with him from my past. It's like that part of my life isn't closed, yet, and it feels like failure. Like if you and I don't get married, Steve's still in there. Inside me. Always in the way. And he's laughing at me. Laughing because he got the last official crack at me since he was my husband."

"But I'm your mate, which is a much stronger bond than that of a husband."

She sighed, growing visibly upset. "I know it's all just semantics, but I can't get past it." Her delicate eyebrows bent in harsh angles as old demons haunted her eyes. "He's the biggest mistake I ever made, and sometimes it feels like his dark cloud is always going to be hanging over me. I just want him gone, you know? Just . . . out of my life. Out of *our* life. And . . . it just . . ." Her growing agitation felt like pinpricks on his arms.

"Okay, ssshh." He pulled her into him and tucked her cheek

against his shoulder, gently rocking her. "I'm not criticizing. I just wanted to hear your reasoning, that's all."

Her fingers curled against his back, but the tension began to ease out of her shoulders.

He'd known for a while that Steve's memory still haunted her. She still hesitated to go out in public. Still grew squeamish about using the credit cards he'd given her for fear Steve could use them to track her down. She'd lived a secret, hidden life for barely a year, but that had been long enough to leave an influential mark on her habits, just as Steve's abuse had left its invasive mark on her freedom, as well as the scar on her stomach from where he'd pushed her onto a glass table, causing it to break and pierce her pristine flesh.

Then, instead of taking her to the hospital, where his abuse would have been exposed, he stitched her up at home. It didn't matter that Steve was a surgeon. Sam had deserved proper medical care and for someone to discover what that asshole had done to her.

She exhaled against his wet skin. "I'm sorry to burden you with my problems when you've already got enough on your plate."

"Burden?" He frowned and pushed her away so he could look into her eyes. "Baby, you're not a burden. Nothing about you is a burden."

She shook her head and dropped her gaze. "But you just found out that your dad is still alive, that you have a brother, and that Rysk and Argon are your ancestors, and . . . you've just got a lot more important things to worry about right now than me and my silly Steve issues."

Wedging his finger under her chin, he forced her to lift her head and meet his gaze. "Let me make one thing explicitly clear. There is nothing — and I mean *nothing* — more important to me than you." He solemnly held her gaze. "And your issues with Steve are *not* silly."

As tough and independent as Sam was, it was easy to forget she needed someone to hold her up from time to time.

"He will never hurt you again." He looked her dead in the eye as he said it. "I will never let him or anyone else hurt you ever again."

And if a wedding was what she needed to know he meant it, a wedding he would give her.

"You have a serious hero complex." She said the words in jest, but the gratitude that shone from her expression made his heart swell.

"Get used to it."

"Bossy."

"Only because I love you." He reached over her shoulder for his body wash.

"Oh, is that what it is?" She stepped backward into the water to rinse off any lingering soap and shampoo.

Micah quickly lathered himself up then rinsed.

"No more thinking about Steve," he said, reaching around her and shutting off the water.

"I'll try." She pulled their towels off the warming racks just outside the shower and handed one to him.

"No trying. Only doing." He gave her ass a light swat.

She leaped away from him, covering her bare bottom. "Hey!"

He briskly dried himself then wrapped his towel around his waist and returned to the bedroom to get dressed.

"I was wondering . . ." she called from the bathroom.

"About?"

"This black ops team you're going to put together."

He buttoned up the fly on his jeans. "What about it?"

"Are you going to need someone with medical training on your team?"

Micah froze with his shirt halfway over his head.

"You know, like a nurse or—"

"No!" He tugged his shirt down and marched to the bathroom. "Absolutely not, Sam."

She'd been rubbing lotion over her arms and abruptly dropped her hands to her sides. "What?"

"You're not going to be part of my team."

She crossed her arms and cocked her head. "Why not?"

"It's out of the question."

Her eyebrows popped. "Out of the question? Are you saying you won't need someone with medical training on your team?"

"It's too dangerous."

"You're forgetting that I was an Army medic, Micah. I've seen combat. I've seen danger. I know how to take care of myself."

He slashed the air in front of him with both arms, pushing them in opposite directions like he was throwing open a set of heavy drapes. "If I need medical personnel on my team, I'll choose someone else. Not you."

Her mouth fell open and she gave him a look like he'd just accused her of cheating on him. A moment later, she whipped off the towel she'd wrapped around her and threw it at him as she stormed into the bedroom.

"Am I not *good enough* to be on your team?" She yanked open the top drawer of her dresser and pulled out a pair of underwear.

"That's not what I said."

But she wasn't hearing it. He'd stepped on her temper and she was on a war path. "I can save your life from drecks, drag you back to my apartment" — she jabbed her index finger at him — "and carry you over my shoulder, I might add" — she shoved the drawer shut — "and provide medical assistance to *you*, but I'm not good enough to provide medical backup for your team?" She pulled on her panties with enough aggression it was a wonder she didn't rip them in half. "It's not like I'd be in the field with you, Micah." She tugged the drawer back open, whipped out a bra, and blew past him to the closet. "I'd be in a medical unit away from the danger, ready to provide emergency assistance if and when it was needed. That's what I did in Iraq and Afghanistan. That was my job. And I was damn good at it."

Hangers scraped loudly over the rod. A moment later, she reappeared, holding a pair of jeans and a peach-and-cream peasant blouse.

"I'm not asking for special favors, and I'm not saying I won't need training. I know I do. But you won't even consider it. Why is that, I wonder?" She tugged on the jeans, beat her chest dramatically, then finally stopped to pointedly meet his gaze. "You big he-man. Me? I'm helpless. Is that it?"

"Sam, you're preg—"

Green fire erupted in her eyes. "So help me God, if you tell me I'm pregnant as if it's a reason for me to shrivel up into a bedridden sissy one more time, I'm going to pack my things and get my own place for the next nine months so you won't be tempted to lay a hand on me. Do you understand me, Micah Black?" She practically shoved herself into her blouse.

"But—"

"No, Micah! Not another word. You can deal with it and get with the program that pregnancy doesn't make me a weakling or get up close and personal with your hand for the next nine months. Those are your options. You decide what it's going to be."

She pushed him aside, marched past him back into the bathroom, and slammed the door behind her, leaving him in dumbfounded silence.

He'd heard pregnancy hormones could cause wicked mood changes worthy of hell's demons, but dayum! It's one thing to hear that it could happen and another to witness it in the flesh. Hell, forget witnessing, he'd just experienced the phenomenon full force.

Typhoon Sam had torn through the bedroom and shredded him.

She had made a valid point about working together, though. She was trained for combat, so it wasn't like she'd be a liability. Not like an untrained doctor who wasn't used to the field. But this was his mate he was talking about. His *pregnant* mate. Every instinct he possessed demanded he keep her safe, and keeping her safe didn't include taking her anywhere near the field, where she could get hurt or worse.

Okay fine, she wouldn't actually be in the field, but she'd be involved. She would be close to the action just by being on his team, even if she was tucked safely away inside some medical bunker far from the actual bloodshed.

The question was, could he function knowing she was there? Or would she be too much of a distraction? Would he feel safer and more comfortable knowing someone he trusted with his life was ready to provide him with medical care should he need it, or would he prefer medical aid from someone he wasn't emotionally attached to, and who wasn't emotionally attached to him? He just didn't know. He wouldn't know unless he gave it a try.

She would be working at AKM, anyway, and wouldn't it be easier to ensure her safety if she were on his team rather than in the new underground facility, especially if the drecks had a mole on staff?

Whether he ultimately added her to the team or she stayed on AKM's official payroll, she would need training first. He wouldn't allow her to even take a test drive on the team without receiving proper training from the AKM medical staff.

The bathroom door slowly opened, and Micah prepared for another round of destruction.

Instead, she gingerly stepped out, her face red, and her brow curled upward over nose. She shamefully met his gaze then threw herself at him, burying her face against his chest.

"I'm so sorry. I didn't mean all that. I don't know why I said it." He grinned and wrapped his arms around her, flattening his palms against her back. Jesus, her hormones were flowing like the Great Flood inside her. "It's your pregnancy hormones."

"Seriously?" She pulled back and frowned up at him.

He nodded. "I can feel them. You're buzzing like a beehive. A very busy beehive." He kissed the tip of her nose. "Lots of honey."

"Only I'm not as sweet." She chuckled then groaned as she dropped her forehead against his sternum. "I'm not even a month in. Am I going to be like this for the next nine months?"

"They're just words, Sam. You didn't hurt me. And you're wrong. Your honey is *very* sweet."

She groaned again and shook her head against him.

He rubbed his hands up and down her back and kissed her hair. "We'll get through it." He hugged her close and rocked her side to side. "But you made a good point."

"No, I didn't."

"Yes, you did."

"No—"

He pushed her away and kissed her to shut her up. When he broke their lip-lock, all she could do was stare at him in stunned silence.

"Maybe I need to rephrase myself," he said. "I've reconsidered your offer."

"You have?"

"Yes, but I can't promise you anything. Complete your training, and then we'll have a trial run. We'll see how it goes. Right now, I don't know if having you on the team would distract me too much to do my job or reassure me that I have someone I can trust ready to take care of me if I should need medical assistance."

"You don't have to do that, Micah. I was out of line."

He kissed her again. "It's too late. I've already made up my mind."

She bit back a smile. "And your word is final, huh?"

"Yep."

Her smile turned into a sexy smirk. "And what if I change *my* mind after I have the babies?"

"Then we'll figure it out then, but for now, get ready to bring your A game, Mrs. Black, because I plan on giving you a tryout when the time comes."

She sighed impatiently. "How many times do I have to tell you that just because you put a ring on it doesn't mean you can call me Mrs. Black? Until we're married, I'm Ms. Garrett."

"Then I guess we'll have to do something about that."

CHAPTER 28

"ARE YOU INTENTIONALLY TRYING TO EMBARRASS ME, Persephone?"

She knew better than to answer. Her father didn't want an answer, anyway. He wanted complete acquiescence. He didn't even seem to care that she'd almost died this morning. All he'd talked about since entering her room was how humiliating her actions were to the family, how ashamed he was of her, how things were going to change if she knew what was good for her, and how if the Chastain family found out about her overdose they might reconsider the arranged pairing between her and Cecil.

Persephone actually liked the sound of that last one, but her optimism was short-lived. If the arrangement between her and Cecil dissolved, her father would just find some other intellectually worthless, physically bankrupt male to mate her off to. Someone more in love with his money than her. She would still be in the same boat she was in now, she'd just be sailing down a different river.

Her stomach knotted with a sour grumble. Now that she was back on the detox drugs AKM used in their overdose and addiction recovery protocol, her stomach had begun to roil with increasing discontent. Her father's angry outbursts weren't helping, either. She was pretty sure she was going to throw up sometime in the next ten minutes. If she was lucky, she'd throw up on him.

He paced at the foot of the bed, his face crimson, his hands wringing the air. "I don't understand what's gotten into you, Persephone. Your mother and I have given you everything."

"Not everything," she muttered.

He couldn't say they'd given her everything when they refused to give her the only thing she wanted: a biological mate.

Her father stopped and spun toward her. "What?" His voice boomed. No doubt every doctor and nurse in the facility heard him. "What did you say, young lady?"

Finding courage from God knew where, she raised her chin. "I said you haven't given me everything."

He appeared affronted, rearing back the way someone might if they'd been insulted. "Is that so? The house? The clothes? The car? Your phone and jewelry? All those designer shoes in your closet? Are those things nothing to you?" Then his eyes narrowed knowingly as he zeroed in on the real issue. "This is about your mating, isn't it?"

She set her jaw and lifted her chin higher without answering. She feared if she did, she would hurl. In record time, her stomach had become a bubbling witch's cauldron with one too many eyes of newt in it.

Her father marched to the side of her bed, ominous and foreboding. "There will be no more talk of biological mates, Persephone. Do you understand me? I'm not taking a chance that some filthy, undeserving male will mate you. Is that what you want? What if he's a drug dealer? Or a criminal? Or, God forbid, a killer? Is that really the kind of male you'd want as a mate?"

Her anger helped her resist her upchuck reflex. "Why does my biological mate automatically have to be someone bad? What if he's a noble male? He could be an upstanding citizen. A male of worth."

"He could be a pauper. Where would you be then?"

"If he's my biological mate, I wouldn't care!"

"You say that now, but when the money dries up and you can't afford a decent evening gown for our annual summer ball, will you be so forgiving?"

Persephone forced the bile back down her throat. "The money and appearances mean more to you than to me. I don't care about evening gowns and summer balls and diamond necklaces."

Her father threw up his arms and barked out a sarcastic laugh. "Then, by all means, when we return home, I will have the servants clear out your closet and give away all your designer gowns, your shoes, your fur coats." Persephone had never worn the furs, anyway, believing them a cruelty. "While I'm at it, I'll have them clean out your jewelry bureau, as well. I'm sure the poor would love to get their hands on them so they can pawn them for money. Let's see how happy you are then."

"Then you'll cancel the arrangement for me to mate Cecil?"

If her father was serious about throwing out all her designer dresses and million-dollar necklaces, she would have no need of them, anyway, if he dropped his quest to mate her off to a wealthy cad. But if he still planned on going through with the mating, there was no way he would get rid of her things. After all, it was all about appearances with her father. He couldn't let his daughter be seen in public, on Cecil's twig of an arm, wearing jeans and a T-shirt. She would be expected to dress only in the finest couture. To wear the gaudiest and most expensive jewelry.

Such was the life of the aristocracy.

Her father's expression creased in both anger and frustration. "I will hear no more of this nonsense about biological mates, Persephone."

For a moment there, she'd glimpsed a flicker of hope, but just like every other flicker of hope she'd tried to grasp, he snuffed this one out, too.

"You are to be mated to Cecil. The arrangements are being made as we speak." He loomed closer, casting his shadow over her. "So here's what's going to happen. You are going to enter the drug rehabilitation program. *Again.* You will clean yourself up, and this time, you will stay clean. Do you understand?"

As usual, her father spoke, and he expected his word to be followed as if it were law.

She stared straight ahead, too busy fighting the nausea to even nod, but her submission was implied.

"After your rehab, you will come home, attend a formal engagement party, and become Cecil's mate." He straightened, took a deep breath that seemed to pull the veneer he usually showed the world back over him, and brushed his palms down the front of his suit.

How vain. She'd been overdosing and dying, and he'd still had time to put on an impeccably tailored three-piece suit. Talk about priorities. It was good to know she rated below Armani, Versace, and Marc Jacobs.

"You have responsibilities, Persephone. You have a duty to your family name."

How she wished her family name was anything other than

Fenton. She used to feel sorry for Miriam, because her father was the king, and despite the king's support of biological matings, he'd once felt as Persephone's father did. He had wanted her to mate a "suitable male," too. As such, he hadn't approved when Io was the one to form a bond to her.

He'd eventually come around, but it had been a hard-fought battle. One that almost saw Miriam's death. But she had survived, she was clean, and she was happy. And the king was happy for her.

Now Persephone was in a similar position, except her father would never bend as King Bain had. Miriam was the lucky one in this friendship. She'd found her match. Persephone would never get that chance.

"You will fulfill your obligations to this family, Persephone. Is that clear?"

She nodded only once, more to get him out of her room than to surrender.

He took the hint. Checking his watch, he told her he would be back to collect her in a few weeks, after her rehab was finished, and then he left without so much as a good-bye, good luck, a promise of visiting her while she recovered, or a kiss on the cheek.

She watched him go, willing her tears not to fall, even as her stomach approached critical mass.

She had no intention of fulfilling her disgraceful obligation to the family, but as far as her father was concerned, she would do as he commanded, without question. She would be the dutiful daughter who had no voice, no rights, no thoughts of her own, no dreams, and no life.

But she *did* have a choice. And when another chance presented itself, she would take her life and leave this godforsaken existence.

Dr. Snow gingerly entered her room. "Are you okay?"

"I'm going to throw up."

The doctor got the puke tray under her mouth just in time, but at least the purge brought relief. Relief that her life was closer to its end than its beginning.

Much closer.

CHAPTER 29

MICAH SCANNED HIS KEY CARD AT **AKM's** BACK ENTRANCE and pushed inside.

The main floor was unusually quiet. Most of the staff had been relocated to the new underground facility by now, but a skeleton crew remained, along with a small medical staff who continued to look after the last of the victims from Bishop's lab. The ones they hadn't yet been able to move because they were still too unstable or critical. Kieran, for example. He was the demon boy with the fucked-up tattoos that could take on a life of their own. Kieran was still being held in an induced coma, and Savill, who had been sliced open from neck to groin, hadn't yet regained consciousness. He'd been traumatized into a coma, and it was anyone's guess how long he would remain that way.

But even if Savill woke up today, moving him to the new facility was out of the question. Micah and Dr. Snow agreed that the secret of his half-vampire, half-lycan blood couldn't leak to the general population, and if he was moved to the new facility, it wouldn't take long for the staff there to see what he was. And then . . . let the leaking begin. Whatever he and Dr. Snow were going to do with Savill, they needed to think of it soon. Time was ticking down.

Now Ronan had joined the do-not-move crew.

And that was where Micah was headed. To check on his brother. Then he would pay Bain a visit and give him his answer.

His footsteps echoed in the empty hall as he made his way toward the break room. Micah had no idea what King Bain planned to do with the building once all of AKM had made the move to the new facility, but he felt a little reminiscent about this old place. They had wrung every last ounce of productivity out of it. The building was severely outdated and too small to house the growing ranks of enforcers and tech personnel needed to keep up with the mounting cobalt epidemic and rising crime. It was also too exposed, out in the open as it was. The new facility had been built underground and included secret passages that connected covertly to Chicago's underground pedway for emergency evac and entry.

The new facility had been finished just in time, too, now that it looked like all-out war was coming.

Micah planned to stop that war and help turn the tide against their enemies with the team he had yet to put together, but it would take time, and he wasn't sure how much time he had before Bishop and Searcy were ready to attack.

After grabbing a cup of coffee — at least the coffee maker was still here — he headed to the medical wing.

He tried not to hurry. He tried to tell himself he didn't care as much as he did about whether or not Ronan was awake. But yeah, *liar, liar, pants on fire.*

Pushing through the double doors, he glanced toward Ronan's room then veered right instead. In the direction of Savill's room. It was the only way he could keep from appearing too eager to see his flesh and blood.

He looked in on the young male. No change. Still not awake. Still in a coma. The last time he'd talked to Dr. Snow about his condition, she'd told him his vitals were getting stronger every day, but they still didn't know when he would wake up. It could be today, tomorrow, or next week. Maybe longer. Or he could take a sudden turn for the worse. Not likely at this point, but still a possibility.

Once Savill woke up, he'd be inside a whole new hell. One where everything he'd known no longer existed. One in which he would have to accept he was an anomaly. The product of a mating that never should have happened. At least according to lycan law.

He turned toward the sound of talking coming from Kieran's room. Trevor? What was he doing here? Oh, that's right. Trevor had a hard-on for demon boy.

Micah quietly stepped to the side and peeked in. Demon boy's black tattoos, which covered his arms and torso, weren't moving right now, but that didn't change the fact that they had. Just last week, those swirls of ink had come to life and crawled all over his skin . . . and sometimes off of it.

Micah shivered as he remembered those tattoos peeling off Kieran's body and wrapping around his arm as he tried to restrain Kieran.

Yeah, that freak could *stay* in a coma for all he cared. Micah had seen a lot of fucked-up shit, but tattoos that leaped off the skin and moved on their own? Fuck that.

He took a sip of his coffee and quietly listened. Trevor was kicked back in a cushioned chair, legs crossed, with a book in his lap. He was reading to Kieran, his voice cool, smooth, and calm.

Trevor had it bad for Kieran if he was sitting with the guy during his time off, reading to him.

The words from the story Trevor was reading were familiar. Micah had read this book. Which one was it? He could see it in his mind, and the name was on the tip of his tongue. When Trevor read the word *shitter*, it clicked. *Christine* by Stephen King. Good book. Great movie.

And perfect for demon boy.

He listened to Trevor read for a couple more minutes then slipped away, toward Ronan's room.

Dr. Snow was in with him, checking his vitals. He imagined she'd been checking them every hour on the hour.

"How is he?" Micah said, noting Ronan's color hadn't improved much.

When the doc looked up, he could see the fatigue written all over her face. Had she even slept?

"Not much change," she said. "He woke up a few hours after you left, but he was in so much pain, we put him back out, especially after he got upset with your father."

"What?"

"I don't know what happened, but Ronan got very upset. From what I was told, Ronan became belligerent, and they were told to leave."

"They?"

"Your dad and the male who brought Ronan in. Rysk."

Micah could only imagine what kind of shit they had tried to throw at Ronan in the short time he'd been awake.

"If they come back, tell them to leave Ronan alone until he's better or they'll have to answer to me. They don't need to unload any of their shit on him right now. He's already got enough to deal with."

Did he like Ronan? Eh, the little shit was growing on him. He still didn't think he could invite him over for tea and crumpets, but blood had to look out for blood, and right now, Micah was the closest thing to an ally Ronan had in the Black family tree. They'd both been lied to and subjected to a lot of fucked-up-the-ass-dry upheaval caused by the actions of those around them.

Micah would be able to forgive and forget in time, but he couldn't speak for Ronan. He hoped his little brother would be able to get over what their father, Rysk, Argon, and even King Bain had done, keeping secrets from him his whole life. Secrets that could have created a different — *better* — life for Ronan had he known the truth.

Dr. Snow replaced Ronan's chart on the footboard and rested her hand on Micah's arm. "He's stable and still breathing," she said. "That's something, right?"

"Fuckin' A it's something." He couldn't hide the pride in his voice. "He's a fighter."

"Just like his brother." Dr. Snow squeezed his arm.

"Is it okay if I sit with him for a while?" His meeting with Bain wasn't for another hour. He had time.

"I don't see why not. Just don't upset him if he wakes up."

"I promise, I won't. And if he asks me to leave, I'll go peacefully."

"You're a good male, Micah." Dr. Snow smiled warmly then nodded toward the back hallway. "I'm going to try to grab an hour or two of sleep, but if anything happens, have the nurse come get me." She quietly slipped out of the room.

Micah approached the side of Ronan's bed and gazed down at his younger brother.

The jagged blue and purple lines still covered his skin, crisscrossing him like mapped rivers. They didn't look like veins, but they were. Micah's stomach churned at the thought that those lines might mark Ronan's body forever like deathly tattoos.

But he refused to believe that was Ronan's future.

"You hear what I said to the doctor, little brother? You're a fighter. And you're going to get through this."

Conflicted emotions battled within his heart as he gazed down at the pale face that looked so much like his in so many ways. But as similar as they were physically, they were worlds apart mentally.

Ronan resented him. Hated him. Loathed him to the point that he'd broken into his apartment and stolen the ankh their father had given him for safekeeping. The ankh that had almost led to his death. If it hadn't been for the timely arrival of Rameses and his brothers, Ronan *would* be dead now, and Micah would have lost his brother before he'd even gotten to know him.

Clearing his throat, he dropped his gaze to his feet, unsure what to do or say. When a member of his team was in medical, he knew what words needed to come out of his mouth. He knew how to act. Because he knew *them*. Malek, Severin, Io, Ari . . . any of them. He knew what they needed to hear. But with Ronan, he had no idea.

"Ummm . . ." He shifted his weight and drummed his fingers on the outside of his coffee mug.

Maybe he could start by sitting down.

Taking a seat in the cushioned chair beside Ronan's bed, he set his coffee on the meal tray placed against the wall.

That was his blood lying in that bed. Surely, he could think of at least one thing worth saying.

Glancing out the door to Kieran's room, he suddenly wished he had something to read, because then he could read to Ronan the way Trevor was reading to Kieran. Perhaps that would have calmed them both.

He rubbed his palms up and down his thighs. "Too bad I didn't bring a book or a newspaper with me," he said lightheartedly. "Not that you want to hear me read, but . . ." He nibbled the inside of his lip as his gaze jumped from Ronan to the beeping monitor on the other side of the bed, back out the door, to his coffee, and back to Ronan. "But at least it'd be better than listening to all this beeping, right? And, hey, I can do voices. Not good voices, but still, you should hear my Ariel or Princess Jasmine." His attempt at humor fell flat.

Ronan looked bad. Real bad. His haggard hair hung over his eyes, and the black scruff on his cheeks, jaw, and upper lip had grown into a heavy five o'clock shadow.

But at least he was alive.

"So . . ." He eyed the stitched-up bullet wound on Ronan's shoulder. "I'm sorry about that. Shooting you, I mean. If I'd known you were my brother, I wouldn't have. But, hey, it looks like you've got some mad skills with a needle. Those sutures look good." It was obvious no one at the medical center had done them, but someone had cleaned up the area around the wound, which looked like it had been bandaged at one point, according to the red lines from the adhesive tape that had been stuck to his skin.

He nodded awkwardly as his mind blanked out on him again.

What would *he* want to hear if he were in Ronan's place and the tables were turned? Probably not a whole helluva lot. He'd probably be too pissed off at the world.

"You know," he said softly, dropping his gaze, "maybe I shouldn't be here right now. Maybe you think I have no right to be." He looked up again, letting his gaze land on Ronan's deceptively serene face. It was the first time he'd looked upon his brother and not seen hatred and resentment flashing back at him. "You probably don't even want me here." He pushed back in the chair and laid his arms on the armrests. "Well, too bad. You're my brother. And while that might not mean anything to you, it means something to me." He crossed his ankle over the opposite knee. "And what it means to me is that there's nothing I won't do to make sure you get through this. In fact" — he snorted — "I gave a pint of blood for you last night. You know what that means, right? It means that not only do we share genes, but my blood really does run through your veins now."

He plopped one hand on his thigh. "So get used to having a brother, Ronan, because I'm not going anywhere. And since you already know from personal experience how stubborn those born with the Black name can be — because I suspect you're just as stubborn as Dad and I are — you know I'll wear you down before you do me. After all, I'm older. Older brothers always win. It's family law." He chuckled at the idea that he could now call himself an older brother. "God, that sounds crazy, doesn't it? Me. An older brother. Who would have thought?"

He exhaled heavily and brushed back his hair. If only Ronan could answer him. He would have liked to hear his smart-assed retorts right about now, because then at least he would know Ronan was getting better.

"By the way, I forgive you for breaking into my apartment and stealing the ankh. I'm sure you had your reasons." He shrugged, uncrossed his legs, and leaned forward again, elbows on knees, gaze locked on Ronan's pale face with the trademark angular jaw males in his family were born with. "I have no idea what those reasons are . . . well, maybe I do a little. It's clear you and our dad don't get along, so I'm assuming that's part of it, but I've never gotten a chance to know you, so I can't say for sure what's happened in your life to lead you down this road." He glanced at his hands, which were loosely joined between his knees. "God willing, you and I will get to know each other once you get out of this place, and then maybe I'll understand your reasons better.

"But you're going to have to cut me some slack, okay? I'm pissed at our father, too. But I also understand his reasons for doing what he's done. For being the way he is." He looked back up. "I've been in his shoes, Ronan. It's not a good place to be. Losing a mate is something I hope you never have to experience. It's a kind of hell it's almost impossible to pull yourself out of. You *can't* pull yourself out of it. The only thing that can is taking another mate. And our father hasn't done that, yet, so he's still swimming in the bowels of hell. It's amazing he's even made it this long without losing his mind, and my guess is you're partly responsible for keeping him from being six feet under. He may not act like it, but he cares about you. He loves you. You've never known the father I knew. You never got to know the kind of male he really is. If you did, you would understand, and you'd be able to forgive him."

He'd never once met a male who'd lost a mate and fully healed. *He* hadn't even been able to. It had taken finding Sam to drag him from his own bout with suffering's insanity to find peace again, but even that didn't rid him of the memories of how agonizing his life had been after Kat's death. And, yes, he would always experience at least some pain from that loss. It just wouldn't dictate his life, anymore. Thanks to Sam.

"I assume you know that I have a mate. Her name is Sam. Well, Samantha, but I call her Sam. We've been together since January. I know she'd love to meet you." No doubt Sam would know just what to say to get through to Ronan. She had that way about her. Hell, she'd become besties with Cordray overnight. If she could turn Medusa into a friend, who knew what she could pull off with Ronan?

"She's pregnant. Twins. Which means you're going to be an uncle." He stood and wrapped his hand around Ronan's. "I know you're angry with me. Ours isn't exactly an ideal family situation.

I know you've been forced to live a shit life. We *all* have. Our father, you, me. We've each had to face hell in one way or another. But we're still standing. We Blacks are strong motherfuckers."

He squeezed Ronan's hand and stepped closer to the bed. "Do you hear me? We're strong. We don't let life beat us. We don't let our circumstances dictate who we are. That's how I know you're going to get through this, my brother. It's how I know you're going to be stronger for it. Whether you want to accept me into your life or not doesn't matter. What matters is that you're a Black. And that means you're one tough son of a bitch. You won't let anything beat you. Not even this." He motioned toward Ronan's prone, unconscious body. "You'll recover, and when you do, you'll be as ornery as the rest of us again."

He took a deep breath and pressed his lips into a determined line. His words had run out, his mind suddenly quiet. All that remained was him, Ronan, and their joined hands. A physical link between brothers.

Micah bowed his head and closed his eyes, willing Ronan to get better, trying to give some of his strength to his brother simply by way of energy transference.

He didn't know how much time had passed when he became aware of another presence in the room.

Opening his eyes, he found his father standing across from him.

"How is he?" his father asked.

"Alive." Micah let go of Ronan's hand. "I heard he woke up last night."

"Yes."

"I also heard he got upset. So upset the doctor had to drug him up."

"Micah—"

"You and Rysk don't need to be making shit worse right now by giving him the big reveal."

"It's time he knew the truth."

"No. It's time he healed. *Then* we can tell him the truth. He's got enough shit to deal with right now without adding our family secrets to the pile."

His father closed his eyes and nodded. "You're right, you're right." He sounded mentally exhausted. Just like the rest of them. "We'll wait until he's recovered to tell him the rest."

Micah checked the time. He should leave soon. "You knew,

didn't you? When I was a child, you knew our bloodline went straight to the king."

Heavy sigh. "Yes."

"You lied about our family tree. You said it had been destroyed. But it hadn't. You knew all along we were part of King Bain's bloodline. You'd been protecting me even then."

His father nodded.

"Bain has asked me to be his crown regent. Did you know that, too?"

"It's been discussed."

Micah wanted to be angry at his father, but he just couldn't find the emotion, anymore.

"You're the one who should be next in line for the throne, not me."

"You know I'm not up to it."

"And I am?"

"You're more than capable, Micah. I always thought you'd make a fine king if the crown had come down our line as it should have. But things as they are between the drecks and vampires, that's not how it happened."

Micah made a motion for the door. "Yeah, well, I hope it never does. God willing, nothing will happen to Bain, and my services won't be needed."

His father nodded absently, drawing his gaze back to Ronan.

"So, you've accepted the title?" he asked.

Micah palmed his watched. "I'm on my way to give Bain my answer now."

His father nodded again, appearing somewhat lost. It hurt to see him like this. So unsure. Dependent even. Like a human with early Alzheimer's who couldn't quite remember where he was or what he was doing there.

But being around Ronan wasn't going to do him or Ronan any good if his brother woke up again. Dad needed to give Ronan some space.

"You have someplace else to be, Dad." Micah took him by the arm.

"No, I don't."

"Yes, you do."

"Where?"

Micah ushered him out the door. "Anywhere but here. Ronan doesn't need you here right now."

"Micah, please . . ."

"Look, Dad . . ." Micah came to a stop a few feet outside Ronan's room. "I forgive you for not telling me you were alive. Okay? I'm done being angry with you about that. I've had time to process everything that was thrown at me last night, and I just want us to get to know each other again. I want us to be a father and son again, but Ronan . . .?" Micah pointed into his brother's room. "He's not ready for that, yet. He needs more time, and he needs you to give him space. You're doing him more harm than good by being here. He's got a long fucking road ahead of him, not just with his injuries, but with everything he's going to learn about our family once he's well enough to hear it." Micah angled his father toward the exit. "Let him heal. Let him get better. And let him figure himself out without you interfering. He's going to have a lot of shit thrown at him, and his life is going to change. Don't expect him to accept it all overnight, and don't expect him to be happy about it for a while."

They walked toward the double doors, his father sullen and silent. As they passed the nurses' station, Micah stopped and asked one of the nurses for a piece of paper.

He scribbled down his address and Sam's mobile then handed it to his father. "I want you to come and live with us."

"Micah, I can't—"

"I'm not asking if you want to, Dad. I'm telling you that you *will* come live with us."

"I don't want to burden you."

Micah shook his head as he felt an unexpected emotion rise within him. Gratitude. Blinking back tears, he pulled his father into a crushing bear hug. "You're not a burden, Dad. You'll never be a burden." He cleared his throat, refusing to let tears fall. "You're my hero."

His father wasn't as successful at keeping his emotions inside, letting out a thick sob as he hugged Micah so hard it was a wonder he didn't crack a few ribs.

"I'm so proud of you, son." He coughed to hide another sob. "I love you."

A lone tear slipped from Micah's eye. "I love you, too, Dad."

Ronan's eyes peeled open barely a crack, but it was just enough to follow Micah's back as he guided their father out of the room and out of view. He could still hear their voices.

His hand felt surprisingly empty now that Micah no longer held it. Cold and empty.

Monumental feats of self-control shouldn't be endured when you're lying in a hospital bed, feeling like death, struggling just to keep your lungs pumping air, but listening to Micah spill his guts while he had pretended to be asleep had been one of the greatest challenges Ronan had ever faced.

At first, he'd wanted to rail against Micah for presuming to know anything about him. To rage against his kindness. To lash out at him for simply being there. But as Micah continued to talk, Ronan's internalized anger quieted. Micah had spoken as if he were proud of Ronan. As if . . . as if . . . shit, just thinking the words was hard. Micah had sounded as if he actually wanted Ronan to be a part of his life, despite all Ronan had done to him and all his angry, spiteful words.

And then Micah had told their father to leave. That he didn't need to be there. Ronan owed him for that. And, God, was all that true about their bloodline? Did royal genes really flow in his blood? He had so many questions. Questions that fueled his desire to heal, because the sooner he did, the sooner he could get answers.

And what about Alexis? He'd promised to spend the day with her. And her motorcycle was still God knew where. It wasn't like he could call to let her know where he was. No one was supposed to know about her. That was the deal.

But he couldn't think about Alex right now. He would get in touch with her as soon as he could. He hated leaving her hanging, probably thinking the worst, but his head was already swimming with enough shit. Most of all, his brother, and all the words he'd just spewed about family, blood, and forgiveness. About how Ronan was going to be an uncle.

Would he be willing to forgive as easily as Micah if the tables were turned? The question was enough to give him pause, and as he swallowed past the lump in his throat, he considered that maybe, just maybe, a place existed for him in this world after all. A place where family was more important than he thought it ever could be.

CHAPTER 30

LESS THAN THIRTY MINUTES LATER, Micah sat across from Bain in his study. The same bottle of brandy they'd drank from last night waited nearby, along with two snifters. Obviously, Bain expected him to say yes.

"Have you decided?" Bain asked.

"I have."

"And?"

"Yes."

Bain's expression remained steady and controlled. "Yes to being crown regent? Or yes to running the black ops team?"

"Yes to all of it."

Bain smiled and reached for the brandy.

"Wait. I have a couple of conditions."

Bain pulled his hand back and placed it over the other on the blotter in front of him. "I'm listening."

"I want the Knights of Justice brought on as out-of-state consultants and given the royal stamp of approval." Micah had heard Trevor talk about his team in Florida enough to know they were highly skilled and regretted their loss of AKM status. His team could make for a tremendous ally as the situation heated up with Searcy, Premier Royce, and the motleys.

Bain's eyes narrowed as he crossed his arms. "I disbanded the Knights years ago, Micah. They operated outside AKM protocol. They were too much like vigilantes."

"Which makes them perfect for what you're trying to accomplish by creating a new covert ops team. They have resources and means beyond ours. Not that theirs are better or that their methods are more effective. They're just different. And if you want me to lead this team, that's what I want. People who will think outside the box and can tap into areas we can't and vice versa."

With a nod of concession, Bain relented. "Fine, consider it done. What else?"

Micah's mind drifted to Sam. To his unborn babies. To the engagement ring she wore on her left hand. To the wedding she wanted. The wedding he'd promised to give her.

Micah stood, uncapped the brandy, and poured a finger's worth in each snifter.

"I have one thing I have to do before I can officially accept." He lifted the two snifters and extended one toward Bain. "And I need your help. Can I count on you, cousin?"

Bain took the glass. "Whatever you need, if it means your *official* acceptance as crown regent, as well as captain of my black ops team, you have whatever you need from me." He raised his glass. "You need only ask."

Micah clinked his glass to Bain's. "Good, because I need your help planning a wedding."

"Ah, Jesus." Bain laughed. "This ought to be good."

Micah downed his brandy in one swallow. His Sam wanted a wedding. He was going to give her the best damn wedding ever.

And then he was going to bring the dreck empire to its knees.

They wanted a war. He'd give them a war they would never forget.

No one fucked with the Black name, and now that he knew he was fighting for more than just himself, it was time to avenge the murders of the ancestors he had never gotten to know.

Time to unleash the power of the Black legacy.

Micah had risen once more.

EPILOGUE

Rameses stood in front of the sarcophagus that held his brother's sleeping form. Memnon wasn't going to like being awakened, but there was no avoiding it. Not anymore. A gate had been opened by a vampire, allowing Hunter to return, and motleys were polluting the planet. And that was just the beginning of their problems.

He turned toward Priest. The male was still weak, but this was his duty. Once Memnon was awake, Priest would return to the healing chamber to complete his rejuvenation.

"Begin," Rameses said with a nod.

The head members of the three families had gathered, as was the custom when pulling the *imeut* from Osiris's Sleep, and stood in ceremonial linen kilts around the gold sarcophagus, all of them wearing their cartouches around their necks. A statue of Isis stood at the head of the sarcophagus, and one of Anubis, the lycans' patron god and ancestor, stood at the foot.

Priest bowed to their god's likeness, uttered a quiet benediction, then began pouring red wine into a bowl made of gold. Once he finished, he lifted a worn leather pouch from the lip of the tomb, loosened the drawstring, and then sprinkled the contents of gold dust into the bowl. Gold was a powerful metal to the lycans. It conducted energy between realms and helped them heal more quickly from their battle wounds.

Next, Priest pulled a cask of purified water — taken from the Nile River — from inside his robes and added it to the bowl. This created the connection to Memnon's spirit, which resided beneath the Sphinx, where the spirits of all sleeping lycans resided within Osiris's chamber until awakened.

Rameses nodded at the others.

Jupiter and Priest's brother, Wrex, of the McClerran clan joined

Dain on one side of the tomblike casket, and the three brothers of the Strauss clan, Reed, Julian, and Barrett, stood on the other. Rameses remained at the foot, overseeing the awakening.

He nodded, and the six lycans on either side of the sarcophagus shifted into their lycan forms, stepped forward in unison, and lifted off the lid, revealing Memnon's prone form. As they maneuvered the mammoth slab of gold to the side and propped it against its assigned panel in the enclosed tomb, Priest dipped his thumb in the bowl then pressed the tip against Memnon's forehead and began chanting in their ancient language.

The awakening had begun.

MEMNON'S AWARENESS JOLTED. His soul was being pulled upward, out of Osiris's Sleep. He traveled through the caverns underneath the Giza Plateau, through Osiris's tomb below the Sphinx, and then through the Great Sphinx itself, the gateway for his people.

Then he was airborne, whisking through the atmosphere, flying through the maze of gateways connecting one to the next. To his ethereal eye, the paths between the gates looked like glowing roadways creating a crisscrossing web surrounding the planet. Wormholes.

And at each intersection was a portal. A gateway he could pass through in his physical form.

But he wasn't being called to just any random gateway. He was being called to the compound. His home. Where his clan resided.

Why was he being disturbed? It was too soon for him to awaken. He wasn't sure how long he'd been asleep, but he knew it hadn't been fifty years. Not even close.

There would be hell to pay for waking him early.

Memnon had made this journey hundreds of times over thousands of years, and only once had he been pulled from his sleep early: when his brother, Hunter, had lost his ankh.

He had been furious at Hunter's carelessness. He should have banished him then, but he'd given Hunter another chance. Only to regret the decision later, when Hunter broke their only law and took a vampire mate.

No longer had Memnon been able to look the other way. Lycans didn't mix with vampires. To do so could end in disaster. There had been no other option than to banish him. A sentence he had hated carrying out. But he couldn't make exceptions. Not even for his closest friend.

The lycan compound built on the steep, rocky hillside overlooking Moon Lake—how appropriate—came into view. His soul homed in on the chanting calling him back, and he dropped through the three stories of brick, steel, and drywall into the basement tomb, where he took root inside his body.

He was back. Back on the doomed planet known as earth. Where he had yet to find anything worth dying for since the age of the pharaohs. And if there was nothing worth dying for, living became a vast wasteland of emptiness.

Filling his lungs with earthbound oxygen, he opened his eyes. The gold ceiling above him came into focus. It was covered in hieroglyphs that told the history of their people. Of the arrival of the lycans on earth. Of the beastly slaves they'd transported from their prison planet to erect the colossal structures once prolific in Egypt.

This had been their gift to the human colonists who'd been brought here from the various corners of the universe to populate earth in what had become known as the great experiment. The lycans, among other godly races, such as vampires and those who had long since vacated Mount Olympus, had been charged with providing humanity with the means to overcome and survive.

At one time, Memnon had respected and loved the humans he and the other lycans had been meant to protect and nurture. Back then, the mortals had been innocent, wide-eyed, and wondrous, despite having no recollection from where they'd come.

Then the humans found religion. And as their fervor for a new savior developed, they grew absurd, dirty, and vile in their *in*humanity. Not just to beasts, but to themselves.

Over time, they came to see the lycans and all supernatural beings as blasphemous, sinful, even demonic. They destroyed great monuments—some of the lycans' finest work—including the library at Alexandria. So much history was lost that day. And so many lives.

Memnon now held nothing but disdain for their species. The human experiment had become the human *plague*. All they seemed capable of was war, as one sect of mortal society preached superiority over another. From the bowels of religious cultism, humanity had grown out of control, infesting the earth with their lust for power and carnage.

If only they knew the truth of their meager place in the universe. They existed by the thinnest of threads on what was now a dying planet that could no longer sustain their catastrophic love affair with greed and destruction.

But he would continue to protect them. He had to. He'd sworn an oath to Anubis.

He inhaled again then slowly exhaled as he pulled himself to a sitting position. Easier said than done after a long hibernation.

His brothers stood around his sarcophagus, looking like the powerful descendants of Anubis they were, stoic and towering. Rameses stood at his feet, his expression stony.

"Why have you awakened me before it's time?"

"Events require your attention."

"What events?"

Rameses blinked. It was the only sign of distress he exposed. "Hunter, among others."

"What about Hunter?" He already knew whatever had happened was not going to please him.

"He's back."

Interesting. Memnon climbed out of the sarcophagus, his body stiff, and rose to his full seven foot height. "How did that happen when he no longer possesses his key and was banished to a prison planet, where only one who holds a key can set him free?"

As a testament to his superior fortitude, Rameses kept his gaze coolly locked with Memnon's. "A vampire found his key and used it."

Memnon curled his upper lip. Vampires. Not the worst beings on the planet—exceptional to humans, to be sure—but creatures he would rather not contend with for a variety of reasons.

"How did this vampire find Hunter's ankh when we could not?"

Rameses's shoulders lifted subtly then fell. "I don't yet know."

"Disappointing."

His brother ignored him. "The vampire managed to open a gate. Hunter came through."

Not one to dwell on trivialities, Memnon pushed for more. "And have you captured him?"

"No."

Memnon's mood soured even further. Being awakened early

was bad enough. Awaking to such a show of incompetence was downright insulting. "Why not?"

Rameses shook his head and dropped his gaze, a sign Memnon had come to learn meant his brother was about to lie. "He knows how to evade us." He lifted his gaze to Memnon's once more. "And we have other, more urgent matters that need attention."

Memnon stepped into the robe two of his clan brothers held open for him. He wrapped it around himself, leaving the belt untied. "More urgent than capturing Hunter and sending him back into exile?" This piqued Memnon's curiosity.

"Mutant werewolves," Rameses said, not wasting any time. "We call them motleys."

Memnon's mind began reconnecting with the minds of his brothers, and, through their memories, he began to see all that had happened while he'd been away, including the rise of this new beast Rameses referred to as a motley.

"Interesting." They had a new enemy to hunt. How exciting.

Memnon's stomach rumbled. He would eat, and then he and the heads of the families would meet, and no one would sleep until someone—first—explained how Hunter had returned from exile, and—second—developed a plan to recapture him. He couldn't let his people think he was weak. There had to be justice for breaking their laws. Then they would discuss these motleys and what was to be done about them. Based on the thoughts coming from Dain and Priest about a vampire alliance, Memnon didn't think he was going to like what had transpired during his hibernation.

"There's more," Rameses said.

Memnon stopped his descent down the gilded stairs, turned his head only halfway around, and burned his black gaze into that of his blood brother out of the corners of his eyes. "Indeed, there is." He had never liked the feeling of cold irritation rolling down his back.

Rameses didn't even flinch. "Hunter has a son."

Clearly, Rameses hoped to gain leniency for Hunter by revealing this bit of information. Memnon knew his brother well. Rameses wanted to find a way to mend fences between him and Hunter, and a son—one not burdened by the sickness that could arise in the child of a lycan-vampire pairing—could be a tremendous asset.

Unfortunately, allowing the child to live would be a sign of weakness and would cast doubt over the law preventing such dalliances.

Rameses's heart was in the right place, but he had forgotten one thing. Memnon no longer had a heart. It had died with his mate over three millennia ago. And yet, Memnon could still smell the sweet scent of myrrh from her perfume when he thought of her.

"A son? Truly?" Bad, bad Hunter. "How did we not know this when Hunter was banished?"

"Someone has been protecting him."

"Who?"

"We don't know. We only found out about him last night."

Memnon started down the stairs again. "Find out who has been protecting him. Whoever it is knows about us. Bring that person and the boy to me."

"What are you going to do to him?" Rameses said, his voice holding the barest hint of concern.

Memnon stopped and pivoted to face his blooded brother. Without a doubt, Rameses was the more merciful of the two of them.

Memnon had once been merciful, too, but those days were long gone. There was nothing left inside him but a black heart to match his black eyes.

"I'm going to kill him."

DID YOU ENJOY READING THIS BOOK?

If you did, please help others enjoy it, too:

Review it.

Recommend it.

Lend it.

If you leave a review, please send me an email at donya@donyalynne.com or message me on Facebook so that I can thank you with a personal e-mail.

Watch for the first of my AKM novelettes, Micah's Bride, in December. Turn the page for an excerpt.

EXCERPT FROM MICAH'S BRIDE

SAM RAN HER HAND DOWN THE WHITE CHIFFON SKIRT of the floor-length dress.

Every woman should feel like a princess on her wedding day, and this dress certainly did the trick. Sweetheart bodice, layers and layers of fluffy, cloudlike skirting, silver beading that sparkled and shimmered like a million diamonds.

How had Micah pulled this off in only a week without her knowing?

"He didn't," Cordray said behind her, obviously reading her mind.

"What do you mean?" Sam glanced at Cordray's reflection in the full-length mirror hanging on the wall of the most impressive marble, gold, and glass bathroom she'd ever set foot in. It was more like a ballroom with a toilet and a sink. But they were inside the king's mansion, so why wouldn't she be surrounded by priceless opulence?

Cordray smiled back at her as she finished pinning the simple lace veil with the pearl-studded tiara into Sam's hair. "Bain did all this for you." She was wearing a royal blue dress that matched one of the two shades of blue in her hair, which fell in loose rivulets over her shoulders, falling almost to her waist.

"King Bain?" Sam's hand when to her throat, covering the Harry Winston diamond wreath Cordray had given her to wear. Each cluster of diamonds was set in platinum and resembled multiple strands of roses.

Cordray fluffed the veil down her back. "Micah made it part of the terms of accepting the role of crown regent, as well as becoming the head honcho of Bain's new black ops team . . . God help us." The last she said under her breath while smirking.

A week ago, Micah had revealed to Sam that he and Bain were distant cousins, that he descended from the vampire race's first king, and that he had dreck blood in him. He'd also told Sam about Bain's request to become crown regent and to run a new covert ops team. It wasn't until a few days later that he mentioned he and Cordray were related, too, a fact he and Cordray were reluctantly become used to.

But she'd had no idea he'd been planning a wedding.

Two hours ago, he had told her they were going to do something special tonight. She assumed they were heading into the city to a fancy meal and a night at the theater, but he drove them away from Chicago, into the suburbs, and then into an area where the houses and plots of land grew bigger with every mile they drove.

When Micah slowed and turned into a gated drive, she assumed they were going to some kind of sex party like the one they'd attended a few months ago when Micah found out Trace was a submissive.

"Micah, I didn't dress for this." She had glanced down at her dress slacks and silk blouse.

"You're dressed fine." The gate had opened in front of them, and Micah accelerated through, along a curving drive that rolled through pristinely landscaped grounds. Pear trees lined the drive.

She had nearly choked on her tongue when she asked where they were and Micah had told her King Bain's home.

At first, she'd thought King Bain was part of the BDSM community and that he was hosting some kind of party, but when Micah escorted her inside, only for Cordray and Tristan's mate, Josie, to whisk her away within seconds, she knew something was up, especially when Micah winked and called after her that he couldn't wait to see her in her dress.

She rotated left then right, admiring the gown from all angles. "That man—male, whatever—never ceases to amaze me."

Josie spritzed more glitter hairspray in her hair. "I always knew he'd make some lucky girl deliriously happy." She set the bottle of spray on the nearby vanity, which held all the makeup they'd expertly painted on her face. "Micah has always been special to me," Josie said, eyes watering. "Thank you for bringing him back to us." She sniffled and pulled Sam in for a tight hug.

Sam's flat belly bumped against Josie's rounded one. Before long, Sam's belly would grow as big as Josie's. Maybe bigger, since she was carrying twins. "I was just in the right place at the right time."

"And thank God for that." Josie pushed away, briefly holding Sam at arm's length, giving her a once-over before brushing away her tears. "My goodness, look at how beautiful you are."

Sam gently patted her own stomach. "Must be the baby glow."

By now, almost everyone knew she was pregnant.

Cordray stepped up behind her and pointedly turned her toward the mirror so she had no other choice than to look at her reflection. "No, Sam. It's you. You're stunning. Your pregnancy hormones have nothing to do with it."

This concludes this excerpt.

ABOUT THE AUTHOR

DONYA LYNNE is the bestselling author of the award winning All the King's Men and Strong Karma Series and a member of Romance Writers of America. Making her home in a wooded suburb north of Indianapolis with her husband, Donya has lived in Indiana most of her life and knew at a young age she was destined to be a writer. She started writing poetry in grade school and won her first short story contest in fourth grade. In junior high, she began writing romantic stories for her friends, and by her sophomore year, she'd been dubbed Most Likely to Become a Romance Novelist. In 2012, she fulfilled her dream by publishing her first two novels and a novella. Her work has earned her two IPPYs, five eLit Awards, a USA Today Recommended Read, and numerous accolades, including two Smashwords bestsellers. When she's not writing, she can be found cheering on the Indianapolis Colts or doing her cats' bidding.

For more information on Donya's books or just to say hello, visit her on Facebook or swing by her website.

www.facebook.com/DonyaLynne

www.donyalynne.com